A DIFFERENT LIFE

A True Fiction About the Power of
Jesus to Save and Redeem

Lorie Evers

A Different Life
A true fiction book about the power of Jesus to save and redeem

For information about this title you can email:
2019differentlife@gmail.com

Published 2019
Printed in the United States of America

Cover photo: Bri Walther
Cover model: Hallie Pennington
Cover design: Sarah Ayling

DEDICATION

This book is dedicated to:

My wonderful husband Michael.
I couldn't have done this without you
and your love and support.
And to my Savior
Without you I would not live-
I love you more than life

CONTENTS

PROLOGUE

October 2002

It was 6pm when Jenna pulled her Toyota land cruiser into her driveway. Samson, her faithful sidekick sat in the passenger seat, tail wagging and ears perked. It had been a long day and she was tired. She loved her job as the administrative assistant to her pastor. She had learned so much and grown to enjoy all the ways she was able to serve.

Samson had just turned two and was finally coming out of his puppy stage. She was grateful for that. He had calmed down a bit and was now fully trained but still had enough puppy playfulness in him that he made her laugh. He was full grown and weighed 110 lbs. And was quite intimidating looking to those who didn't know him. He'd finally grown into his huge feet. If he stood on his hind legs he could put his front paws on her shoulders. He shed a lot, but she didn't mind. He was always there offering comfort and loved her no matter what kind of day she had. He was such a blessing in her otherwise crazy life. She was glad that she was able to take him to work. She was in the office most of the time by herself and he was great company and a good watchdog.

"Ok buddy, release. Let's go in and get some dinner." He was trained to enter or exit her vehicle at her command. He would sit eagerly waiting for the word, his ears perked forward and a little wrinkle on his forehead, waiting for the signal. Sometimes he could hardly contain himself wondering if he was going to be allowed to go with her or be left behind. He was very smart. When she put him in the truck if she said, "we are going to work" then he was excited and eager to get out when they pulled into the church parking lot. If she said, "we are going to church" he would relax and sit patiently as she went inside for service. All the kids would run up to her after service was over asking if they could get him out of the truck. He loved them and was always excited when one of them set him free. He'd lick their faces, wag his tail wildly and run around the churchyard then run straight for the door to find Jenna.

As they walked into the house, B.C. her cat met them as usual. Samson would give him a good sniff all over. Thoroughly but very cautiously. It was their ritual whenever Samson came home with Jenna. B.C. and Samson had a love/hate relationship. One minute they were best buds, curled up on the couch sleeping, the next Samson was bobbing and weaving trying to avoid the cat claws. It was a ridiculous sight because Samson could have put one paw on the cat and held him down or picked him up and flung him. But he never took advantage of the size or weight difference. Jenna had no intention of getting a cat but B.C. (Brat Cat, named because he was a complete brat) showed up on her deck in the middle of winter. It was thirty-two degrees outside, she'd gone out to get some wood for the stove and there he was. Shivering in the cold, meowing his head off. She brought him in intending to find his owner the next day. She tried, but no one claimed him, so he stayed. Samson didn't mind at all. But B.C. wasn't sure he wanted to share his new home with a dog. After a few tussles and some scolding by Jenna, he decided that he would let the dog stay.

Jenna was looking forward to putting on her pajamas, feeding the animals, eating her dinner and crashing. She still had health struggles and all she had been through had taken its toll on her body. Although things had changed in recent months, she was still worn out and recuperating.

The phone rang...

THE BEGINNING

November 1964

J enna's parents were young when they got married. Her mom, Cindy, was 15 and pregnant and her dad, Mitch Clark, was 19. Cindy was 5'8 ½", weighed about 117 lbs., had brown hair, blue eyes. Mitch was 6'1" and weighed 165 lbs., had blonde hair and blue eyes. They were barely adults themselves and they were getting ready to bring a child into the world. Cindy's parents weren't happy about that fact, especially her dad, Jim Stevens. Although her parents were divorced, her dad was very involved with Cindy and her brother, Mark. Her mom Esther lived in her own universe. She was usually in her room with some ailment or with her nose in a romance novel. When the news hit Cindy's dad that she was pregnant, it took a lot of coaxing and convincing to keep him from physically hurting Mitch. Esther tried to persuade her to go away, have the baby, come back and Esther would raise the baby as Cindy's sister. They got married instead. They kept the wedding small and for family only.

Jenna Clark came into the world March 1965. She weighed in at 7.5 lbs. and had a head of black curly hair. They lived in a rented house in Long Beach, California.

The early part of Jenna's life was typical in most ways. There were bouts of colic, ear infections, sleepless nights and all the "baby firsts". Mitch, who worked for Cindy's dad, came home most nights sober. There were a few exceptions. Cindy began to see a pattern; if he drank, he was violent. Then she realized that even without alcohol he could have an explosive temper. This shouldn't have come as a surprise to her since he came from a violent family. Mitch's dad was constantly yelling and physically beating him and his brother. But, Cindy was young and ignored the red flags while they were dating. When you live under the same roof, things become difficult to overlook.

After being married for three years, Cindy got pregnant again and gave birth to Rachel. Jenna had a little sister.

Not long after that Cindy began to realize that Mitch was very controlling. The rules were, he could do what he wanted, when he wanted but she needed to be at home where he knew where she was and what she was doing at all times. At first, she didn't mind. Jenna and Rachel were small, she didn't have many friends and the only place she went besides the grocery store, was to her moms. She didn't know how to cope with it. She had small kids, no job and no real work experience. Besides, it was the 60's and 70's; you dealt with your troubles and kept them to yourself. She had no idea that later in life, the same isolationism and controlling behavior would-be put-on Jenna and Rachel.

Since the girls were three years apart, they played together all the time. In Long Beach, Jenna and Rachel would ride their bikes up and down the driveway, play in their bedroom, beg for ice cream from the ice cream truck that came everyday in the summer selling every kind of ice cream imaginable. They got a dog when Jenna was three, Sadie. Sadie was a German Shepherd and Doberman mix. She was very protective of the girls but gentle and sweet around kids. She would bark and stand between the girls and the end of the driveway because she knew they weren't supposed to go past the end of the driveway while playing. She also loved the ice cream truck and always got her own special ice cream to eat with the girls.

When the girls were five and two, Cindy went to work for her dad's business. The girls went next door to Leana, their African American babysitter. She was a fun babysitter. She loved the girls and they loved her. She pierced the girls' ears with a needle, thread, ice cubes and a potato behind the ear lobe for support. The girls laughed when Leana painted her house wearing a pair of old underwear on her head so she wouldn't get white paint specks in her black Afro. She was strict with the girls but always made them laugh. They felt safe and loved by her and her husband.

They played hide and seek and gymnastics in Grandpa Jim's house. He had a big house with a very long hallway that led to the master bedroom. It was perfect for running down and then jumping onto the bed and doing summersaults or flips. They gathered at his house for big family get-togethers for the holidays, lots of relatives, food and fun playing with cousins. Jim had remarried when Cindy was pregnant with Jenna. His wife Heidi was from Denmark and always made the best chicken and dumplings every Christmas.

They had a few fun family vacations when the girls were small. One summer they hit all the big attractions, Disneyland, San Diego Zoo, Sea World and Knott's Berry Farm. They would take a picnic to save money with homemade fried chicken, potato salad, deviled eggs and iced tea.

Grandma Esther had also remarried around the time Jenna was born and lived in a small house with a huge backyard that the girls would run and play in, get lost in the tall grass and pretend they were in a jungle. Esther always had cats, which the girls loved. They weren't allowed to have a cat because Mitch hated them.

MOVING AND GROWING UP

When she was seven, the Clarks moved to Lake Town, California, a nice, quiet residential neighborhood with green lawns, tall trees and kids down the street to play with. They moved into a two-bedroom house, so the girls shared a room. They had Sadie, the family dog, a yard to play in, good schools and, for the most part, a regular life. Their mom and dad still worked for Cindy's dad, so the girls went to a babysitter down the street. Her name was Carol. Carol had two kids of her own and was a nice person that took good care of the girls. They hated going to a sitter. No matter how nice Carol was, she wasn't their mom. They wanted to be at home with their mom.

Jenna had brief memories from those years, her mom taking care of her when she was sick and being picked up from the babysitter. She was always happy to see her mom, give her a hug and go back to her own house. Cindy worked in an air-conditioned office, she smoked, and the two smells blended together; it gave her mom a distinct smell. Jenna loved that smell; it was her "mom" smell. Cindy made the girls breakfast every morning before they left for school and always made them hot tea. Cindy's family was from Texas, so they drank hot tea and iced tea instead of soda or water. Cindy loved to sing, and country music was her favorite. Jenna liked to hear her mom sing even though their taste in music was different. When they were cleaning the house on Saturday's, they always had music playing and she was always singing. Of course, if her mom selected the music it was country with maybe a little 50's sock hop thrown in. If Jenna had her way, she'd listen to the music Mitch loved which was the music she loved. Mitch was more of a Creedence Clearwater Revival/Led Zeppelin/Doors kind of music lover.

They visited with Esther, "Grammy" as they called her, at least once a month. Every Fourth of July, Esther, Ray, her husband, and Jenna and her family would barbeque ribs, make potato salad, deviled eggs, chocolate cake and homemade ice cream. The girls took turns churning the ice cream. They loved to help and then eat and enjoy their hard work. Mitch was good at barbequing and the girls got to help with all the prep work. When it was dark, they'd drive to the local park and watch fireworks.

Grammy had moved from her house with the tall grass to an apartment because she couldn't keep up with the grass any longer. Sometimes the girls got to spend the night with her, and they'd stay up late laughing, talking and eating cinnamon rolls.

Thanksgiving was spent with Esther in her small apartment that barely held everyone. It was small, cozy and full of safety and comfort.

They went to visit all the grandparents for Christmas.

Athletics came easy to Jenna. She played girls softball and flag football with the local parks and did well. Mitch encouraged her in those sports, especially baseball because he and his brother had played baseball most of their young lives. She was the fastest kid on the elementary school playground next to Billy Garcia. They were always racing to see if they could beat each other.

Mitch's controlling oversight of the girls didn't allow them to play much with the other neighborhood kids. So, they made up games to play in their room. They did covert gymnastics in the small closet in their bedroom. They found if they moved all their clothes to one side, they could use the bar just like they had on the playground. When mom would find little black footprints on the wall, she would scold them, but they would do it again. They had to burn off energy some how even if it meant putting little black footprints on the wall in the closet. They also found if they climbed on top of their dresser it made a perfect springboard to do flips onto the bed. The girls would spend hours in their room playing, talking about the day when they'd be able to have a big farm of their own with horses and lots of dogs. They'd play records and sometimes watch the black and white TV they had in their room. They built blanket forts and played cops and robbers. They both loved playing with Barbie's and had lots of accessories. Sometimes they would put on rock concerts to an invisible audience, singing into the vacuum cleaner and a broom to songs by Creedence Clearwater Revival.

Rachel was much smaller than Jenna. She had small bones, was much shorter and not the athletic type. She just wasn't very coordinated. She loved to climb trees, ride her bike and play with her friends, but sports were not her thing. Both girls were blonde haired and blue eyed, but very different in all other aspects. Jenna didn't mind having her little sister tag along. She felt protective of her because she was the oldest and Rachel seemed so fragile and small. Rachel's hand was half the size of Jenna's. She never understood the significance that had for her, but some how it was very important. Because she was smaller it made Rachel seem very vulnerable. She reminded Jenna of a little tiny bird that couldn't fly or fight off predators and Jenna felt it was her job to fight them for her.

At ten, she fell in love with gymnastics. She was a natural. Because she was athletic, flexible and willing to try anything, gymnastics came easy to her. She begged her mom and dad to enroll her in classes offered at the local high school-- it was free, within walking distance, only one night a week and it would give them something to do. After much begging, she and Rachel were enrolled. Rachel didn't really care about gymnastics; she just wanted to be with her big sister.

After the first year of free gymnastics, Jenna wanted to go to a special school for gymnastics. She was competitive and wanted to go to the next level. The teachers said she showed promise and the thought of being able to compete gave her a thrill. She'd thrown herself into it. She practiced all the time, in the living room, the front yard whenever and wherever she could. She loved watching gymnastics, especially the Olympics. She was already too old to try for the Olympics, but she didn't want to give up.

But, no matter how much she pleaded and begged the answer was no. "We don't have the money and we don't have the time to drive you all over the place for lessons and competition. Don't ask again." Her dad's words were final. She felt frustrated and disappointed. She didn't understand why he wouldn't even check into the cost and as for the time, they never went anywhere. He went to work, came home and stayed there, usually on the couch, until Monday came, and he had to go to work again. She knew that in a few years she'd be too old, and it would be too late. She had already moved to the advanced class in the short time she was involved. She didn't want to re-enroll to continue learning and repeating the same things. If she continued, she'd only be allowed one more enrollment because she was reaching the age limit anyway. So, she had to quit. She filed the dream away. It was a short-lived dream.

The isolation and control were becoming more pronounced in Jenna's life. It was the first of many "no's" to come. They came with little or no explanation and sometimes they were flat out illogical. Her father would become more and more possessive, controlling and isolating as time went on.

It was perplexing, frustrating and caused her great turmoil. She always felt as though she'd done something wrong, but she could never figure out what that something was. She tried harder but it didn't change.

IT'S WHAT
GRANDPAS ARE FOR!

Grandpa Jim, Cindy's dad was the fun, happy, "my grand-kids can do whatever they want" kind of grandpa. He could also use a very stern voice if they got out of hand, but most of the time he just let them be kids. He was half Native American, so he had a full head of jet-black hair, high cheekbones, always looked tan, with a solid build and big strong hands. He worked hard and was always in shape. He could be very intimidating but none of the kids were ever afraid of him. He commanded respect and had his share of brawls as a young navy sailor. But Jenna always felt safe with him.

He loved horses and owned several. He would go out riding almost every weekend with family and always invited Jenna and Rachel to go. Once again after much pleading, her parents agreed, with a stipulation, "we are not buying you a horse!" She went every other weekend to the stables. They lived in the city, so they had to keep the horses stabled some-where else. The trails were not the most picturesque, dirt mostly, but they provided a safe place to ride. At one end of the trail there was a riding ring, at the other end there was a store with the best beef jerky around.

She rode a Shetland pony named Stormy. He came by

that name honestly because he had quite a temper. He was not above pinning you against a fence if he was in a bad mood. Nor was he above taking off running straight up the hill to the stables if something spooked him. He also only had two gears, slow plod or full run. She loved the full run. It took a lot of prodding to get him there, but it was well worth it. All in all, he was a good beginner horse for eleven-year-old Jenna. She was the only one that ever rode him. He was a little roly-poly but very cute and just the right size for her first efforts.

Her grandpa owned a horse that only he could ride. She was a wild Thoroughbred and Quarter horse, with only one goal, run! Not just run, she would run so hard and fast she'd be lathered up and down her neck and still prancing and dancing to go for more. He'd have to hold her back just so they could walk as a group. After a while he'd have to let her go to work off some of her energy so they would race from one end of the trail to the other always with grandpa pulling out ahead. Of course, it took forever to even get Stormy to run but once she did, it was a race. Most of the time Grandpa would get to the designated finish line and have to wait for everyone else to catch up. But it was still so much fun to try and beat him.

They had fun times at the stables and always ate lots of food that they never had at home. Grandpa always brought soda and little miniature wieners in a can, both things that Cindy wouldn't normally feed her girls. But it was Grandpa, and after all, it wasn't every day.

After about a year of going to the stables, which her parents hated, especially her dad, the day she had hoped for came. "Jenna, how would you like to have Della as your very own?" Grandpa was smiling at her with a twinkle in his eye.

"Are you serious? You'd let me have her? All my own?"

She could hardly believe it. What about her parents? Little did she know that her mom and dad, more her dad than anything, had argued for weeks with Grandpa, but Grandpa won out. It was hard to argue with him. Especially if he was the one footing the bill for the horse and willing to take on the responsibility of training Jenna.

She knew, that Della belonged to her grandmother, but a back injury had prevented her from riding. Della had basically been stable bound for over a year. She was beautiful, about 17 hands high, a black Appaloosa with faint white spots on her rear haunches. She needed to be groomed and checked out by the vet, but she was Jenna's. The first time she took her out, Della was a little timid but once she tasted freedom she loosened up. Della loved the trails especially when the other horses were around her. She seemed to find some sense of security with the others around. Jenna could understand that, they spoke the same language. She spent so much time alone and certain people made her feel more secure. Her grandpa was at the top of that list.

She discovered that she loved to ride bareback. The blanket and saddle put so much between her and the horse, she didn't like it. She loved the feel of Della's muscles moving and working and the connection it gave them. Riding gave her a sense of freedom and without the saddle those feelings were intensified. She felt like a real horseperson riding bareback. She had strong legs and was easily able to hold on, even when Della was in a full run. She had gymnastics to thank for that. She also liked the fact that she didn't have to try to maneuver the saddle and buckle it down, especially in the summer when it was so hot, and the saddle was heavy. She hated trying to cinch it up. Della would always puff herself up so that the saddle looked tight, but it wasn't. Then when she'd try to get on, the saddle would come sliding right at her and she would almost fall right on her butt. Della would just turn her head as though she had no idea how that had happened. Besides, the saddle made Jenna hot and she figured it had to make Della hot too, so she left it off. She needed a boost up by her grandpa without the saddle, but she didn't mind.

She learned how to groom her, clean out her hoofs, wash her down, put her away and feed her. The only thing she didn't like was putting the bit in her mouth. She was always scared she'd get bitten. One good chomp and she'd be missing a finger. Della was already famous for standing on her foot when she was trying to groom her. She'd try to push her off, tell her to move but Della would casually turn her head, look at Jenna then look away, pretending to be deaf. It would have been funny except she was on her foot! Grandpa would say, "push her off" and go back to what he was doing. Although she was strong for her age, she was no match for Della. So, when she decided to stand on her foot, rear up or take off running, Jenna would battle but at 5'5 and 105 lbs., most of the time her Grandpa would have to help her. He wanted her to learn. He never let her be in danger but knew she had to learn how to handle Della by herself.

Her whole life became about riding. She read up on horses, talked about horses and dreamed of owning a ranch some day with horses, dogs and wide-open spaces. She would let the horses and dogs run free on the property and she would ride everyday. No one would hurt her, and she would finally get to experience the world. She didn't have much in the way of friends, but she had her grandpa, Della and her dreams. She dreamed of showing her someday, maybe in the barrel races. It gave her a sense of purpose and belonging, as though she was part of the world, that she had something to contribute and something to do that other horse people could relate to. Riding, talking about horses, learning about them made her feel alive.

She had so much fun with her grandpa.

Rachel liked going out to the stables and playing with her cousins. She didn't ride much but got dirty and had a lot of fun. Jenna and her older cousin used to play tricks on Rachel and the younger cousins. Like the time they convinced them to let them put them on the horse walker and hang them by their belt loops. They had fun for about forty-five seconds until the belt loops broke and they landed smack on the ground belly first. Jenna got into trouble for that one.

Then suddenly everything changed.

TRAGEDY STRIKES

I t was July. She was twelve; she was down the street at Carol's house when she saw her mom and dad drive by. It was earlier than normal for them to be getting home from work. They didn't stop and her mom never looked her way. She went inside to tell Carol that she and Rachel were going to go home.

But Carol said, "Jenna, you and Rachel have to stay here for awhile, your dad will come get you later." Carol's face had a look of concern, her brow was wrinkled, and her eyes looked a little red.

"Why? They're home. We should be able to go home. What's wrong with my mom?" Jenna was taught to never talk back to adults, but she was confused.

"You just need to go outside and wait until I tell you that you can go home. No more questions." There was such finality in Carol's voice that Jenna turned and walked away.

Jenna was confused and felt sick to her stomach. Nothing came to her mind that would explain the situation or take away her frustration. She couldn't imagine why her mother had driven past her and didn't stop to get them and why they were home so early. Add to that, Carol wouldn't let them walk home. It was her house, her parent's; she should be able to go home if she wanted. Carol's expression was difficult to read and gave her no hint as to the reason.

About two hours later, Carol sent them home. Nothing

could have prepared her for what was waiting. Her mom sat on the couch staring straight ahead and her dad looked bewildered.

"Kids" he began with shaking in his voice, "your Grandpa Jim is dead."

Simple as that. No long explanation or drawn out story, just dead. No one had ever died before. What did it mean? How could this be? When could she see him? All these questions and more raced through her mind but nothing came out of her mouth. Now she really felt sick to her stomach. Her whole body seemed to be in rebellion. She couldn't speak, she couldn't move, what was happening?

Finally, she found her voice "What do you mean he's dead? What happened to him? Where is he? Do I get to see him?" He was her favorite person. She felt safe with him. Nothing could hurt her if he was around, now she was being told he was gone. She couldn't comprehend what she was hearing.

Her mom sat still and silent. She never looked at Jenna or Rachel. She never spoke, she barely even moved. Her eyes were red and starring straight ahead.

"He had a heart attack at work today and he went to the hospital, but they couldn't save him, so he isn't coming back ever again." His face was distressed as though he was tired and had been worrying but he was matter of fact.

A few tears ran down his face and then he caught them.

"Your mom is going to be very upset for awhile, she'll need your help around the house, and you can't bug her." He wasn't trying to be mean, just setting the record straight with the facts. Taking care of the business at hand. Trying to handle a situation that he had never been prepared for. He had no idea how life was going to change for them, their jobs or their family.

She had never seen her dad this way. He seemed very upset, but he didn't want it to show. Someone had to take charge of the situation at hand. For now, it was left to him.

Both girls began to cry and longed more than anything

for the comfort of their mom, but it didn't come. She was lost in her own pain and would remain that way for years to come. Jenna wanted her mom. She wanted to comfort her and to be comforted by her. She yearned for her mom to tell her it would all be OK, but there was only silence. To Jenna, her mom seemed to have shrunk down to a frail little girl. She was so lifeless and wounded. Jenna didn't understand most of what her dad had said to them, but she could see that her mom wasn't the same.

The next few days passed by in haze of tears, quiet and emptiness. As if there was no life in their house anymore. The world seemed to be shallow as though it had been silenced.

Then the viewing and the funeral came.

Jenna had never been to a viewing or a funeral before. It was a strange silent world of hushed tones and good manners, dress up clothes and funny smells. She had never seen a dead person before either. Looking at her Grandpa lying there so quiet and still. He looked like himself. His hair was combed in its usual way, he had on his favorite suit and a sweet smile touched slightly at the corners of his mouth. He had the same rugged good looks and tan skin that he always had. He looked like he was sleeping. As Jenna, Rachel and their cousin stood looking at him, she tried to will him to open his eyes. To sit up and grab her in a big hug and everything would be normal again. The girls stood looking for what seemed like an eternity as their parents and relatives filed in and out and talked in secretive voices out of their hearing. He never opened his eyes. He just continued to lie there sleeping. Only he wasn't sleeping.

At the funeral Jenna and Rachel wanted to be with their mom but were told they couldn't, they would have to stay with Grammy and sit in a separate section. Cindy was physically there but was just out of reach to the girls. She was shut up inside of herself and no one, not even Jenna and Rachel were allowed in.

When the funeral was over, they had to go to the graveside. She had never been in a cemetery before. It seemed to be such a sad yet beautiful place. Full of lush green grass, big towering trees, lots of small, winding roads to walk or drive on and flowers on headstones scattered throughout the cemetery. And it was quiet. So very quiet. Again, the girls had to stay with Grammy while their mom and dad were further away in a different car and different place. Jenna felt the finality of the place as they lowered her Grandpa's coffin into the ground. She realized that this would be the only place she could ever visit him again.

They got through the funeral and the shock of it, but it wasn't over for Jenna.

About a month after the funeral her dad called her into the living room and asked her to sit down.

"Jenna, we have to sell Della. We don't have the time to take you out to the stables, we don't have the money to care for her and your mom doesn't ever want to go out there again. So, we have talked to the stable owners to ask for help in finding a buyer for her. We have to go out there next weekend to talk to them." Her dad's voice was matter of fact and without much compassion. His face was expressionless, and his tone was clear, there would be no discussion.

Didn't he realize this was the only thing she had left of her Grandpa? Didn't he understand that was her horse and she loved her? Della was the only thing she had that she could call her own. Della was the only thing she had to connect her to the world outside. Everything else in her life consisted of her house, her yard and her room. Now Grandpa was gone, and they want to take Della away. She couldn't bare it. She ran to her room and threw herself on her bed crying so hard her gut hurt. No one came to comfort her, no one came to talk it out with her, they had decided and that was that. So, she was sold. It didn't seem to matter to anyone else that her heart was broken.

She felt she had no one and nothing in the world. Her whole world was rocked. Her mom wasn't the same person anymore. She barely spoke, she cried all the time, she couldn't handle simple tasks at home and work was unbearable for her. Everyday there reminded her of the dad she missed that would never come back. She had taken to reading constantly. She always had her nose in a book and seemed oblivious to anything around her. It was her way of escaping the pain and emptiness she felt. Her dad had been so important to her and she had felt a sense of security knowing that he was always there for her, but now he was gone, and she was broken. Jenna felt sad for her mom.

Jenna was cooking almost every meal, doing the dishes, the laundry and cleaning the house. Rachel was completely beside herself. She was only nine and didn't understand all of it. Jenna became Rachel's mom, not by choice but by necessity. Mitch worked, watched TV and not much else.

Because Cindy was lost inside her own soul, Mitch had lost his wife. He couldn't control that, but he could do everything in his power to try to keep from losing his daughters. He became even more controlling over them, which led Jenna to feel more and more isolated. It seemed to her that she lived inside a glass house that was soundproof. She could see out and watch the world go by. See people living their lives, being alive, but no one saw her or heard her. She had no voice. She couldn't join them or participate in life except within the confines of necessity.

One month after Grandpa Jim died, Elvis Presley died. Her mom was a huge Elvis Presley fan. She had all his records, knew all his songs and even got to see him in person one year for her birthday. Jenna and her mom were watching the funeral on TV. It was a sad, difficult time, it seemed the whole country was mourning and weeping. It was especially hard for Cindy because she was still dealing with the loss of her dad. At the end of the funeral, "Memories" sung by Elvis himself began to play. She could hear her mom softly singing along. Jenna turned to see her mom sitting in the chair with tears streaming down her face singing. She was singing for the memories that were locked away in her heart, memories of the dad she no longer had.

Jenna lost her mom, her grandpa, her horse and her happiness all in one fell swoop. She was alone.

Jenna missed her mom. She needed her mom.

CHANGING TIDE

S trange things happen in families when tragedy strikes. Jennas' parents were no exception.

After Grandpa Jim died the girls didn't want to go to Carol's anymore. They wanted to be home. It felt safer. After much discussion, they agreed to let them be at home after school with Jenna in charge.

As her mom withdrew more and more, Jenna became increasingly responsible for the duties of the house. She became the little mom. Every day when she got home from school, she waited for Rachel outside to make sure she got home safe. She did her homework, got Rachel going on hers and then started dinner. Dinner had to be done by the time her mom got home from work at 5:30. After dinner she and Rachel would clean off the table, feed the dog, do the dishes and finish homework. On the weekends, it was chores. She had to clean the bathrooms, dust, vacuum, clean her room, clean the kitchen and do the kitchen floor.

It was always a challenge to get Rachel to accomplish anything. She was easily distracted, hated cleaning, loved to invent games with whatever she was supposed to be cleaning and was slow as molasses. They'd finished an addition to the house around the same time that Grandpa Jim died. That meant the girls had their own rooms, so Rachel was solely responsible for her room. She invented the game of "cleaning Rachel's way". That meant that everything that was on the floor either went into the closet or under the bed. At first glance the room looked clean, but upon further inspection you would find the clutter had simply been gathered together and relocated. Rachel didn't care if she spent all day in her room cleaning because she would usually spend all day in her room anyway simply because she wasn't allowed to do much else. If the chores weren't done, the room wasn't clean or she'd gotten into trouble for something, she'd be confined to her room. So, she learned to entertain herself.

Because Cindy had checked out and Jenna had become the little mom, things began to change with her dad. She couldn't remember exactly how it started but she began to realize that she felt very uncomfortable around her dad. She didn't want to be left alone in the house with him. Just the thought of that would cause her whole body to become tense and her stomach to get all knotted up. She would get so anxious that she couldn't eat.

Then things began to accelerate. First it began with dressing and undressing. She had to hurry and change as fast as she could before he could come into her room. He didn't always touch her, but he leered at her and made comments about her 13-year-old changing body.

He began to pay special attention to her. He wanted to take her with him to do things. He picked up the hobby of CB radios and wanted her to be involved. They would sit out in his car late at night talking on it. Inevitably she'd find herself being told about the thing's boys wanted from her, of him being the only one she could trust, of the time that would come when some boy would want to have sex with her. He told her that when that time came, if she would go to him, he'd teach her the "right way" to have sex. When he kissed her goodnight, it lingered too long. When he gave her a hug it was too firm, too long and he would press his body into hers.

She was not allowed to lock the bathroom door when she took a shower. He was free to enter any time and would look in on her and comment about her body and ask her questions that made her feel self-conscious and very uncomfortable. She tried to time her showers, dressing and undressing to when he wasn't home, or he was asleep. She was grateful for the times that he came home from work and passed out on the couch. Then she could dress and undress without fear.

She had to make adjustments and calculations in her daily life. She had to put a great deal of forethought into everything she did. It had to be well thought out, well planned with every angle thought through if she was to have the maximum amount of self-protection.

With all the turmoil going on in her house, she had a hard time at school. Not because of the schoolwork, she was an A/B student easily. It was socially that she had a hard time. She didn't feel that she fit in anywhere. There were clicks of people, the athletes or jocks, bookworms, surfer/stoners, bully/troublemakers and then the regular kids. Where did a smart, introverted, controlled, molested by her dad, with a mom who'd checked out and a sister to protect, kind of kid really fit in? The answer was nowhere!

She had a few friends that she'd gone to school with since second grade that were at her junior high and would attend the same high school as her. In elementary school things were different for her at home. Everything had changed since then. None of her friends knew that, but it was the truth and it was a truth that she kept to herself. It was hard enough for her to think about it and face it but to say it out loud to someone just wasn't done. No one talked about that kind of stuff. How do you begin that conversation? She didn't know. So, it was better to just try to fit in on the outside regardless of the inside.

Over the summer between seventh and eighth grade she had started smoking. Both her parents smoked, and her dad had offered her a cigarette one late night when the two of them were up watching Don Kirshner's Rock Concert on T.V. Smoking didn't seem like a big deal to her because her parents smoked. But it did make her feel kind of cool and grown up, she had never felt cool in her life. During the summer a few of her friends had started to smoke and party. Jenna didn't know that because she wasn't allowed to see them during the summer. When eighth grade started, they picked up where they'd left off and hung out together. Since her friends smoked, they thought it was great that Jenna had started. Then they offered her pot. She had no desire to take drugs, rebel against her parents or be out of control for even a moment. It was too risky for her at home and she was deathly afraid of her dad. There was no telling what he would do if he found out she did something like that. But she was so tired of being an outsider; she wanted to belong, somewhere. She wanted to be accepted just because she was a person. Not because someone wanted something from her. To be liked by someone, loved even, a group of people that she could be a part of and feel like she belonged. So, she started to smoke pot. She felt like it was her only way of being a person, a real live person that was participating in the world. She didn't think beyond that. If she had, she probably would have walked away because her reasonable, ultra-responsible, logical self would have kicked-in and told her to scram. So, she smoked cigarettes, smoked pot a few times a week before school and cussed when she was around her friends.

At the end of eighth grade she had everyone sign her yearbook. Unfortunately, because of her choice of friends, she became one of the surfer/stoner crowd. Everywhere in her yearbook there were references to that. Well, her dad got a hold of it.

It was the last day of school and she had just gotten home. She was in the kitchen looking in the fridge for something to eat.

Her dad was in the living room.

"Jenna have you been smoking pot?" He was cool as a cucumber.

She froze in place. She would not lie to her parents. She had to answer, and she had to face him. *Move legs. Move!*

She stepped into the living room and saw that he had a half smirk on his face.

"Yea, I have a few times." She was so scared that she felt like throwing up.

"OK. Well, I'm not going to tell your mom. We'll handle this between us. If you are going to smoke pot, then I don't want you doing it on the street where you could get busted by the cops. Only do it at home and not around your mom or sister. I also don't want you smoking pot you get off the street. It could be laced with PCP and that stuff is dangerous. I'll buy it for you." He was calm and matter of fact about it.

What in the world was his problem? If you had given her a million chances to guess his reaction, she would've gotten all million of them wrong. His face gave nothing away. She didn't know if he was trying to trick her or if he was serious.

"Um, OK." She didn't know what to say. She felt like she was in the twilight zone.

Jenna went to her room and tried to process what had just happened. She didn't really want to smoke pot; she certainly didn't want to do it with her dad. There was no way in the world she would ever smoke pot with him. The thought of that was weird and scary. She wanted to roll up into a little ball and die.

She didn't realize it at the time, but it was just another way to control her. It was a way to be "inside" with her and her friends. As cool as it sounded, it was the exact opposite. Over time, he would repeatedly try to talk to her about it, get her to smoke with him and try to get her friends involved. She tried to avoid the topic.

That was the only trouble she ever really got into. She continued to smoke cigarettes and pot, but she had been given permission. She could live without them both quite easily; they were just tools to her. If she didn't have cigarettes or pot it didn't matter to her, but to be part of the crowd she needed them. She never changed anything she did, how she behaved at home or her grades. She still did what she was told, just like before. But even with those tools, she didn't fit in with them. She wanted to be like everyone else, she just wasn't. She wanted to be popular, hang out with other kids, have fun, be adventurous, have cool things to talk about, but she wasn't like other kids. The other kids went to the beach, hung out at each other's house, went to parties, football games and had sleepovers, but not Jenna. No matter how much she tried to become part of the world, she was always just a spectator. She laughed at their jokes and played along with all their antics but, at the end of the day, they'd go home and continue to be kids and she'd go home to her chores, her room, her dad and her thoughts.

By the time Jenna was fifteen, she'd grown into a young woman. She was tall at 5'7 ½", long blonde hair, hazel eyes and 115 lbs. She was well proportioned and just long all over. She wasn't gangly though; she was very trim, athletic and graceful. Her body was a place of conflict for her. On one side she was very self-conscience about it due to her dad bringing so much attention to it and on the other she was a teenage girl realizing her potential. Although she felt that what she saw in the mirror from the neck down was decent, she never considered herself to be pretty. She saw a forehead that was too high, a jaw that was too long, eyes that were too small and had too much eyelid. Her friends all wore make-up and it made them look prettier. No matter what make-up she put on, she still looked the same, so she didn't bother except for mascara. Her hair was straight and thin, so it didn't do anything but lay there. It was the 80's and Farrah Fawcett had set the world on fire with her feathered hair. Jenna's hair didn't feather.

Her friends were all much prettier than her and always had boys barking at their heels. She did not. Boys never seemed too interested in her. She had a few that she wished were interested in her, but she knew they were way out of her league, so she kept it to herself. If she was honest, she was afraid of boys. She knew she didn't want to have sex with them. She'd been told over and over "all boys want from you is sex". It was drilled into her that they didn't care about who she was as a person or her feelings, just sex. She also knew her dad would come unglued over her having a boyfriend. She would never be able to leave the house with one on a date, so she was afraid. Her dad constantly asked her about boys. Did she have a boyfriend? Was there a boy she liked? Did any boys like her? She didn't have a life; how could she have a boyfriend. She was scared and introverted, that equals a single girl without much hope.

DEF-CON 4... GET A FILING CABINET

That winter everything drastically changed. Rachel was at camp for the week, her mom was at work and her dad was on vacation for a week at home.

One day she came home from school and sat down on the couch to do her homework. He began asking her uncomfortable questions about her body and she tried to ignore them. He got up and left the room. The "feeling" started to creep up in her throat, the feeling that was all too familiar and way too much a part of her everyday life; fear, strangulation, like a trapped animal with no hope or help for escape. There was a tension in the air you could almost see.

"Jenna, could you come in here for a second, I have something in my eye and need your help." He was in the bathroom. To say she felt scared is an understatement. Every fiber of her being tensed up and every alarm sounded in her head, "run for your life". She was immediately nauseated. She was terrified and wanted to refuse but she went. She had to. She had been taught her whole life, obey your parents and respect authority. Under most circumstances that is acceptable and wise, just not always.

"OK, coming." She put her homework down and moved toward the bathroom.

Their bathroom was small, not much room for two people. The sink was right next to the door, the bathtub/shower was behind the door and the toilet was in the corner. If you were standing at the sink with the door open, you could not close the door without moving away from the sink. When she got to the bathroom, he was standing at the sink looking in the mirror messing around with his right eye.

"What is it?" she asked without moving into the bathroom. The hallway outside the bathroom wasn't very big so she didn't have much wiggle room but everything inside of her screamed, "DON'T STEP INTO THE BATHROOM!"

"I don't know, you will have to come in here, so you get the best lighting." He was insistent.

She moved further into the bathroom and he maneuvered himself between her and the door and shut it. She was trapped! Now the sirens were so loud in her head she couldn't even hear herself think. Her whole body went numb and tense at the same time.

"What are you doing? I want out." Jenna tried to sound calm and respectful even being filled with so much fear.

"I just want to see you naked. Take off your clothes." His voice was calm, as though he was asking her to take out the trash and as if the whole scenario was perfectly normal. He was walking her back into the corner of the bathroom. He was between her and freedom and safety. He had a hungry, lustful look in his eye that she'd never seen before and it was pushing her to a place of sheer terror.

"I just want to see what you look like down there; I'm not going to hurt you." He had her pushed up against the toilet, which sat in a small cubbyhole of the bathroom.

She couldn't remember what she said or how she managed to get out, but she did without any physical harm coming to her. The mental and emotional damage was another story. What happened between then and the time her mother got home was a blur. When her mom finally got home, she told her what had happened. They all sat down in the living room and her parents talked as she lay on the couch crying from the depth of her soul. She wanted to be far away from her dad. She wanted to talk to her mom and be ushered into safety with the peace that nothing would ever happen to her again. She didn't want to hear their conversation. She wanted to be protected and feel safe. She felt neither.

"You either have to go to counseling or move out." Her mom sounded firm and absolute. She was stroking Jenna's hair and trying to calm her while talking to Mitch. She was trying to sound authoritative but not push him into a rage.

"I don't need counseling; I don't want to go talk to some shrink. I said I was sorry-- that should be good enough." He wasn't yelling, he just sounded defiant. He wouldn't look at Cindy. He sat in his favorite chair, feet up looking away as though it was the least important conversation of his life.

"If you won't go to counseling then you will have to move out. I mean that." Now she was pushing.

"Fine, I'll go to counseling." He was not convincing, but it was settled according to them.

Jenna got up to go in the bathroom to wash her face. Her mom sent her dad in after her to make sure she was OK. That was the last person she wanted to have help her, but she was so distraught she couldn't speak to protest. When she got into the bathroom her legs went out from under her. She had been crying so long and so hard that she had hyperventilated and was in the process of fainting. He caught her and got her on her feet again. She wanted to resist but didn't have the strength.

Her soul hurt way down deep. She had never felt so alone, empty or afraid. Her universe was spinning way out of control and she had just been hurled out into space. Suddenly everything in her life went gray. All the lines were blurred. Nothing seemed clear anymore. Nothing seemed to have a place. It was all out of order— no black, no white, nothing but gray. She had no idea how to deal with the whole situation. She no longer felt safe in her own home. She had no one to turn to and nowhere to run. Who could she tell and what was she to do?

No answers came. Only silence.

She didn't realize it, but she was about to discover the skill of filing things away in her brain. She never purposed this, it just happened. Because there were no outlets for what had happened, her brain began to file. There were many things in her life that her dad could and would control but her mind was not one of them. Every event, every disappointment, hurt, you name it; it would all have its proper place in the filing cabinet. It was the only coping mechanism she had. Without an outlet it all had to go somewhere, or she would have exploded. So, it got filed.

This one event was going to take a whole filing cabinet by itself.

NOTHING CHANGED

After that incident they went to counseling. Her dad went twice. They never told the counselor what happened, and the counselor never got anywhere with him. Her mom never pursued the issue. The rest of the family went for a few months. They talked about the anger that was ever present in the house. The outbursts of violence had always been there, but they had gotten worse since Grandpa Jim had died. The telephone repairman repeatedly had to come out and replace the phone that had been ripped off the wall. It happened so frequently; they started charging to fix it. In those days, the phones attached to the wall, weighed about five pounds and repairs were usually free. The screen door had been pulled from its hinges several times. There were many dinners that had ended up on the floor from the table being overturned. Lamps were broken, stereos kicked in and screaming matches were the norm. The neighbors were all familiar with the sound of Mitch slamming out of the front door, getting into his car and peeling out of the driveway. On one occasion, Cindy had been the one to try to leave with the girls. As she was pulling out of the driveway, Mitch, screaming at the top of his lungs, lunged at the car and flung himself onto the hood to stop her from driving away. Cindy kept backing out of the driveway. Mitch realized that she was not going to be stopped and finally jumped off the car. The girls were frightened but mostly embarrassed. What would all the neighbors think of them? One time when Jenna was in high school, the neighbor kids were out late, in the middle of the street with a bon fire. Mitch was asleep, was awakened by the noise and in his white t-shirt and tightie-whitie underwear, yelling at the top of his lungs, ran out into the street to tell them to put out the bon fire and go home. He not only looked ridiculous but sounded like a raving lunatic. She went to school with some of the kids. Jenna wanted to crawl under the bed and stay there.

Without any intervention or consequences, he continued to invade her personal privacy. He persisted in entering her room while she was dressing or undressing, looking at her in the shower and made numerous attempts to get her to participate in things that should have been reserved for his wife. He still hugged and kissed her inappropriately and made lewd comments about her body. He made her feel like she was always one step away from being in a dangerous and inescapable situation. She was very self-conscience of what she wore in front of him. She constantly felt she needed to cover herself up but could never accomplish it. She hated the feeling that no matter what she wore or what she did, she was always at risk of being violated, either in word or in deed. She would ask her mom to speak to him, to please make him stop barging in on her when she was dressing or in the shower, she'd say OK, and nothing would change.

He had always been a controlling person even with Cindy, but it was getting worse. From the time Grandpa Jim died, everything seemed to get worse. She was to watch her sister during the summer. She was not allowed to have friends over, go anywhere or spend the night anywhere because she was responsible for Rachel. Rachel could play with her friends that lived on the street, but Jenna couldn't. Sometimes her dad would make surprise visits or phone calls in the middle of the day to check up on them. She couldn't go to the beach in the summer with her friends even if she took Rachel. His reasoning was illogical at best. The dog may bite someone,

someone will break their leg and sue us, you could drown, and you might get lost, reasons Jenna never understood.

If she had been a real troublemaker, a bad student or had disobeyed them profoundly, it would have been understandable—all the restrictions, suspicions and mistrust, but Jenna wasn't like that. She did everything that was asked of her. She was an A/B student, she didn't talk back-- that would have landed her a slap across the face. She was respectful and did all that she could to please her parents. No matter what she did, she just could not seem to get her dad's approval. If he disapproved or was angry for some reason, he would give her the silent treatment, sometimes for days and she wouldn't know why. He would lay a set of criteria for her to meet so she could go to a football game with kids from school. She would meet that criteria and he would say no, oftentimes without explanation. Sometimes the explanation was an unmet criterion; one that she was unaware of. The rules were always changing. When she'd try to reason with him, he would get angry and not speak to her for days. If her mom tried to intervene, he'd get angry with her, blow up and give everyone in the house the silent treatment. Sometimes the battles just weren't worth the effort.

She was not resentful of Rachel; she loved her and was glad to be her protector. She would rather stay around the house than leave her sister alone with her dad, lest she meet the same fate as Jenna. Since Rachel was three years younger than Jenna, she had begun to develop when the bathroom incident took place. So, she saw it as her duty to protect her little sister from harm.

Her dad always picked on Rachel. Nothing she did was ever good enough. All his anger seemed to be at times directed at her. Jenna tried to keep her out of trouble. She would even cover up things that Rachel did. Like the time Rachel broke a light in the garage, Jenna took the blame instead of letting her sister get in trouble for it. She was willing to take care of Rachel; she just wanted to have something to look forward to in return, to enjoy things like other kids.

There was nothing to look forward to, just a black, cavernous hole in her soul. Sometimes she felt that she would be swallowed up by it. Other times, she wished she could dive into it and simply vanish.

IT'S ALL IN MY HEAD

Because she spent so much time in her room, alone, music became everything to Jenna. It was the perfect escape to help calm and mask the constant knot in her stomach. So many songwriters could express her feelings, dreams and desires. She was well rounded in her musical taste. James Taylor, Prince, Neil Diamond, The Doors, Led Zeppelin were all in her collection. She loved to spend hours listening to her music, writing poetry and dreaming of the day she could be free. She wondered what other people felt, what they thought, how they lived. Did others have the same hole in their soul as she did? Did others feel that they were watching the world go by without participating in it? Were other people as conflicted inside as she was? Did they have the answers? Did they feel like they belonged? Somewhere? Anywhere? She would have run away, but her dad threatened her more than once that if she ever ran, when he found her, he would kick her backside all the way home. He was very colorful in his description and she got the point. She was afraid of him. His temper was explosive and unpredictable, and she didn't want to set it off.

She went to school and tried to be as much like the other kids as possible, but the end of the day always came, and she'd make the lonely walk home to her house and her room. When Friday came, she tried to avoid the "what are you going to do this weekend?" question. The worst was after summer vacation. They would all come back with tales of beach parties, summer romances, vacation trips, movies and all kinds of surfing fun. She never had anything to say. So, she withdrew into her mind and her room. She was so lonely. She felt like she was invisible. She felt lonely at home and at school even with all the other kids around. Sometimes that made it worse. No one really knew her and what went on inside. She pretended to be having fun when she was at school and could pretend to be like them, talk like them, laugh at what they laughed at, but inside she was alone.

Her junior year she gave up pot. She decided it was stupid to continue to do something that she didn't like, was of no lasting benefit and in the end would only cause her harm. It wasn't hard to give it up, she never owned it and it never owned her. It was only a tool. The tool was no longer useful. Her dad had tried to keep her engaged in conversation about it over the years, but she wouldn't go there. She never smoked pot with him. That was just weird! He wanted to be her friend and have something to use against her all at the same time. She *wanted* a dad. She needed a dad. The friends she used to hang out with who smoked pot had all moved on to harder drugs, gotten pregnant or dropped out. She'd also started dating Brandon who didn't use drugs, hated drugs and smoking. She still smoked but not around him. She got involved in drama and dance. She loved them both and they gave her a sense of release. Drama was especially satisfying. She had a deep well of emotion to draw on and loved to play characters that allowed her to tap into that. But once again it got squelched. Neither drama nor dance lessons would come. She was already too tall at sixteen to be a ballerina and her dad didn't like her being away for rehearsals, fittings or performances. So, she gave up on those activities too. More dead dreams and unfulfilled desires to add to the growing pile.

When things happened that made her frustrated, angry, or feel completely hopeless she would clean. She would clean the house, her room and even the cars. She would rearrange the furniture, clean out cabinets, anything to release the pent-up emotion she had. She could not strike out in any way or she would be punished so she tried to be constructive in her release to keep herself from exploding or going insane. Ever so responsible, she was not going to do anything to rock the boat. She had a clean room for a teenager!

She couldn't keep a diary because her father had, on numerous occasions, found it, read it and then used it against her. The final straw on that was an entry she had written in frustration over her situation. She had let her teenage emotions out on paper and written "I hate him...I could just kill him. He is so unfair." He had discovered it unbeknownst to her. One night she was sitting on the edge of her bed, feet dangling, talking on the phone to Brandon. Suddenly she heard his footsteps coming down the hallway. She had her own phone and phone line that she paid for. The only reason she could have it was her dad got tired of her being on the house phone. It was the only real communication outlet she had.

"I gotta go Brandon, I hear my dad coming." It was 10:30 at night and she didn't want to hear the guff that her dad would give her or answer his fifty questions, so it was easier to hang up the phone.

"No, I want to talk to you, just put the phone down and we can finish talking after he leaves."

"OK, hang on then." She sat the phone down on the other side of her bed, away from the door so it was out of sight.

Suddenly, the door burst open and a knife landed on the ground right between her feet and stuck in the carpet. It all happened so fast she couldn't even react.

"You want to kill me? Go ahead here's your chance. Pick it up, go ahead—kill me if you want." He was yelling. The blood vessels in his neck were bulging and his face was beet red. He was shaking, he was so mad at her.

"What are you talking about?" She was bewildered.

"You know exactly what I'm talking about." He was seething.

She honestly didn't know. She sat in stunned, petrified silence. She couldn't speak. He continued his tirade of her hating him, her no-good-wet-back boyfriend, and anything else he could verbally throw at her. Her mind was racing through the roll-a-dex of possibilities that could have set him off.

Suddenly it dawned on her. "Have you been reading my diary?"

"I found it by accident."

By accident? She knew that was a lie. She had hidden it in the very back and very bottom of her underwear drawer. He must have found it the day before and been stewing on it because she'd only written three days ago, and she'd been home all day.

"I was looking for some pictures that I needed, and I found it. I see you want to kill me, so do it." He spit out the words at her.

She said nothing. There was nothing she could say. No matter which way she went, she'd be wrong, and he'd continue to yell, so she was silent.

He finally bent over and picked up the knife and stormed out of her room.

She knew there was nothing she could do about it. He was lying. She was the kid, and he was the parent. She decided from that point on, no more diaries.

Now she had no one. Not even "Dear Diary".

She was so shaken and embarrassed that Brandon had heard the whole conversation.

"What just happened Jenna?" Brandon sounded angry.

"You heard the whole thing; you know what happened. He's insane. He threw a knife at me and it landed right between my feet and stuck in the carpet. I can't deal with this." She was shaking.

"He threw a knife at you? I want to punch his face in. He is insane Jenna. He's got problems. Are you OK? Do you want me to come over there?"

"Are you crazy? He'd kill you if he saw you. I just need

to get off the phone and go to sleep. I'm sorry you had to hear that. I don't even understand why you put up with me when you have to deal with him. I love you, I gotta go." She was crying now. Her worst fear was that Brandon would run the other direction. Why would he stick around with her when there were a ton of other girls that would jump at the chance to go out with him and their dads weren't psychotic?

"OK, I love you. I'll talk to you tomorrow." He was angry but what could he do?

She hung up the phone and lay in bed crying and shaking. What kind of dad throws a knife at their kid? Why didn't her mom do something? If only she could run. All she could think about was turning eighteen and leaving, the only draw back to that was Rachel. How could she ever leave Rachel?

Often at night she would lie in bed and cry herself to sleep. She always felt that if her Grandpa were alive, this kind of stuff would not be happening to her. If he had found out about the bathroom incident and so many others, he would have put a stop to it. Or maybe if he were still alive her mom would feel she had someone to help her or somewhere to go and it would all be over. She would cry out to God or whoever might be listening, "Why did you take my Grandpa, this would all be over if he was here."

Even though no one else in her family went, she continued to see many counselors off and on over the years. One that she began to see when she was about seventeen had given her the option of turning her dad in. She had never realized that was an option. She'd never told anyone so she never knew that she could turn him in and put an end to everything. Thoughts raced through her mind all in a split-second. Thoughts of freedom, peace, safety and maybe even a normal life but in the end it all came down to one final overwhelming thought. If she did, every bad thing that happened after that would be her fault, so she declined.

CHANGE IS COMING

It was August and she was getting ready to enter her senior year. She'd been dating the boy of her dreams for about a year. Brandon was two years older than her, played football, attended the local college and was one of the hottest guys she knew. He was beautiful, half Greek and half Italian and had the best of both. Olive skin, green eyes, brown curly hair and dimples. She had been in love with him since she first met him at thirteen years old. He was the older brother of her best friend at the time. The moment she saw him her knees went weak, her heart raced, and she felt butterflies in her stomach, the good kind! They became friends but Jenna dreamed of the day that he'd see her as more than a friend. It took him a few years to realize that she was the one he had dreamed of. He was slower than she had liked, but eventually he came around. He'd dated other girls but no matter who she saw him with, she always knew that one day, he'd be with her. She always felt that he would be the one she'd marry. She didn't obsess over him or anything; she patiently waited for him to fall for her. Because of her dad, dating for her was not like dating to the other kids. Dating for them meant that Brandon went to her house; they talked, watched TV or played a game. They rarely ever got to go to a movie and never to the beach, a party, or hang out at his house. But, for her, the fact that Brandon liked her and saw something in her that he valued, was all that mattered. She was hopelessly in love with him. She constantly had to push back the thoughts that he was going to find someone else. She didn't believe she was pretty enough for him, fun enough or anything else "enough" for him. Especially considering all they had to endure with her dad.

Her dad hated Brandon. He hated the very idea of him. He refused to talk to him, wouldn't even look at him when Brandon was at the house. He criticized Brandon every chance he got. The only reason she could have Brandon over was because of Cindy. She had fought Mitch tooth and nail over it until Mitch just gave up. But he made the whole house pay for it with his attitude.

Brandon was the one splash of color in her other wise gray world.

Things were the same at home. She had grown used to all the uncomfortable things that her dad did, if anyone ever gets used to that. Maybe numb to it would be a better description. It was her lot in life, there wasn't a thing she could do to change it. So, everything that came her way she filed it and moved on. He still invaded her shower time, dressing time, hugged and kissed her too long and she still complained to her mom about it. Her mom still read all the time. Jenna still took care of the house and Rachel, nothing ever changed.

She was working a part-time job, which gave her more time out of the house. That had come about at sixteen, because she had needed money for school clothes. She couldn't believe that her dad had allowed her to get a job, but then again, he didn't have to pay for her clothes anymore either. Besides with a job, he always knew exactly where she was and what she was doing.

She started noticing that her dad was gone a lot. She didn't mind because it gave everyone a reprieve. But this guy who never dressed up for anything, never went anywhere or wanted to go anywhere except to work, was suddenly getting dressed up and going *fishing?* Every night! Jenna may have been only seventeen, but she wasn't stupid. She had grown up fast and could see the obvious; her dad was seeing someone else.

After some drama and a long drawn out battle, her parents got divorced. She was sad for her mom, but happy for the peace and quiet as well as safety it provided for her and her sister.

From that point on life got crazy. Once she graduated from high school, she went to work full-time to help support her mom and sister. She was working retail in the mall and at eighteen was already an assistant manager in training. Her mom was only thirty-four at the time, attractive and wanted to experience what she had missed out on by getting married and having a baby at fifteen. She was out dating every weekend; Jenna was raising her sister and they had to move. Her mom had decided to sell the house that the girls had grown up in and move to Orange Park, California. Rachel wasn't doing well in school and Mitch was still in town with his new girlfriend and soon to be wife. That was too close for comfort for Cindy. Neither Jenna nor Rachel wanted to move. They had to get rid of their beloved dog, most of their furniture, leave their friends and for the first time live in an apartment.

Eventually, Brandon decided he didn't want to be tied down. After almost four years, she was devastated. She didn't understand it. He called her one-day and told her that he needed to move on. How could he do this to her? What was wrong with him? What was wrong with her? She loved him more now than ever before, how could he leave her? She had never believed in sex before marriage but had given herself to him because she thought she was going to marry him. They had been dating almost two years before she'd made the decision to have sex with him. There was a long list of devastations in her life. Her one shining moment of happiness had now been tarnished and added to that list. She had never been happier than when she was with Brandon. Just to think of talking to him on the phone made her heart flutter and her palms sweat.

They had so much fun together, so many memories.

Once her parents had divorced, they had a lot more freedom to do fun things, hang out together, go to the movies, plays, the park, be a normal couple. Brandon got along well with Rachel and Cindy. He'd become the big brother Rachel never had. It was very helpful to Cindy to have a guy around the house to fix things, help with Rachel and they all laughed and had a lot of fun together. He preferred to be at Jenna's house instead of his own. She was the longest relationship he had ever had. Now he was gone. Out of her life and onto the next thing. In her mind there would never be anyone else. First, she didn't believe that she would ever attract anyone like him ever again. Secondly, she didn't believe she could love anyone the way she did him. The butterfly in the stomach, weak in the knees, sweaty palms and giddy girl smile feelings had never gone away, even after four years. Now he had left her. She felt the dark, empty vacuum in her soul once again. She tried on numerous occasions to win him back. She would stop by his house, call him and even tried to use her body to get him back. Nothing worked.

How would she ever find that again? The answer in her mind was a resounding, "you never will"!

LOSS

Since graduation and the break-up with Brandon, Jenna was working between forty-four and sixty hours a week. She threw herself into work. She learned, worked, worked some more and was determined to excel at whatever she did. She was finally able to go as far as she wanted and make her own decisions. That meant there wasn't a lot of time for anything else.

She had a hard time getting over Brandon and if she was honest with herself, she didn't want to get over him. She wanted him back and wanted her dream to be fulfilled of marrying him. She started to date a little, but it was more casual than anything serious, no one measured up. She'd go out on one or two dates with someone and that was it.

At twenty she was introduced to Todd. Her friend Sharon was the matchmaker.

Sharon and Jenna met when she was thirteen. Sharon was ten years her senior. She first met Cindy's older brother, Mark. She then became fast friends with Cindy's mom Esther. So, she spent a lot of time at her house and became part of the family. She was like an older sister to Jenna and Rachel. She was an interesting person. She was part Native American Indian and had a lot of the old school superstitions and traditions. She didn't look it. She had blue eyes, almost porcelain skin and medium brown hair. Her cheekbones, however, gave it away. She also claimed to be supernaturally gifted. She never said she was psychic or anything like that but claimed that she could read people by objects they had held or see things about people and sometimes in dreams, see the future. At some point she told Jenna she was a white witch. Apparently, that meant she did good to people with her gifts or abilities. At the time they met, she told Jenna she worked in an office for a record company and knew a lot of rock and roll stars. At thirteen, Jenna was completely enthralled by her. Sharon loved the girls and took them out shopping, bought them make-up, took them to restaurants, brought them special gifts when she traveled and was always willing to listen to them and try to help them with their struggles. She knew of the molestation by Mitch but not until Jenna was seventeen.

"I know this really nice guy who you should meet. He loves the same music you do, never been married, has a job and a great sense of humor." She had that twinkle in her eye and the look that said, "I won't take no for an answer!"

Why did Sharon feel like she needed a nice guy? She still hadn't recovered from Brandon. Some new guy wasn't going to make that happen. No amount of fairy dust would work on that wound.

"OK, but I hate blind dates and I don't want to get involved with anyone." The argument fell flat.

So, she met Todd. They dated and the next thing she knew, she was living with him in an apartment. She then found herself pregnant. She had never intended to live with him, so she had not intended to have sex with him so no need for the pill. She had caved a couple of times, but it was the night that, for the first time in her life, she got drunk. It was her twenty-first birthday. They had gone out with the drug dealer/friend who lived in apartment B. The dealer/friend had rented a limo and the whole deal. They went out to a few clubs to drink and dance. She was drinking Kamikazes and dancing all night. She had no idea how many she drank or that she was even drunk. Todd had taken advantage of the situation and now she was pregnant.

"I'm pregnant."

"Are you sure?" he asked only out of courtesy. She had been barfing every single morning. As soon as her eyes opened enough to let in the light she had to run to the bathroom.

"Of course, but I'll go get a pregnancy test if you don't believe me."

She went and got a blood test. Two day later the phone rang.

"Congratulations, you're pregnant."

"Thanks." She hung up. What was she going to do now? She'd never thought about this. Once again, she felt empty, alone and hurled out into space. How could this happen to Miss Responsibility? How could she be so stupid? A few profanities ran through her mind as she chastised herself for letting this happen. Jenna didn't even know why she was with him in the first place. He used drugs, hung out with drug dealers, and was rude to her family and all around just not her type. She had sunk to a new low in her life. How was she going to deal with this and most of all did she even want to? The answer was no she didn't want to deal with it. She tried to compartmentalize, but a baby wasn't going away, and neither was morning sickness. No filing cabinet in her head was big enough or efficient enough for that.

Todd was raised Catholic; she was raised nothing. He wasn't ready to be a dad and settle down. So, he borrowed the $250 bucks from the drug-dealer friend in apartment B and convinced her to have an abortion. Her mom went with her to Planned Parenthood for the initial consultation. No one told her that at three months the baby already has a heart, limbs, eyes, and can feel pain. They never told her what the impact would be like on her life, the risk involved, or that it was a human being she was killing. Nor did they explain the emotional aftermath, the physical shockwaves and the lifetime of regret that came with the decision.

The day came and again her mom took her. As she sat in the waiting room, she almost got up and left. She had been having dreams every night seeing a baby in her womb, but she didn't know what it meant, and she was scared. As she pondered leaving, they called her name. She was terrified and the nurse that helped her into the room with all the other girls was cold, informal, short and sharp with her words. She wanted to run but her feet wouldn't move. She wanted to flee but this woman was an authority and you can't run from that.

The whole ordeal felt like she was on a conveyer belt turned up to high speed. She was ushered into the room, put on a table and told that it would only take a few minutes. They stuck a needle in her arm and before she could protest, ask a question or think she was out and waking up in another room feeling like her guts had been ripped out. She was told to get dressed and go home. She felt the black hole consuming her and physical pain like nothing she had ever known.

She had trouble physically after that. She kept getting vaginal infections. She went back to Planned Parenthood on several occasions, but they kept telling her it was a yeast infection, or she was allergic to her detergent. Finally, after about a year she went to an O.B.G.Y.N and found out that her cervix was eroding. She had to have an in-office surgery where they froze her cervix. The doctor said it would feel like bad period cramps. Jenna thought to herself you're a dude; how would you know? It hurt worse than any period she'd ever experienced. When she went to get off the table, she almost fainted. The doctor told her that if she had waited much longer or they didn't do the procedure, she'd never be able to carry a child. It was all due to the abortion.

Everything changed after that. Not just her relationship with Todd but everything in her life. It wasn't anything that she could put into words, it just changed and not for the better. He treated her as if it was all her fault and all his guilt was placed onto her. She had never known anyone who had an abortion, never had any counseling regarding it or the aftermath so what happened to her was completely beyond her. So, she did what she knew how to do, she compartmentalized and moved on. It would be eight years before she would truly see and understand the impact that having an abortion had on her. Eight years before she would be able to deal with it and heal from it.

The relationship wasn't great to begin with. She tried to make it work but he didn't treat her well. He complained that her cooking wasn't like his mom's. He used drugs even when she asked him not to. He was reckless too. When he drove her car, he drove too fast, weaved in and out of traffic and took unnecessary risks. He flirted with other girls and treated her without much respect. Eventually she threw him out because he was cheating on her. It was the sixth sense she had developed over the years that had busted him. Sometimes it came in handy. Although learned under harsh and difficult circumstances, it did give her an advantage at times, sometimes a painful one, but nevertheless an advantage.

She vowed never to live with anyone else again.

RAFAEL

J enna still lived in Orange County. It was 1988, she was twenty-four and had been working for a car insurance company for three years. The company had gone through a ton of changes and she had grown and shifted with it. She was smart, hard working and willing to learn. She was also willing to go above and beyond the call of duty if something needed to be done. Jenna never did anything in the gray; she threw herself into whatever she was doing, all black, all white but no gray. She had been forced into gray growing up and never wanted to live there again.

When she left retail, they had just asked her, at twenty years old, to manage her own store but they had cheated her out of a much-needed vacation, so she quit. She took an office job for a change and chance to learn. She devoured as much knowledge about the industry as anyone would teach her. She would talk to anyone that would answer her questions. She found herself working in claims. That was where she met Rafael. She first met him when she was still living with Todd. He was Spanish and French. He was ten years older than her, about 6'1" about 190 lbs. He had dark hair, dark brown eyes and medium brown skin. He wasn't particularly muscular. In fact, he looked kind of squishy. Like a big, fuzzy teddy-bear that you could snuggle. He was soft spoken, gentle, smart and very funny. He was fascinating to her because she'd never met a man with those traits. He also took the time to teach her things that helped her do her job better and later helped her advance to an office manager. He treated her like a person, not an object. He was the only man except Ray, her step-grandpa, that had cared to listen to her, ask her questions, explain things to her, and treat her like an adult. He was gentle like Ray and she liked that. She sat three cubicles behind him. She was a clerk and he was an adjuster.

She'd known him for about a year. She'd kicked Todd out and been living on her own for about five months. No one ever told her how unwise it was to date someone in the same office as you, especially if that someone is in any way your superior. So, she got involved and eventually, against her own resolve, moved in with him. Everything went well at first. He exposed her to culture. He loved to travel, go to the theater, eat fine expensive food, buy expensive things, and she benefited from his wealth and generosity. He loved to take her shopping and buy clothes with her and for her. He listened to her and treated her as though she were smart, funny and interesting. They went on vacations and weekend trips to fun places. They took a two-week vacation to Cabo San Lucas and stayed at a beautiful resort. It was amazing except for the night they were riding in a cab on their way to dinner and got stopped, questioned and searched by the Mexican Federales. Apparently, the President was in town and they were lined up along the highways and stopping and searching everyone. Fortunately, Rafael spoke fluent Spanish so not only could he communicate with them but also understood what they were saying. She was just grateful she didn't end up in a Mexican prison!

They went to fabulous places to eat; he bought her jewelry; they talked about everything and enjoyed each other's company. They loved to watch football and she cooked for him as often as possible. Because of her home life she had never had the chance to experience a lot of things. She finally felt like she was getting to experience the world. The gaping hole in her soul was still there but she was at least enjoying life a little and hoped over time it would go away. He knew all about her past, including her dad but not the abortion. Jenna never talked about that to anyone.

After they'd been living together for a while, she talked him into getting her a dog. She hadn't had a dog since her parent's divorce, and she loved dogs. She was heartbroken when she had to get rid of her dog to move to Orange Park and she wanted one again. He finally gave in and they went to the pet store. Jenna's dogs had always been mutts, which was fine for her. But Rafael, being Rafael, had to have a purebred. They went and decided on an adorable little black and white Shitz Tsu puppy. They named him Captain Jack because when he ran, he ran with one back leg stiff, so he looked like a peg-legged pirate running down the street. He was a piece of work. He ate anything and everything except Jell-O and Pepto-Bismal. If it hit the floor it was his and good luck trying to get it back. She knew about the Pepto because she had a basket of red, Styrofoam apples on the coffee table for a Christmas decoration and he ate them. So, he had a stomachache and the vet told her to give him Pepto Bismal, which he spit out and refused to eat. One summer she spent a week sifting through dog-poop trying to recover a half-carat diamond necklace that he'd gotten a hold of and ate. Rafael had given that to her, and he was not happy about that incident. One-time CJ ate a peroxide soaked cotton ball that she'd dropped on the floor. When she called poison control, the guy on the line laughed at the fact that the dumb dog would eat it. But he assured her it wouldn't hurt him. He was always getting himself into trouble. He managed on several occasions to get a coat hanger stuck around his middle and would run around wildly trying to get it off. He loved to chew on the high heel portion of Jenna's shoes. So, she would often go to work dressed for success, with little puppy chew marks up and down the heel of her high-heeled shoes. He was crazy! He kept her laughing at all his antics, and he was very cute.

This time she had finally scored the one she would

marry. There was only one small problem. He wasn't divorced from his first wife. She had left him. She "didn't want to be married and tied down anymore." He was devastated. He had wanted kids, she didn't. He'd planned on being married to her for the rest of his life, and she'd changed her mind. At first Jenna felt that it was only a matter of time as the divorce was in process when they started dating.

Then after about two years she started to feel panic well up in her again. Things changed. He went places without her, kept secrets from her, had phone calls that she was not privy to and the divorce was at a stand still. There was that feeling again. The feeling that her life was about to come crashing down on her and she had no ability to stop it. She had a knot in the pit of her stomach that would not be ignored no matter how much her mind tried to reason it away.

She applied her best deductive reasoning and detective skills and couldn't figure out his problem. She'd even discovered the code to his briefcase and checked inside of it to see if she could find something, nothing!

"Where are you going again?" she was sick of him spending weekends elsewhere.

"I am going to my sisters if you must know." He sounded annoyed. His face was firmly set. He had a way of looking and saying things to her that made her feel like she was five, stupid and not worth the explanation.

She didn't believe him, but she had no proof. For as nice as he could be, as giving as he could be, when he wanted to be obstinate and difficult, she couldn't make headway no matter what she did.

"When will you be home?" She tried to sound nonchalant and sweet.

"I don't know, and it shouldn't matter to you. I'll be home when I get home." His back was toward her and he was picking up his car keys.

"Will you call and let me know?" She knew he wouldn't, but she asked anyway. What was she missing? She couldn't find a shred of evidence for where he was going or what he was up to. She had her suspicions that he might be seeing his soon-to-be ex-wife. She didn't see how he could be going out with any other woman other than her. His ex had the inside track on him; after all they were still married and had been married longer than she'd even known Rafael. He wasn't the one who'd wanted the divorce in the first place. It made sense.

"I'll see you later." He left, hopped into his little red Miata and drove away.

She was moving between rage and an emotional melt down. She was so sick of this. Would the emptiness and darkness of her soul ever go away? Would anyone ever just love her? Would she ever be able to trust anyone, ever? Was happiness meant only for those people living outside of the glass box she lived in? She could tell it was crumbling right in front of her eyes, but she was unable to stop it or explain it, so she filed it.

Then she decided that she would go to her mom's house for the weekend and when he tried to call, if he tried to call or come home, she wouldn't be there. She was sick and didn't feel like being at home alone anyway. Going to her mom's wasn't exactly high on her list of things she wanted to do, but she could rest on her mom's couch. Maybe her mom would make her some food or some hot tea. Captain Jack loved to go places, so he'd be happy. So, she left. Give him a taste of his own medicine.

Sunday night she got home, and he wasn't there. Great her plan to get back at him had failed and worse yet, it hadn't even been discovered. There's nothing worse than trying to get back at somebody and they don't even know it!

They no longer worked together. In the last six months he had taken a teaching job and she went to work at the Orange Police Department in the City of Orange. She was the clerk for the homicide detectives.

One Monday evening, after they got home from work the bomb dropped.

"I'm moving out." He smiled and walked away.

She sat in stunned silence and then began to cry. "Why, what did I do? I know we have been fighting a lot lately and you think I'm being nosy, but do you have to move out? Can't we just work it out?" She was desperate to not allow another relationship to fail. She went through the file cabinet in her mind. What had happened and what could she say now to change his mind?

"I have a place already, I will be packing my stuff and moving in two weeks. I love you and we can still date but I'm moving." His voice was firm and final.

He was moving to be near his sister and his nephews. His sister had a house about three blocks from where she and her family lived, it was empty, and she was willing to rent it to him. It was an hour away from their current residence together.

"I just don't understand, why you are leaving?" She was beside herself now. He already had a place. How could that be? She had been right; there was something more than his 'going to visit my sister' routine.

Three long-term relationships and all three ended in heartache for her. He was ten years older than her and more mature, wasn't that supposed to make a difference? They had been through so much together. Job changes, two moves, all the ups and downs and shenanigans of his soon-to-be ex-wife, they loved each other and still he was leaving. Why did life have to be so hard and hurt so much? Why did she have to feel the black hole? Was she just a freak and only meant to have misery in her life? Her mind began to reel, and her heart began to shut down, time to open the file cabinet and start filing. It was the only way she knew how to live and how to survive.

He moved out.

She was left with a half empty house, her dog, and a broken heart. Again.

1991

Sharon knew all about everyone of Jenna's boyfriends from Brandon, all the way to Rafael. She felt bad about the Todd fiasco and swore off setting Jenna up on blind dates from that point on.

Now here they were again, another crash and burn for Jenna.

"Everything in my life sucks." Jenna sat in the chair opposite her friend Sharon weighing her next statement. "If this is all there is, I don't want to do this life."

Jenna wasn't a drama queen or one to make off-the-cuff radical statements nor was she a person that would do something totally rash. She was just angry. Angry and hurting.

Sharon realized that her friend's statement wasn't just about Rafael, but years of rejection, hurt and pain that had built up inside. Although it sounded a little fatalistic, Sharon knew the source of Jenna's words and that she wouldn't do anything stupid or try to hurt herself. She just needed to blow off some steam, so she didn't explode.

Sharon took a deep breath, "I know it seems that way now, but it won't always be this way. You know as well as I do, guys are jerks, not all of them are as bad as Rafael, but still they can be jerks. Besides, look at you. You're tall, thin, blonde, blue-eyed and beautiful, you can do better than him any day. Look I've been in a relationship with Rick for three years now, it has its ups and downs, but we're happy."

Jenna was not comforted. She held back from making a sarcastic comment. Sharon and Rick had a relationship, if you could call it that; they rarely lived under the same roof or even in the same state. How did that compare? She knew Sharon meant well, but it felt empty. She was frustrated and irritated. She had butterflies in her stomach, her jaw was clinched like a tight wire and arguing the point was useless.

"OK, so now what? I'm twenty-six, almost twenty-seven, Rafael moved out, I'm left with the house, a fat rent, a new car and I'm jerked around once again. I had always planned on being married and living on my farm by the time I was twenty-five. I'm more than a quarter-of-a-century old. Not only am I not married, I don't even have a boyfriend anymore."

Sharon knew that her words sounded empty to her friend. She knew trying to console her was pointless. When Jenna got in this state there wasn't much she could say.

She'd been down this road before with Jenna. She knew the whole story of the abuse, control, disappointments and a missed childhood. It broke her heart to see her friend suffer. To have happiness elude her once again made her feel sad and helpless. She knew there was nothing she could say. There wasn't anything she could do to change things for her friend; nothing could make up for the damage that had been done. She didn't have a magic wand to wave or a crystal ball to look into. She simply had to listen and allow Jenna to go through whatever she was going through and try to be the best friend she could be to her.

For Jenna every time she had to add another check mark on her, "I've been rejected" list, she was forced to replay her whole miserable life over again in her mind. That was a movie she didn't want to see the first time and she had replayed it thousands of times.

"He wants to date. Are you kidding? I just gave two years of my life to this guy, he drops the bomb on me that he is moving out, with no real explanation and says we can date.

Do I just look stupid? Do I have 'use me and throw me away' written somewhere on my forehead? And now I have all these bills. I can't pay my bills and still eat. I won't be eating anyway because he took the refrigerator, the dining room table, the bedroom set, the T.V., stereo and the washer and dryer with him. I certainly don't have the money for a new fridge, or anything else for that fact. I have the couch and love seat I started with, my dishes, towels and my dog! I can sleep on the couch. I'll be hungry but not tired. How does someone say they love you, leave you high and dry and then say, 'we can date'?" She was on a tirade. The anger was seething out of her like a teapot when it's boiling.

Every muscle in her body was ridged and every sentence was punctuated with a curse word. She felt so betrayed. Oh, how she hated gray and here she was again. No explanation to put into a category, no clear line of demarcation, only a gray, ambiguous, "I'm moving out." Was life ever going to be black and white for her? Did there always have to be this fog she was fighting to get through? Wasn't there supposed to be right and wrong in the world? Didn't anyone have the answers?

"Can your mom help you? Maybe you can get a roommate or something." Sharon was trying to help.

"I guess I can ask her, but this is just crap!" Jenna didn't want to ask her mom. Since the divorce, Cindy had been dating the same guy and was gone every weekend. She had checked out of mommy mode and into relationship mode. Cindy and Rachel had a good relationship, but since the divorce Cindy always seemed to have an edge to her when it came to Jenna. It was frustrating for Jenna, she felt she had no one, not even a mom. She knew her mom loved her, but there was just tension.

Jenna was pacing and chain smoking. Smoking always made her feel better, but chain smoking gave her a sense of power and courage to continue her tirade. "Who does he think he is? Just wait until he calls and wants a date, I'll be busy, or I may not even return his phone calls." She let out a few profanities to punctuate her sentence.

"Well, you'll get over this and move on. You're strong and a survivor. Look you have a great job at the Police Department, you look hot in your new car, you're smart, and have a lot to offer anyone. You can take care of yourself and don't need him anyway. It's his loss not yours." Sharon loved her friend and knew that she'd get past it and move on, she always did. She'd seen Jenna go through a lot over the years and saw her as a survivor. Jenna didn't want to be a survivor she wanted to be whole, to be loved and to have the empty void filled. She wanted to feel alive.

Jenna didn't end up being as strong as she'd originally professed to be. For the first few months after Rafael moved out, he'd call her every night to talk to her about her day and they'd laugh and she'd cry because she missed him, felt so alone and didn't understand why he left. You'd think she'd have gotten a clue or at least been so mad that she didn't ever want to speak to him again, but no such luck. She ended up trying to date him at first. She still loved him and hoped that he would see that he didn't want to live his life without her. They went out a few times. She went to his new place a few times and stayed the night with him. They celebrated Christmas together, had a few laughs but eventually he began to pull the same stunts. He'd tell her he was going to call her at a specific time on a specific day, the time would come and go, and he wouldn't call. She'd try to call him, and he wouldn't answer the phone. When she'd finally get a hold of him, he'd always have some lame sounding excuse. So eventually she began to do the same to him. She wouldn't answer the phone when he called, she'd be busy when he wanted to get together and finally, he just stopped calling. So, after the end, it lasted another eight months. She still had no idea as to why he'd ended it and now it didn't matter, she was done.

1992

Around the time Rafael was leaving Jenna, she found out her dad had abused Rachel as well. She had failed to protect her little sister. When she found out, she was so enraged and so broken she almost crashed her car while driving on the freeway. She had foolishly thought that somehow, she had been able to keep Rachel from suffering the same fate as her. All those years and Rachel never told her. She never said a word or confided in Jenna until now. She failed at the single most important job she'd had, protecting her little sister. She was a lousy protector. It killed her to think of tiny, fragile little Rachel being subjected to the perversion of their dad. She wanted to kill him. The things Rachel told her were almost unbearable to hear. She felt like she was going to go insane thinking of everything that had happened to Rachel, and then add her failure as a big sister to keep Rachel safe. It felt like more than Jenna could bear. Why had he gone after her? Wasn't Jenna enough? Couldn't he have left Rachel alone? How did she not see it? How could she have done better? Why hadn't she ever asked Rachel before? She couldn't file fast enough to keep the pain from searing her heart.

She hated men.

That had pushed her over the edge. Now at twenty-seven she was done with men. No one could blame her. Abuse at the hand of her father, a broken heart at nineteen and several failed relationships had caused her to believe that any relationship she entered was doomed and she'd had enough. She didn't want to marry out of fear that she'd marry an abuser. She couldn't bare the thought of her children being abused by their dad and going through all the anguish that she'd been through. She believed that she would literally kill someone for that. She didn't want to end up in prison for the rest of her life for any reason.

The second scariest thought to her was that she'd become the abuser. After all she'd been through, she had a great deal of hate and anger pent up inside of her. She didn't understand all the anger. It didn't come out very often, but it was there. She was terrified that she'd have children, they'd be crying, acting up, or simply being children and she would lose control, fly into a rage and do serious damage. No one could guarantee that her kids would be safe. Nothing could sway her. She couldn't fix the problems inside of her, so she chose to move away from relationships and the idea of ever being married. All the counselors in the world hadn't been able to change her, heal her or help her sort it out. She felt better for dumping on them, but she was still the same person when she left their office, as she was when she went in. She wanted to change, but the execution was always elusive.

She had quit smoking, drinking, and having sex outside of marriage. Not because she thought it was wrong; she didn't see any further use for those things. Drinking was too scary because she could lose control. She couldn't risk another guy taking advantage of her. She'd also blacked out once. Rafael and Jenna had been at a Christmas party and she was drinking. She didn't remember much about that night, but Rafael didn't speak to her for a week. When he finally did, he told her that she'd cussed him out. She remembered nothing. That scared her to death. She wasn't a heavy or frequent drinker anyway, but if that could happen once, it could happen again and she wasn't going to be that out of control, ever! Smoking, well, she simply decided that being a wrinkled, crusty woman that smoked through a hole in her throat was not her idea of glamorous. Sex was something she never completely enjoyed. Even with all the therapy, she always felt dirty, even if she wanted to be sexy and alluring it just ended up making her feel cheap and ashamed. She had sex because she was "supposed to" in long-term relationships, it was expected. It was always an irritant in her relationships, so she gave it up. She dated but would not allow it to be serious or go any further. Logical, black and white-compartmentalizing Jenna; that was that. It worked out fine for her, not so well for the men. She didn't care; she didn't like men all that much anyway. Women friends and a few casual guy friends were enough. Besides she had Rachel.

GIRLS BEING GIRLS

B y now Rachel and Jenna lived together. Rachel had moved in to help after Rafael left. She was tired of living with their mom and wanted to get out on her own. The house was big enough with three bedrooms and two bathrooms and even had a built-in pool, which in Orange County, California came in handy. Both girls had to take a part-time job along with their full-time one to supplement their income. It was the only way they could pay rent and eat. Cindy had bought them a new fridge so they could grocery shop. They would have moved, but to find a place that took the dog and then to come up with first, last and security on their own, was impossible. They didn't live extravagantly. They had their rent, utilities and pool upkeep. They both had car payments and of course insurance, gas, food and her little dog. Most of the time they ate tacos, bean burritos, hamburgers, and occasionally some chicken. Sometimes all they had were potatoes and green beans. Jenna never could figure out how it ended up being green beans, she was never a green bean fan, but they were cheap, so they ate them. They shopped at the discount stores and thrift stores and tried to be as thrifty as possible. Fortunately for them both, their jobs were not very far away from where they lived so they didn't have to spend a fortune on gas to get to work.

Rachel had suffered a great deal in her life from the things that happened to her at the hand of their father. She took a different route then Jenna and seemed to have a much harder time with life then Jenna. She was more outspoken. If Rachel didn't like something or someone made her mad, she let it out. She was not above telling off someone in the grocery store if they seemed to be staring or made a rude comment. Although she was smaller than Jenna, at 5'4" and 95 lbs. with zero muscle tone, she would pick fights with people bigger than her. Jenna was always trying to get her out of jams or keep her from getting her face smashed in. It seemed whenever they went to a club or a concert they always ended up by the drunkest, rudest girls who would spill beer on Rachel or make a snide remark and Jenna was always stepping in the middle to keep her sister from a full-on brawl. She was beautiful, funny, energetic, and witty and wasn't afraid to use her sexuality. Jenna ran from it, Rachel embraced it. She had long-and short-term relationships and was willing to move on easily if someone was not worth the fight. She made Jenna laugh. She was quick witted and always had funny, sarcastic things to say. Rachel was also more sensitive. Her feelings were easily hurt, and she constantly struggled to believe she had value. She was the more girly of the two. She loved to fuss with her hair and make-up. Her hair had wave and body to it so she could change hairstyles easily. Her skin tone was much fairer than Jenna's and it allowed her to change her hair color from platinum blonde to brick red and still look beautiful.

Even though they were grown women, Jenna still felt very protective of her little sister because Rachel still seemed so vulnerable.

They were more like best friends than sisters. They had a lot of fun together and did mostly everything together. They had private jokes between them, they both loved animals and their music. In one year's, time they'd gone to over twelve concerts, everyone from James Taylor, Prince, Gun's n' Roses to Skid Row, even Neil Diamond. Getting dressed up, hanging out together and going to concerts was something they lived for. They would skimp on groceries to save for a concert. They also loved driving up to Hollywood to walk the Strip, check out the stores and clubs. There were several clubs they liked and were always looking for the newest and latest local band to hit the scene. Sometimes they got lucky and some of the big names would show up to play at a local club.

They weren't wild by definition. But they did a few crazy things that they could've gotten into a lot of trouble doing, but miraculously didn't.

One time they went to a club to see a friend of theirs play. They were all dressed up in their black mini-skirts, high heels and hair all done. They were on their way to their car when three guys were making their way into the club.

"Hey, you guys leaving so soon?" They had directed their question at the girls.

"Yeah, we were leaving, why?" The girls had nothing else to do and it was only 10:30 PM.

"Well, if you come back in, we'll buy you a drink." They were cute. *Three of them and only two of us, OK, here goes.* So, they went back inside with them.

The girls introduced themselves and found out the guys names were Frank, he was the oldest, Doug his little brother and Jeff.

"What are you drinking?" Frank was talking to Jenna as he gave her the once over with his eyes.

"Neither one of us drink but I'll take a soda." Jenna smiled and said, "Thanks."

Jenna thought he was cute. He was taller than Jenna with her heels on; so he was about 6'1, around 190, shoulder length blonde hair and blue eyes, maybe 25 to 29 years old. The other two, Doug and Jeff were both blonde as well, a little thinner and a little shorter but rock star all over. Doug decided he liked Rachel. They hung out at the club for about an hour listening to the music, watching people dance and making small talk.

"Hey, we're hungry, want to go get a burger?" It was Doug. By now the boys had three or four beers in them.

"Rachel, you want to get a burger?" She gave her the look that said, 'I will if you want to but if you aren't up for it, we can go home'.

Rachel read her signal but didn't want to go home, "OK, yeah I'm hungry too."

"Great, we can go to Tommy's and get some grub and go back to our house. We have a pool table and we could hang out." It was Doug's idea.

So, Jenna drove her car with Frank in it and Rachel got in the car with Doug and Jeff. They went to the popular local burger spot and loaded up on fries and burgers then headed back to the house where all three of the guys lived.

They lived about eight blocks away from where the girls had grown up. It was an upper middle-class neighborhood; the house was like the one they'd grown up in; it was a nice house. It was full of musical instruments and sound equipment. Apparently, they worked with a few up and coming musicians and did the mixing and recording for them. They ate and the guys drank more beer, one thing led to another and Jenna was out in the garage playing pool with Frank and Rachel was in the bedroom making out with Doug. Jenna's mind wandered from time to time onto Rachel, she had to check on her to make sure she was safe. She didn't bother knocking but went right into the bedroom to check on her. She didn't want her to be taken advantage of or manhandled.

Next thing the girls knew it was 5:00 o'clock in the morning.

Now Jenna was usually Miss Responsibility. Under normal circumstances she'd never have gone with three guys that she just met who were drunk, back to their house until 5:00 o'clock in the morning with no one knowing where she was. Taking Rachel along was totally out of character. Jenna trusted her instincts. She felt they'd be safe, and they made it out unscathed. It was foolish. At the time, she didn't think so, but it was.

In the spring they decided to get tattoos. It was Jenna's

idea.

"Hey, lets get a tat!" Jenna was hoping for a positive response from her sister. She got it.

"OK, I know just what to get. When do you want to do it? We should both do it at the same time. That will be so cool." Rachel was excited.

"What are you gonna get?" Jenna asked, glad that Rachel was on board.

"I'll get a penguin on my ankle." Rachel loved penguins and had an entire collection of stuffed ones in her room.

"I haven't totally decided yet what to get. I think maybe a dolphin jumping through something. I love dolphins. If I get to be reincarnated, I want to come back as a dolphin." Jenna loved nature and animals. Since dolphins were one of her favorites that seemed like a good choice.

"I think I'll have money this Friday to go, I get paid and should have a few extra bucks. What do you think?" Rachel was looking over her checkbook with excitement.

Jenna grabbed hers, "Yep, I get paid at the coffee house so I could swing a few. I wonder how much they are?"

"How much will you have? I'll have about $40."

Jenna did a quick calculation, "I should have about $40 as well. Hope that's enough."

Friday came and the girls called a couple of guy friends they had, hopped in Jenna's car and drove to Hollywood. They looked at several tattoo parlors and found one that seemed like the right place. They looked around and Rachel found what she wanted right away. It turned out, they only had enough money for one, and so Jenna let Rachel go first. Although she was much smaller than Jenna, she almost broke Jenna's hand squeezing it to keep from screaming while Waldo Lusky was inking her. What name would you expect from a tattoo artist on Hollywood Boulevard? Waldo was tattooed from one end to the other with a giant spider web covering the top of his foot. He looked like a biker and scary as could be, but he was very kind and gentle with Rachel. Rachel was brave and never cried, until they got in the car, she cried all the way home. It turned out beautifully, full of color and very cute on her little thin ankle. She was so proud of it. She loved to show it off. Jenna would have to wait for another day.

Jenna also began to think about her future and what she wanted to do with her life. She decided that she liked police work and was interested in solving crime. She loved the idea of working for the FBI. She talked Rachel into taking some night classes with her in Criminal Justice at the local college. She had set the challenge in front of her to work her two jobs, take classes and get into shape to pass the physical examine and get hired by the FBI. She was twenty-seven and if she was accepted by her thirty-fourth birthday, she was in. She had nothing in her background to keep her from it, so it was a matter of learning and training.

Goal set.

SEARCHING IN
THE DARKNESS

L ife seemed pretty good. No one was controlling her. She didn't have to answer to anyone. She could do what she wanted; go where she wanted, talk how she wanted, and she didn't need some guy around. She felt that maybe for the first time in her life she could figure out what it was like to live outside the glass. There was one problem. She was horribly empty inside. Nothing ever seemed to make it go away. Everyone else seemed to have fun doing the same things she did, but some how it didn't satisfy her. Although she told herself that everyone must have this gaping hole in their heart, she couldn't quite leave it alone and she could never quite believe it either. She lived her whole life feeling empty deep down. There must be something she was missing.

She'd learned to ask a lot of internal questions, mentally going over everything until she figured it out. She was always learning. She watched T.V. specials on everything, from orphans in Romania, to why serial killers do what they do and everything in between. She read constantly, fiction, romance and non-fiction. She had a very acute sense of her surroundings. If she entered a room that was familiar to her, she could tell you if the slightest thing had been moved. With all her learning, compartmentalizing, black and white acute observation skills, she couldn't solve the emptiness. She had this feeling that there was something more that was always just beyond her reach.

From the time she was twelve she had been a reader. Because her mom was a reader, she had access to books all the time. Cindy didn't care what Jenna read. Jenna was mature for her age, articulate and smart so her mom figured she could handle it. She began to read everything her mom read except the Harlequin Romance novels; she hated those. She loved Stephen King, Anne Rule, Ann Rice, Danielle Steel and Dean Koontz. Because of the books she read and the movies she watched she had a fascination with the supernatural. In her endeavor to fill that empty, gaping hole she tried the occult. She already had that connection with Sharon. Now she had another friend who was a medium, read Tarot cards and did astrological charting. Her name was Maggie.

One Saturday, Jenna went to Maggie's house with several other friends who were into all that stuff and had a séance. Jenna was nervous but excited. They all quieted themselves and waited. Maggie did her "trance" thing and Jenna waited.

"Jenna there's someone who wants to speak to you. He's here in the room now."

Jenna felt a cold chill run down her spine and the presence of some one or some thing next to her. She couldn't move. Every hair on her body was standing on end. She didn't know what to do or say. She was thrilled and scared to death at the same time.

"Is he next to me?" She already knew the answer.

"Yes, he has left our world. He has dark hair; I see him next to a piano and a gold statue of an eagle on the piano. He wants you to know that you'll be all right. Don't be afraid. He's watching over you."

Jenna didn't know who it was. It didn't sound familiar to her at first. Then it dawned on her. Sharon's long-time boyfriend Rick had died suddenly about seven months before. He loved to play the piano, was Native American and had a statue of a gold eagle that sat on top of his piano. It was Rick. She had never even met him. He knew about her because of Sharon. She knew about Rick only from Sharon's description and the information that she shared. She was impressed.

She told Sharon about the incident and Sharon confirmed that it was Rick. Sharon explained that he felt a special need to watch over Jenna because she had told him about her and all the difficulty that she had in life. He was assigned as her protector.

So, Jenna decided to follow in Sharon's footsteps and try to become a white witch. She had the connections, the desire and the spiritual sensitivity, which she was told was very valuable. There was a shop down the street from her house with books, instruments and everything she needed.

She tried it, still nothing. Just emptiness. She decided it needed time. She continued to pursue it even though it was not fulfilling her.

Then one day at her part-time job someone walked into her life that would radically alter her life forever.

"Beloved, do not believe every spirit, but test the spirits, whether they are of God; because many false prophets have gone out into the world." 1 John 4:1 KJV

COLGATE AND A TWELVE-STRING

J enna still had a part-time job at a local coffee house that had recently opened. The coffee house worked perfect with her full-time job at the police department and it was fun.

Working there was like eating comfort food. The air smelled wonderful, like coffee, baked bread with sugar all melted into one glorious aroma. She loved the fact that after working only a short shift she could smell that comforting, warm fragrance on her clothing long after she got home. She had regular customers that she loved. The Friday night guys who came in to play music to hone their craft and earn some extra cash. The quirky guy, John, who believed he could heal you with the heat of his hands over your liver. The owner, Roy, had traveled all over the world with his wife. He had great adventure stories to tell, a love for food and coffee and a great sense of humor. He was kind of a dad-like figure, always asking about Jenna's life. Checking in on her. She liked talking to Roy. He didn't try to hit on her, which she was grateful for. There was a Special Forces-Navy Seal that she worked with for three months. His name was Chuck, or so he said. He was young, blued eyed, physically fit and very intriguing. He had just returned from a mission and was on leave for three months. He still had training everyday and had to stay in shape, but he was bored, so he got a part-time job. She loved to verbally spar with him. He was very witty and sarcastic. The fact that she could tell jokes with the best of them and cuss like a sailor helped in her sparing. If Roy got in the middle of it, it became a verbal firefight. She went out with Chuck once, to a movie, nothing happened. She was so disappointed. Even though she had sworn off men, she still dated here and there and making out with a Navy Seal would be a cool story to tell. She found him so intriguing and sort of dangerous. But, so out of reach.

It was a Friday night when Jenna walked into the coffee house to the sound of an acoustic guitar playing and someone singing. As she rounded the corner, she saw the face that was connected to the voice. Her knees went weak at the sight of him. That hadn't happened to her since she was thirteen, the first time she met Brandon. He looked to be in his early 30's. He had dark shoulder length hair, piercing blue eyes and a smile that would make Colgate and any dentist proud. His facial structure was like Brad Pitt, strong, nice lines with dimples. He was about 6'1" with a strong, medium build, about 195 lbs. and in good shape. His name was Trevor Stone. He was auditioning for Roy to play at the coffee house. He played a twelve-string guitar like a sweet violin. He could play any song you threw at him.

Jenna went to work behind the counter but couldn't take her eyes off him. This was a guy she had to get to know. That night he approached the counter, flashed a brilliant Colgate smile and asked for some "water, room temperature, no ice." He explained that ice water makes your vocal cords freeze up which of course is not conducive to singing. She noted that for future use. While she was quite taken with his smile, she couldn't help but notice a pin he wore on the lapel of his jacket it simply said, Jesus. She dismissed it.

He got the job. Good she thought, she'd see more of him. There was something about this guy that seemed so different. She couldn't explain it. She felt somehow that he could see right through her. Although that unnerved her, she was strangely drawn to him.

"No one can come to Me unless the Father who sent Me draws him..." John 6:44 KJV

NOT WHAT
YOU THINK

The following week, Friday arrived. Trevor was taking the place of the usual Friday night guys. The owners were letting them switch off to see who could draw bigger crowds.

He walked into the coffee house carrying his guitar wearing that crazy smile, cowboy boots, a blazer and that Jesus pin. "How are you?"

Jenna was glad to see him "Good, would you like some water, no ice?"

He smiled that smile. "You remembered. I'd love some water. It's warm out there today."

This routine went on for several weeks. She found out that he liked to be called Trev instead of Trevor. A few conversations happened of no real significance. He was a little evasive when asked about his personal life, never talked about a girlfriend, didn't wear a ring and some how always moved the conversation around to some other topic. No matter how much Jenna flirted he just didn't take the bait. Then came the day.

"You busy tomorrow night?" He sat down at the counter.

"No, I have no plans, maybe go out to Hollywood and

walk the strip with some friends, you know see who's playing, but nothing set in stone. Why?" Her heart was racing.

"I play at the Black Angus lounge on Saturday nights, thought you might like to come out and hear me play." He always had a hint of laughter around the corner of his eyes and in the sound of his voice.

"Sure, that sounds great. I'd really like that." She could hardly control her thoughts as they raced through her mind. What did this mean? What do I wear? Did he finally notice me? He is so far out of my league. What is his angle? How can I go? I'm so awkward around him? She was distracted her entire shift and could hardly sleep that night.

Saturday, she went through her wardrobe several times trying to decide what to wear. She finally decided on a black skirt, just above the knee, a yellow button up shirt, black stockings and pumps. Jenna looked in the mirror to survey the results. She was tall and had an athletic lean build and was still well proportioned. But the three-inch heels added to her height and made her legs look even longer than they already were. Honestly, she hadn't changed much since high school. She still didn't like her forehead or jaw; she still didn't think she was particularly pretty. Mascara was still her go to for make-up. She loved big earrings and lots of rings on her fingers. She kind of went between the hippie-rocker look and the high-fashion look depending on the occasion and mood. This time she opted for high fashion. She had put on some make-up and decided she needed one more thing to finish the outfit. She added an ankle bracelet for effect and drove nervously to the restaurant.

When she arrived, she went to the lounge where she found an entire table of groupies that were there for Trev. The first thing she noticed was the drinks— actually the absence of them. At every other table in the bar, the people had alcoholic drinks in front of them except the groupie table. The second thing was the real problem, a few guys, but mostly girls. Great. Competition. Awkwardness. One of the girls, Renee, seemed to know "all about Trev". He was already playing a set. He motioned for her to sit at the table with the others. She sat directly in his line of vision so that her legs, which she crossed, with the little gold ankle bracelet were noticeable. He nodded approval. Finally, she thought, I'm making headway.

She should've chastised herself for even caring about this guy. She had, after all, sworn off men and now here she was trying so desperately to get his attention. He was a hard customer. She usually didn't have so much trouble. Not that she went out of her way to act that way, but she knew she could get attention if she tried. She had known that since she was 13. She could illicit catcalls and wolf-whistles just walking down the street. She always looked older than she was, which when you're a teenager, is a bonus. This was some how different. Maybe that's why it meant so much to her to get his attention, because he was so resistive. Oh no, she thought, maybe I'm turning into one of them. You know the kind of girl that goes after a guy just to see if she can conquer? She'd never been like that. In fact, she was still scared of men because the issue of sex always came up. She dismissed those thoughts and went back to concentrating on Trev.

His first set was done. He was on his way over.

"I like your ankle bracelet." He motioned with his head.

"Thanks. You sound great." She tried not to sound nervous.

"Did you meet everyone? This is Renee, Josh, Kim, Kenny, Carol, and my manager Connie. This is Jenna everyone." He sat down.

Everyone started talking about this and that. Jenna felt totally out of place. For all the confidence she seemed to project, she was an introverted person who felt socially awkward. Being at a table with a gorgeous, talented guy and a bunch of groupies was way out of her comfort zone. Jenna's thoughts were racing, *put me in a stadium with 20,000 screaming Guns and Roses fans and I am in my element. Not here! Not with groupies and all their groupie talk. Why am I so stupid? I am way out of my league. I should make up an excuse and leave.*

She was too chicken to leave. She was taught to be polite and respectful. She was stuck. Awkward, uncomfortable and insecure, but stuck.

Then someone directed a question at her.

"So, what do you do?" it was Renee.

"I work for the Orange County P.D. I am a clerk for the homicide detectives there."

"Wow, I bet that's exciting. Do you like it?" This time it was Connie, the manager.

"Yes, I love it. Sometimes it's a little scary, but I love all the guys I work for and it's challenging for me." Jenna tried to watch her language as she spoke. These people seemed to speak without using colorful language to punctuate their sentences. She used colorful language as part of her normal conversation. Working for detectives didn't help that any. She was not afraid to tell the jokes, make the points or challenge. It was all part of the wall she had built up to protect herself. She was smart, eager to learn and advance in her job but wanted them to know she could banter with the best of them. Even if she was scared to death inside, never let it show! This was different.

Trev went back to his set. The conversation died down which she was grateful for. She felt like an outsider with these people. There was the window again. She hated feeling like she was looking at life through that stupid window. She was sick of that window, but she had no idea how to break it. They all knew each other and seems they had for some time. They had been Trev groupies for a while and knew more about him than she did. She didn't like that. She didn't have the upper hand in this situation and that made her uncomfortable.

After his last set was over, he came back to the table. Jenna noticed that they all had the same bracelets on. They were simple, hand made thin black leather with some plastics beads, a green one, red, black and white.

"What are those about?" Jenna pointed to the bracelet.

"Here would you like one?" Trevor took his off and gave it to her.

Wow, he gave me his. Cool! As she surveyed the landscape, she decided she would be the first to make an exit. She put the bracelet on, said her polite goodbyes and left.

Well, that was a disappointment. What the heck was that all about? I barely had a conversation with him. The safety of the group kept him at bay, no hope for the future, a failed attempt! As she drove home, she scolded herself for even caring. Besides this guy was way too good looking and charming for her. Who did she think she was? She was not very attractive; she had a great figure but so what. Lots of girls had that plus more! She could never land such a beautiful person. Besides, did she want a guy that was prettier than her? Who would want that! OK, Jenna, let it go! Go back to your original plan, no guys, and no worries!

"Verily, verily I say unto you, except a man be born again he cannot see the kingdom of God." John 3:3 KJV

SARA

Monday came and off to work she went. She was doing her normal Monday morning filing when Sara Roberts from evidence came by. Sara and Jenna were friends. Not close, but they had coffee occasionally and made small talk. She didn't know much about her. Sara was single, lived on her own and was from the mean streets of Philadelphia. She was a beautiful black woman, about 5'5", 120 lbs. and wore her hair in braids all over her head with a single colored bead at the end of each braid. Her face was beautifully shaped, and she had deep, dark brown eyes. It was hard to tell how old she was, she didn't have a single wrinkle; she seemed ageless. Jenna assumed she was around 30 just based on what little she knew about her. She dressed very conservatively but carried herself in a very confident way. She kept to herself mostly but when you spoke to her, she was very friendly and sweet. She did her job well but there was always something very different about her that Jenna could never put her finger on.

"Hey Jenna, I have some paperwork for Detective La-Cross. I guess he forgot it on the counter. How was your weekend?" She handed her the papers.

"It was fine. I worked on Friday as usual and went to hear a friend play on Saturday, kind of non-eventful. How about you?"

Sara was about to answer the question when she noticed the bracelet Jenna was wearing. She grabbed Jenna's wrist, "Where did you get this?" She had a serious tone to her voice.

"Oh, my friend Trevor gave it to me. He is the one I went to see on Saturday. Why?"

"Do you know what this is?" she was still holding her wrist. Her eyebrow was raised, and she had that slight head-tilt that showed her attitude.

"No, it's just a bracelet, I thought it was cool." She pulled her wrist away and tried to sound dismissive.

"We need to have coffee. When is your break?" Sara was not letting it go.

"Um, well, it's 9:30 now, I can go at 10." Jenna was curious but puzzled. Why was this a big deal and why did Sara care?

"OK, I'll be here at 10 o'clock and we can go talk."

Ten o'clock came and there was Sara ready to go. They left the building and went across the street to Mel's, the little coffee shop where everyone from the department hung out. It was a little mom and pop place owned by a husband and wife. They served real home cooked food, big portions, great prices and excellent coffee. It was an excellent place for a coffee shop because Mel and his wife Carol loved the police and being able to serve them. They knew most everyone on a first name basis. They had heard and seen it all. They loved to listen to the stories and felt protective over the men and women who frequented their establishment.

They found a table and sat down. Sara didn't waste any time.

"Why do you have this if you don't know what it means?" Her words were critical, but her tone was curious and baiting. Her Philly attitude was coming out.

"I told you, I thought it was cool. Trevor took his off and gave it to me and that was that. I didn't think anything of it. I don't understand what your problem is? Why do you care what I wear anyway? I don't appreciate your insinuation that I shouldn't be wearing it." Jenna was irritated at her and although she didn't raise her voice or pepper it with language her tone conveyed it all.

"I didn't mean to sound that way. I just think I need to explain to you what it means. These beads all stand for something. It's the salvation message. The black bead is for sin, the red for the blood of Jesus, the white for new life and the green for growth. Usually only people who are Christians wear them." She had both eyebrows arched this time and added an "mmm" with a head bob at the end.

"Oh, I see. You mean this has something to do with religion? I didn't know that. What does all that stuff mean anyway? I don't understand." Jenna toned down her attitude.

"Not religion. Jesus isn't a religion He's a person, He's God and He died for your sins. You see, you and I are sinners, we can't keep the Ten Commandments, and we can't keep God's law. We are incapable of the perfection, which is required by Him to get into Heaven. He loves us and wants to have a relationship with us. According to the Bible we have sinned against God. We were born sinners and He is the only one who can repair the relationship. Without Him we will all go to hell when we die. We deserve death; God's judgment is on us. So, in order to make a way for us he sent His only Son, Jesus Christ to live a perfect sinless life, die in our place, shed His blood, and be buried in a grave and three days later He was raised from the dead. That is what those beads mean."

Jenna sat there in silence trying to wrap her brain around what had just been said. She couldn't comprehend it. It was just a bracelet given to her by a super hot guy who she desperately wanted attention from. Now all this heaven, hell, sin and death symbolism was getting thrown at her. What did Trevor have to do with that, and what was his part in all this salvation stuff? Did he know what it meant? Did his groupies know or were they all just part of the "hey Trev wears it so it's cool" crowd?

Break was over and Jenna went back to work. She pondered this whole scene over for a couple of days and then filed it in the 'never going to open again' cabinet of her mind. It was just a bracelet and who cared about all the other stuff. She didn't need complications or more junk to think about, she had enough in her life. She was just trying to survive.

"But God demonstrates His own love toward us, in that while we were still sinners, Christ died for us." Romans 5:8 KJV

ONE LATE NIGHT

The following Friday, Jenna went to work at the coffee shop as usual. The band didn't get done until midnight. This meant she would be there cleaning until at least 1 a.m. The harmonica player, John, was flirting. She wasn't in the mood, but she humored him.

"Everyone has left, do you need a ride John?" she was being polite.

"Yes, if you would be willing. I live about 25 minutes from here. The buses don't run this late and I don't have my car."

She finished cleaning up at 1:30 a.m. He lived more like thirty minutes away on a dark lonely road that she should have been more worried about than she was. Sometimes her bravado got the best of her. So, here she was in the car with a guy she barely knew, out in the middle of nowhere and no one knew where she was. Not smart Jenna. They talked and then the move came. He reached over and got a little too fresh.

She pulled back and with all the bravery she could muster said, "What are you doing?"

He looked insulted and with the why-are-you-playing-hard-to-get tone said, "Oh, come on Jenna, what's the big deal?"

She shot him another look, "It is a big deal."

She hated that. She felt stuck but didn't think she should have to feel that way. Why did men always feel they had a right to her? Going through the stuff with her dad gave her the feeling that she didn't have a right to say no and no matter how much she didn't want to she had to yield. But she was sick of feeling that way...sick of feeling like she had no rights over her own body...sick of feeling like she should be forced to allow her body to be used by men at their bidding just because she was a girl with an attractive figure and knew how to dress for it.

She finally got the point across that she wasn't going to give it up and he left her alone.

She realized it was four in the morning. They had been sitting talking and she was exhausted. She'd been up since seven the previous morning, worked all day and then all night. She was uncomfortable in her little sports car and wanted to go home. She had two hours before she was supposed to go stand in line with her sister to get tickets to the highly antici-pated Guns and Roses/Metallica show! Two of their favorite bands and she wasn't going to miss out on that. She had prom-ised Rachel that she would be the one to get them up so they could stand in line and hopefully get good seats. She had to exit. She told John thanks for the talk and finally got him out of the car. She drove home thinking about how stupid she was to take him home in the first place. Why had she opened her mouth? Well, lesson learned.

She finally made it home, woke up Rachel, chugged some hot coffee and donuts and went and got in line. They got their tickets and got home around 8 a.m. Jenna was exhausted and fell into bed. She was in a dead sleep when the phone rang at 1 o'clock in the afternoon.

"Hello." She could barely open her eyes.

"Jenna, this is Trevor. Did I wake you? Do you know what time it is?"

Her eyes were open now. For several months she had made no real progress with this guy. She had given him her number weeks ago, but he'd never bothered to call. She had gone to watch him play at Black Angus, talked with him at the coffee house and finally given up any intentions. Now he was calling.

"Yes, I was asleep, I just got to bed at 8 o'clock this morning." She tried to sound more alert.

"Wow, were you out all night?" He was asking questions. That's good. He's curious.

"I worked until one, was out with a friend until four and then stood in line for tickets to GNR until 8. What made you call me today anyway? Is everything OK?"

"I just wanted to talk to you. Do you want me to call back later when you have had some sleep?"

"No, I'm awake now. I'd rather talk to you anyway." Boy would she rather talk to him than sleep, she could sleep anytime. She could hardly believe it was his voice on the other end. Control yourself Jenna, he's still out of your league.

"OK. I was just wondering if you've ever thought about heaven or hell and where you will go when you die." Just as sweet and wonderful as he always sounded. There was that hint of laughter at the end of his words, like he had something wonderful that made him smile and laugh all the time, it would sneak out every time he spoke and then that Colgate smile. That should be his nickname she thought, Colgate.

Jenna was shocked but it didn't stop her. She let it bounce off and she kept on rolling. The filing cabinet came in very handy. "No not really. Why do you ask such a weird question anyway?" This was not the way she wanted the conversation to go. What was up with him? Had he gone weird on her or what?

"I just care about you and if you don't know Jesus when you die you will go to hell and I don't want you to go to hell, so I thought I'd ask you. You might want to give it some thought. If you want to talk more, call me OK?"

"Uh OK, sure I'll think about it." She could tell he was done with the conversation. He hung up after Jenna said goodbye. What the heck just happened? Did he just call her and then tell her she was going to hell? What is wrong with everyone? Why did he just dive right into the whole deal, no soft pedal, no warmup, just heaven, hell, you should think about it and then click?

She tried to go back to sleep but it kept bugging her. She tried to remember what Sara had told her about sin and heaven and the Bible and all that, but she couldn't remember. As much as she tried it wouldn't leave her alone. All weekend she kept going back to it. What did it all mean? Why was all this stuff coming at her and what was she supposed to do with it? She decided that on Monday she would ask Sara again.

"And He said to them, "Go into all the world and preach the gospel to every creature." Mark 16:15

NEW BEGINNINGS

Monday came but she had changed her mind. She decided she didn't want to know what it all meant. She didn't see any reason to pursue it. He could believe what he wanted to believe and that was that. It was already clear that nothing was going to come of their friendship so who cared. The filing cabinet had worked and that was all there was to it. At least that's what she thought.

Friday rolled around and so did the coffee house. There he was, in all his tall, dark and handsome way looking at her with the question on his face. "Did you think about what I asked you?" He never said it out loud, but she could read it, so she pretended to be illiterate.

A few weeks went by and she let it go and he never brought it up again. But he still had that look in his eyes. Maybe she was imagining it, but it was driving her crazy. She decided the safe thing to do was talk to Sara.

"Sara, do you want to have lunch today? I've been meaning to talk to you and if you're free, I'd love to chat." She was sort of hoping to get a no but wanted a yes just to shut Trevor up. Well, at least the looks.

"Yep, I can do that. Where do you want to go? Mel's or the sandwich shop down the street?"

"The sandwich shop." Jenna didn't want to go to Mel's; too many familiar faces, too much noise and too much chance of someone overhearing their conversation, which would shut Jenna right up.

The rest of the morning went quickly and without much distraction.

They walked to the sandwich shop, placed their orders, got their food and sat down. There were only a few people in the shop, so they sat in the corner away from the others.

"So, I was thinking about our conversation about the bracelet and all that other stuff. Then Trevor called me the other day and threw all this heaven and hell stuff at me and said if I don't know Jesus and I die, I'll go to hell and he cared about me and didn't want that to happen and had I ever thought about it." Jenna barely took a breath. She had to get it all out at once or it wasn't going to come out. Her sandwich was sitting untouched and she didn't care. "I wanted to know about that and what he was talking about. I mean is he right? Is that true? Where does it say that and how does he know that?" She was glad to get it out in the open.

"Wow, I guess you have been thinking about it and you have had it thrown at you quite fast haven't you? He's right. It's in the Bible. He must be a Christian so he's telling you about Jesus and the Bible. Obviously, he cares enough to tell you the truth, as hard as that may be to believe." Sara was cautiously answering her questions for fear of scaring her away and over-whelming Jenna. "Remember I told you that we are all sinners. The Bible says in Romans 3:10 "there is none righteous, no not one." In Romans 3:23 that "all have sinned and fallen short of the glory of God" and Romans 6:23 that "the wages of sin is death." All of us were born sinners because of Adam and Eve. They sinned in the Garden of Eden and so according to Romans 5:12 "through one-man sin entered the world, and death through sin, and thus death spread to all men, because all sinned." None of us can escape it. We all break God's law or the Ten Commandments. He didn't design it that way, but through man's choice we are all lawbreakers. We are separated from Him. We have no way to get to Him, have a relationship with Him or make it right. We are all destined for hell. That is why we are empty inside. Why we are always looking for fulfillment in everyone and everything. We're empty and lost without Him."

Sara held her breath waiting to see Jenna's reaction.

Jenna heard what Sara said, but couldn't grasp it. There were so many questions that started assailing her mind. It was like a machine gun going off in her head. She couldn't even catch them to file them let alone speak them. What was happening to her?

"OK, so you're telling me that I'm a sinner, heaven and hell are real and I'm going to hell?" Simplified, but clear and concise. Her voice reflected the shock and disbelief of it all.

"Yes, that is what I am telling you. But I'm only the messenger. In reality, it's Jesus who's telling you. He wrote the book, made the rules and the statements. He's the one we have to answer to." Sara was being very gentle with her.

"Who is Jesus?" Jenna couldn't believe she was having this conversation. Was she crazy? Had she suddenly lost her mind? Her mind was the one refined, controlled tool in her life and now it seemed to be going crazy on her. It was like her brain was in total rebellion, acting all on its own. She couldn't believe the things that were coming out of her own mouth. It was like she was outside of herself, listening to someone that was supposed to be her but wasn't. She knew it wasn't drugs; she had stopped using when she was in high school. What in the world was happening to her?

"He's the Son of God. Jesus said in John 3:16 "For God so loved the world that He gave His only begotten Son that whoever believes in Him should not perish but have everlasting life." He came to die in your place, take your sin and give you eternal life and forgiveness of your sins." Sara was studying Jenna for any sign of resistance or anger, but all she saw was curiosity mixed with confusion. This was going to take more than one conversation. Beside that, their lunch hour was just about up.

"OK, I seriously don't get all this stuff but maybe we

can take our break together later and talk some more?" Jenna couldn't believe what she was saying. She had gone mad. No matter how hard she tried to tell herself to stop the train, she couldn't do it and honestly, she didn't want to. It was unexplainable. She felt so much conflict inside. She'd never thought about all this stuff before, never ever heard it, and now, some how she knew it was true.

Jenna couldn't stop thinking about it. Questions kept coming to her. Weeks went by and every break and lunch hour was spent with Sara talking to her, asking her every question that she could possibly think of. She asked about the Aborigines who had never heard of Jesus and did the Bible talk about creation and sex outside of marriage? What did it say about abortion and child molesters and what about serial killers? Sara answered them all to the best of her ability. Quoting Bible verses that she knew and if she didn't, she would look it up and get back to her. She would explain as best she could and listen patiently to Jenna's further questioning. Now Jenna really felt like she was on an out-of-control freight train. She was so lost in the questions and things coming out of her mouth she didn't even know herself anymore. She had given up trying to stop the locomotive. It was completely out of her control. Is there anyway to stop a train moving a thousand miles an hour? It was moving too fast to jump and there was some unseen force that was compelling her to stay on the train. Pushing her forward.

One day, after work they went to the mall to have dinner. As they sat there having their usual Jesus and the Bible talk, Sara stopped mid-sentence.

"Jenna, do you believe what I've been telling you? What I've shown you in the Bible?"

"Yes, I believe it." Jenna couldn't believe what had come out of her mouth. She *had* lost her mind!

"If you believe it then why don't you write down all the sins that you can think of that you have done in your life?"

Jenna pulled out a napkin and a pen. She began to write.

Abortion. Fornication, (sex outside of marriage). Cursing. Lying. Stealing (only once when she was 12, but she did steal). Using the Lords name in vain. Adultery, which she didn't think was fair. Rafael was the one who was married, but according to the Bible she was an adulterer. The list went on. There were a few that she had to ask if they were sins or not, but it was quite a list. She got done and was proud of herself for being able to write it out and acknowledge it.

"You can see that you're a sinner, you said you agree with and believe all that the Bible has to say, so what are you waiting for?" Sara was being very sweet and very gentle but also very direct. It was a challenge, put right on the table.

"I guess I'm scared. I guess I just can't believe that Jesus would accept me and scared that I'm not good enough for Him or that I'll believe and find out it's all a lie." Jenna was shaking inside. She knew that Sara had been speaking truth to her. She couldn't explain that, she just knew. She also knew that she desperately wanted to have the big black hole in her soul filled up and to stop feeling so alone in the world. She wanted her life to have purpose and direction. To be acknowledged somewhere by someone, that she mattered and that her life was meant to be about more than people using her and her suffering. She needed to be loved because she was Jenna Clark not because someone wanted something from her. She longed for clarity, truth, clear lines and black & white. She wanted to be full, instead of empty. She desperately wanted to stop hurting deep down inside and to have hope. She needed hope.

"It's all true. He loves you and knows everything about you. He has seen every teardrop and heard every cry. He sees the dark hole in your soul and knows the emptiness you feel, and He wants to heal you and wants to give you a wonderful life both now and in heaven. He died to save you and to let you know that you have value to Him." Sara was praying silently in her heart that Jenna would hear and respond. "Why don't you ask Him to forgive you, you have nothing to lose and everything to gain."

"OK, but can we go to your place?" Jenna felt timid but did not want to delay any longer.

"Sure." Sara was hopeful and excited.

They got in Jenna's car and drove to Sara's. They sat on her couch and held hands. Sara looked her in the eye and with tears said, "I want you to pray with me. You just repeat after me and I will lead you." Jenna shook her head yes.

"Dear Jesus, I know I'm a sinner. Please come into my heart and forgive me. I believe that you're the Son of God that you died on a cross for my sins, that you were buried and raised from the dead. I want You to live in my heart and be my Savior and Lord. I want to follow You and serve You. I want to go to heaven. Thank you for forgiving me and for loving me. Thank you for coming to live in my heart. In Jesus name, Amen."

It was July 16, 1992 at 10 p.m.; she would never forget that moment.

Jenna opened her eyes and looked at Sara who had tears streaming down her face.

"Is that it? Am I forgiven; do I get to go to heaven? How do I know it worked? I don't feel any different." It was hard to accept that it was that simple.

"It really is that simple. You must believe it by faith not by your feelings. I have been praying for you for two years that this day would come."

Jenna was shocked at what she'd just heard. No one had ever told her that before. To her knowledge no one in her entire life had prayed for her. What an insane thing to hear.

"You have? Why?"

"Because I knew you weren't saved. I could see that you were miserable and most importantly because Jesus told me to pray for you." She smiled. Her Philly attitude was coming out again. Very matter of fact, a hint of streetwise and a lot of spunk!

"Jesus told you to pray for me?" That one blew her out of the water. Jesus told someone to pray for her. Maybe He truly did love her and maybe He really was real.

"Here let me call my friend and you can talk to her, she's a Christian too and she can tell you that your prayer worked." Sara got up.

"But I just don't feel any different." Jenna was sitting on the couch watching Sara and waiting for something to kick in.

Sara was already picking up the phone and dialing. "Hey Debbie, I just led my friend Jenna straight to Jesus and she says she doesn't feel any different, can you talk to her for a second?" She handed Jenna the phone.

"Hi, Debbie, um, I don't know what to say except I said this prayer and Sara says I'm saved but I don't feel any different, is it that simple?" She sounded so foolish even to herself.

Debbie let out a little giggle, "It is that simple. You have faith that He heard you and accepted you. If you meant it from your heart and believe it, He accepted it. You'll feel different, just give it time and you'll start to notice the changes. It's a marathon not a sprint, a relationship not a set of religious rules. You read your Bible, pray, get set up with a good church and watch what He does with your life."

"I will. Thanks for talking to me. I hope we get to meet some day."

"We will, if not here then in heaven. God bless you and remember Jesus loves you." Debbie hung up.

Wow, what an evening. It was late and they had to work the next day. Jenna said her good-byes and gave Sara a hug. That was something new to her already, but she was grateful to her friend and all that she'd done and shared with her over the last few weeks. She'd been so patient.

"Just keep saying, 'Jesus, I believe you're real and that I'm saved'. The devil wants you to doubt. He's a liar and the father of lies. He hates you because he hates Jesus. We'll talk more about that later. For now, trust Him."

Jenna got in her car and drove home. All the while she kept saying out loud, 'I believe you are real and that I am saved' over and over. She slept better that night than at anytime in her life. She had so much peace and a sense of knowing that some how everything was going to be all right in her life.

Sure enough, the reality hit when she woke up the next morning. The next two weeks of her life she felt like she was walking on a cloud and all she could think about was Jesus.

It was as though a great burden had been lifted off her. She felt as light and free as air. Euphoric. She'd never felt that way before. The gaping hole in her soul was gone. She didn't feel empty or alone inside. She felt in fact, that she had the best secret in the world and wanted to shout it to everyone. She didn't just feel happy; she felt joy for the first time in her life. She knew that she had the Truth in her soul. She had purpose and she belonged to Him. She didn't know what her life would be like or where He would lead her, but she had her Bible to give her clarity and hope. Hope that was dependent upon Him, not her.

She went to work, both jobs, started to read the Bible she had been given years before as a gift. She couldn't think of anything but Jesus. It was like a ticker tape continuously running around her brain and it just said, "Jesus." It was amazing that she accomplished anything. Her job was intense and required a lot of attention to detail, a good memory and the instant location of information at any given moment, and she did it some how, but that was all a mystery itself. She could not stop smiling and she slept peacefully and soundly every night.

"Therefore, if anyone is in Christ, he is a new creation; old things have passed away; behold, all things have become new." 2 Corinthians 5:17 KJV

HARD THINGS

It was August and a month had gone by since she said the prayer and asked Jesus to save her. She read her Bible every day and for hours on her days off. She spent time in prayer for her unsaved family and friends. She was attending a local church and feeling for the first time in her life, that life might just turn out wonderful.

However, her balloon was about to get popped. Rachel had noticed that Jenna was gone a lot, seemed happier in a different way and knew that there was obviously something going on that she wasn't telling her. Rachel had a steady boyfriend and so she was gone a lot too, but it didn't take her long to realize that Jenna was keeping something from her. After all, the girls were best friends and didn't keep secrets.

"What is going on with you? You're acting weird and I know there's something you're not telling me." Rachel was doing the dishes and had the sound of barely restrained anger in her voice. Her face looked hurt and angry. If she was afraid, she didn't let it show.

Jenna knew this day was going to come. She stepped out in boldness with the lightest tone she could muster, "Well, I found God; I met Jesus and said a prayer and now I follow Him." There, she'd said it.

Rachel turned on her with anger, hurt and such venom that she almost dropped the dish she had in her hand. It caused Jenna to take a step back. She'd seen the movie *The Exorcist* when she was about twelve and when Rachel turned on her it reminded her of the scene where the girl's head spins around. Thankfully she didn't puke green stuff on Jenna.

"Don't you tell me about God. What has He ever done for me? I don't want to hear it, don't talk to me about it at all. What, so now you're some Jesus freak or something?" The hurt in her voice was deep.

Jenna was shocked at the amount of anger that was being directed at her. She couldn't understand why her sister was so angry with God. They had never discussed God in their family. His name was used as a curse word but never in any other way. She felt so free and joyful how could her sister not want that?

"Why are you so angry at God?"

"Why? Because He took the only thing I've ever had that was mine and that I wanted more than anything else in the world. He took Ben from me. If that's the way He is, I want nothing to do with Him." With that she stormed off and slammed her bedroom door. She had never seen so much pain in her sister's face before. It broke her heart.

Ben was Rachel's baby that had died when she was five months pregnant with him. Jenna knew how bad she had wanted the baby. Her sister had felt that having the baby would be the answer to the tragedies of her life and the emptiness it had left inside of her. The baby would be someone that she could love and that would love her unconditionally. Everything had been fine until she went for a check up because she hadn't felt the baby moving. They did an ultrasound and saw that the baby had died. It was a terrible blow to Rachel and then she had to go through labor knowing her son was already dead. Jenna never realized how angry her sister was at God over the loss of Ben. The thought had never even occurred to her because they'd never discussed the existence of God. Jenna had been so caught up in her own pain and anger over her abortion, that at the time, she didn't realize the pain Rachel was in. Now she saw the raw truth of her broken little bird. It crushed Jenna. Her sister was hurting, she knew that Jesus was the answer to that hurt and Rachel wanted nothing to do with Him. Jenna felt helpless and went to her room and cried. She knew there was nothing she could do but pray for her little sister.

"Do not think that I am come to bring peace on earth. I did not come to bring peace but a sword. For I have come to set a man against his father, a daughter against her mother, a daughter-in- law against her mother- in- law. And a man's enemies will be those of his own household." Jesus, Matthew 10:34-36 KJV

"IF THEY HATED ME..."

Home was not the only troubled front. Jenna was starting to get a lot of flack at work as well. The detectives she worked for were great and didn't seem to have a problem with Jenna's changed demeanor. It was the part-time person that was helping Jenna that was the problem. Her name was Kathy. She began helping Jenna before Jenna had accepted Christ. She was assigned to another department and was on loan part-time to help Jenna with the workload. She seemed to be a happy person and they'd had a few laughs and got along fine. However, after Jenna got saved everything seemed to change. She noticed that Kathy seemed to be short with her all the time. She didn't talk much and wasn't the same pleasant person she'd once been. Then one day she got called into the supervisor's office. Jenna never got called into the supervisors' office.

"Jenna, are you sharing the workload with Kathy or just giving her all of the typing to do?" Barbara sat across the desk from Jenna. Her gray hair was pulled up on top of her head, her glasses were resting halfway down her nose, and her plump hands were folded on top of her desk. She was a heavy woman in her late 50's and always looked like she was mad at the world. Right now, that angry face was staring at Jenna.

"We share the workload. Is there a problem?" Jenna was cautious.

"Yes. Kathy says that the officers come to you for help and to answer their questions. She feels that you're not allowing her to help them."

"Well, what am I supposed to do if they come to me and ask me their questions? I'm here all the time and so I know about a lot of the things they are working on. So, naturally they ask me." Jenna was trying to be respectful and not sound irritated, but it seemed so simple and ridiculous. The guys did ask her their questions. She was there every day working with them and taking care of stuff for them so naturally they'd ask her. It seemed so elementary and yet here she was getting in trouble for it.

"Well, you need to make sure you're sharing other responsibilities and not giving Kathy all the typing. She needs to help them as well." Her voice was very firm and sounded like she was on the edge of yelling.

"OK." Jenna wasn't sure how to resolve a problem she didn't feel even existed or one that she had no control over. Was she supposed to tell the officers "ask Kathy" when they came to her? It didn't make sense. Kathy never talked to Jenna about the problem. She only spoke to the supervisor, who in turn, called Jenna into the office.

Jenna dreaded the days she knew Kathy was going to be there. She constantly felt like she was doing something wrong, only she had no idea what it was. As a result, whenever Kathy was there, Jenna did the typing, but she couldn't tell the officers to stop asking her questions. They needed to be helped and the pettiness of someone else wasn't going to prevent them from getting the help they needed to do their jobs. In Jenna's logical black and white brain there wasn't a solution because a problem didn't really exist. It was so ridiculous and absurd.

She got called into the supervisor's office four or five more times over the next couple of months all for the same type of petty issues. Then one day Kathy came in and said it was the last day she was going to be there to help Jenna. She was short and rather angry about it.

Jenna couldn't help but feel relieved. She'd have to handle the extra caseload but that was more manageable than dealing with Kathy and her tattle-tailing pettiness.

Unfortunately, the same supervisor remained for another 6 months and she kept finding reasons to call Jenna in. She had never had any trouble with anyone, at any job, ever. She had been at the job for over two years when she accepted Jesus, so she had a track record. Then suddenly she was getting flack. In fact, she'd started out as a simple typing clerk and moved her way up to unit clerk. The position she had with the detectives was one that she'd help to organize. They originally handled all their own paperwork and cases, but it wasn't working, they were too overwhelmed. So, they'd asked Jenna to help them organize and set up a system to help with the workload so they had more free time to work on their cases and she could take care of the details, organization, locating files and documents they needed.

She hated getting in trouble. Because her dad was always accusing her of things she never did, she was always getting into trouble for breaking rules she never knew existed. She now had a built-in hypersensitivity to being unjustly accused. It was extremely frustrating to her. Just like with her dad, there was no way for her to defend herself. She went to extreme measures to follow the rules and please her superiors. When someone was mad at her or accusing her, it caused her so much internal stress and strife she couldn't eat. Now, added on top of all of that, she wanted to be a good witness for Christ.

"For we do not wrestle against flesh and blood, but against principalities, against powers, against the rulers of the darkness of this age, against spiritual hosts of wickedness in the heavenly places." Ephesians 6:12 KJV

BAPTISM

J enna still had Sara. Sara would stop by her desk and encourage her, check in on her and remind her to keep her mind focused on Jesus.

She still had her part-time job at the coffee house. So, she still saw Trevor. He and his gang of groupies were all very happy when Jenna told them she'd accepted Christ. She would go to his manager Connie's house, and hang out with the groupies that were now her friends. Sometimes she would go and listen to him play at a coffee house or lounge. Now that she was a Christian, Trevor opened up more and she got to know him a little better. The first thing she noticed was his ability to tell people about Jesus and use the weirdest objects to make his intro. One time they were going through a Jack N' The Box drive through and he ordered an iced tea with a straw. When the server handed it to him, he took the straw and some how used it to tell the person at the window about Jesus. Jenna couldn't even begin to figure out how he did it, but he did it all the time, everywhere they went, with anything he had handy. She also recognized his musical genius. He was one of the few people that she knew of that played a twelve-string acoustic guitar and he played it very well. He could play any song you asked him to, and he wrote his own songs. His songs were always about Jesus. They were beautiful. He had been an up and coming musician in Houston, Texas before he gave his life to Christ. He was well-known and had an agent; unfortunately, he'd also developed a serious cocaine problem. He'd hit rock bottom, lost his music gigs, his agent, his potential record deal and all his money. That led him to Jesus and ultimately salvation.

She had known a few musicians in her life, and they tended to be, well, different. She had to stop by his apartment one time to drop something off and he invited her in. For a bachelor pad it was pretty clean but there were yellow post-it notes, and legal-size papers taped all over the cabinet doors and walls. They were either ideas for songs or the beginning lyrics to a song. His bathtub was full of newspapers. The room where he wrote his music was rigged with a string from the light switch, through a series of different objects to the bed, so if he was writing and got tired, he could turn out the light without getting up. Different. He also had conversation issues. In other words, it was hard to have an actual conversation with him. Musicians live in their own artistic ADHD world. He could talk about music and Jesus but not much else. Even those topics were difficult. Sometimes you'd be talking to him and five minutes in, his eyes would glaze over because he'd drifted off into his own world. It was very frustrating. Sometimes she felt she'd be better off just having a conversation with herself; she might get further. He had a real passion for Christ and reaching people with the Gospel message. But his social skills beyond that left something to be desired.

Because of his handsome looks, amazing smile, his talent and genuine love for the Lord, the girls were all over him. Jenna had to fight feelings at times herself. She knew that she wasn't his type but more importantly, that he'd drive her insane, their relationship would never work as anything other than friends. She now understood the "something different" about him that she had sensed before. Of course, she hadn't come to either of those realizations until after she became a Christian.

She was grateful for him and the others, especially Connie his manager, because the few friends she had before, mysteriously left when she got saved.

Rachel and Jenna were still roommates, but they didn't hang out the same way they used too. She was angry with Jenna for her new-found faith. Rachel worked a lot and was with her boyfriend every weekend, so the girls were growing apart. That broke Jenna's heart. She loved her sister and wanted them to do things together, hang out like they used to, only now in Jesus. She wanted Rachel to know Jesus and to be healed from all her hurts, to be whole and to have the peace that she had. She also didn't want her sister to go to hell if something were to happen to her. But it was a subject that for now was off limits. All she could do was pray diligently and fervently for her sister.

Losing her friends and her sister was difficult. But Jenna had never felt so much peace, joy and fulfillment in her life. The black hole was gone; she missed her sister, but she felt full and more complete. She had hope now. She knew that she'd have difficulty in her journey, but she felt so clean and free because of Jesus so it was worth it to her. He was worth it all. He loved her enough to die on a cross, pay for her sin, love her when she was sinning against Him and pursue her until she bowed her heart; there wasn't anything in the world that would cause her to turn away from Him. All the counselors over ten years could never accomplish what Jesus had accomplished in a spilt-second.

Jenna still had the same passion for music she'd always had. So, she immediately needed to find a radio station to listen to and get Christian music. She needed music in her life and she desperately wanted to be taught the Bible. She could not get enough of it. Fortunately for her she found KWAVE, a radio station that was owned and operated by Calvary Chapel. She didn't know who they were, but Sara told her that it was a good station and that she could learn the Bible. She listened to it every time she was in her car and at home in her room.

One day while driving into work she heard the announcement that Calvary Chapel Costa Mesa was doing their final summer baptism at Corona Del Mar beach at a place called Pirates Cove. She was beside herself. She could be baptized at the beach, which for her was an amazing concept. She loved the ocean. It was power under restraint, calming in its sound and peaceful in its power.

As soon as she got to work, she hunted Sara down.

"Sara, I just heard that they're doing a baptism down at the beach tonight at 7:30. I really want to go. You told me I needed to be baptized. But I'm supposed to work at the Coffee House tonight." She was so excited.

"Can you call them and tell them you can't come in?"

"I don't know what to do. They'd be fine without me, but I know they won't let me off." Jenna was frustrated. She knew it was wrong to call in sick because she wasn't. She couldn't tell them she wanted to be baptized because she knew they wouldn't let her off for that; it was the last one of the summer, she didn't know what to do.

"Well, I think you should call them and try." Sara wasn't going to tell her to lie.

Jenna made the decision, called and told them she wasn't feeling well. She knew it was wrong, but she was so excited about getting baptized, the excitement over-rode anything else. They weren't happy but what could they say?

"Will you go with me? You led me to Jesus, and it would be awesome if you went with me. I'm kind of scared and don't want to go alone."

"I would be honored to go. If we could stop at my house so I can get a coat and if you have a camera, I could take a picture for you." Sara was so excited for her.

"OK great. Just come back to my desk at 5 o'clock and we'll go. I'll have to go home and get something to wear. What should I wear? I don't want to just wear my bathing suit."

"Something conservative. Maybe a pair of shorts and a shirt over your suit." Sarah was so happy to be part of Jenna's journey.

From the moment she prayed with Sara and accepted

Jesus, she had a deep conviction about what clothing she wore. She made sure her shirts weren't too low; her skirts weren't too short and about half of the clothes in her closet were now in a bag going to the thrift store. That was one of many things that Jesus changed in her without her praying about it, asking for it or even being aware of it. She no longer used profanity. Not because she tried, it had just disappeared. Which was an amazing feat. Only God could do that. She used to use the "f" word like a verb, noun and an adjective. The word never even went through her head anymore. She didn't want to listen to the music she used to listen to. She loved GNR and Metallica, but she couldn't listen because of the feelings it invoked in her. That hadn't happened before. She noticed the lyrics now too. Now when she heard them, she realized how destructive, sexual, violent and ungodly they were. At one point, when she was about nineteen, she was listening to her favorite rock station and heard that the Christian Coalition was ranting about how bad rock music was and apparently there was a trial going on to see if a particular band was responsible for the suicide of a fifteen-year-old boy. She was so angry. They were spouting how the music caused violence, suicide, destructive behavior, drug use and that parents should not let their kids listen to rock music. She was yelling at the car radio. She had listened to that music for years and she hadn't suffered any dire consequences. Now, with her spiritual eyes open, she could see the influence it had on her and the effect it had on her emotionally and even physically. She believed that it was destructive. It stood to reason in her mind that what goes into your brain, ultimately affects your life. She only wanted to put godly things into her mind.

They made it down to the beach where the crowd had gathered. She had to climb up rocks and then down again to get to the cove where they were baptizing. There were several pastors in the water, a crowd of people on the beach that were singing worship songs and lines of people just at the edge of the water waiting to be baptized. She had opted to wear her bathing suit with a pair of shorts and a shirt over it. It was around 7:45 p.m. when she got in line. The sun was sitting low on the horizon, it was a clear day, the air temperature was around 73 degrees and the water was in the 60's. She was slightly nervous but very excited. Sara had explained to her that being baptized wasn't a requirement for salvation but was an act of obedience to the Bible. Jesus was baptized at the beginning of His ministry by John the Baptist and He told His disciples in Matthew 28: 19 to "go and preach the Gospel and to baptize them in the name of the Father, the Son and the Holy Spirit". She explained to her that going down into the water and coming up was a public witness that her old life was dead and buried with Christ and she was being raised into new life with Jesus.

She stood there in anticipation as she watched person after person go into the water, go under and come up beaming. Every time someone would come up, there was at least one person standing on the shore cheering wildly, most often the whole crowd would go crazy. The energy on the beach was electric. She couldn't believe how many people were there. There were so many people that the cove was completely full. She looked around and saw smiling, happy, joy filled faces that cared about the strangers they saw in the water. No one cared about being cold. They made room for each other to pass by with smiles, congratulations, hugs and tears. The pastors tirelessly baptized person after person as if each one was the only one. She imagined heaven must be like that. Selfless. Cheering for each other and full of joy.

As she stood waiting her turn, she realized just how crazy this would seem to some people. Only a few months ago she had been standing in line for tickets to GNR/Metallica after she'd been up all night with a harmonica player. Now here she was standing in line, on a beach, with hundreds, if not thousands of people, waiting to get baptized. The thought brought tears to her eyes. God was so amazing. To think He saw it all, knew that she'd be standing on this very beach and was willing to bring her to this point, it was all beyond her comprehension. She thought *He must have been laughing in heaven watching me stand in that line, knowing all along I wouldn't even be going to that concert, instead I'd be standing here waiting to get baptized.*

She finally made it into the water and up to the pastor. He asked her if she had accepted Christ as her Savior and if she understood baptism. She told him yes. He asked her to cross her arms and hold her nose and he prayed for her. She couldn't even tell you what he'd prayed, she could only think about going in the water. He leaned her back all the way down into the water. She was only under for a few seconds but in those seconds, she felt the presence of God, saw a light shine into her eyes and her heart began to fill with joy. As she came up out of the water, she felt like her heart was going to explode. She could hardly catch her breath. Not from being under too long but from the overwhelming sense of joy that was inside of her. She saw Sara on the beach, smiling and waving wildly at her, holding up a camera!

"That was so awesome!" Jenna was bubbling over and threw her arms around Sara.

"I'm so proud of you!" Sara didn't even care that Jenna got her wet when she hugged her.

Sara was such an encouragement to Jenna. She was in awe of God's work in Jenna's life. She would always tell her, "God's gonna do something big in your life, just wait, trust Him and believe His Word." Although Sara had been a believer for about ten years when Jenna met her, she had never led anyone to Jesus before. She prayed for many, shared with many, but it was the first time she got to follow through. She had told Jenna that a few days after their prayer time together. Jenna was honored to have been the first. For Sara, it was like having her first child. Now to see her get baptized was so overwhelming for Sara she began to cry. Tears of joy and relief that her two years of prayer for this girl had paid off, in a big way, like hitting the heavenly lotto! Sara had often wondered if her labor in prayer was going to break through the hardness of Jenna's heart. She had confidence that eventually it might, she just wasn't sure if she'd be around to see it. Sara had great confidence in her God; it was Jenna that had worried her.

They made their way back to the car. Although she was dripping wet and the sun was setting, she didn't even notice the cool air. She felt like she wanted to stand on top of the tallest building somewhere and shout to the world, "Jesus loves you! I got baptized! It was amazing!" What an awesome night it was for her. She was so grateful for her new life and the friend she had in Sara. How did she ever live her life without Jesus? She didn't know the answer to that question but what she did know was that she never wanted to live her life without Him again.

"For whosever will save his life shall lose it; but whosever shall lose his life for My sake and the gospel's, the same shall save it." Mark 8:35

"Likewise, I say unto you there is joy in the presence of the angels of God over one sinner that repents." Luke 15:10 KJV

NEW LIFE

I t had been almost a year since Jenna had accepted Christ.
There were many changes happening in her life.

She had been baptized, found a church she could
call home and was learning a lot.

She had a lot of internal work being done as well. After
the two weeks of her Jesus saturated brain, she began to realize the weight of her own sin and the need to forgive. It
wasn't anything anyone said to her; it was a simple work of
the Holy Spirit in her life. She began to see her sin in light of
the holiness of God. She needed to forgive her dad. She didn't
understand it all, but she began simply. In her heart she knew
she had committed terrible sins against Jesus. She understood
that in the eyes of God she had committed murder when she
chose to abort her child. When she weighed that against what
her dad had done, she could not stand before God and choose
to hold onto her pain, unforgiveness and anger. She had killed
her child as a person who didn't know Jesus and had made her
decisions without regard for the life she was taking. She was
doing the best she could with what she had, and she realized
that it was no different for her dad. He was acting like a person who didn't know Jesus would act, without much regard
for the consequences or for the other person. It didn't make it
OK or right, but she knew that she was no better than him. She
understood that there was not a sin scale where one sin was
worse or weightier than another. The ground was level at the

cross and she had to choose to forgive or she would be in bondage to the pain and anger her whole life. So, in her prayer time she purposely told the Lord that she forgave her dad and asked Jesus to save him. She knew it would be a process and had no idea what that would look like. She only knew what she had to do in that moment. Forgive.

She found that she loved prayer and took every opportunity she had to pray; before bed, on the way to work, driving in her car, on her breaks and any prayer meeting she could go to. She had discovered a few other people in her office were Christians. She felt like she was part of a secret club that worked within the police department. They prayed for each other and for their co-workers that didn't know Jesus. Sometimes she prayed for the people that came in or people she would see in the case files. She could see their lives were messed up and they were hurting. It made her sad to see them trying to fix their problems with anything other than Jesus. Sometimes seeing the people and their emptiness and sadness was the most difficult part of her job. On more than one occasion she ended up in the bathroom crying because she came face to face with someone, either victim or criminal, that seemed so empty, sad, hurting and lost. Sometimes she could feel their broken hearts and it was more than she could bear. She knew it was the Lord allowing her to experience that. His heart broke for them. He had bled and died on that cross 2,000 years before so they either wouldn't have to experience those things or if they did, He could heal them. If only they would let Him. That was the hardest part, they had to let Him. She could do nothing but pray. If the Lord had told her to go to them and share the Truth, she would have in a heartbeat, but until then, she could only pray and weep.

There were some that were harder to handle than others. Meth addicts were difficult. They all had the same paranoia about people watching them, the government spying on them, microchip implants in their teeth, and they'd write long rambling letters. They were all the same. She began to think of it, as the "meth-demon" because they all had the same thought processes, wouldn't sleep for days, wouldn't eat and over a very short period would age ten years. Most of them ended up being homeless and stealing, even from their own families, just to get money to buy the drug.

She had a hard time with the prostitutes and strippers. It broke her heart to see women trapped in that life. She knew that none of them aspired to live that life when they were little girls. So many of them ended up dead, murdered or over-dosing on drugs. After what she'd been through with her dad, she knew it had to be hell for those girls to have to sell them-selves or take off their clothes for men who cared nothing for them except to use them for their own pleasure.

It crushed her to see men who were cross-dressers sell-ing themselves, believing they were women trapped in men's bodies. She knew that Jesus loved each of them and that His plan and design for their lives was much better than theirs. She also knew that He valued each of them and saw their lives to be worth far more than what they believed it to be.

Every time a new file came across her desk she won-dered if the people involved knew the Lord or had the oppor-tunity to meet Him. Life was so fragile. The darkness of the sin-sick world was sometimes overwhelming for her. It could be so emotionally draining. Before she was a believer their problems didn't bother her. Bad guys were supposed to get caught, victims were supposed to get justice and that was the way the world was supposed to work. But now by the end of every day she was ready to go home and get away from all the suffering. She was so grateful for Jesus, His Word, church and the people she had around her that loved Him. Thankful that in God's economy there will be justice one day.

She had to quit her job at the Coffee House because her job at the department had changed. She had more responsi-bility; they were working overtime a lot and had changed her hours. She couldn't keep up the pace working both jobs, espe-cially with the new schedule. She was working a 10/80. She worked Monday through Thursday for ten hours a day, Friday was an eight-hour day, the same the following week with that Friday off. She had tried it for a while. The only way she could get through was to sleep on her one-hour lunch. It was starting to take its toll on her health. She was getting sinus infections a lot, which meant she missed work. She only had so many sick days and couldn't afford to be off without getting paid. So, the part-time job had to go.

Jenna also quit her night classes in Criminal Justice at the local college. She realized very soon after being born-again that working for the FBI was not His plan for her life. It wasn't a conversation they'd had; she just lost the desire and drive. Once she realized that she'd lost that, she knew it was because of Jesus. So, she gave up the classes. It was strange to her that all the other dreams in her life that she'd been forced to give up on were so crushing to her but not this one. The only explanation she had was Him. She didn't know what the future held for her, but she knew that His plans were always better, even if they were different.

Sara left the department and moved away but the Lord provided a new co-worker, Michelle Hunter. Michelle was a believer. She had been following Jesus for about 20 years. She had gotten saved at 17 and never looked back. She was very sweet. She worked hard and was willing to learn whatever there was to learn. She was married, had a young son and was returning to work after being a stay-at-home mom. They were both excited to learn the other was a Christian. Michelle was very encouraging to Jenna. She would listen every morning when Jenna came in as she replayed the sermon she had just heard on the way to work. Michelle loved her youthful enthusiasm concerning the things of the Lord. Jenna would ask her questions, talk to her about what she was reading, share with her what she was learning at church and at times, cry on her shoulder for the difficulties she encountered. Michelle would listen, sometimes give advice and always encouraged her to keep growing. Jenna was so grateful for her. They prayed for each other on a regular basis, sometimes even at work on their break-times if needed. The other people in the office started calling them the "God Squad". They got along like they'd known each other their whole lives. They laughed together, comforted one another, helped each other and were very thankful for being put side by side in their cubicle. The girls grew to love each other and would prove to be invaluable to each other over time.

"For I know the thoughts that I think toward you, says the Lord, thoughts of peace and not of evil, to give you a future and a hope." Jeremiah 29:11. NKJV

MIKE

For all the positive things that happened during her first year, there was also difficulty.

Before Jenna became a Christian, she had reconnected, quite by accident, with an old high school friend. His name was Mike Weber. He was two years ahead of her in high school but had dated one of her closest friends. He was the cool guy with a 1968 Camaro Super Sport that you heard coming from two blocks over. He was tall at 6'1", slender build, sandy bleached-blonde hair, permanently tan with light, piercing blue eyes. He was happily married, was at her office training for six weeks with the gang unit, then left. They'd had lunch once to catch up on all that had happened in the twelve years since they had last seen each other. No big deal, just two friends who chatted and then parted ways. That was not going to be the case the second time around. It was July and a new round of transfers had just arrived at the station.

Jenna was walking through the reception area on her way to her desk when she saw a familiar face.

"Mike is that you?" Jenna wasn't sure because she could only see his profile.

"Jenna? Hey, you're still here." He looked the same once she saw him straight on. He looked surprised to see her. What was he doing back here?

"I still work here. What are you doing here?"

"I got stationed here to work with the gang unit."

She noticed the ring on his finger was missing. "How's your wife?"

His face dropped. "She moved out. She decided she wanted to go back to school, have a career and there was no room for a husband or a family."

Jenna could see he was hurting. When they had talked a year ago, he spoke in a very loving manner about his wife. Clearly, he still wanted to be married and was broken and hurting over her decision.

"I'm so sorry Mike. That's awful. I wish there was something I could say that would make it right. I know there isn't anything. Sorry." Jenna was at a loss. He was hurting and she knew from their conversation a year ago that he was not a believer. At the time they'd talked astrology and reincarnation because that was where her head was back then.

She wanted to tell him about Jesus and let him know that there was hope in Him.

"Maybe we can go to lunch and talk about it?" No one told her that even stepping in the direction of a male that was not a believer could be a danger zone. She had no intention of dating him, she just saw a broken, hurting person who could benefit from the love of Christ.

"I'll come by your desk and get you at noon. Is that OK?" A little of the wind had been knocked out of his sails since the last time they talked.

"Yup. I gotta go back to my desk. See you at noon." She turned and left.

They went to lunch. They talked about his life, his marriage and she even shared about how she had become a believer. He listened and so did she. But that wasn't the end of the story. They found they liked talking to each other. She saw them as friends. They went to eat, walked on the beach and he even went to church with her a few times. Things didn't stay that way. She wasn't sure how it happened but suddenly they were kissing and holding hands and going to lunch every day and dinner several times a week, including the weekends when he wasn't out on patrol. He was one of the nicest guys she had ever dated; polite, not pushy, and thoughtful. And he wasn't pressuring her about sex.

She knew it wasn't the wisest thing to be emotionally involved with him. He was still technically married. She couldn't help herself. She couldn't reconcile how it was wrong when he was so nice, they had fun, they weren't having sex and he was a good person. No one told her the scriptural reason or challenged her on her involvement. She was on her own. There was a still small voice inside telling her she needed to flee. She didn't recognize it nor did she listen. Instead, she decided she needed to confront the issue of Jesus head on and see what happened. She did. It fell flat. Mike explained to her that he'd gone to Sunday school at his parents' Baptist church his whole life and no one had ever told him about being born again. She explained from the Bible how important it was and how without being born again his sin would not be forgiven and that Jesus loved him. He politely told her, that he believed differently and if his church hadn't taught him about being born again then it must not be necessary. She was stuck. She had no further argument to that. She let it go. They kept dating.

They'd spent a brief time together on Christmas. He'd been with his family and she was with her mom and sister down at Grandma Esther's for the day and then they had dinner at her house later.

"What are you doing for New Years?"

Jenna shrugged, "I don't know. Nothing probably. I'm not really into New Year's Eve parties." She hoped that he had plans for them, but she wasn't going to ask.

"Well, I'm not either. Let's have dinner, get a bottle of Champagne and watch a movie at your house."

"Sure. What time?" Staying home with him and a movie was the ticket. She had always hated New Year's. Growing up every year was the same. There was never a new beginning; it had always been the same old Jenna inside no matter what year it was. She never went to parties because she had never understood the big draw for people...her life was just on repeat so what was there to celebrate?

"I'll come get you at 7 o'clock." He kissed her and left. He was late for his shift. He had been working the night shift but was going to be off for New Year's.

New Year's Eve arrived. He picked her up, they went and had a nice dinner and drove to a liquor store to purchase the champagne. He wanted to watch *Basic Instincts*. The movie had been out for about two years and she'd seen it in the theater with the Navy Seal, Chuck, when if first came out, before she was a Christian. It wouldn't have been her choice, but she let it go. They went back to her house. Rachel was gone for the weekend with her boyfriend, so they were alone. They put in the movie and curled up on the couch. The movie got over about 11:00.

"Ready for some champagne?"

"Yeah sure, I'll get some glasses and you open it." Jenna got up to get the glasses out of the cabinet and Mike went to the fridge. He popped the cork and poured each of them a glass.

"To you and old friends that are new friends." He smiled that perfect smile he had.

"Cheers." She clinked his glass.

They went and sat back down on the couch and chatted and sipped their drinks waiting for midnight.

"Look, 15 seconds left. Let me refresh our drinks and we can toast at midnight." He got up and got the bottle, poured them both a full glass and sat back down next to her. They counted it off.

"10, 9, 8, 7, 6, 5, 4, 3, 2, 1...happy New Year!" They clinked glasses and kissed.

Jenna had barely gotten her glass away from her mouth when he kissed her again. In the commotion she spilled champagne down her mouth and her neck. Just as she was about to wipe it away, he stopped her.

"I'll get that for you." He leaned forward and began to

slowly lick it off her neck.

Her first instinct was to pull back, but she resisted and allowed him to continue. He continued and then they began to kiss again. She realized that if she didn't stop him that it was going to continue and go a lot further than she wanted.

"You have to stop." She was breathless.

"You really want me to?" He said with a sly smile.

"You need to before something else happens." She was trying to get off the couch now and move away from him. She knew she had to move away before she caved in and then later regretted it.

"You're probably right. I'll go. It's late and it's probably best." He sounded slightly disappointed.

He got up and walked toward the door. She gave him one last kiss and moved him out the door.

Jenna had never felt the way she was feeling. She couldn't even identify it. She ran to her room, changed her clothes, got into bed and pulled the covers over her head. She wanted to hide, be invisible, run away, do something but she didn't want to face Jesus. She was so embarrassed and ashamed of her behavior. She knew that God saw everything she did, nothing was hidden from Him and He had just seen it ALL! She began to cry, which then turned into convulsive sobs. She cried out to the Lord begging for His forgiveness and asking Him to help her. She knew that she couldn't see Mike anymore if she wanted to continue to follow Jesus. It was difficult for her to tell if she was more upset because she had failed so miserably in her walk with the Lord or because she knew that she had blown the chance at winning him to Christ. She knew the next day she had to deal with it and tell him their relationship was over. She totally accepted the fact that he wouldn't understand her reason, he couldn't understand, because it was based on the Bible and he didn't live his life according to that book.

The next morning, January 1st, she woke up with dread in her heart. She knew she had to call him right away and tell him they were done. What a way to start a new year!

"Hey Mike, how are you this morning?" She was trying to fight back the tears and keep her voice even.

"I'm fine. Are you OK? You sound upset." Part of his job was reading people; he'd just read her like a dime store novel.

"Uh, um, actually no, I'm not. I have something to tell you and it's super hard for me. I just need you to listen so I can get it out. I can't see you anymore. I realized last night that I must make a choice between following God and going out with you. The Bible says that because I'm a believer I'm not supposed to be involved with a person who is not a believer. I'm sorry that I let it go this far. I like you a lot and love spending time with you. You're a super nice guy and we've had so much fun together. I must make a choice and I have to choose Jesus. I'm sorry...I really am!" She was crying uncontrollably now and could barely get the words out. "I didn't mean to hurt you; this is all my fault. It's just what I believe, and I must go with that. Please forgive me." She could barely breathe.

He was silent for a moment. "OK Jenna. I understand. You have to follow what you believe in and I don't want to ask you to change that. I wish we could continue to date. I really like you and think we're good together. But, I understand. That's your belief and you must follow it. Don't be sorry. I'm not mad at you or anything. We can still be friends and I'll see you at work, OK?" He sounded so sweet.

She had no idea how he truly felt or what was going on inside of him. She couldn't stay on the phone to find out. She had to hang up before she changed her mind. She didn't want to change her mind; she wanted to be true to the Lord. She was miserable the rest of the day thinking about how she had failed. She knew that once she had confessed to the Lord and followed through that she was forgiven but she felt so dirty and ashamed. She wasn't very old in the Lord and already she'd had such an epic failure. She chided herself because she had refused to listen to the warnings of the Holy Spirit. She knew better than to trust herself when it came to relationships, even as a Christian.

She also felt bad because he was just coming off the pain and loss of his wife and now she'd hurt him.

The next day was Sunday. She went to church and was determined to pour her heart and soul out to the Lord in worship.

She sat down. The worship team came out. Everyone stood for the first song. The song began to play, and she lifted her hands and sang at the top of her lungs. She kept thinking in her mind, *I'm sorry Jesus, so sorry*. Please forgive me. About a third-of-the-way through the song she was lost in the worship. She wasn't thinking about how dirty she felt or how sorry she was, she was just singing to Him who had redeemed her.

"You are forgiven my child." She heard it in her ear as though He was standing right behind her with his mouth right against her ear. Her heart almost stopped. She knew beyond a shadow of a doubt that Jesus had just spoken to her. He knew what she needed to move on from her sin and He gave it to her.

Now she was crying tears of joy and thanksgiving for the special gift she'd just been given. She needed to know she was forgiven because she had failed. She hated failing.

Monday came and she was driving to work. She felt as though a tight band was wrapped around her head and her heart. She felt weak, fragile and very vulnerable. What would she do when she saw him? She didn't have the confidence that she would stand on what she'd already told him. What was she going to do? How would she get the victory over this? She didn't want to go back into a relationship she'd just exited, back track on what was said, or fail this test.

"Father, please break this bond that has been created between Mike and I. I have allowed it. I am emotionally attached to him. I feel weak and if you don't break this bondage, this hold that's around my heart and mind, I'll fail when I see him. I admit that I'm in bondage. My mind is flooded with thoughts of him right now, my emotions are going crazy and I know the devil wants me to fail. Please help me."

She waited for something to happen. It didn't take long. Within a minute she felt free. She couldn't explain it other than, free. When she saw him, as she inevitably would, it would be OK. God had broken the hold and given her the strength because she'd cried out to Him for it.

She did, of course, eventually see him. They worked in the same office. He treated her the same, flirty, sweet, gentle and acted as if nothing had happened. She was nervous the first time, but she had the victory. She was able to continue to work with him without difficulty. That could only be Jesus.

"Do not be unequally yoked with unbelievers, for what fellowship does light have with darkness or righteousness with un-righteousness." 2 Corinthians 6:14KJV

ALEXX AND
THE GANG

Before she reconnected with Mike, she'd stopped spending so much time with Trevor and his group. She liked them all and loved Connie, but she began to realize that their lives revolved around Trevor. They went to whatever church Trevor was playing at on Sunday, whatever coffee house or lounge he was playing at and when they weren't there, they were all at Connie's house listening to Trevor play. She didn't want to follow Trevor around like a lost puppy; she wanted to follow Jesus. So, she'd decided to strike out on her own. She started to go to church every night of the week. Going to church, working and taking care of Captain Jack pretty much filled up her life.

She had slacked on church while she was dating Mike. Now that he was out of the picture, she went back to her routine of being in church every night of the week. She threw herself harder into Bible study, worship, prayer and following Jesus.

It was difficult to be at home alone every weekend. She found out that Calvary Costa Mesa had a concert every Saturday night in the summer. Even though it was hard for her, she went one Saturday, all by herself. She was determined that she was going to have fun even if she did it alone.

She was standing in line listening to the other conversations around her when behind her she heard a female voice discussing one of the bands she used to love, GNR.

"I used to love that band but since I got saved, I don't listen to them anymore." The female voice sounded to be about Jenna's age.

She turned to see the face that the voice belonged to. It was a girl that looked to be around 25. She was much shorter than Jenna, maybe 5'4" at the most. She had shoulder length hair that was very curly. She had a medium build and looked like she could hold her own in a fight. She was smiling with a big Jesus smile that made her blue eyes sparkle. She seemed tough with a softened edge to her. Jenna could tell right away they were alike. There seemed to be a kindred spirit sort of floating in the air. She could tell this girl was spunky and had a lot of guts. Jenna liked that. Jenna never butted into other people's conversations, especially strangers but she couldn't help herself.

"Excuse me. Did you say you used to listen to GNR? They used to be one of my favorite bands too!"

"Yea, I loved rock and heavy metal. You name it, I probably listened to it." She was smiling at Jenna now. "My name is Alexx, short for Alexandra".

"I'm Jenna. This is my first concert here. Have you been here before?"

"This is my first time." Alexx was outgoing and put her at ease at once.

"Are you here by yourself?" Jenna was hoping she was so they could sit together.

"No, I'm waiting for some friends. We're celebrating a birthday. But you can sit with us. You'll like them; they're cool."

"Are you sure? I don't want to butt in or anything." Jenna didn't want to be the awkward third wheel in the group and feel like she was imposing on anyone.

"No way, it will totally be cool with them."

They continued to talk while they stood in line. Alexx and most of her friends had all gotten saved around the same time as Jenna. So, they were all new to Christianity and how it all worked. They had met at a home bible study that was being led by a Bible college student who was going to be a pastor after he finished school. They met every Friday night at Alexx's dad's house in Huntington Beach.

Soon, the rest of the group arrived. There were men and women, different ages, obviously different backgrounds, but all had the same "Jesus loves me" smile on their faces. Jenna hoped they'd like her.

"Jenna, this is Susan, Rick, Chris, Cindy, Lucky and Dave, he's my dad." She smiled a big smile at that introduction.

"Hi everyone." Jenna was nervous but they were all laughing, talking and joking and tried to make her feel at ease. Jenna thought it must be awesome for Alexx that she and her dad were both saved, hanging out together at a concert.

They all sat together and enjoyed the concert. Afterwards, Alexx and Jenna exchanged numbers and decided they would get together and hang out. They also invited her to the Bible study at Dave's house.

The next Friday came and Jenna went to Alexx's house to pick her up for Bible study.

"Come on in, I'm just finishing something for my grandma. I live with my mom, stepdad and grandma. I help take care of her when my mom is at work." She followed Alexx into Grandma's room. She was sitting in her chair watching Jeopardy.

"Grandma, this is my new friend Jenna." Grandma turned and nodded.

"Hi, it's nice to meet you. You're watching Jeopardy, I love Jeopardy, and sometimes I can even guess the answers." Jenna didn't know what else to say even though that sounded dumb, she hoped it would make Grandma smile. It did.

"Let's go in my room so I can get some stuff. Have you ever heard of Guardian?"

"No, who are they?" She was curious.

"You'll love them, here listen." She leaned over and clicked on a tape player and an amazing sound came out. Sounded a little like GNR but she could tell the lyrics were about Jesus.

"Wow! They're awesome. That's a Christian band?" Jenna couldn't believe it.

"Yes! You can borrow this tape and I'll make you another one. I have a couple other's here you'd probably like. I had to find some Christian Rock to listen to. Sometimes I can't handle the mellow praise music. I need to feel it—you know what I mean?" Alexx said the last part with a kind of growl in her voice and Jenna knew exactly what she meant. Before she was a Christian, there were many times she needed to "feel it" and those were the times she'd put in her favorite and turn it up as loud as she could. She could see how this band could do that for her.

They talked at length during the drive and found their lives were very parallel. Alexx had a Brandon, had an abortion at the same age as Jenna, had a hard life growing up, a filing cabinet of her own, partied, loved the same music and the girls were instant best friends.

Over the next year the girls were practically inseparable. They spent all their time together. Alexx was at Jenna's house every weekend. Rachel was still gone every weekend but when she was around, her and Alexx got along well. Alexx had a younger, unsaved, kind of wild sister too, so she understood both sides of the coin. They both spent a lot of time with the rest of the Friday gang as well. There were potlucks, BBQ's, concerts, beach outings, prayer times' that lasted until two in the morning and great friendships that were forged. Alexx and Jenna went to church together, went through a Post Abortion Counseling Education Bible study together and even burned all their old books, concert stuff and drug paraphernalia together. That was an interesting time.

"Hey, Jenna, I was thinking, I've got all this stuff from

before I was saved. You know, concert mags, my favorite co-caine mirror, a bunch of vinyl and some occult books. I don't want to give it to anyone, I don't want to throw it away, let's go down to the beach and throw it in the fire pit and burn it." She said it with such enthusiasm and a little devilish sneakiness in her voice.

"That's a cool idea. I have a ton of stuff too and I want it out of my house. When should we do it?" Jenna was excited now.

"Well, this weekend is the long weekend so I'm off on Monday. Let's go at like six in the morning before anyone else is there and do it."

"Sweet, I can do that. Wow, that'll be fun!" She'd had all this stuff and didn't know what to do with it. She'd already gotten rid of her inappropriate clothes and all the cassette tapes she had, but the books and vinyl she didn't know what to do with, so this was perfect.

Monday came and the girls got up at 5 a.m., poured some coffee, loaded up Alexx's car and drove to Corona Del Mar, the same beach where she had been baptized. Seemed appropriate!

They put all the stuff in the fire pit and tried to light it but every time they did, the wind would kick up and blow out the fire. The stuff just didn't want to burn! Finally, they got it going and burnt it all up, including the mirror.

Jenna had no idea what was about to come her way. It started the night of the bon fire. She'd go to bed, start to fall asleep then wake up with a sudden terrifying fear, hearing noises outside, feeling like someone was watching her. It was like a dark cloud had descended on her house. She wasn't getting any sleep. She was barely functioning as a person. She had a job to do and bills to pay. It was worse when she was in the house alone. She went to the Bible study group and asked for prayer. They were so faithful to pray for each other and to encourage each other. Finally, after about six months she was talking to an older lady at her church about it and the answer came.

"You are under spiritual attack. When did all of this start?"

Jenna told her about the book burning incident and how that same night all her sleeping issues had started.

"You are being attacked by the devil. You have to pray through it and ask Jesus to give you the victory." She was so sure of herself.

Jenna had never thought of that before. It made sense on one hand but in her logical black-and-white brain it didn't. But her life was based on faith in God now, not her logic. She was so tired from all the sleepless nights; she figured it was worth a shot. That night before she went to bed, she called her new friend and they prayed. When Jenna hung up, she prayed again. She asked the Lord to protect her, to bind back the enemy and give her sleep. Finally, after six months she was able to sleep the whole night through, but she wasn't going to quit praying about it just to make sure!

"God sets the solitary in families: He brings out those which are bound with chains..." Psalm 68:6

NOTHING STAYS
THE SAME

L ife was good. Jenna had a great group of friends that she loved, a best friend that she had fun with, a good job, a place to live and she loved Jesus. If life could only stay that way, but change is inevitable.

She'd known Alexx and the others for a little over a year now. She'd become close friends with Susan, and Dave was like a dad to everyone. They'd grown to love one another through all the prayer and time they spent together. They'd all been through so much, growing pains, fun times, family difficulties but they'd stuck together.

Alexx had told Jenna, from the beginning of their friendship, that she knew she was going to get married someone day and that she was going to marry a pastor. Jenna was a little envious of the fact that Alexx was so confident of that. Jenna still hadn't decided if she could risk marriage even as a Christian. She certainly knew she couldn't or wouldn't ever marry a pastor.

Enter Joshua. Joshua was in Bible College and had joined the Friday night group. In a very short time, he and Alexx were married. He was perfect for her. They had the same ideals, same sense of humor, same stubborn pursuit of God, they both loved kids and wanted a house full and so they got married. Jenna was the maid of honor at their wedding; she cried most of the way through it. She was excited for her friend but knew that things would be drastically different. They'd already changed as Alexx went from spending all her time with Jenna to spending it with Joshua, which was completely understandable.

Alexx and Jenna would soon be separated by miles and grow apart. She was grateful for the rest of the group and their friendships. She would grow to love them and depend on them as a lifeline, especially over the next year.

Jenna had been struggling for some time with sinus infections. They were getting more frequent and harder to get rid of. Then one morning she woke up to get ready for work.

"Rachel, can you come in here for a second?" Jenna was in her bathroom looking in the mirror in disbelief.

"Yea, what's up?" Rachel came into her bathroom and stopped dead in her tracks. She saw right away what was bothering Jenna. Sticking out from the side of her neck were three lumps. One large one and two smaller ones, they were in a cluster on the side of her neck just under her jaw line.

"Um, what the heck is that?" Rachel was trying not to sound freaked out but not doing a very good job.

"I don't know. I woke up, came in here, looked in the mirror and there they were. I don't feel weird or anything; they're a little sore, but not bad. What the heck should I do?" Jenna was kind of smiling. It was a nervous habit she had. When she was scared or freaked out, she'd sometimes get a nervous smile. She hated it because she always thought people must think her to be insensitive or sadistic.

"You need to go to the doctor. What if it's cancer or something?"

"Yea, I guess you're right." She called into work and then called the doctor's office. She got in right away. He didn't know what to make of it. He gave her several options, none of them good. Cancer, Lupus, Hodgkin's all possibilities, but he ran blood tests and would get back to her. She went home thinking, about dying and going to heaven. She was so thankful that she knew the Lord, but what about her sister and other family? The nervous smile crept back across her face.

Well Lord, it's up to you. I have no control over this and I'm kind of scared but if I die at least I know I'll go to heaven. Help me not to freak out. It was all she could say in the moment.

Rachel came home from work and headed straight for Jenna's room. Jenna was sitting in the dark, motionless, half scared and half excited. She really had changed.

"Well, what happened? What did he say?" Rachel was trying to stay calm but was very anxious and the fear came through in her voice.

"He doesn't know, he thinks it could be a couple of things and none of them are good. He's gonna call me tomorrow or the next day with blood results." Jenna was trying to keep the nervous smile off her face.

"What are you going to do?" Rachel was frozen in the doorway.

"Well, nothing I can do. I know I'll go to heaven if I die. I'm not saying I'm ready for that. I'm mostly scared about going to the hospital. I hate hospitals. Don't worry though Bean, I'll be alright!" She tried to sound reassuring. Jenna had started calling Rachel "Bean" when she was about fifteen and Rachel was twelve. Rachel and Jenna made up songs and nicknames for each other and one day Jenna made up a song and called Rachel Bean, and it just stuck.

"I am freaking out. I don't want you to die, what would I do? I'm glad you know your going to heaven or whatever, but I'm not ready to lose my sister." She was trying not to cry and simultaneously control her anger. She was the scared little bird that Jenna loved so much.

Jenna reached out and hugged her sister. She felt so bad for her. She didn't have the same peaceful confidence that Jenna had because she didn't know Jesus. She knew that if Jesus took her, it would be hardest on Rachel and although she was excited at the thought of going to heaven, she was sad to think of leaving her sister behind without her knowing Jesus. *Lord if you take me, please don't let Rachel become angrier, please use it to save her.*

The next morning, she woke up, had a 103 temperature, her throat felt like it was covered in sandpaper that had been lit on fire and she could barely move. She felt like she'd been run over by a truck. She was back at the doctors that morning and he gave her antibiotics; he was still waiting for the blood test. This began a full year of sickness. A full year of constant antibiotics and doctor visits. Missed work. Barely able to get out of bed and eat. Missing church every week. Miserable. Frustrated. Questioning. Every time she would start to feel a little better, she'd go to work and within two weeks she'd be out again. She was already thin at 123 lbs. but went down to 116 simply because she was so sick, she could barely eat. She was not a frou-frou girl and under ordinary circumstances she could get up at 7 a.m., shower, and be ready to leave the house by 7:30. Now she had to get up at 6:30 just to try to get out of the house by 7:30. She'd have to lie on the bed and rest after she took a shower because it exhausted her.

She had every one of her friends praying for her.

"I don't understand why I am so sick. Why don't the doctors know what's wrong with me? I'm going to work sick just because I've used every available day I have and I have to work because I have to take care of myself, no one is going to do it for me. Why is the Lord allowing this to happen? I feel so alone, and I don't know what to do." She was sobbing uncontrollably into her hands while Susan had her arm around her listening.

Susan had experienced a long illness before she was saved. She understood what it felt like.

"I don't understand it either, but I know that God loves you. I have been where you are. I know it's hard and scary, but I know He has it under control. I love you; I'm here for you. I will help you with whatever you need. Just let me. Maybe that's part of what this is all about; you allowing other people to help you. You're like me; you take care of yourself because no one else ever has. You don't trust people and you don't want to let them in. I get that. But in God's economy, that won't work. You have to let people in because if you block them, you will inadvertently block Jesus. You can't separate the two." Susan sounded very gentle but very sure of the truth she was speaking.

Susan prayed for her. She prayed that Jenna would feel the love of God and let people love her. She prayed that Jenna would accept that there were people that genuinely cared for her and that she'd trust God and allow Him to work in her life.

Jenna had been battling for about ten months with her illness. She still had no answers from the doctors. She was just constantly sick, always on antibiotics and tired down to her bones. She felt broken, discouraged, frustrated and yet determined as ever to move forward trusting the Lord had a plan, even if it seemed silent and dark. Her strong-willed determination that she had developed in the world transferred over beautifully to Jesus. It could have been a real detriment, but Jesus had turned it to her advantage; she was relentless in her pursuit of Him and going back was not an option. She was all-in! Even if she was crawling in.

One day she was writing in her diary and asking Him to help her and complaining that she didn't understand. She heard His still small Voice tell her "Look at June 23rd". She knew the voice. She turned to June 23rd. It happened to be June 23rd a year prior; she was rather inconsistent with her diary. She read it and began to weep. In that entry she had asked the Lord to take the wall down, to heal and change her heart and she didn't care what it cost or what it took, she just wanted it gone. From the time she accepted Christ, Jenna had a great awareness of two major things in her life. First, she had to forgive her dad for everything that he'd done and secondly there was an invisible wall that she could feel that separated her from everything that Jesus wanted to give her and keeping her from being as close to Him as she wanted to be. She knew she was saved, forgiven and belonged to Him but she understood that all the years of hurt, sin, pain, loss and trying to deal with it her own way, had not only created her filing system, but had built up an internal wall, brick by brick. She felt like the wall was 9,000 feet tall and went on forever. She hated it. So, in the youthful exuberance of a young Christian, she had asked God to take the wall down and heal her from everything that had come her way or that she had created on her own. She had no idea what that would look like, feel like, act like or taste like, she only knew she wanted it and needed it. Desperately.

As she was reading, she heard His Voice again, "I'm answering your prayer."

Her unidentifiable illness did not go away for another two months and after it did, she would never regain her health completely, but she had joy and hope because He, the Almighty God of the Universe, was answering her prayer. Not in the way she would've picked but He heard her. He understood the desperation of her soul, listened to the cry of her broken, beat-up heart and was answering. She had prayed for healing, asked others to pray for healing and it hadn't come. Now she understood why. He was doing a spiritual healing, not a physical one. She would never be the same again, physically or spiritually.

"You number my wanderings; Put my tears into Your bottle; Are they not in Your book?" Psalm 56:8 KJV

GENERAL PATTON

During the time of her illness, she spent as much time as she could with the Friday night gang because she needed their support and encouragement. Part of that group was a guy named Steve. Steve was sort of a hippie. He never wore shoes, had shoulder length dishwater-blonde hair, blue eyes, 6-foot-tall with a muscular build. He was originally from Ohio and lived in a house with three other guys. He walked everywhere because he didn't own a car and didn't see the need to. He was quiet, loved the Lord, read his Bible constantly, had a sharp, witty sense of humor and was an animal lover.

Jenna noticed him looking at her more than once. She was intrigued by him simply because he was so earthy, and she was kind of a hippie herself. They had similar backgrounds in music, and both had a passion for the Word of God. They started talking more, hanging out more together even though they were in a group. They decided they liked each other and that maybe it was God's plan for them to be together. They talked for hours about the Bible, life, the future, everything. They went to church together and eventually began to talk about the possibility of marriage. She even bought a dress.

Jenna was fine with everything at first. But she started

to feel a little tension inside that was a blast from the past. She tried to ignore it, but it persisted.

Then one day a big red flag popped up and the tension turned into fear.

"I'm reading this great book on World War II about General Patton. I was thinking about how much it reminds me of marriage." Steve sounded very enthusiastic and couldn't wait to tell her what he'd been thinking.

"How does that relate to marriage?" She was perplexed.

"Well, General Patton was in command of his troops. He was well respected and feared. When he spoke, the men listened and instantly obeyed. If he said jump, they jumped. They listened and obeyed him without hesitation or reservation. The Bible says that husbands are the head of the household, that wives are supposed to submit to their husbands in everything and the children are supposed to obey the parents. So, that's how I want our house to be. I expect that you'll obey me and when I say jump you jump." He was dead serious and said it very matter-of-factly. Like it was a normal everyday conversation.

Jenna almost jumped out of the car they were sitting in and ran screaming down the street. She was in shock, full of fear and couldn't believe what she was hearing. She couldn't believe this was coming from a Christian man and was torn between the reality of the Bible and the fear of being controlled in that way.

"You really believe that's what marriage is supposed to be like? Like running a military troop? That your family, that I, am supposed to just jump and obey your every command?" She was fighting back tears and working her way up to a rage.

"Yea, the Bible uses military terms in describing the marriage relationship. I do expect that from my wife and kids." He was calm, polite, and unassuming in his delivery.

She opened the car door and ran out. They happened to be parked across the street from a park, so she ran and sat on one of the benches and burst into tears.

He got out of the car and slowly walked over to her. He had a look of total bewilderment on his face.

"Jenna, I don't understand why you are so upset." He sat down next to her.

"Are you kidding me? You don't understand? Why would any woman want to be controlled and bossed around like a child or a soldier? Why would I want to be treated like that?" She could barely breathe.

"I don't understand." He sounded so confused and shocked. He really didn't get it. She could hardly believe what she was seeing or hearing.

"I have to go, and I don't want to talk about his." She got up and ran to her car and left. He could walk home. He only lived a block away from the park, but she wouldn't have cared if he had to walk ten miles, she was leaving.

She drove home and as far as she was concerned didn't care what happened. She was feeling all the familiar feelings of her youth. Is that what God wanted for her? Did He want her to live under a controlling husband? She couldn't reconcile that. She was young in her faith and didn't understand everything about submission or marriage according to the Bible. She felt so scared inside. She felt like a trapped animal. She didn't know what to do, where to go or how to resolve it.

She wouldn't take his phone calls for the next few days. She needed time to think and pray. She decided that she'd give it a few days to cool off and then see what happened. The next time she saw him, six days later; she didn't say anything about their conversation. He was sheepish and asked her if she wanted to talk about it and she told him no.

Everything went fine for a few weeks. Then one Sunday she went to pick him up for church and was five minutes later than what she had intended to be. When she got to his house he was gone. She couldn't figure it out at first, and then she drove to the church and saw him in the parking lot. Then she understood. He'd left because she was late. So, she drove home. She had calculated that he would have had to leave his house at exactly the time she was to be there in order to make it to church. He'd not been willing to wait even five minutes for her. She was furious.

"Hello". Jenna picked up the phone.

"Why were you late and why didn't you go to church?" He sounded mad.

"Well, I was exactly five minutes late and you'd left. You couldn't wait for me five minutes? So, I came home. You couldn't wait for me; why should I go to church with you? That was childish of you and I'm not going to play your stupid games." She was so angry she could hardly contain herself to sound civil.

"Well, don't be late next time. If I say you need to be here at 9 a.m. that's what time you need to be here. Not 9:05, hope you learned your lesson." He sounded so smug.

"For real? You hope I learned my lesson. OK!" She hung up.

Again, she gave him a week of silence. She was working so hard to reconcile in her mind what was right and wrong. She had talked to Michelle about it and told her the things he was saying. Michelle felt Jenna needed to get away from him because he was controlling, and it would only bring Jenna misery if she pursued it. Jenna was waiting for her release from the Lord. She had felt that God had directed her down this road and so she felt He was the only one that could release her. Now, she was beginning to question if He had in fact directed her at all. Part of her struggle came from the past. She'd been taught to obey and what little she knew about marriage in the Bible, she knew that if she was married, she was supposed to submit but the past and the truth were all mixed up in her mind and it was creating a cloud of fear. Fear of being controlled and fear of not obeying the Lord; the thought of being disobedient turned her stomach.

Once again they resumed their relationship. A few weeks went by without a problem. Then one day it came to a boil.

The phone rang. "Hello."

"Hey Jenna, I need to go somewhere can you come get me?" He sounded a little edgy.

"No, I can't, I'm right in the middle of something and I can't leave."

"Well I need you to give me a ride so you're going to have to stop whatever you're doing and come get me." Now he was being bossy.

"I told you I can't! You're going to have to call someone else." She was starting to get irritated.

"I'm telling *you*; you need to do it. I'm not calling anyone else." Now he was angry.

"I'm not doing it and don't talk to me that way." She hung up. Now she'd had enough.

The phone immediately began to ring. She knew who it was. She let the answering machine get it. He proceeded to call incessantly for the next ten minutes. She'd let the machine get it, he'd hang up and call right back. Someone else happened to get a call in there and while she was on the phone, he continued to call and beep in. Finally, he left a message.

"I can't believe you won't pick up the phone. You are being so rebellious and rude, and I will not accept your behavior. You need to pick up the phone Jenna. You need to repent of your attitude. I know you can hear me." He was furious.

Now she knew that she wasn't going any further with him. She called him two days later and told him she didn't want to talk to him, see him or hear from him for two weeks. She was going to pray and seek the Lord to see if being in a relationship with him was what Jesus wanted for her life.

She did just that. She concluded that the Lord didn't want her to be in this relationship and she realized He wasn't the one who had directed her there in the first place. It had been her flesh, feelings and longing to have a godly man. Probably born out of her missing Alexx and wanting what Alexx had with Joshua. She realized that God's plan for marriage was not Steve's plan for marriage. She was grateful for that!

She was sad at the thought of telling him but sadder that she'd gone off track yet again all because of a dude!

"...it is hard for you to kick against the goad." Acts 9:5

LITTLE WOMEN

J enna had come to the place where she was excited at the
thought of having a godly marriage and believed that with
Jesus, she could have a successful one. That excitement
and hope had caused her problems. When she was against marriage it wasn't an issue, now she'd gotten herself involved with
a guy that wasn't the Lord's will and felt defeated and fearful that she'd never get married. She'd bought the dress and
started making plans, now she saw it hanging in the closet as
another empty dream.

"Hey, they did a remake of Little Women and it's showing this weekend, do you want to go and see it with me?" Michelle was trying to get Jenna out of the slump she'd been in
ever since her breakup with Steve.

"Um, I guess so. I probably won't be very good company
but, I'll go." Jenna didn't feel like going to the movies or anything else for that matter. She was having such an internal
battle.

They went to the movies and then to Marie Calendars'
for dessert. Michelle was such a sweet person. The movie was
enjoyable, and the dessert was awesome. By the time they got
back to Michelle's house Jenna was in a little better mood and
a little more talkative.

"What is it that's really bothering you Jenna?"

"I guess I just want to get married and have a godly
husband. I see couples in my church with godly marriages,

women with godly husbands and I want that for my life. I'm almost 30 years old, I hate being alone and yet I feel like God isn't going to bring me a husband. I don't know why I feel that way, it's something inside that I can't explain." She felt like she was going to cry.

"Have you given your desire over to Him? You know, asked Him to take it and told Him you're willing to wait for His timing?" Michelle was being gentle, but Jenna could tell she was going somewhere that wasn't going to feel gentle.

"No!"

"Why not? Are you afraid?"

"Yes, I'm afraid. I'm afraid if I give it up to Him then it's a dead dream. It'll be in the ash heap where every other dream I've ever had is. It will be gone and done." Jenna was crying now.

"Why do you feel that way and say that? If that does happen and He never brings you a husband can't you believe by faith that it's the best thing for your life? His will is always the best for our lives and if that's what He has for you, you'll be the happiest person on earth, because He'll give you joy." Michelle was trying to encourage her.

"But I thought you weren't supposed to give up on your dreams. After Brandon and then Rafael I gave up wanting to be married. I didn't want to be hurt or marry an abuser and I was sick of men. I didn't want to end up divorced either. So, I gave up my dream, let it die, and buried it. After I got saved, it took a while for me to allow myself to consider the possibility. I've seen godly marriages and they are amazing. I also figure that if Jesus picks him out, Jesus is in the middle of it and we are following Him, it won't end up in divorce, I won't marry an abuser and we'll make it. It feels like death to me. Letting the dream go is letting it die and dead things don't come back to life." Why couldn't Michelle see what she was asking was so painful and impossible?

"Well, maybe the Lord wants you to give it up so He can give it back but, in His timing, and with the person He's picked out. Sometimes He asks us to surrender something to see if we're willing and to see if we love Him more than the thing He's asking us to surrender. Sometimes He asks us to surrender because if we don't, we'll hurt others and ourselves. In the world we are told to dream and hang on to those dreams, let no one take it, but in Christ we are told to surrender our lives and allow Him to have His way. Then, as we do that, His desires become our desires and then He fulfills them."

Michelle cared about Jenna and had been walking with the Lord much longer than her, so she had experience and wisdom.

"I hear you. I'll pray about it and try to let it go." Jenna had an internal war going on. She knew what she was hearing was truth and that it was right, but she couldn't reconcile it in her mind; she couldn't wrap her brain around the instruction she was receiving.

"Let me pray for you now. Dear Lord, please comfort my friend Jenna. Please help her to surrender her dreams to You. Help her to see that You love her and have her best interest in mind. You have a perfect plan for her life. Your Word says You have plans to give her a hope and a future. Lord, show her she can trust You with her dreams. Give her peace and bless her. In Jesus Name. Amen." Michelle hugged her.

Jenna went home that night and sat on the floor beside her bed, as was her habit. She bowed her head and prayed.

Lord, I am so scared to pray this prayer but here goes. I give You my desire and dream to be married. I am willing to give it up to You and let You have it. I am willing, if it is Your will, to be single for the rest of my life. I realize Lord that I have made bad choices my whole life. My track record since being saved isn't great either. So, apparently, I'm incapable of making a good decision when it comes to men. If You do want me to be married, I want You to pick him out. Wherever he is now, please save him if he isn't saved and if he is, please cause him to want to love You, serve You and follow You more than I do. I am willing to serve You, follow You and love You no matter what. I want to be married; I don't want to be an old cat lady who sits on her porch and talks to her 25 cats. I want to have a godly man in my life and to share my life with someone. But, if that is not Your will for me and it is better for me to be single, I am willing. I do ask that You help me to be content and satisfied in You. I don't want to feel like I'm missing out on anything. In Jesus Name. Amen.

She went to bed.

"If any man will come after Me, let him deny himself and take up his cross daily and follow Me." Luke 9:23 KJV

U-HAULS & TODDLERS

1995 was an interesting year for Jenna. She'd laid down her desire to be married and the Lord had given her peace about whatever happened. The Friday night group had broken up. Several of the people had gone their own directions for work, marriage and then having kids. The leader, Brian, had moved to Colorado with his wife after graduating from Bible College and so the group no longer officially met every week. They would, on occasion, get together for potluck, prayer and just hanging out. Jenna had been attending the same church on Sunday mornings and had gotten connected with a ladies Saturday Bible Study.

She loved her church. She had made friends with all the ladies at the Saturday morning study. The leader was a woman in her late 50's. Her name was Jo. She'd come from a hard, difficult life and when she accepted Christ had made a radical transformation from bartender to Bible teacher. She was an amazing woman. She had such a love for the Lord it just oozed out of every part of her. She had gray hair and blue eyes that sparkled with the love of Jesus. When she said His Name, her eyes lit up, she beamed with a huge smile and you could always see a hint of a tear drop. She was a little taller than Jenna and had a heavy build. She reminded Jenna of a grandmother that you could tell all your secrets to, get a big warm hug and then she'd make you cookies. But she was equally tough and didn't mess around when someone was off the track. She was an awesome Bible teacher and loved to spend time in worship and prayer. The first time Jenna met her was at a women's retreat she'd gone to with her church. Jo was one of the speakers and the moment she started to talk about Jesus and the Bible, the way she explained it and the love she had, Jenna was captivated and connected. In fact, right after she'd finished, Jenna ran up to her to tell her how much she had enjoyed her teaching. With her torn jeans, long blonde hair, bare feet and bouncy youth, she must have been a sight.

"I loved your study. It spoke to me so much. This is the first time I've been on a retreat with this church and only my second retreat ever. Do you do a women's study or something because I'd love to hear you teach again?" She was gushing but didn't care.

"Well, thank you. I do teach a women's study on Saturday mornings at the church. I'm glad to know the Lord used me to speak to you." Her face had a look of shock and amusement. She was a little hesitant but at the same time didn't want to seem rude. Jenna found out later, after they were friends, that after Jenna bounded up to her and gushed all over, Jo had thought, "this little rebel isn't going to like my study with a bunch of old ladies and she probably won't even show up." They laughed about it later.

Jenna did show up. All the ladies there were older than her. She was 30 and the next closest one was probably about 50. They all accepted her, graciously. The ladies all became like a mom to her. They were godly examples to follow and the lifeline that would hold her together in days to come. She fell in love with them and they with her. Every Saturday she'd go at 10 a.m. and sometimes they wouldn't leave until

2. They worshipped, studied the Bible, prayed and sometimes prayed and worshipped for several hours after the study, and of course they fellowshipped. They always had special Christmas potlucks, birthday celebrations and became very close to one another. They shared one another's burdens, tragedies and triumphs.

She also threw herself into serving. She began to help on Sunday mornings in children's ministry. She landed there completely by accident. A friend of hers served a few Sunday's a month and one Sunday her friends' helper didn't show, she was desperate and asked if Jenna could help, so she did. It was the 3 & 4-year-old class. There was an average of twenty-five of them all in one room for an hour and a half. She was overwhelmed and knew nothing of Sunday school. She'd babysat a few times as a teenager, but this was different. She had fun. She helped a few more Sundays with the other teacher and then the director approached her about taking over teaching the class. Both teachers were leaving.

"You want me to be the teacher for this class?" She was shocked.

"Yes. Would you pray about it and get back to me? You'd have to do it every Sunday for now until I can find someone to switch off with you. You would do it second service and you'd have at least one helper if not two. Pray about it, think it over and let me know." She sounded so positive.

Jenna was scared to death. First off, she didn't think she was the Sunday school teacher type. The old Jenna certainly wasn't. Secondly, she didn't think she could teach them. She wasn't a teacher. But she told the director she'd pray about it so she did.

"I'll do it. I'm scared that I won't be a good teacher but I'm willing. I believe it's what the Lord wants me to do. When do I start?" The Lord had spoken to her when she was reading her Bible and she came across 2 Timothy 1:7 "For the Lord has not given us a Spirit of fear, but of power, love and a sound mind." She knew the only thing keeping her from doing it was her own fear. So, she stepped out in faith.

"Great. You can be in the class the next three weeks with the current teacher and then she'll be leaving. She can show you the routine and where everything is. Thanks so much for being willing." She was relieved.

Six months into her first year Jenna had fallen in love. She'd fallen in love with the kids, with the opportunity she'd been given to share Jesus with them, with serving the God that had done so much for her and with teaching. She'd done some street witnessing, served Thanksgiving to the homeless and a few other things, but consistently serving every week was amazing and she loved it.

"I just wanted to let you know that you don't have to look for someone to help me out. I'll teach the kids every week myself. I want to be able to be with them every week. Is that alright?" Jenna hoped it was because she didn't want to go even one week without being with them.

"That's great Jenna. I'll put you on the calendar every week and stop worrying about giving you a break unless you tell me otherwise." She was grateful to give up the search. It was hard finding people to serve in Children's Ministry. Now she didn't have to worry about that class.

She loved acting out the stories for the kids. They got so excited and loved to be a part of acting them out. Jenna had kids that came and went. Some came every couple of weeks, others she saw only once but there were those that came every week. She grew to love them and got to know their little personalities. The kids that were there every week grew to love her too. They drew pictures for her, brought her presents, told her the things they wanted for Christmas and shared some of their heartaches with her.

She had a favorite little girl; her name was Amanda. She was a tiny little petite girl with brown curly hair, big blue eyes and dimples. She was so sweet. She always wanted Jenna to pick her up. When she'd arrive at class she'd go running to Jenna and say, "Teacher Jenna, teacher Jenna, I've missed you" and throw herself into Jenna's arms. If she saw her in the sanctuary, she'd do the same. Then there was Patrick. He took a strong liking to Jenna. He was a little blonde, curly haired boy that was built like a small tank. He always had some story to tell her about his adventures with his dad and his army trucks. The kids made her laugh, cry, rejoice and see the world in a whole new way. Jenna loved to see their little hearts grab a hold of the Bible story she was teaching. Listening to them pray brought smiles and sometimes tears to her eyes; she felt privileged to listen and hear their little hearts. She loved them more than she could of ever imagined.

That year brought about a lot of change for Jenna at home as well. Rachel decided to move out on her own. She'd never lived by herself; she went from living with their mom to living with Jenna. The three years that they'd lived together since Jenna's salvation had been difficult at times. Jenna tried to be the big sister/friend to Rachel that she had always been but because of Jesus there was a divide and Rachel wasn't crossing over it. Rachel spent a lot of time with her boyfriend, but when she was there, she stayed in her room and watched TV. They discussed the bills, animals, meals and work schedules. Jenna tried to ask her about her life and sometimes Rachel would open up but most of the time she'd just get the brush off.

"I'm going to look for a place to live. I think it's time I moved out, so you probably need to look for another roommate or an apartment yourself." She was scared but trying to sound brave. Rachel hated to say things to Jenna that could be deemed confrontational. As much as they were friends and sisters, there was still something that existed between them from Jenna taking over the mom role toward Rachel. If Jenna came across as "mom-ing" her, Rachel was immediately defensive.

"Um, OK!" Jenna didn't know what to say. She was sad at the thought but excited for her sister, and yet unsure how to respond so Rachel wouldn't feel scolded or defensive.

"So, yeah, I'm going to start looking. I'll take the cats if I can." They had accidentally acquired five cats. They had the mommy cat, Miss Kitty, so named because she was very small and had a huge attitude. She got pregnant before the girls could get her fixed. So, she had four kittens and they were so cute the girls couldn't give them up, presto-five cats. They had lost two to coyotes. The girls had no idea that living in a concrete jungle, coyotes still prowled. They were heartbroken at the loss.

She still had Captain Jack and with the cats they had a full house. The cats and dog were worth hours of entertainment. They played chase; the cats usually won that game. The cats were always bringing in "gifts" through the doggie door for the girls. Miss Kitty herself once brought in a full-grown dove, still alive and unharmed. She traipsed it through the house all the way back to Jenna's bedroom. Jenna got her to let it go and then it flew all over the room before she finally caught it. She had feathers on the ceiling for months. They brought in lizards, mice, rats and birds. Because of the tender heartedness of both girls they were constantly trying to capture and release them while they were still alive and relatively unharmed. They got bit numerous times by the tiny lizards that Miss Kitty was so fond of catching. Once they had to ask the man next door to help them catch a mouse that was behind the fridge, poor little thing ended up getting shop-vac'd.

Rachel was still so fragile. Jenna realized she'd always feel protective of her. She was scared for her and how Rachel would handle living on her own. Although she was twenty-seven, she'd been able to stay under the shelter of their mom or Jenna and now she was leaving that shelter. Rachel wasn't very good with money and living with them had given her a safety net. She'd never had to keep a house on her own, shop on her own, pay her bills on her own and now that was all about to change. She knew that it was pointless to try to change her mind. If this was God's plan, Rachel would find a place, if not she wouldn't. Jenna knew she could leave it in His hands, and it would be safe. She also knew she had to give Rachel over to Him once again. God loved her more than she did and wanted her to be saved. She also understood that sometimes people must go down long hard roads before they turn to Jesus. Jenna didn't want to see that with her little sister, but she didn't have much say in the matter. It was time to look for another place for her and CJ to live.

A few months went by and Rachel told her she'd found a place. She'd be moving out in one month. Jenna had looked a bit but hadn't found anything. She would have to step up her game now. She went and looked at Rachel's new apartment. It was a small place with a kitchen, bedroom, bathroom and small living room. She could have the cats and it was close to her work. It was an older place. It was once a house that had been divided to make two small apartments. It seemed like a safe place for a single girl. They began to divide up the kitchen supplies, did some thrift store shopping and asked their mom to provide anything she could. There were a few people at Rachel's work that had some furniture they were willing to let her have. She'd broken up with her boyfriend, which Jenna was happy about. Jenna never really liked him because he didn't treat Rachel the way she felt she should be treated. She would truly be on her own.

The month went by quickly. Moving day came. Jenna rented a truck, loaded it up and helped her move in. Cindy came and helped too. They accomplished it all in one day. They helped her get things set up and unpacked. Jenna was excited for her and Rachel was excited as well. When it was time to leave, they both teared up. It was difficult to let go. Jenna had a feeling that it was going to be hard but good for both of them. Maybe they could go back to being close since the tension of being in the same home would be gone. She was hopeful.

Jenna had to get a place. She'd been looking, but now it was time for her to put in her notice to the landlord because she couldn't pay the rent on her own. She prayed constantly for the Lord to provide the right place for her, a place where she could have her dog, her washer and dryer and a garage for her car. She also wanted to be safe; she'd be living on her own. She faithfully looked in the paper, called on places and went out looking at every possibility. Nothing! The days were approaching where she'd have to move. Everyone that she knew constantly asked her if she'd found a place. When she would tell them no, they would proceed to tell her all the things she could do and should do and be willing to do. She was constantly checking back with God and every single day she kept getting the same message, "Wait and trust", through sermons, her daily reading and her calendar. She had a tear off calendar on her desk with Bible verses on it. Every day was about trust in some way. It began to be comical to her. People kept pressuring her and she kept waiting and looking. She'd found a few places that fit some of the things she needed, but not all. Some just didn't feel very safe.

Her thirty days was up, and she had no place to go. She called her landlord and told him the situation. He told her not to worry, she could stay there for another week and he'd prorate her rent. That was on a Tuesday.

Thursday evening, she went to look at an apartment, well a loft. It was perfect. It was part of a four-plex. It was around the back of the building and right next to the garage that would be hers. She could have her dog; her washer and dryer and she'd be safe. It was in an older part of town. The streets were lined with huge Oak trees and lots of places to walk CJ.

"Wow, this is really cute. I love it." She had stepped through the door into the living room. Straight ahead were the stairs that went up to the loft/bedroom and the bathroom. To the right, the living room and a breakfast bar that connected the living room and kitchen. The kitchen was small but would work for her. There was a back door that led to the service porch where she could put the washer and dryer. Everything would just about fit and what little didn't, she could put in the garage if she needed to.

They discussed the deposit, utilities, first and last. It was all a little overwhelming, but she knew somehow that this was the place the Lord had prepared for her. She felt His peace as she walked in. There were a few hurdles to overcome but she knew He'd take care of them if it was His will for her to live there.

"There is one thing I need to tell you. I don't know what my credit score will be. I had some financial trouble due to job loss. I've gotten it all taken care of, but I don't know what my credit report will look like. I also don't have the full deposit but if I can add an extra $100 a month to the rent to pay off the rest of it that would be helpful." She said it with humility and confidence because she truly believed that being humble and honest was what the Lord wanted from her. She was a little embarrassed, she'd always had perfect credit and was proud of the fact that she always paid her bills on time and wasn't in debt. But when she and Rachel lived together, Rachel had lost a few jobs and it had been a financial stress on them both, so she had gotten behind on the one credit card she had. Everything was out of her control, so she decided honesty was the best way to go.

"Well, I'll run the credit score and let you know. If that checks out, you can have it. When do you need to know and move in by?"

"Well, if you could let me know by tomorrow and I could move in on Saturday that would be great. I was supposed to be out of where I am now on Tuesday. I have to work and so moving this weekend is really the only time I have."

"I think I can do that for you. I'll call you tomorrow." They shook hands and parted ways.

It was in His hands now. All she could do was wait. The next day was Friday and her day off. She spent it packing and waiting. Finally, at 2 o'clock she got the call. Her credit score was great, and the place was hers. She was so excited. He had come through for her. He'd even fixed her credit score! She called Rachel to set up a time to meet so they could pick up the U-Haul. She got it and the next day they packed up her belongings and moved her in.

When she'd rented the U-Haul, she did it on sheer faith. She didn't have any money. She had to put the rental amount on her credit card, which she only used for emergencies. They told her she had to bring it back with a full tank of gas or they would charge her for a full tank at almost double the going rate for gas. She didn't have money for even a drop of gas. So, she prayed. She asked the Lord to help her. She wasn't sure what that looked like, but she knew the whole deal was on Him, so He'd take care of it.

She drove the truck from the U-Haul place to home, loaded it up, drove it to the new apartment, then back to the U-Haul place and the gas gage never moved. She got to the U-Haul place and handed them the keys.

"Did you fill it up with gas?" the attendant took the keys from her.

"Um, no. But it's full." She said with a smile as they looked at her like she was crazy.

"How is that possible? Carl, go check the gas gage in the truck parked at the curb." He threw him the keys and a sideways glance of disbelief.

"I know this is hard to believe but I'm a Christian. I don't have any money and so I prayed and asked God to take care of the gas. He did. So, I did what I needed to do and the gas gauge didn't move, it's a miracle." She smiled at the attendant and waited for Carl to return.

"Yep, it's full." Carl put the keys on the counter.

"OK, I don't get it, have the gas gauge checked. You can go." The clerk just shook his head.

Jenna was rejoicing. Rachel was in shock and God got the glory.

With all of that going on, she went to work one day and got an unexpected shock.

Michelle didn't show up for work. She went to check

with their boss to see if she'd called in.

"Have a seat Jenna." She sounded somber and hesitant.

She sat down and her brain went a thousand miles an hour in a split second with all the possible scenarios.

"Jenna, Michelle's husband died. She went out to the living room this morning because he wasn't in bed and he was on the kitchen floor dead. They think he had a heart attack. She won't be in today." She looked like she was going to cry.

"OK. I.... I guess there's nothing I can do right now, I'll just try to call her later maybe. Thanks for telling me." She was in shock. She got up and went back to her desk. She was fighting back tears. She wanted to talk to her friend. Tell her she loved her and let her know she'd be praying for her. She wanted to help her. She waited until her morning break and called the house. She was able to talk to Michelle's brother and found out that her husband had died in the middle of the night.

When she finally got to speak to Michelle, her heart broke for her friend.

"Jenna, I feel so guilty. Brad and I had a fight last night. When I was in the shower, the Lord told me to go apologize to him, but I didn't. I was so mad at him I didn't want to talk to him. I should have obeyed the Lord. He never came to bed. He was mad so he sat up in his chair watching T.V. He got up to go into the kitchen at some point and died. He was lying on the kitchen floor and.... and... and ants were all over him. I never got to say good-bye or apologize. I should have listened." She was sobbing. She could barely get the words out. She was so heartbroken and guilt- ridden. Jenna could hardly keep the tears back herself.

"Oh, Michelle, I'm so sorry. I wish I could say something, anything else but I'm just so sorry. I'm sorry you had to find him that way." Jenna was speechless and she knew that words weren't what her friend needed anyway. There'd be time for words later. Right now, she just needed someone to love her and listen.

"Jenna, it was so awful to see him like that. I can't get the picture out of my mind."

"Do you want me to come over there?"

"No, my brother and my parents are here with me. Thank you for being willing. I am so tired right now; I need to go lay down. I'll call you tomorrow." She sounded spent.

"OK, I love you and I'll be praying for you."

"I love you too and thank you."

They hung up. Jenna cried and prayed and cried some more. She couldn't imagine what her friend must be going through, all the pain, guilt, and the images. It was all so sad and awful.

Michelle and Brad were married for seven years. They had one son who was five years old. Now she'd have to raise their son by herself. Their marriage was difficult at times, but Michelle loved the Lord and her husband. She worked at keeping their marriage strong and making a nice home for Brad. Brad owned his own business and worked very hard to support his family and provide for them.

Jenna went to the funeral. It was beautiful. She'd never been to a Christian funeral before. They sang worship songs, the pastor shared the Gospel message of Salvation by faith in Jesus Christ, then family and friends got up and shared memories and fun stories about Brad. Although it was sad because he was gone and everyone would miss him, it was more of a celebration over him moving on to heaven.

Over the next few months, Jenna tried to help her friend as much as possible. She called her, prayed with her, tried to encourage her, listened to her when she needed to talk and tried her best to love her with the love of Jesus. Jenna felt privileged to be able to be a part of her friend's life and what was going on in it. She'd felt honored that Michelle trusted her, loved her, confided in her and that she could walk through such a tragedy with her friend. It was also a true testimony of the power of God to get a person through something so difficult. Michelle continued to love and trust Jesus even though it was hard and painful.

"But I would not have you to be ignorant, brethren, concerning them which are asleep, that you sorrow not, even as others which have no hope." 1 Thessalonians 4:13 KJV

JACK JENKINS

I t was August 1995. Jenna got to church at 8:15 a.m. and made her way to the front pew, which is where she always sat. She was waiting for Jo. They always sat next to each other. She had to sit in the front row because she couldn't pay attention to the sermon sitting anywhere else. She had tried but found she was constantly distracted by what other people were or weren't doing. Things that most people wouldn't notice, but she did. So, she finally gave up and started sitting in the front row.

Jo finally showed up and they sat down and chatted for a few minutes. The worship team came out and began to sing. Everyone stood to sing along with the first song and when it was over everyone sat down for the next four or five songs. While she was in the process of sitting, she noticed that a man had sat down at the end of the pew. She knew most everyone that sat in the first few rows because the same people sat in the same place every week. She'd never seen him before. She dismissed it. She'd come to the place where she was content with being single and in fact didn't want to even entertain the idea of a guy. She'd given up the "Oh Lord, is my future husband here today?" prayer.

The Bible study started and as the pastor was sharing, she was looking down at her Bible and out of the corner of her eye she could see him sitting there. He was looking over at her.

She silently prayed, *Lord, I don't want to be distracted by some guy. Please make him stop looking at me. I don't want to move away from where I am with you, I am happy being single and don't want to have to deal with a situation.*

The sermon was over, the congregation stood to sing the last song with the worship team and then they were dismissed. She turned to talk to Jo. She had about ten minutes before she had to go to her class and greet her kids. As she was standing there talking to Jo, she noticed that Jo diverted her eyes to someone behind Jenna. Jenna turned to see what had distracted her and when she turned to look over her shoulder, it was him, the guy in the black slacks, white shirt, and looking all business-like. *Oh no! He was right behind her, moving toward Jo.*

"Hi Jack, how are you?" Jo stepped into him and gave him one of her famous big-momma-Jo hugs.

"I'm good. How are you?" He was hugging her back. After they were done hugging, he stepped back and looked right at Jenna. He looked nervous.

"Jenna, this is Jack Jenkins. We both go to the same hair-dresser, Sherry. Jack this is Jenna. Jenna teaches the 3 & 4-year old's' second service". She smiled.

"Hi Jenna, nice to meet you. I just saw Sherry yesterday and got a trim." He seemed uncomfortable but nice enough. "So, you teach Sunday school? That's awesome. Kids are great. Do you like it?" He was about 5'11, 225 lbs., he was thick. His arms and legs looked like he'd played sports and were very muscular. He had a barrel chest and his legs looked like a line-backer. His hair was brown with a hint of red, thick and wavy, it was combed back, short around the ears, business like, he had brown eyes and a mustache. He was ruddy looking.

"Yea, they're great. I love it; been doing it about a year now. The kids are so amazing and fun. They say crazy things sometimes. Sorry, I gotta go or I'm gonna be late. I need to get the classroom ready. It was nice to meet you." She just wanted to get away from him. She didn't need the complication, temptation or to even give off the vibe that she was interested. She just wanted to get to her class and her kids.

She had to go to the bathroom before class. As she was inside the stall, she saw familiar feet pacing up and down the bathroom.

"Jo, is that you?"

"There you are, sweetheart." She sounded impish.

"Yes, I had to go to the bathroom. Why are you here and what are you doing?" If you'd given Jenna a million years, she couldn't have come up with the response that she was about to get.

"I'm looking for you. I have to tell you something. Want to know what it is?" She sounded almost giddy.

"Um, no actually I don't because you sound too happy right now and I'm afraid of what you are about to say." Jenna was being sarcastic with her friend.

"You know Jack? You are never going to guess what he just said to me. After you left, he said, 'who is that? She's beautiful. Is she married?'" She was giddy.

"What? Don't tell me anymore, I'm not listening, lala-lala!" Jenna stepped out of the stall. Her friend's face was beaming with joy.

"I told him no, you weren't married and then he said, 'I want to ride up on a white horse and sweep her off her feet. I'm gonna marry that girl', can you believe that?" She was beside herself.

Jenna didn't find the same humor in it that Jo did. She was a little mad and scared at the same time. She didn't even know this guy and he's talking about marrying her. The nerve.

Jenna rolled her eyes and said, "Whatever, I don't want to hear anymore. I have to go to class. I'll see you later." She dashed out of the bathroom leaving Jo standing there.

Why in the world was she so unnerved? Who cares what this guy said, who cares what he thinks, he's just some dude! Shake it off and move on. She was distracted the whole time she was trying to teach her class. She was going to call Jo when she got home.

"Jo, I need to talk to you about that Jack guy." She was scared and was holding back tears.

"I've known him for a year or so and he's a great guy. He was so excited about you; he thinks you're beautiful." She was so happy about the conversation.

"You don't think this is from the Lord do you?" Jenna's tone was questioning at the same time one of disbelief.

"What if it is? The Lord may have this in mind for you. Wouldn't it be awesome?" She sounded hopeful.

Jenna was crying now. "It can't be from the Lord. I don't want to be distracted, I am happy being single and I don't want to get married." She could hardly get the words out.

"Why are you so upset? If it is from the Lord, it'll be the best thing ever. I don't know why you're crying. All he did was say hi and say you were beautiful, and he wanted to marry you." She was holding back a smile.

"I have to go. I don't want him to bother me. I'm not interested. If he talks to you again about me just tell him I'm not interested." She was trying to get off the phone.

"Well, I'm sorry you're so upset. You just need to trust the Lord and whatever He has for you. I'll talk to you later." She hung up.

Jenna wasn't going to think about it anymore. She was going back to her life of following Jesus, serving Him and working. She was single and happy about it.

She didn't see him for two weeks. She was grateful and relieved over that. She thought maybe he had moved on or gone to a different church. Then one Sunday she was in her classroom. Service was over and the kids were all gone. She was cleaning up and vacuuming the floors. She looked up from the vacuum to see Jack standing in the doorway.

"Hey, what are you doing here?" She sounded surprised because she was. She tried to keep the fear and anger out of her voice. She didn't want him invading her space or her life.

"Oh, I just stopped by to say hi." He smiled nervously.

"How was church today?" She was deflecting the conversation away from her.

"Good. I just stopped by to say hi. I'm leaving tomorrow for two weeks vacation. I'm going to Arizona." He sounded sheepish.

"Oh, well have fun." Why in the world did she care? Maybe by the time he got back he'd forget about her. Maybe he'd forget the way to her classroom. Weird! She went back to cleaning and he left. She breathed a sigh of relief.

Jenna went on with life. She worked, took care of CJ, went to the ladies Bible study and taught her kids. She didn't really care about Jack Jenkins and forgot about the time.

Three weeks had gone by. She was in her classroom vacuuming. She was talking to the Lord about the kids and how grateful she was to serve Him and teach them about Him. She stopped in her tracks.

"He's coming by and going to ask you to lunch." She heard the still small Voice but did not have time to process the reality of what she'd heard or to ask what her response should be. She wanted to ignore the Voice and in fact questioned if indeed it was the Lord, then she noticed he was standing in the doorway.

"Hey, do you need any help?" *He looks tanner; I guess Arizona would do that.* He was smiling. He had his Bible in one hand, the other one shoved into his pants pocket. He was wearing black jeans and a button up shirt trying to act as casual as he looked even though it was obvious he was nervous.

No, I want you to go away and forget you ever saw me.

"Um, sure. You can put the rest of the chairs on the desk and empty the trash for me while I finish vacuuming." She didn't want him hanging around but couldn't be rude. In the old days she would have told him to get lost, politely but she would have done it. Now, everything had changed, and the Holy Spirit wouldn't let her tell him to hit the bricks.

"OK." He started putting the chairs up. She didn't know what to do or say so she just kept working. If only there was more to clean, like enough to keep her distracted for a week.

Finally, she was done with the floor and had to move on to put the art supplies away. She longed for the noise of the vacuum so she wouldn't have to talk.

The silence was awkward.

"How was Arizona?"

"Hot. It was fun though. I swam a lot and hung out in the hotel room. Just kicked back, got some rest and played some golf." He was taking care of the trash.

"I couldn't handle that kind of heat. It gets too hot for me here sometimes; there is no way I'd go to Arizona."

"Yea, I don't think I'll go back there either. It's hot. Say, I was wondering if you wanted to go get a sandwich or something for lunch, if you're free that is." He sort of blurted it out like he had to or it wasn't going to move from his thoughts to his mouth.

She didn't know what to say. She was shaking inside. She felt that it would be rude to say no. She realized the Lord had told her this was going to happen and before she knew what she was doing, she said yes. They agreed to meet at Marie Calendar's around the corner from the church. She was so irritated with herself the whole way there. Why had she said yes? Did the Lord want her to say yes? She should have asked Him before she opened her mouth. Well, she'd lay it all on the line and then he'd back off.

They got to the restaurant and went in. As they sat down, he looked at her with a look that said, "I'm so stupid" and said, "Um, I feel terrible, but I just tried to get $20 out of my account for lunch and the machine wouldn't let me. I was going to buy you lunch and I can't. I'm really sorry. I feel like an idiot."

"It's OK, I'll get it." Wow, what a way to start.

They sat at lunch and talked. They chatted small talk at first. Where they were from, how long they'd been saved, where they worked. Then she turned the conversation more personal.

"So, I just need to tell you that I don't believe in Christian dating. I feel that if God wants me to get married, He'll bring that person to me and I'll know. I don't need to help him by trying on a bunch of different shoes if you know what I mean. I also don't believe in kissing or having sex at all before marriage. The next time I kiss a guy is going to be on my wedding day. I don't believe in long-term dating or long-term engagements either. I think the temptations are too great and the risk is too high." She was very matter of fact and hoped that it would send him packing.

"Really? I totally feel the same way. I have been down the dating road and don't want to go there again. I believe when God sends me the right one, I'll know it and that will be that." He sounded impressed and solid in his belief. He looked a little surprised. He clearly wasn't offended but didn't look like he was ready to run off either.

Rat's, that didn't do the trick? This guy wouldn't quit.

Jack sat there in amazement looking at Jenna. He was awestruck. In his opinion she was the most beautiful woman he'd ever seen. The first thing he noticed was the color of her eyes. They weren't blue and they weren't green. They were a collage of blue/green/gray with tiny specks of brown. He was taken with her stand on dating and everything else. He'd never met a girl like her. She wore her hair straight with a bandana that pulled it away from her face. Her hair was long, to the middle of her back and blonde. Her eyes sparkled when she talked about the Lord and she had a beautiful smile. She was so conservatively dressed he couldn't tell what her shape was like. She was wearing light blue leggings, sandals and a white and blue baby doll top that covered her all the way to mid-thigh. He figured she might be a little overweight and was trying to hide it by the clothes she wore. He was enjoying talking to her immensely and could have sat there all day. He truly believed that the Lord had told him the first day he laid eyes on her that he was going to marry her. He wanted to get to know her better but was afraid to ask for her number. He was scared she'd say no. Her confidence in the Lord and her strong stance on His Word was attractive but intimidating. He'd met a lot of Christian women, but he knew he'd never met anyone like her.

The waitress brought the bill and she took care of it.

"I better get going. We've been sitting here for two hours and I have a dog I need to take care of. Thanks for the chat." She started to get up. She was ready to go.

"Um, could I have your number? I totally understand if you don't want to give it to me, but I'd like to call you and get to know you." He was sheepish again.

Jenna reacted before she could think. "Sure." She wrote it down and said her good-byes. The whole way home she was mad at herself. Why did you do that you idiot? You should have just told him no and that would have been it. What in the world is your problem? Think--Jenna--think!

He called her on Tuesday. They chatted for a while and then he called her the next day and the next. Pretty soon, he was calling her every day. It was September now and she'd met him in August. She'd kept the fact of his existence to herself. She didn't want to talk about it or even get into a discussion with herself about it until Jesus told her what to do. Everyday she prayed for the Lord to remove him out of her life if he was not the one she was supposed to marry. She was tired of making stupid mistakes and tired of being hurt. Most of all she was tired of being disobedient to the call of God. She prayed and he kept calling.

They talked about everything. He was divorced. His wife had cheated on him and left him. She'd taken everything they owned. He went bankrupt because she'd forged his name, ran up a bunch of expensive purchases and used his social security number to take out a boat loan and now he was living with his parents. He had been a terrible drunk during their marriage and accepted responsibility for her misery. After the divorce he'd hit rock bottom. He'd grown up in the Catholic Church, he even had family members that were priests' and nuns', but Catholicism had left him empty. His niece had invited him to church, and he'd heard the Gospel message.

When Crystal Lewis began to sing "Come Just As You Are" God melted his stony heart and he got saved. He'd been saved about two years and was six years older than her. He worked at a machine tooling company as a sales manager. He'd grown up in California and played sports his whole life. By his own admission, he was a sports addict. He'd become fascinated with sports at the age of seven; football was his favorite.

They talked a lot about the Bible and spiritual things.

"Um, I know neither of us want to do the whole dating thing, but my birthday is coming up this Saturday, the 23rd and I was wondering if you'd have dinner with me?" He sounded reluctant but hopeful.

"Well, I guess so. Where should we go?"

"How about Olive Garden? I'll pick you up at 7 if that's OK." He was controlling his excitement.

"That's fine. I like their food and I love their salad and breadsticks. They're the best!"

"Great. Just give me directions and your address and I'll see you then."

Now it was time to talk about it with Michelle. She went to work the next day and told Michelle about him. She talked about the funny things he said; he had a great sense of humor. How they talked about the Bible and how well they got a long. When she finally stopped talking it was Michelle's turn.

"You know you've told me all this stuff about him, but you haven't told me what he looks like." She was smiling.

"I didn't?" Jenna hadn't realized it, but she never really thought about what he looked like. She'd told the Lord some time ago that He could pick out the person she was to marry, He knew what she liked and didn't and more importantly what she needed. She'd left it up to Jesus, she never even thought about it.

"Wow, I guess I haven't. I don't really think about what he looks like. I just like who he is. He makes me laugh. He opens doors for me. He listens to me. He asks me questions, makes me feel that what I think and say matters. We have similar thoughts on so much and I guess I never think about it. Well, lets see. He's about 5'11", medium build, brownish eyes, light brown hair. He has a mustache, pretty muscular, a great smile--he's cute I'd say."

"Do you think he's the one? You've not even entertained the idea of getting married for almost a year now. Are you nervous about Saturday?" Michelle was smiling at Jenna and teasing her a little bit too.

"I am kind of nervous. I don't know. I keep asking the Lord to move him out of my life, make him go away but he keeps coming back. I don't know what to think. But I do know this, if it is from the Lord, He is going to have to give me scripture to let me know or I am hightailing it out of this guy's path."

"Well, I'll pray for you." Michelle was so faithful to pray for Jenna; she so appreciated her friend.

"For the mountains shall depart and the hills be removed; but My kindness shall not depart from you, neither shall the covenant of My peace be removed, says the Lord that has mercy on you." Isaiah 54:10 KJV. Given to Jenna 9-9-95.

WHAT JUST HAPPENED?

Saturday arrived. Jenna opted for a pair of jeans, her cowboy boots, a black shirt and leaving her hair straight and loose.

Jack came and picked her up right on time. He was shocked when he saw her. He'd never seen her in anything except long loose dresses or leggings with long baby doll tops that covered her. She definitely wasn't overweight and trying to hide it. She looked beautiful.

They got into the car and started to drive.

"I have to tell you something. I know this is going to sound totally weird, but I know I'm supposed to tell you. I couldn't sleep at all last night. I was tossing and turning all night long. I kept praying to go to sleep, but the Lord kept me awake and told me a few things that kind of blew my mind and when He got done, He told me I had to tell you when I picked you up tonight." He sounded scared and nervous and was cautiously glancing at Jenna to see her reaction.

"Just, shoot. Tell me whatever it is you have to tell me. It can't be all that bad." At least she hoped not. Crazy! She tried to be nonchalant about it. She couldn't imagine what on earth he'd have to say to her but if he said it was from the Lord, she'd listen.

"Well, here goes. The Lord told me if I ever drink again that I wouldn't be able to hide it. You'll know when I do, and I won't be able to get away with it. He told me that if I ever look at pornography again that you'll know that as well. If I try to deceive you in anyway, He'll tell you. He will expose everything I do, every time I do it. He told me I had to tell you that and although I wrestled with Him all night about it, He wouldn't let me sleep until I was willing to submit myself to Him and agreed to tell you." He was breathless as he finished.

Jack's mind was reeling with thoughts, *God also told me I was going to marry you, but I'm not going to say that out loud so, we'll just leave that part out because you don't need to know that. There is no way on the planet that is coming out of my mouth! Besides I know I can talk God out of it or at least pretend He didn't tell me that.*

"Wow! So, when was the last time you drank or looked at porn?" Jenna didn't know what to think of this whole deal except that it was out of left field. Why would God want her to know all of that? What on earth would possess Jack to care if she knew about his habits?

"Two years ago, right before I got saved." He was driving so he couldn't look at her and was glad for that. He was very uncomfortable about the topic.

"Well, I guess I don't know what else to say. Hopefully you never do either of them again. It would totally hurt your walk with the Lord and obviously, He doesn't want you trying to go back to it." She was perplexed but wanted to move on.

"Yea, I don't want to go back. I was miserable when I lived that way."

Jenna didn't see a need for the conversation to go any further, what else was there to say about it anyway.

They were at the restaurant now. They had a nice dinner. They talked about their lives before being saved, talked about abortion and she told him about hers. She'd come to the place that she knew she was forgiven, and the Lord had done a major healing in her heart and soul through the PACE

(Post Abortion Counseling Education) classes. Jenna learned so much about herself and the impact of abortion on her life and the lives of other women through the class. They had a workbook that was full of personal, thought provoking questions and Scripture to guide, heal and to show God's thoughts and perspective about abortion, when life begins and forgiveness. They did the homework every week and then met in small groups to discuss the homework. Jenna had no idea of the pain, anger, hurt, condemnation and grief that she had locked inside of her over her abortion. When she'd found out, a few years after her abortion, that Rachel was pregnant, she'd reacted inwardly with such rage. She could never figure out why until she went through the class. There were times when she was doing the homework that she'd get so angry or so grief stricken she couldn't proceed until she'd prayed through whatever the issue was. She'd gone through a grieving process over the loss of her child. She'd never done that nor had any idea how to until the class. She felt as though it might have been a girl and named her Elizabeth. She took great comfort in the fact that she'd be with her one day in heaven. She only had regret now. She'd have that the rest of her life. Regret that she'd never see her baby grow up or experience the impact of Elizabeth's life on her or the world. But she knew she was forgiven. She'd let go of the anger and hurt already so she could talk about it. He received it well and was very gracious and compassionate toward her.

Before the "date" they had only talked on the phone and occasionally chatted at church, after the date he'd stop over for dinner after work occasionally, but they talked every day on the phone.

About three weeks later, it was Tuesday, October 18th and Jenna was home sick from work. She'd been sleeping most of the day but around 2 o'clock in the afternoon she called to see how Jack's dental appointment had gone. He was supposed to have a root canal. She'd prayed for him the night before over the phone that the Lord would heal him. She had a phobia-type fear of root canals and understood his apprehension about having one, so she prayed.

"Hello", he answered the phone and sounded fine.

"Hey it's me."

"How come you're home, are you sick?" He didn't even sound like his mouth was numb.

"Yea, I woke up feeling terrible, so I stayed home. Hey, I was calling to see how your appointment went. You sound fine. Did you have your dental work done?" She expected him to at least sound like his mouth hurt.

"Um, well, no. I went there, and my dentist wanted to check my tooth one more time before he prepped it and when he did my tooth was fine. He x-rayed it and couldn't even find the crack that had been there. I guess your prayers worked and God healed me." He was excited and relieved that he didn't have to go through the root canal.

"Wow! That's so awesome. I'm so glad you didn't have to go through all that. What are you doing now?"

"Well, I've just been at home, in my office, doing Bible study and praying. I had the day off, so I've just been spending it with the Lord."

"That's cool. You sound kind of weird, is everything OK?" She couldn't figure out what she heard in his voice, but it sounded like he had something to tell her that he didn't want to tell her, so he was avoiding it.

"Really? Wow, I'm fine. I don't know why you'd think there was something wrong." Man keep it together, she can tell.

"I can just tell. Just tell me what it is. Why are you acting weird? It can't be that bad." She hated secrets.

He hesitated.

"What if the Lord was asking you to do something that you didn't want to do, but He was speaking so clearly to you, you couldn't avoid it? But you don't want to do it?"

What in the world was he talking about?

"Well, if God is telling you to do something you need

to do it. Why wouldn't you want to? Are you just scared?" It seemed logical to her; it was God they were talking about after all.

Her boldness in Christ scared him. He didn't want to tell her what the Lord had spoken to him and asked him to do because he was scared but the reason he was scared was not what it would seem. She intimidated him. She seemed so spiritually mature, so bold in her faith, so confident in her God. She seemed to have so much confidence as a person, she carried herself tall and self-assured, not stuck up, just confident. She was easy going but tenacious in her faith. She loved the Bible and as far as she was concerned, there was no moving off it to the right or left. God said what He meant and meant what He said--non-negotiable! She was out of his league.

But Jesus would not relent. He was persistent in His direction to Jack. Jack was fighting every step of the way. If he had to tell her there was no way he was going to tell her over the phone. Besides, there was still time, maybe he could get out of the whole thing.

"Yes, I'm scared. I don't know what is going to happen if I do it. I'm equally scared to disobey. But what if I follow through with it and it turns out bad or I completely mess it up? I don't want that." He sounded apprehensive.

"If the Lord has asked you to do something, you have to obey. It's not your problem to worry about the results. Your job is to obey Him. If you don't, you'll be miserable. If you step out, He'll take care of the rest. We can't be concerned about the outcome of His directions; we have to be concerned with immediate obedience and leave the rest to Him. Besides whatever it is, you can only be blessed by it. Whatever it is He will give you the ability and desire you need. He's not going to send you to Africa and make you miserable. Are you going to tell me what it is or not?" She couldn't stand it.

"I will tell you but not on the phone. I'll come over around 5 o'clock and bring you some soup and we can talk. Will you pray with me?" If he was going to follow through and obey the Lord, he had things to do.

They prayed and hung up. She had three hours to sit and stew on what was going on with him. She thought and analyzed and reanalyzed and finally concluded the Lord was asking him to go be a missionary somewhere and he was going to be leaving and didn't know how to tell her. There was no other logical explanation. He told her he wanted to teach the Bible in school, he'd had teaching experience before, so that must be it. *Well Lord, I guess You are finally answering my prayer to take him out of my life if he isn't the one. Wish You'd have done it a little sooner before I got to know him and got a little attached. I am falling for him and that is my fault for letting that happen. Just move him quickly and don't drag it out. I thought maybe he was the one, but if You're taking him away then OK.*

She heard the knock at the door. Her heart jumped. She was going to have to face it and there was nothing she could do about that. Just get it over with Jenna, answer the door, be cool and be thankful that its only been two months and not two years.

"Come on in" she could tell he was stressed. "So, what's the big news? You gonna tell me now?" She just wanted to get it over with.

"Can't we eat first? I'm starving" He was wound like a clock but trying to play it cool.

"Sure." The silence was thick and neither of them wanted to look at the other.

They sat on the couch and ate soup and grilled cheese sandwiches. They were sitting side-by-side and Jenna was looking down at the floor. She had a hard time looking at someone in the face when they were going to tell her something hard. It went back to her teen years. She began looking at the floor when her dad would yell at her or give her some long explanation for why she couldn't do some activity she'd asked to be able to do. It was self-preservation. If she looked at the ground, her face was somewhat hidden and she wouldn't give herself away if she was mad, sad, or frustrated. If she'd showed any of those emotions to her dad, she might have gotten slapped. So, she looked down. She couldn't look at Jack, she was afraid.

"Jenna, today when I was at home studying and praying the Lord began to speak to me and I fought him for several hours because I was scared. After we talked this afternoon I decided to do what He'd asked me to do no matter what. So, Jenna will you marry me?" He stuck a ring box with the lid open in front of her.

She didn't respond immediately. Her mind was trying to register what had just happened. When her brain finally caught up, she put her hands over her mouth and looked at the shiny diamond ring in the box.

"Oh my goodness, oh my gosh, I can't believe it, yes I'll marry you." She was crying and finally "saw" the ring. It was not what she expected. Well, she'd not expected a ring at all! He'd picked it out himself. It had four rows on each side of three diamonds in each row in a baguette style with a single solitaire diamond in the middle. She took it out of the box and put it on her finger. It looked beautiful and very sparkly. She didn't know what to think or how to feel or what to say. She hugged him and he looked relieved.

"I didn't know what you'd say. I was afraid you'd say no." He had tears in his eyes. He'd gone to the jewelry store and picked out the ring after they had talked on the phone.

"I can't believe we had that conversation earlier. I talked you into asking me to marry you and I didn't even know that was what I was doing--that is so weird and funny and crazy. I was so scared about what you were going to tell me."

"What did you think I was going to say?"

She was laughing now. She felt so ridiculous she was embarrassed to even tell him what she was thinking. Her analytical mind got the best of her and she'd never, in a million years, have come up with the big question being popped. That was not even in the running!

"I thought you were going to be leaving because God called you to go be a missionary somewhere." She was laughing through the tears now.

He started laughing as well. "Seriously? Wow that *is* funny. How in the world did you ever come up with that?"

"Well, what else was I supposed to think based on all the stuff you said? That was the logical conclusion." They talked and laughed for a few more minutes. She was still in shock.

"We need to call Jo; she should be the first person to know." Jenna was already picking up the phone and dialing.

She called Jo. She was elated. She wanted credit for the introduction and matchmaking. Duly noted! She called her mom and her sister next. They weren't so elated. To them, Jenna was being stupid. She'd only known this guy for two months and now they were engaged. Jenna knew they wouldn't understand. She couldn't expect them to. She'd prayed and prayed and trusted in the Lord. If it was meant to be, it would be OK, after all He is God and knows all from beginning to end. She wasn't going to let them ruin her joy. They didn't say anything; they just had a tone to their "Oh congratulations" that said it all. She was a little disappointed but let it go.

"Now that we're engaged, do we get to go on dates?" Jack was being funny and serious at the same time and had a little smirk on his face.

"I guess so. Since we're going to be married, that changes the rules!" She was trying to sound serious but couldn't help but smile.

"Well, thank you very much for your concession." Now he was teasing.

"Seriously, we have to talk about the boundaries, and we should probably set a date."

"I agree. No kissing not even on the cheek. Hugs, hand holding?"

"Yes, but we have to be careful. I don't want to mess anything up for us or have us be embarrassed before the Lord."

She'd already had enough of that to last a lifetime.

"Yep, I agree. I know as the leader I am responsible for that more than you. So, we will be aware and careful. We should pray about the date. What do you think? I know I don't want to wait forever to marry you."

"Yes, we should pray. God knows when He wants us to get married. He already has it all planned so let's pray and ask Him to confirm it by His Word." She couldn't believe it. Married. Wow.

"Agreed."

They began to pray about it, separately and together every time they talked on the phone or were together. They had called Pastor Mark, their pastor, the night they got engaged and told him the news and had asked him to officiate their wedding. He told them he would be honored, they needed to go through pre-marital counseling and let him know the date they decided on. He told them he'd be praying for them and for the Lord to speak to them about a date. The following week they were talking and they both felt the day was to be January 27th, three months from their engagement. They also agreed to continue to pray and to throw out a request to the Lord. They would ask for confirmation through His Word, they'd approach Pastor Mark and ask him if he had a thought concerning a date, if he came up with the same date, it would be set.

Two days after their conversation Jenna was driving home from work. The same time and same way she did every day. She pulled up to a red light and stopped. There was a car right in front of her and when she saw the license plate, she almost fainted. The license plate said, "Psalm 27 1" she knew it was the Lord.

That Sunday after service they approached Pastor Mark and asked if they could speak with him.

"Sure, can you meet me in my office in about twenty minutes?"

"We'll be there." Jack grabbed Jenna by the hand, and

they walked toward the church offices.

"What can I do for you two?" Pastor Mark was one of the sweetest, godliest men that they knew. He preached God's Word with boldness, integrity, power and love. He was an unassuming person. He'd grown up in Southern California, a surfer kid and at 50 something, he still loved to surf. He wore Hawaiian shirts and casual slacks. His hair was salt & pepper now and he had a smile that would make anyone feel at ease. He had a lovely wife, Shary; he spoke about her with great passion and affection. He talked about how much they loved the Lord and prayed together and how she'd changed him over the years with her kind, gentle ways.

"Well, we were wondering if you had a thought as to the date of our wedding." Jack was apprehensive.

"Hum let me look at my calendar. How about January 27th?"

They looked at each other with shock and amusement. January 27th, 1996 would be the day.

"That sounds great! That was the day we thought of too. So, what do we need to do now?" Jack was taking the lead, great.

"Well, Calvary Costa Mesa has pre-marital classes. You need to get enrolled and complete it. Start making your plans and let me know when you've finished the classes and if there is anything I can do for you. May I pray for you?"

"That would be great."

They held hands, bowed their heads and prayed together.

"Your eyes saw my unformed body; all the days ordained for me were written in Your book before one of them came to be." Psalm 139:16 NIV

PLANS AND PURPOSES

The date was set, the plans were in motion, but there was just one tiny problem, they had no money. Their parents didn't have money and they weren't going to go into debt just to get married. They were going to have to pay for it themselves and if they couldn't afford a wedding, they certainly weren't going to be able to afford a honeymoon. So, they did what came naturally, they prayed. They asked the Lord to give them wisdom, guidance and provision. They had no idea how that was going to happen, but they trusted that He had a plan and therefore He had provision for those plans to be fulfilled. After all, it was His idea.

They were going to get married at their church, which was free, she had her dress and they could live in her apartment, check and check. It was everything in between that they needed to figure out.

It was November and Jenna was sick again. She'd barely recovered from her October bout and it hit again. She'd never regained her health since the year she'd been so sick. She'd been home for two days already and could barely get off the couch. She'd been sleeping and woke up to the sound of the phone ringing.

"Hello."

"Hey Jenna, how are you feeling. You sound terrible." He was on his lunch hour and had called to check on her. She'd given him a key to her apartment two days earlier because she needed some things from the store, Captain Jack needed to be taken out for walks and she was sleeping a lot. He was going to bring her some things after he got off work, so she assumed that he was calling to get a list.

"I feel terrible. How are you? How's work going today?" Her voice was raspy and tired.

"Me? I'm great. I called to tell you something that you won't believe. I got promoted back in April to National Product Sales Manager. Today I got my paycheck and along with my paycheck was a bonus. Apparently, I was supposed to get it back in April because of the promotion, but someone in Human Resources messed up and I never got it. But, I got it today. It's a two-thousand-dollar bonus."

"Are you kidding me? That's so crazy. God is so amazing!" She could hardly contain her emotions. She knew that He'd take care of it somehow, but she never expected that. He has His purposes for everything, and Jack didn't *need* the bonus back in April; he needed it now and now is when he got it. They'd have a wedding!

They began to plan. They made lists, talked about colors and flowers, who was going to be in the wedding party, a cake, where they'd have the reception, could they even afford one and what about tuxes, photographers and decorations? God took care of everything. Jack had a friend from high school that did wedding invitations; he knew she'd give them a great deal. One of the ladies at church had a daughter who was training to be a florist and she'd give them a discount. Jack's younger sister would decorate the church and reception hall, Michelle had a great photographer she could recommend, and her mom, Cindy, was going to pay for the rest of Jenna's bridal wear. There was still the reception hall to find, the cake and the honeymoon, but everything else was falling into place. Jack could pay for some things out of his paycheck and so could Jenna; they just had to be thrifty.

A few weeks later, Jack came over after work so they could work on wedding stuff and eat dinner together.

"Hey Jenna, how are you?" He stepped inside the door and gave her a hug.

"I'm good, how are you? How was work?" She'd only been home about 20 minutes when he got to her apartment.

"Work was great. I had an interesting day. I was wondering how you feel about Hawaii?"

"I don't know. I've never been there. I suppose it would be cool to go there, why do you ask such a lame question?" She was in the kitchen getting food ready and wasn't looking in his direction.

"I wanted to know how you felt about going there for our honeymoon?" That got her attention. He was trying to conceal a smile that said 'I know something you don't know' but not doing a very good job of it.

"I'd feel awesomely blessed to go to Hawaii for our honeymoon, but we don't have the bucks to do that—remember? We are kinda broke." She couldn't figure out what he was up to.

"Well, that is where we're going. Today, I'm sitting at my desk and the phone rings. I pick it up and it's my friend Scott. He says to me, 'I hear you're getting married, is that true?' I say, yes it is, why? He says, 'where are you going for your honeymoon?' I say, 'I have a great room at Motel 6 reserved for two nights' why are you asking me these questions?' He says, 'How would you like to go to Hawaii, on me for your honeymoon, you have to have a honeymoon and it will be my wedding gift to you and your new bride'. So, we talked, and he is going to make all the arrangements for five nights in Kauai, a car, a condo and airfare. Can you believe it? We're going to Kauai for our honeymoon." Now he was beside himself, grabbed her swung her around and was grinning from ear to ear.

"Oh my gosh! I can't believe it. Jesus is so awesome; are we really going to Kauai for a honeymoon? I don't even know what to say, I am completely blown away. Every time something happens it just confirms over and over that we are supposed to get married doesn't it? He just keeps giving us miracles." She was crying. She couldn't believe the goodness and blessings of God that were being showered upon them. It was hard for her to accept that she was going to get married, that Jesus had brought her to this place and this person, and He was just pouring out His grace. She felt like she was on a conveyor belt that was set at high speed. She couldn't get off and didn't want to.

They continued to make plans and look for a reception hall. They had narrowed it down to a few places, but they had to look at them, check the dates and prices. It turned out the weekend they were getting married was super bowl weekend, so everything was crazy around town. They checked into several places and they were either too expensive or booked. They had one last place and if it didn't work out, they were at a loss.

They made an appointment and went and looked at it. The room looked perfect, the price seemed right, they had one more hurdle, the date. So, they told them what day they would need it and the response was the same, "that's Super Bowl weekend, I doubt it's available." They checked anyway. The place was booked every weekend solid for six months before and after, except that day! And because it wasn't booked, they gave them the prime rate for the date.

"And My God shall supply all your need according to His riches in glory by Christ Jesus." Philippians 4:19 KJV

FRIENDS.
CONFESSIONS.
A REQUEST.

During all the activity, Jenna of course had shared it all with Michelle. Michelle couldn't have been happier for her. They talked all day long at work about the wedding plans, the fun they were having learning about each other in pre-marital class and the future. Jenna was scared about being a good wife. She hadn't had a godly role model and although she'd asked the Lord to heal her and prepare her for marriage should the day ever come; she knew she still had a lot to learn. She was grateful for her friend and that Michelle could be trusted. She'd asked her to be one of her bridesmaids and Michelle had gladly accepted. Her sister was her maid of honor and Susan from the old Bible Study group was her third. Jack had his guys all settled so the wedding party was in place.

Jack and Jenna had discussed at length her walking down the aisle. She'd not had any real contact with her dad since her parent's divorce. Jenna and Rachel had distanced themselves from him. They were grateful that they were able to choose in their own free will if they had contact with him or not and chose not to. He'd never apologized for what he'd done and in fact denied that it ever happened. Jenna had confronted him via letter when she was with Rafael. Mitch's new wife then called Cindy and read her up one side and down the other and told her as far as they were concerned Mitch was dead to the girls, he'd never done any of those things and the girls were liars. So, that was that. Jenna didn't have anyone else. She was going to walk down the aisle with Jesus. In her mind and heart, He was the only one who had the right to give her away. He'd chosen Jack and she'd walk with Him down the aisle. Jack understood, Michelle understood and no one else's opinion mattered to her.

They'd signed up and started their pre-marital classes. It was a six-week course and they didn't have much longer than that. It was going well. They were learning a lot about each other, had to share about their past and all the things they'd been involved in. They talked about the people they'd been involved with and what type of relationship they had, how intimate they'd been and what had happened to them. It was true confession time! Jenna had no problem with it. It didn't bother her at all. The only thing that was hard for her was she wished she could say that she was a virgin. She couldn't change that, but if she could, she would have. She felt very comfortable talking to him and she had nothing to hide. The Lord had already done a great work in her, just like she'd asked Him to. She told him all about her dad, Brandon, Rafael, Todd, everything. He told her about the girls he'd dated before his first marriage and after he'd gotten saved. They had a great time in class and enjoyed the time together.

Since he had a key to her apartment, he would sneak in there periodically while she wasn't home and leave her notes around the house. He'd tell her how much he loved her, how excited he was to be her husband and to live the rest of his life with her. He was very clever and would leave them in odd places and pun off the objects that he'd put them on. He left a note in the medicine cabinet that said, "When I feel sick you are the medicine that makes me feel better." He put one in her closet that said, "I'm hung up on you." It was very sweet and made her laugh. She'd never had anyone treat her that way before. He sent her flowers and took care of CJ when she was sick. He was definitely a keeper.

When they first got engaged, Jenna had told Jack that she wanted Rachel in the wedding party, but she knew it would be uncomfortable for Rachel to be around all the Christian people. Jack encouraged her to pray that God would use it to bring Rachel to salvation. So, they decided together the only wedding gift they really wanted was Rachel's salvation. They began to pray together and in their own prayer time that the Lord would give them that one wedding gift. It was a request that Jenna had been making for almost four years now. Rachel didn't seem one step closer, any softer or less resistive to the Gospel, but Jenna continued to pray for her. She had no idea what was going on in her dad's life. Her mom was very antagonistic about anything to do with church, the Bible or Jesus. Her family was part of her prayer life whether they liked it or not.

"Pray without ceasing." 1 Thessalonians 5:17 KJV

THE WEDDING THAT ALMOST WASN'T

A s a Christian the thought never remotely crossed her mind that she'd marry someone with an ex-wife. So, Jack having an ex-wife was an unexpected twist in the tale. At first it wasn't an issue for Jenna. Then one day, for some unexplained reason, the reality hit her that she was marrying a divorced man and all the baggage that goes along with it.

She started to second-guess the whole situation. She didn't know if she wanted to marry someone with those issues. It didn't come up very often but when it did, she could tell he had a lot of hurt, anger and bitterness toward her. She'd taken him to the cleaners and cheated on him. Jenna couldn't blame him. She figured that it would come up in the future when they were more into their relationship and she wasn't sure if she could handle it. She knew from being in relationships before that the past could rear its ugly head at very inopportune times and interfere on a regular basis. She'd already been through that once with Rafael and didn't want to go through it again.

She was about forty-five days away from getting married, the invitations, reservations, and arrangements had all been taken care of and she was getting cold feet. She was scared and wanted to run as far away from Jack Jenkins as she could.

She was sitting on the couch one day trying to hash it out with the Lord.

"Jenna, there are two roads before you. Your road of running away, which you can choose to follow, and I will still love you and you will be my child. The other road is the road I have chosen for you. It looks dark, scary and uncertain but it's the road I've chosen for you. If you'll go down that road with Me, I'll be with you, bless you and work it all out for your good. You must choose which road you will take." The voice of the Lord was gentle, kind and yet very clear. She had a choice to make.

She sat in silence for a few minutes thinking about what He had said. She wasn't a gray person. When she'd come to know Jesus, she'd given Him her life. She wanted nothing more than to know Him, love Him and obey Him. She couldn't imagine what would happen if she chose to go her own way. She knew she would regret it and that she'd live with that regret and the "what ifs" the rest of her life. She was given a choice but in her mind there really wasn't one. She couldn't go her own way no matter the cost.

OK Lord. I will go down Your road, but You have to help me. I'm afraid. I will trust You. I don't understand why You've chosen this road, but I believe You will work it out.

Jack wouldn't know for years how close they came to never walking down that aisle together.

"And we know that all things work together for good to those who love God, to those who are the called according to His purpose." NKJV Romans 8:28

THE IN-LAWS

J enna's mom and sister were not particularly happy about her marrying Jack so soon after them meeting. They didn't feel that they'd known each other long enough to make a lifelong commitment and at the very least they should wait a year before they got married. Jenna listened politely and went on her way. At this point in her life all that mattered was being obedient to the God that she loved and that loved her. If He was sending her on this journey at breakneck speed, then it was the journey she was going to take, she just had to put on her seatbelt. It didn't even seem abnormal to her that they met in August, got engaged in October and would be married in January. She was thirty and would turn thirty-one a month after they were married. She'd lived her life long enough on her terms and now she wanted to live on His terms. So, although there was some fuss and muss from family members, Jack and Jenna were doing what they believed to be the will of God.

Sometimes it was hard to be a Christian. There was a time when she wanted to tell her mom off, but that wasn't what Jesus wanted her to do. Her mom hadn't protected her when she was growing up; now, she wasn't supporting her as an adult. It hurt her that her mom wasn't willing to trust Jenna and her choice. She was supporting her in that she was willing to buy her a few things, but Jenna wanted more than that. Her mom tried to give her marital advice, which was laced with the bitterness of her failed marriage. Jenna let it go in one ear and out the other. She wanted her mom to be proud of her. But there was nothing she could do about it.

Jack had met Rachel and Jenna's mom. They'd gone out to dinner together to meet each other. It went well because Jack had a way of talking to people. Being a former salesman, he could talk to anyone about anything without a problem. Nothing that Rachel or their mom said flustered him or threw him off, even Cindy's colorful language. She constantly used the Lord's name in vain. It drove Jenna crazy; every time her mom said it, she cringed inside. But Jack didn't flinch, at least not outwardly. He made them laugh and Rachel was excited about having a brother-in-law. The idea that one day she might be an aunt thrilled her. Her mom seemed excited about the possibility of being a grandma some day.

Meeting Jack's family was a little scary for Jenna. She didn't do well around new people; especially those she needed to make an impression on. Her first meeting was a birthday party for Jack's grandmother and the whole family would be there. Jack's dad, Phil, who everybody called Poppy, had been a severe alcoholic for the first 20 years of Jack's life. He'd been diagnosed with a brain tumor when Jack was 8. He'd been a functioning alcoholic up to that point but after the diagnosis he began to drink heavier due to severe headaches. In those days' treatment methods were far less advanced so there weren't many options. He'd been told he would only live about a year. He was still around and now he was sober. He'd worked in the State Penitentiary system as a correctional officer until his cancer overtook him. He had a wicked sense of humor, loved practical jokes, playing cards and playing with his grandkids. Jack's mom, MaryJo or Nanny, was a school nurse. She'd worked in a hospital for quite awhile and then switched to school nursing and part-time at the hospital. She had to support the family because Poppy's brain tumor had incapacitated him enough that he couldn't work. She loved her family and was very proud of them. Jack was the spitting image of his mom.

It was her side of the family where the strong Catholicism stood. She had an aunt that was a nun and a brother studying to be a priest. She had been diagnosed with Lupus some years before and struggled to care for herself, work and take care of Poppy. She adored her grandkids and Jack was her only son, so she was very partial to him. They were all nice and polite to Jenna, but they all drank a lot, which made for some uncomfortable incidents.

She made it through the first meeting alive. She'd met, aunts, uncles, cousins, everyone. She hated that she felt so self-conscious around people when meeting them. She still felt like she never fit in anywhere and was socially awkward. Although it appeared to everyone else that she was a confident person, she was exactly the opposite. The only thing she had confidence in was Jesus.

She was grateful that she'd met his sister before hand. Carol seemed to like Jenna and according to Jack, so did the rest of his family.

"I can do all things through Christ which strengtheneth me."
Philippians 4:13 KJV

A FEW GLITCHES

T he wedding plans were moving along. Everything was coming together. Jenna had her dress in for alterations, the rest of her things were purchased, the flowers, invitations, reception, the photographer, the cake were all getting their final touches. December was a busy month with wedding plans and Christmas. It would be the first Christmas with the in-laws.

Christmas went without a hitch and January came. Jenna had her bridal shower. Michelle, Susan and Rachel all planned it together. Jenna was very clear that she didn't want anything distasteful, rude or vulgar and she hated the games they made you play at those things. In truth, she didn't even want a bridal shower, but the girls in her wedding party had insisted, so she conceded. She hated being the center of attention and it made her uncomfortable to think it would be all eyes on her. It turned out beautifully. The only people there that weren't Christians were Cindy and Rachel. The women embraced them, loved on them and made them feel at home. They had lunch, ate cake then they went around the room and each lady shared how they'd met Jenna and something about her that was special to them. It was a real blessing and honor to hear her friends share about their love for her. She got beautiful gifts, mostly very pretty and tasteful negligees, they were all feminine and lovely.

It was really happening; she was getting married.

Finally, it was the week before the wedding. She had her hair and make-up appointments all set. She'd picked up her dress from the seamstress, the cake was ordered, the final count for the reception was in and it was Jenna's last day at work before the wedding.

"Are you nervous at all?" Michelle was asking Jenna, knowing full well that the answer was yes.

"Yes, a little. I just don't want anything to go wrong." Jenna was nervous. She'd never been married before or planned a wedding and now she was doing both.

"You'll do great. Everything will turn out beautifully. The Lord will take care of everything and you guys will be blessed. I'll be praying for you and so will many others."

"Thank you. We have been praying that our wedding will glorify the Lord. Getting married is important but the most important thing is Jesus and people hearing the Gospel message. There are going to be a lot of non-believers there and I want them to hear about Jesus." Jack and Jenna had specifically been praying for the Lord to be glorified in the wedding ceremony and in their lives. They'd asked Pastor Mark to give the Gospel message and let everyone know that it was their desire for Jesus to be honored.

"God will honor that. You have desired all along for Him to be glorified and He will honor that and bless you for that. The most important thing is that the message is given, you guys have an awesome wedding and the rest is up to Jesus." Michelle was always so encouraging and always brought everything back to the Lord. It was one of the reasons Jenna loved her so much, and she was a faithful and wonderful friend.

"Thanks, I will remember that. I hope the people that come from the office will really hear and maybe get saved."

When she'd gotten engaged, everyone in the office was excited for her. They "ooh'd & aaahh'd" over her ring, then the 20 questions came. They were all in shock that she'd only known him for two months when they got engaged and getting married three months later was even more shocking to them. Michelle understood because she knew that Jenna and Jack were praying. She'd been with Jenna on her whole journey through all the ups and downs and knew all about Jack. She also knew Jenna. She knew that at this point in her life she wasn't going to move without the go-ahead from the Lord, so if Jenna felt that it was the right thing, she trusted her friend's relationship with the Lord. It was great to have Michelle's support personally and professionally; she knew Michelle had her back.

Just then her desk phone rang. It was the receptionist out front. There was a package for her at the front desk.

Jenna went to the front desk to find a beautiful bouquet of long-stem red roses. They were from Jack, the card said, "I love you and I am so excited to be your husband and to live the rest of my life with you. Jesus loves you and I want to show you how much He loves you. Can't wait for Saturday! Love Jack."

"Oh my gosh Jenna they're beautiful!" Michelle was looking over the roses. "Yes, they are, aren't they? He's so thoughtful!" Jenna was truly blessed.

It was Thursday and her last day of work before the wedding. She had all her work wrapped up and Michelle knew all the loose ends that needed to be taken care of. She'd cleaned her desk off and was ready to head out. The next time she'd sit at that desk she'd be Mrs. Jack Jenkins; how weird was that? She still couldn't completely grasp that whole concept, it seemed so surreal to her, but she was getting married. Her supervisor had already made a new nameplate for her desk with "Jenna Jenkins" on it. She was going to have to change her name everywhere!

Friday night came and the rehearsal was set. They went through the ceremony, so everyone knew where they were supposed to be. It was a surreal experience. They laughed and joked and finalized the decoration plans with Jacks little sister Carol. The wedding rehearsal and dinner were done.

It was late and Jenna was going to have to talk to Jack about the wedding night and she wasn't looking forward to it. She was not on the pill simply because she'd been on it in her younger years and it had messed her body up. She was a believer now and wasn't planning on being sexually active, so she didn't need it and she and Jack had discussed it and decided against it. She had no control over her monthly cycle.

They left his parents house and Jack drove Jenna home.

"Um, Jack, I have to tell you something that isn't going to be very, um, well, very, wonderful for you to hear." They were sitting in his car outside her apartment.

"What is it?" He sounded apprehensive.

"I may start my period at some point between now and our honeymoon." She had that nervous smirk on her face, and it came out in her voice.

"What! Are you kidding me? How did this happen?" His hands were on the steering wheel and they began to clinch around it. He went from zero to eight in less than a second. Not the reaction she was expecting. He was angry!

"I don't know. I calculated it out and thought when we set the date it would be fine, but I have no control over my body. What am I supposed to do? I'm sorry; I didn't plan it this way you know. Even if I do, it will be OK. Don't worry about it. Try not to be mad. Please?" She tried not to sound pleading.

"Yeah, sorry. I lost my temper. I know it will be OK. Just try to get some sleep. Is Rachel coming over to spend the night with you?" He was still mad but realized that he couldn't take it out on her, he tried to change his tone.

She understood his frustration. I mean after all he was a guy, a Christian guy, but still a guy. They'd been seriously together for three months, had refrained from even kissing, but the sexual tension was clearly in the air. He was looking forward to the wedding night and so was she.

"Yes, she should be here any minute, she went home to

get something." She wanted out of the car. His reaction had caught her off guard. She wasn't showing it, but she was about to cry. It all seemed so unfair and yet just typical of her life. She didn't want to let her brain go down that road and be in despair the night before her wedding. There was truly nothing she could do but pray. Pray that he would not be mad and disappointed and that she wouldn't feel guilt and pressure to try to solve the problem.

"You better go in and get some rest. I'm sorry Jenna. I love you and I'll see you at the church tomorrow OK?" He gave her a hug and she went in.

Captain Jack greeted her at the door as usual. He was always excited to see her. Dogs, so loyal and loving no matter what. Rachel was going to take him to her house while they were gone on their honeymoon. He loved Rachel and would get to see his kitty friends again.

She went in and changed her clothes and decided she needed to do the dishes. She was washing a glass when it popped on her hand and cut her on the knuckle of her right index finger. *Great Lord, I just cut myself on my right hand. I'm right-handed; couldn't it have been the left one? Please make it stop bleeding, I don't want to go to the ER and get stitches the night before my wedding. It's deep, and I'm here by myself. Could you please help me?*

She called Jack; Nanny was a nurse after all. When he got on the phone, she told him, and he freaked out. He hated the sight of blood; guess you don't talk about that in pre-marital much! Who knew? He talked to his mom and they decided they could put a butterfly bandage on it, and it would be fine except it was going to throb like heck while she was trying to sleep. So, he ran over with some bandages and got it all fixed up. Just as he was leaving Rachel showed up.

"Jenna, what in the world happened?" She looked shocked but not surprised.

"I was washing dishes and a glass popped on my hand, so now I have a cut on my hand, the night before my wedding."

She shrugged and made a face.

"Why in the world did you feel you needed to wash dishes? You're supposed to wear gloves anyway, so you don't mess up your nails! You could have left them for me for goodness sake. You're the only person I know that would do that!" Rachel had one hand on her hip, shaking her head and rolling her eyes. She was scolding her but, in her mock, disgusted voice trying to conceal a smirk, that was Rachel.

"Yes, I know all that, thank you very much! Now how in the world am I going to wash my hair in the morning? You might have to help me Bean! At least it's not my ring hand so it won't be photographed! I got that going for me."

"Yeah there is that!" She was so sarcastic sometimes.

Just as they were getting settled the phone rang.

"It's 11 o'clock at night. Who in the world is that?" Jenna answered it.

"Hey Jenna, this is Pete." Pete was the photographer.

"Hey Pete, everything alright?"

"Well, yes. Except I was looking at directions to get to the church tomorrow and the address that is on the invitations is wrong. If it existed, it would be right smack in the middle of Disneyland."

"What! Are you kidding me? Hold on, I'm going to get one and get a church bulletin. I checked that stuff like three times. Hang on please." She ran to get an invitation and a bulletin to check the address. Sure enough, she'd transposed a number. Instead of the address reading 720 it read 270. Great! Now no one will show up to the wedding.

"Oh, my gosh Pete. It is wrong. It's supposed to be 720. What am I going to do? Now everyone will get lost and no one will be at the wedding." She was panic-stricken.

"Can't you call someone and have them put up signs or something?"

"Yes, I'll try I guess. Thanks for the heads up, I'll see you tomorrow."

She hung up the phone and started crying. Now what?

Rachel heard her crying and ran up the stairs. "What's the matter now?"

Jenna knew Rachel didn't handle stress well, but she had to tell her. "The address to the church is wrong. I have to call Jack."

She said a short silent prayer and picked up the phone before Rachel had a chance to respond.

Jack picked up the phone, "Hello."

"The address to the church is wrong on the invitations." She was still crying.

"What? No way! What should we do?" He sounded stressed but tried to mask it.

"I don't know. That's why I'm calling you."

"Jenna, it will be fine. Let's pray and then I'll call Carol and ask her to put up some signs in the morning. God will get the people there. Ok?"

"OK."

They prayed together and then he called Carol. She and her kids were going to put signs out so that everyone that was in the general vicinity could find it.

She took two Advil and crawled into bed. She propped a few pillows underneath her hand to keep it from throbbing and prayed.

Jesus, please help me to sleep. My mind is racing, my finger is throbbing, I'm afraid no one will be there, and I desperately need sleep for tomorrow, it's going to be a long day and I don't want to be stressed. Will You please get everyone there that should be there? Please help me to get to all my appointments on time and to the church on time. Keep the enemy at bay and please bless our wedding. Thank You so much for all You have done in my life. I am so blessed and so grateful for You and for Jack. I want to bring honor to You in my life and in my wedding. I ask again for my sister's salvation. Please give me strength to walk down the aisle and be by my side. Thank You for making everything come together and providing for us. Please help Jack to sleep and not be nervous. I love you Lord. In Jesus name, Amen.

"Be anxious for nothing, but in everything by prayer and supplication, with thanksgiving, let your request be made known to God; and the peace of God, which surpasses all understanding, will guard your hearts and minds through Christ Jesus." Philippians 4:6-7 NKJV

THE BEAUTIFUL DAY

J enna slept for about six hours. She woke up and low and behold, her period had started. Great. *Well Lord, you planned this and you're in charge. I don't want it to ruin my day. Help me to accomplish what I need to accomplish and not be tweaked out over my stupid period.*

Rachel had to help her wash her hair, but she managed the rest of her shower by herself. She made some oatmeal and got dressed. She threw on her jeans and a lightweight button up flannel shirt. She didn't want to have to pull anything over her head once she got her hair and make-up done. She was taking her oatmeal with her, she'd learned to eat oatmeal, drive a stick and not spill it or wreck her car.

She gave Rachel last minute instructions.

"Alright, I'm going to my appointments. I'll be back here by noon so we can all go to the church. Make sure you're ready except putting on your dress. Make sure Captain Jack is fed, goes potty and is good to go until you get back here after the wedding. Make sure you eat something because it will be awhile before we get to eat again, and I don't want you passing out while we're standing up there. I have all my stuff together, so we need to make sure it all goes in the car with us to the church. Here's the numbers and appointment times for me in case you need to get a hold of me. That's it! We good?" She got it all out in one breath. She was calm but wired.

"I got it. Don't stress. I'll remember everything, just go and get back here. I'll have some food for you when you get back here so you can eat on the way to the church. Mom, Susan and Michelle will all be here by 11:30 and we'll be waiting for you." Rachel was excited for her sister. They may not have agreed on a lot of things at this point, but she honestly wanted her sister to be happy. Rachel wanted everything to go right for her. She loved her big sister and wanted her to have a beautiful day. As far as she was concerned her sister deserved happiness even if she thought she was rushing the whole deal.

Jenna got into her car and looked at the clock, it was 6:45 a.m. and she had to be at the hairdresser by 7:15, she'd make it. She opted to travel to her appointments by herself. She wanted to spend that time with the Lord. She decided that she would pray in her prayer language the whole way.

She got to her appointment and the hairdresser began to work her magic. Jenna had searched everywhere for a hairdresser. She didn't know exactly what she wanted for her big day and she'd hoped that a beautician would be able to help her. She'd tried three others before she finally got to the one that she liked. They'd done a dress rehearsal for her hair so they both knew what to expect on her big day. Jenna's hair was past the middle of her back now. She hated her hair pulled completely off her face because she didn't like her jaw line and forehead accentuated. She wanted an upsweep to go with her veil, but her hair was heavy all piled on top of her head. So, Kathy took her hair and divided it in half from the top of her ear up she had a ponytail and a secondary one underneath. She left delicate tendrils around Jenna's face that she curled and perfectly placed. Then she took small strands from each ponytail, curled it and placed it with bobby pins. She then placed Jenna's veil on her. It was a half-crown of beading and pearls that sat on top of her head. The veil was long in the back, it fell past her behind and she'd opted to have a veil covering her face in the front. Two hours later, her hair was done, and the veil was in place, minus the actual tulle that she could stick on later. She looked like a quarter-of-a princess.

Next, she was off to the make-up salon. Michelle had a wonderful girl, Sherry that did her make-up for her; she'd been going to her for years and trusted her. As her wedding gift to Jenna, Michelle paid for her make-up appointment for the day of her wedding. Jenna had already had a consultation appointment and liked her and trusted her. Again, she prayed the entire way in her prayer language. God gave her traveling grace so there was little to no traffic and she breezed from one appointment to the other.

Sherry was waiting for her. She began the transformation and an hour later she was a different person. Jenna never wore make-up; so, when she looked in the mirror, it was like looking at another person. She was astounded at the difference. Because she wasn't a make-up person, she'd asked Sherry to use natural earth tones. You couldn't even tell that she had foundation on, her eyes were gently lined with a brown liner and the eye shadows were shades of brown and tan. She used black mascara to make her eyes really stand out and gave her a subtle shade of pink on her lips. She couldn't believe the difference...she was on her way to becoming a bride.

Jenna was now on her way back to the house. She'd make it on time. She prayed the entire hour back to the house and was rejoicing in the favor that God had given her. She pulled into the driveway, the limo Jack had ordered to take them to the church was waiting and all the girls were waiting inside. As Jenna stepped into the limo all she heard were gasps.

"Jenna, you look amazing"

"Wow, you are drop dead gorgeous!"

"Honey, you look beautiful" Cindy was tearing up at the sight of her daughter.

"Hey, no one is allowed to cry and make my make-up run. Thank you all that you think I look fabulous but if you make me cry, I won't look fabulous anymore. It will then be on all of you that the bride looked like a raccoon! I'm starving." Jenna was joking with them. They all laughed. The mood was light and full of excitement.

"You look as cool and calm as I have ever seen you. Aren't you nervous?" It was Susan.

"No, not at all. I feel totally calm and I'm excited. I started my period for everyone's information, how's that for a wedding gift?" She was laughing.

"You are the only person in the universe that could happen to Jenna, I should have expected as much. You seriously have the worst luck ever. What the heck happened to your hand by the way?" Susan was looking over at Jenna's hand and laughing at the calamity of her friend.

"I know. I cut my hand washing a glass last night. No lectures please! That's not the worst of it. The address on the invitations, well, it's wrong. I tried to calculate for my period, but Mother Nature doesn't live by my calendar and well, hopefully that is the only faux pas for my wedding. Every wedding has them I guess!" She was in good spirits and felt at peace. It had to be because of her time spent in prayer with the Lord. She was grateful for the peace and that she could just enjoy everything without being stressed.

They arrived at the church and they all piled into the nursery that had been transformed into a bridal dressing room. She took care of her monthly problem and began to get dressed. Once she had her dress on and her accessories she went and stood in front of the mirror. She got a lump in her throat. She looked like a fairytale princess. Although she'd picked her dress out when she was engaged to Steve, the dress wasn't about him, it was about her. The moment she had tried it on and looked in the mirror she knew it was the one. Now to see it with everything else in place, she knew she'd made the right choice.

The dress was white with beading and pearls on it. The shoulders were gathered, and it had long sleeves that extended over the top of her hands with lace and beading. The bodice was cut to fit her slender shape and came down to her waist where it then flared out into a full gown with a long train. There were pearls and beading around the bottom of the dress and down the middle of the back where it buttoned all the way up. It was a princess gown. And she looked like a princess. She couldn't believe her eyes. There she was standing in a wedding dress all dolled up and ready to walk down the aisle. She barely recognized herself.

Jenna heard the door open and turned to see Jo enter the room.

"Hey Jo, how are you? I'm so glad you came into see me before the ceremony. What do you think?" Jenna was beaming at her friend.

"My darling girl, you look like a princess. Look at your eyes. I've never seen them look so beautiful. You are stunning. I'm so happy for you and Jack." She was starting to get teary eyed.

"No crying. I don't want to ruin my make-up. Can you go check on Jack please? Make sure everything is going OK on his end and tell him when we kiss up at the altar, he can't grab my face; he'll ruin my make-up. We still have pictures to take afterwards and I don't want palm prints on the side of my cheeks." She made a fish-face and Jo laughed.

"Yes, I'll go check on him for you sweetie." Jo left.

Cindy was standing in front of Jenna, "Honey, I want to tell you that I think you look beautiful. I'm happy for you and I wish you all the happiness in the world." Her mom was trying not to cry as she held Jennas' hand. She was looking at her daughter dressed for her wedding and her mom heart made a guest appearance.

"Mom! No crying. I'll start if you start! Thank you for being here with me and for my dress. Do I really look OK?" She so wanted her moms' approval. There was still a little girl inside that wanted her mom to be proud of her.

"I've never seen you look as lovely and radiant as you do right now." Cindy gave her a hug and then distracted herself with helping Rachel.

Jo returned. She was laughing.

"I saw Jack. Jenna, he's as nervous as a cat. I've never seen a groom so nervous in all my life. I told him you looked beautiful and he started to cry. He looks handsome in his tux. You are so calm and he's pacing the floor!" She was laughing and shaking her head at the role reversal.

"What on earth is he nervous for? I hope he holds it together up there. Usually it's the bride that faints or something, I hope it's not him!" Jenna was surprised to hear he was so nervous. Jo wanted to go and find a seat, so she said her good-byes.

Jenna looked around the room. The girls were all dressed and ready. They had their hair done, their make-up all in place and they looked lovely. Jenna had chosen a deep purple velvet dress for the girls. They were simple dresses with quarter-length sleeves and slightly puffy in the shoulders, a sweetheart neckline, a slight form fit to the bodice and slightly full skirt that was tea length. She loved purple and had been blessed that at the time she got married the winter colors were all out in the stores. The dresses were such that the girls could wear them to a Christmas or New Years party if they wanted. She'd given them each a pearl necklace to wear with their dresses and their flowers were white and purple roses.

Jack was pacing like a wild cat. He couldn't believe that he was going to marry Jenna. She was so amazing, and he felt so unworthy of her. He was nervous and couldn't stop sweating and simultaneously trying not to breakdown and cry. There was so much she didn't know about him. He silently prayed. *Lord, I need Your help. I know You've called me to marry this beautiful daughter that You love. I know that You desire me to be a godly husband and I want to be, I just know I fall so short of being that godly man/husband. Everything in me right now wants to run but I know that isn't what You want, and I love this girl so much. She is beautiful, smart, godly, and so much more mature than I am, and I don't want to hurt her, let her down, or anything else. I am going to have to walk out there any minute. I need Your help; I can't go out there without You. Please help me to hold it together.*

It was 1:55 p.m. and they were minutes away from start time.

Everyone had cleared out of the room except the wedding party.

"Places everyone places, we start in five." Linda, the wedding coordinator came in to get everyone together and make sure everyone was ready.

Jenna was grateful for Linda. She was a ducks-in-a-row person so it gave Jenna comfort to know that everything would be in order and someone else was taking care of the details. That meant she didn't have to worry about anything but getting married.

Linda led them out to the hallway just outside the sanctuary doors. Jack was upfront with Pastor Mark. Linda opened the doors, got the wedding party in order and then the music started. The guys escorted the girls down the aisle. Once they arrived on stage the double doors were closed as Pastor Mark began to share the Gospel message and talk about Jack and Jenna, their lives and pending union. Jenna stood just out of view listening to Pastor Mark. She continued to pray in her heart while she waited. Pastor Mark finished and then prayed. As his prayer ended, he had everyone stand and the wedding march began to play. She was standing holding her flowers and trying not to pace. She'd been calm all day but when she heard the first notes of the wedding march she began to choke up. She got a golf ball in her throat and was about to completely breakdown. Linda saw it all happen and immediately spoke up.

"You can't cry now Jenna, you're about to walk down that aisle and get married. Now take a deep breath and step up to the doorway as soon as I open the doors. I want you to pause there for a count of five then walk down the aisle to meet Jack. And don't forget to smile." She was calm and reassuring.

The doors opened, the audience was standing, and Jenna

took a deep breath.

Jesus, you are my Eternal Husband, Father, Savior and Friend. I am about to walk down this aisle and have my life forever changed. I am asking You to walk right beside me. Please hold me up, please be with me and please help me so I don't fall apart. I am so grateful You are with me right now. Thank You for Your presence.

The sanctuary looked beautiful. White tulle and bows lined the aisle. The stage was large with a dark brown carpet and four steps that led to the top, the stairs went all the way across the stage. The lights were dimmed for the audience and on the stage were two large brass candelabras. The candles were lit. Flowers that matched Jenna's bouquet were draped down the candelabra's along with white tulle and a white bow. Everything looked serene. The whole room seemed to have sort of a haze like you were looking at it through a cloud. Carol had done a fabulous job decorating it. It was warm, beautiful and very classy.

Here we go Jesus.

She stepped up to the doorway as the music played, she paused for the five count as Pete was snapping pictures like crazy. She didn't see it at all. She began to walk. As she did, she felt as though she was floating on air. She was looking at Jack aware that there were people all around her, looking at her, but all she felt was Jesus walking her up the aisle, delivering her to Jack Jenkins. She did notice Jack's tux and he did look handsome, just like Jo had told her.

Jack couldn't take his eyes off Jenna. From the moment the double doors opened he could hardly breathe. He thought she was beautiful on a normal day but now she had gone way past beautiful, she was breathtaking. He couldn't believe he was standing there at the altar waiting to be her husband. Jack hoped he could remember to breathe and not totally fall apart. He also hoped he could follow along with Pastor Mark, right now he couldn't even remember English. He had hamsters in his head and spaghetti for legs. *If this girl gets any prettier I'm gonna pass out. Come on Jenkins, hold it together and breathe, don't make a total fool of yourself up here.*

When she arrived, she looked at his face and he was crying. He whispered into her ear, "You take my breath away."

They stepped up to the altar. Jenna handed her flowers to Rachel. Jenna's flowers were mostly white roses with a hint of purple and a long trailing array of flowers that cascaded down the front of her dress as she held them.

She turned and took Jack's hands. Pastor Mark began the wedding ceremony and vows. Jenna was fine until she had to repeat after Pastor Mark and once again, she began to choke up.

"I, Jenna take thee Jack to be my lawfully wedded husband, to have and to hold, in sickness and health, for richer or for poorer, 'til death do us part..." she was holding back the tears and her voices was starting to sound like Kermit the frog. *Jesus help!*

After the vows, Pastor Mark handed Jack the microphone and told him to share the Gospel with the audience. Jack was shocked. This wasn't planned and he could hardly speak. He quickly shared and then handed the mic back to Pastor Mark like it was a poisonous snake.

They continued through the ceremony, stepped to the back of the stage and took communion together and lit the unity candle. They returned to their spot at the front of the stage.

"Jack and Jenna wanted to honor Jesus with their lives and have remained entirely pure during their engagement. Which means they haven't kissed at all until now, so without any further delay, ladies and gentlemen for the very first time, Jack you may kiss your bride." Pastor Mark was beaming.

Jack reached forward and kissed Jenna. It had been difficult at times, but they had made a vow to the Lord and to each other that their first kiss would be at the altar. He didn't touch her face, but he didn't let her go quickly either. The audience began to make a lot of noise. Jenna started to feel embarrassed.

He finally let her up for air.

"Ladies and gentlemen, I present to you Mr. & Mrs. Jack Jenkins." They turned to face the audience, Jenna grabbed her flowers from Rachel, and they stood there holding hands, smiling and waiting for the cheering to stop. They heard their exit music and began to walk back down the aisle as Mr. & Mrs. Jenkins with Pete snapping pictures and the audience cheering.

They spent the next hour in the sanctuary taking pictures. Jenna's cheeks hurt from smiling. She had to make a pit stop with her mom before leaving for the reception to take care of her period. If someone had been able to video the moment it would have been hilarious. She had a full-length dress, a huge underskirt, white stockings, a long veil and high heels she had to navigate to take care of her monthly visitor. Her mom's arms were full of dress and skirt and veil trying to help her. When it was all said and done, she was just grateful that neither she nor any part of her dress had landed in the toilet. It was Jenna after all.

Eventually they made their way to the reception. The reception went well. Everything turned out beautifully. Carol had done a fabulous job decorating. There were white table clothes on the tables and beautiful centerpieces. They had a DJ, toasted with Martinelli's Sparkling Apple Cider, danced and had a great time. They didn't get to eat much of anything because every time they went to take a bite of food, their guests would clink their glasses to signal they wanted the newlyweds to kiss. The cake turned out beautifully. It was a three-tiered cake. They had gotten two tiers of chocolate and one tier of spice cake. Each layer had a vanilla mousse filling, butter cream frosting and it was decorated with pearls and lace. It matched her dress and veil perfectly. They had agreed before the wedding that they would not smash cake in each other's faces. Jenna didn't want to have cake all over her dress. They saved the top tier for their first wedding anniversary.

Finally, it was time to go. They got into Jacks car, it was now 6 p.m. and they were both tired and hungry. Jack had rented a room for them near Disneyland. They were going to stay there for one night and then the next day drive to Los Angeles to stay one night, then leave early Monday morning for Hawaii.

As they were parking at the hotel, a large 15-passenger van pulled up next to them. Jack went around and opened Jenna's door to help her out. She was still in her dress. As she got out of the car the van began to unload. It was full of eight-year-old girls dressed in their soccer gear. As Jack was helping Jenna out of the car, the little girls were in awe.

"Look mommy, it's a princess." One little girl said to her mother with all the wonder and amazement of a little girl that had just seen a princess at Disneyland.

"Yes, she is a princess." Jack was beaming at his new bride.

They got to the door and he carried her across the threshold. She didn't want to take her dress off, remove her make-up or take her hair down. She knew she'd only be this made up in this dress for this one day. She'd never experience this day again. It would never be duplicated, and she didn't want it to end. She wanted to stay in her dress as long as possible. But he was waiting, they were hungry, and they were both tired.

Jenna had to take a shower to get all the make-up and the day washed off of her.

"Jack, I need help getting these bobby pins out of my hair."

"Hang on, I'll be right there."

They spent the next half-hour taking bobby pins out of her hair. It seemed like she had hundreds of them. There were so many that Jack started to get cramps in his hands. They had a good laugh about it later.

They were so hungry they ordered take out burgers, fries and shakes. Eventually they settled down to their wedding night. It wasn't what he'd dreamed of because of her period and Jenna felt bad for her new husband. She did what she could to make it as wonderful, romantic, and fulfilling as she possibly could. He seemed to appreciate her efforts.

They went to Hawaii and had an amazing time. They enjoyed the sun, scenery and each other's company. They shopped and ate. She introduced him to bagels and cream cheese. So, every morning they had bagels, cream cheese and fresh local coffee. Kauai was beautiful. She was so grateful for the Lord and to see His creation and all of His majesty displayed in nature. She'd always loved the beauty of the ocean and nature and being a Christian only enhanced it for her. They took a lot of pictures and saw all the sights. They didn't do the tourist things like snorkeling, boat trips and the helicopter ride. She didn't like boats and they didn't have the money for those things. But the trip was amazing, and they loved it.

Scott had truly blessed them. The condo was beautiful, right on the beach. They had a car to drive around in and spending money from monetary gifts they'd received as wedding presents.

Jenna was so grateful for all the work the Lord had done in her heart before she ever met Jack. She'd prayed and prayed for the Lord to heal her of her sexual issues that had been created by her dad and all the other men in her life. She'd pleaded for him to heal her and to allow her to have a healthy marriage if she was ever to get married. She didn't want that to be an issue in her marriage like it had been in every other relationship she'd had. God was faithful. He'd brought her amazing people to support her, given her a desire and hunger for His Word and brought different books into her life that helped her walk through the healing, forgiving and letting go process of all the junk from her past. It wasn't always easy. She hated reliving many of the events because it was painful. She had her ups and downs and it took time and concentrated effort. There was a deep well of pain and wounding that she had to allow Jesus to bring up so He could heal her. She didn't know exactly how healed she was until she got married, God had answered her, and she was free to love and be intimate with Jack without the old baggage and without reservation. The honeymoon was beautiful. Everything they had waited for was well worth it.

"Therefore, if the Son makes you free, you shall be free indeed." John 8:36 NKJV

NOW THERE'S A MARRIAGE.

They returned home and had a family gathering to open all their wedding gifts and to bring all the family up to date on the honeymoon.

They returned to work. The first week back was hectic. They were both trying to get caught up on work.

"Jenna, I have something I wanted to share with you so can we take our morning break together today?" Michelle was glad to have her back.

"Sure, lets go at 10 and get some toast and coffee at Mel's. I'm kind of hungry." Break time came and they went across the street to Mel's and ordered coffee and sourdough toast with extra butter. They toasted it to perfection.

"So, what's up?" Jenna was curious.

"Well, after you guys left the reception and everyone cleared out, Susan and Rachel and I gathered up the presents and took them back to your apartment. We sat around talking about the day and one thing led to another and your sister started asking questions."

"Questions? What kind of questions?" She was curious now.

"Well, she was asking me about the Lord. It started when she asked me about when Brad died. She wanted to know what happened and all of that but then she was asking me how I could be happy and still follow the Lord when He'd allowed my husband to die like that. Then she was asking Susan about her marriage. Why she stays in it when her husband is such a jerk. How can she be so happy and follow Jesus when He lets her marriage be so awful and allows her husband to treat her so terrible. So, we were able to share with her about the love of Jesus. She was asking a lot of questions about the Bible and Jesus. It was pretty cool. I think Susan is going to ask her to go to church with her. I think she might go." Michelle sounded so excited and so hopeful about Rachel. She knew all about the situation between Jenna and Rachel, about Ben dying and all that the girls had been through. Michelle had been praying for Rachel to get saved.

"Wow, I can't believe that she asked and then listened. She'd never listen to me. When we lived together, she knew about you and Susan, but she never asked me questions or anything like that. That is amazing. I am so blessed the Lord used you to share with her. What powerful testimonies you two have because you have continued to love and serve the Lord through such difficult and painful circumstances. Thank you so much for being willing to share with her and answer her questions. I love you and I'm grateful you were there for her." Jenna was fighting back tears. She'd been praying for four years for her little sister and she had asked the Lord for that wedding gift, maybe she was going to get it. She couldn't wait to tell Jack; he'd be so excited.

She told him when he got home from work that night. They praised the Lord together and prayed that Rachel would go to church with Susan and give her life to Jesus. She'd have to remember to call Susan and thank her.

It was hard to return from the honeymoon back to the real world. It was inevitable; they had jobs, bills, CJ and life to live. They couldn't wait to get home at the end of the day to see each other. She would usually get home before him and start dinner. They enjoyed learning about each other, catching up on their day, making dinner and eating together every night. They played Yahtzee, read their Bibles, prayed and went to church.

For all of the wonderful things about being married she was having a hard time adjusting to being a wife. When she was single, she could eat whatever she wanted when she wanted and could have her personal schedule arranged to her liking. Now she had a husband and his schedule, dinner, groceries for two, laundry for two, and a dirty house that needed to be cleaned and still work her crazy schedule. She still had major health struggles, so she didn't always have the energy she needed. She still got sick easily and often. When she was single, she could nap whenever she wanted and rest if needed. If she was feeling under the weather and needed to be down a few days she could let her house go, eat simply and stay in her pajamas. Jack didn't mind the pajamas, but he was only going to eat tuna fish sandwiches for dinner so many times. Marriage was definitely an adjustment. She had to meet out her energy and prioritize it. This meant she had to give up serving in Sunday school. She gave the Children's Ministry Director a month's notice to find someone to replace her. She was very understanding. It was hard for Jenna, but she had to put her husband and marriage first.

One day Jack came home with a long face.

"Why the long face? Did you just lose your best friend?" Jenna was in the kitchen starting dinner.

"No, but almost as bad. I was informed today that I am going to have to start traveling again for my job. They want me to train the guys and be at the shows to help promote new products. So, I will be leaving for my first trip on March 2nd and be gone for a week. I have to leave on a Saturday and return on a Saturday because the airfare is cheaper." He sat down on the couch with a look of total defeat. Jenna didn't understand why his reaction was so extreme. It was true, they'd only been married a short time and he was going to be leaving, that stunk, but it didn't seem like the end of the world.

"The second? My birthday is on the eighth and we've never celebrated my birthday together. Why are they making you go out on the road again? I thought you weren't supposed to have to do that now that you were management?" She was irritated now, realizing he'd be gone for her birthday.

"I don't really know. The only thing they told me was that the guys in the field aren't selling enough tooling and need to be refreshed on sales technique and new product. I hate traveling." He was still sitting on the couch with his head in his hands looking at the floor.

"Well, I guess we have no choice, it's your job and that's what they want. I'm bummed I'll be spending my birthday without you." She went and sat next to him and put her arm around him, kissed him and silently prayed for him.

"The fining pot is for silver, and the furnace for gold: but the Lord tries the hearts" Proverbs 17:3 KJV

BLINDSIDED

The 2nd came and Jack left for his trip. Jenna had secretly packed a cute, flirtatious card in his suitcase for him to find. She'd called the hotel where he would be staying and ordered a beautiful fruit and cheese basket for his room. She knew he'd be lonely and missing her and she wanted to cheer him up and to bless him.

He had to fly to Washington State and work in Western Washington for the week. He flew out late on Saturday, so he called her when he got to his room, but they only talked for a minutes because he was tired. Since cell phones didn't exist, the only way to talk to him was to catch him in his hotel room.

For her, it was like she'd never gotten married. She easily slipped back into being single and fending for herself. She got up and went to church on Sunday. She hung out after church and talked for a while and then made her way home. She tried to call Jack as soon as she got home but he didn't answer so she took a nap.

She called him again at 5 p.m.

"Hello"

"Hey it's me. What are you doing?" Jenna was glad to hear his voice.

"Oh, just flipping through the channels on the T.V. What are you doing?" His voice sounded odd.

"I'm getting ready to look for food, I'm hungry. I called

you earlier, but you weren't there, where'd you go?" She was looking in the fridge for dinner.

"Oh, it must have been when I went to get lunch. Sorry I missed your call."

"Did you get my card and the basket?" She hoped they were a blessing to him.

"Oh, yea I did. Thanks, it was great. You're so thoughtful." He tried to sound enthusiastic but didn't pull it off.

"Are you OK? You sound kind of weird or something." She wasn't alarmed but she'd never heard his voice sound the way it did.

"Um, yeah just tired I guess. I was watching the game a little bit and I guess I'm just tired. I should go and find something for dinner. I'll try to call you again before I go to bed but if you don't hear from me it's because I fell asleep. OK?" He wanted to get off the phone. Now.

"Um, sure. I love you and I'll talk to you tomorrow after work."

"Yeah, love you too." He just wanted to hang up.

Jack was struggling. He hated where he was mentally and spiritually. He hated lying to Jenna. He'd been struggling from the moment they told him he was going to start traveling again. He arrived in Washington with the battle even more intense. He wanted to watch the basketball games, do his job and get home. Simple. But there was a part of him that was fighting hard against keeping it that simple. It was the old Jack. He wanted to silence that voice, but he couldn't. The old Jack was fighting for control and he knew if that Jack won, Jenna would find out, she'd suffer, and life would spin out of control. God had already told him that before they were married. He didn't want to hear her voice right now. He loved her more than anything but when you love someone, you can hurt them. Deeply.

The rest of the week went the same. She'd talk to him; he'd sound weird and explain it away. Her mental skills were working overtime to try to figure out his problem.

It was finally Saturday and he was returning home. She was glad he was coming back and couldn't wait to see him.

"Hey, you're home. I'm so glad to see you." Jenna threw her arms around him and kissed him. His response was a little half-hearted. He was trying to look like he was glad to see her but not doing a very good job.

"Hey good to see you." He put his suitcase down and wouldn't make eye contact with her.

"You look extremely tired. Didn't' you sleep well while you were gone? Are you hungry? Can I get you anything?" She was working on unpacking his suitcase and trying to catch him up on everything. She was sorting his clothes into laundry and dry cleaning and trying to put everything back to normal.

"Jenna, I have to tell you something. I really don't want to, and I'm embarrassed to have to tell you what I'm about to tell you." He was looking at the ground.

"Alright Jack, what it is?" She felt the giant butterfly take flight in her stomach.

Jack had been in torment the whole week he was gone. He couldn't help but remember the conversation he'd had with Jenna when they went out on their one and only date. God had told him that she would find out when and if he ever drank or looked at pornography. It kept ringing over and over in his head. He was going to have to tell her. The conviction was so intense he felt like he had a thousand-pound weight on his chest. He wanted to talk to her because he loved her and missed her but every time he heard her voice the conviction was intensified. It was a battle every day, all day long. He didn't want to tell her but knew the Lord would not let him off the hook. So, he resigned himself to the fact that he was going to tell her, but he wanted to do it in person.

"When we were talking on the phone on Sunday and you said that I sounded weird you were right. I sounded weird because I'd been drinking. I got drunk." He was crying and looked totally dejected.

Jenna didn't know what to do or say. She was completely blindsided by his confession. Drunk! That had never entered her mind.

"Oh, wow, is that the only day you drank?" She was in information collection mode.

"Yeah. On Saturday when I got there all of us were sitting around talking about the schedule for the week, what was going to happen at the show, and someone sat a beer down in front of me. I took a few sips and left it. After everyone went to their rooms I went and bought a case of beer and went back to my room. I drank a few and saved the rest for Sunday. I'm sorry Jenna, please forgive me, I'm so sorry. I feel like a total loser and I'm sorry to have to tell you this stuff."

She'd left information mode and now she was crying. She couldn't believe it. She was reeling from the shock but felt compassion for him and his pain. She didn't know what to think or say.

"I forgive you. I'm sorry you did that. I wish you would have called me and told me you were struggling. I could have prayed for you. I prayed for you while you were gone but had no idea that was happening." She was crying harder and felt scared but didn't want to let on. They prayed together and he asked God to forgive him and to help him stay sober.

The Lord had taught Jenna long before she was married about forgiveness and how to walk through that process. This was a major test of that discipline. 1 Peter 5:7 says "Cast all your cares upon the Lord because He cares for you." In practical application she'd been taught to pour out her feelings, good or bad, to the Lord. She was honest about her feelings even when she was angry. She told Jesus exactly all that she felt about Jack's drinking. Jesus said in Matthew 6:14 "For if you forgive men their trespasses, your Heavenly Father will also forgive you." So, she chose by faith to forgive Jack for the pain he'd caused her, for lying to her and for getting drunk. In Second Corinthians 10:5, "Casting down imaginations, and every high thing that exalts itself against the knowledge of

God, bringing into captivity every thought to the obedience of Christ." Next, she would take all her thoughts, the fearful "what if" thoughts, the angry ones and the conversations in her head, and give them to the Lord and she would ask Him to fill her with His Holy Spirit so she could love Jack and move past the incident.

She had to walk through that process more than once in the weeks that followed. She didn't want to allow the incident to build a wall between them or between her and the Lord.

Jack struggled. He would seem fine at times and then he would begin to shut down. Other times he seemed defeated and angry.

There were times when she'd lay in bed tossing and turning because she couldn't turn her brain off. She hadn't had that happen in a long time and she hated it. She would start to have conversations in her head with Jack or fear would rise up and grab her by the throat and she'd be awake for hours. She would have to walk through the whole process again before she would finally get to sleep. It was an intense battle at times.

While she was battling, he continued to be moody, depressed, sorry and angry. He just couldn't seem to let it go.

Then he came home with the news that he was going to have to travel again at the end of March.

"Again? Is this going to be a monthly thing or what?" Jenna was scared.

"I don't know Jenna, but I know that at the end of March, which is in a week and a half, I will be gone for another seven days." He looked totally defeated.

"What are you going to do about the drinking? Do you think you'll be OK?" She had no idea of the struggle he had inside. She wasn't accusing but inquiring minds want to know!

"I think I'll be alright. I'm going to have them take the TV out of my room and I'm going to read my Bible and I'm taking a couple of other books to read and my journal. I'll be busy most of the time and when I'm in my room I'll read. It will be OK. I don't want to drink again, that was awful. It was humiliating and embarrassing to have to tell you. I don't want to go through that again and I don't want to sin before God." He sounded hopeful. But in reality, there was an intense war raging inside of him. He didn't want her to know how bad it was.

God please help me. I don't want to drink again but when I travel, I always end up drinking. I don't want to face Jenna again and have to tell her. Please help me to be strong and not drink, I know it's what I've always done when I'm on the road, but could You make this time different?

"Well I'll be praying for you and remember if you are struggling just call me and I'll talk to you and pray for you. I want to help you through this. If you don't have the T.V, you won't have sports, so you'll be fine. I'm going to have faith in the Lord." Jenna didn't see why it would be an issue for him. He'd been sober for almost three years and one blip on the map shouldn't spoil that.

"Submit yourselves therefore to God. Resist the devil, and he will flee from you." James 4:7 KJV

ANSWERED PRAYER

I t was a Friday night; mid-March and the phone rang.
"Hello."
"Hey Jenna, it's Susan. How are you?"
"I'm good. A little tired, you know the end of the week and all that stuff. How's everything on your end?" Susan had a very difficult marriage and Jenna felt bad for her. Her husband had repeatedly left her to use drugs and at one point, went to live with his ex-wife. He was mean when he was home and treated Susan terribly. They'd both gotten saved at the same time and were walking with the Lord when they got married but shortly after the marriage, he turned on her and went back to his old life. Jenna prayed for Susan all the time and more than once had been the shoulder for her to cry on and the one to help talk her through the pain and difficulty.

"Oh, you know same old same old. He's gone right now so although that stinks and I know he's using; it does give me peace and quiet. But, that's not why I'm calling you. I'm calling you to let you know I talked with your sister a little while ago and she said she'd go to church with me on Sunday." She sounded excited.

"No way! Oh my gosh! I can't even believe it. That is awesome. I hope she gets saved and we can hang out again and she'd be so much happier, and I know I'm babbling but I can't believe it!" Jenna wanted to cry, happy tears.

"There is one thing. She doesn't want to sit with you and

Jack. She wants her and I to sit together. She feels like if she is sitting with you, she'll feel pressure and you'll be mad at her or something."

Jenna was deflated. She'd prayed for four years for Rachel. She'd cried gallons of tears over her and gone out of her way to keep from being frustrated, angry or anything else with her. She would never go to church with Jenna and now they'll be in the same building, but she couldn't sit with her.

"I understand." She felt sad and disappointed. But what could she do? At least she was going to church and maybe she'd hear the message and give up the fight.

"I'm sorry Jenna I know that must hurt. But try to understand. I'll let you know what happens as soon as I can OK. I'm sorry, I didn't mean to hurt your feelings." She did sound sorry.

"It's not your fault. You do what you need to do. I'll be praying for you both. Hopefully I'll see you on Sunday."

"Thanks, I'll talk to you later. Bye."

Jenna told Jack and they prayed, and they continued to pray through the weekend. Sunday finally came.

Jenna and Jack sat up front together. Jack ran into Susan in the lobby on his way to the bathroom and she told him where they were sitting. When he got back to the front with Jenna he told her. They were sitting in the back row, middle section. The whole entire service Jenna prayed. She prayed for Pastor Mark and the words he shared, and for her sister to hear God speaking to her. She asked the Lord to take away any fear that Rachel had and to give Susan the words to share. Jenna realized about halfway through the service that it was communion Sunday. On communion Sunday, Pastor Mark always gave an invitation for anyone that wanted to accept Christ to do so before communion was served so that they could partake. He always led them in the sinners' prayer and asked for a show of hands if anyone wanted prayer. Jenna knew that her sister would hear a clear presentation of the Gospel and be given an opportunity to respond. She hoped that Rachel would answer the call of God.

Lord, please help my sister to hear Your voice. Please bind back the enemy that would try to distract her and keep her from hearing You and keep her from salvation. Please cast the enemy away. Give Pastor Mark the right words today, the words that are perfect for my sister. Jesus, please save her. You love her more than I do, You want her to be saved more than I do, You died for her. Help her to turn to You and live for You. Please give Susan wisdom and the right words. Please Lord, save her. In Your Name, Amen.

Pastor Mark gave the invitation just like Jenna knew he would. They took communion together and finally service was over. Jenna couldn't find Rachel or Susan after service. She was nervous, anxious, excited and hopeful but they were no-where to be found. Finally, after looking everywhere she gave up and they went home. She didn't have to wait long, and the phone rang.

"Hello"

"Hey Jenna, it's Susan. Sorry you couldn't find us after service. I bet you looked everywhere."

"Yes, I did, what happened?" She could hardly stand the suspense.

"She accepted Jesus. She was having a hard time after service, so we went and talked. She didn't want to see you right away because she was scared. She said she's going to call you. I'd let her call you and tell you. She feels kind of over-whelmed, I think. She doesn't want to disappoint you and she's a little apprehensive because it's all new to her." Susan was trying to help Jenna see where Rachel was and prepare Jenna for the conversation.

"Um, OK. I'm not quite sure what do to with that, but I'll let her call me. I wish I could have been there. I can't believe she finally did it." Jenna was crying. She was overwhelmed at the reality that her little sister was now going to be in the Kingdom with her. She'd prayed for this day for so long and it finally came. They talked for a few more minutes and then said their goodbyes.

Jenna didn't know what to do. She wanted to call her sister and talk to her about Jesus and start the ball rolling to restoring their relationship, but she had to wait, Rachel had made the rule; she'd follow it. She was excited but couldn't help but feel a little disappointment and hurt that she hadn't been there, and that Rachel was putting a distance between them.

Jenna told Jack the news and they rejoiced together and prayed for Rachel.

They'd gotten their wedding present from Jesus after all.

"...the effective fervent prayer of a righteous man avails much." James 5:16 KJV

ON THE ROAD AGAIN

J ack left at the end of March as scheduled and was gone for a
week. He drank. He was miserable and Jenna was broken.

She didn't know what to do. She'd never dealt with
anything like this in her life. She couldn't figure out in her
logical brain why God would have her marry this person when
He knew all along what was going to happen. She couldn't
understand what Jack was so unhappy about, what she had
done that would cause him to drink. Why wasn't Jesus enough
to make him happy? Why was their marriage not worth his
being sober? She knew God would not violate His word and
His Word told her in 2 Corinthians "to not be unequally
yoked..." so it stood to reason in her mind that Jack must
be saved but why in the world would he want to get drunk?
What was so terrible? She was constantly battling in her mind
trying to answer these questions and at the same time practice forgiveness, surrender and walking in the Spirit, it was
exhausting!

Jack was miserable. He hated hurting Jenna. He hated
that his drinking affected her and that it was an issue. He tried
to convince himself that if he didn't have to travel, he could
get it under control. Maybe if he read his Bible more or prayed
more or memorized more Bible verses, he'd stay sober. Then
on the other side of the coin, he was planning and looking at
the sports page to see which games he wanted to watch while
he was on the road. It was a vicious cycle that had played it-

self out in his heart and mind since he was twenty years old, only now the Jesus factor changed everything. Before Jesus he could drink and plan and not feel bad. Now, he felt like a thousand-pound weight was sitting on him. Even thinking about it was miserable. He no longer enjoyed it. But he kept planning.

They continued on the same destructive train for months. He traveled every month without a break and drank every time he traveled. As time progressed, he began to drink on the weekends and on Monday nights when he was home. He was still a huge sports fan, especially football. He also loved basketball, golf and baseball. During basketball season or baseball season he'd go to the bar on Saturday or Sunday and during football season he would go on Sunday and Monday. Sometimes when the seasons overlapped, he'd be gone all weekend and come home only to sleep. Jenna would get up on Saturday or Sunday morning and find a note that usually read something like, "Went to watch the game, be home later tonight, love Jack." Sometimes on Monday's she'd get a call at work near the end of the day saying he wasn't going to be home; most of the time she'd get home and just find a message on the answering machine.

At first, she had no idea where he went or when he'd be home. After awhile a pattern began to develop. He'd be gone by 8 in the morning and get home sometime between 9 and 11 p.m. He would stay at the bar all day long drinking, watching sports and reading the sports page. They would talk about it at times. He would apologize, read his Bible and go to church. He would call ahead and have the TV taken out of his room so that he couldn't sit and watch movies or sports, only to have it brought back in when he arrived. He would give her the company credit card and his ATM card, ask her for help and she'd pray and do all that she knew to do spiritually and still he drank. He was obviously miserable but some how it still wasn't enough to make him stop.

At times he seemed broken and repentant. Other times he was stoic and angry.

He began to throw accusations at her. He would tell her she was the worst Christian he'd ever seen because she was crying or sad over the situation. Other times he would accuse her of being self-righteous and prideful. The worst were the sexual accusations. He began to accuse her of withholding from him, not caring about their sex life, calling her a cold fish. Those cut her to the heart. She had prayed so hard to be healed, loved him and shared her body with him. It frustrated her because seven days a month he was gone, five days a month she had her period so that only left so many days for the marriage bed. She knew that his accusations were baseless. She wasn't the perfect Christian, but she knew that she was being obedient to the Lord to the best of her ability under the circumstances.

Jenna didn't know what to do. She tried to reason with him but there was no reason in him. She tried to be silent and not retaliate, he only got angrier. When she would get angry, he would mock her. She was at a loss.

She felt so betrayed, broken, frustrated and weighed down by it all that at times she thought she'd literally collapse. She hated to be falsely accused, had no way to defend herself and nothing could stop the painful arrows of accusation that were hurled at her. She couldn't make sense of it all. For her logical, black and white brain there was no reasonable, rational explanation for any of it and yet it persisted. The Lord would not let her file it. When things came at her she'd try to file only to find herself separated from the Lord, without His peace and without His strength. She couldn't bear up under the difficulty without Him and His peace and strength, so she'd go through her process of forgiveness, repentance, surrender and asking to be filled with His Spirit. She wanted to shut down, desperately, but Jesus wouldn't let her.

As time went on in their first year of marriage, the pattern continued. She eventually had to tell Jo and Michelle because she needed prayer support and couldn't carry the pain, burden and difficulty by herself. They knew something was wrong; she looked tired and didn't carry the newly married joy. She knew that the battle would be won in prayer and yet she had to be careful, she wanted to guard her husband. She knew that the Lord would want her to choose those she told very wisely. She wasn't to go around gossiping and complaining about him and the situation. So, she told them. They were shocked and heartbroken and listened like Jenna knew they would. They were very careful in what they said to Jenna; they didn't bash Jack or criticize, nor did they tell Jenna what to do, they were godly women and that was exactly what Jenna needed around her.

There were times when Jack, the Jack she knew when they got married, came out. He would send her flowers, leave her a note, take her out to dinner, cook dinner with her or sit and pray with her. They would have times of laughter and joy, but with Jack, there was always something lurking underneath. It was as though they were not joined at the soul, as they should be. There was an invisible wall that divided them; Jenna hated it and could not understand it.

She could tell he was the most miserable of all people, yet he would still drink. She noticed certain patterns of behavior that told her when he was about to take off and get drunk. Then there was the "feeling". At first that was all she could describe it as. She'd get this feeling down in the pit of her stomach and it would tell her he wasn't going to be home when she got there or that he'd be gone when she got up and it proved itself out time and time again. Soon, however, she began to realize it was Jesus. He was giving her the gentle nudge of His Spirit to pray and letting her know to be prepared. She hated the feeling but was grateful for it at the same time. God cared about her. She needed that reminder because at times, she felt like He had abandoned her.

They lived on a budget and everything was budgeted down to the last few dollars. They had money some months to go to a cheap dinner but for the most part, they lived paycheck to paycheck. So, it was frustrating and scary to Jenna when

Jack's drinking habit increased, and he began to play tricks with the finances. He would take money out of the ATM even though the money was technically spent because the checks were in the mail. He called to find out when the tax refund would hit and took money out with the expectation the refund would cover it, things that made her crazy. She'd pray and ask God to watch over their money and not let anything bounce!

It was harder than anything she had ever gone through in her life. Considering her life, that was saying a lot.

"Beloved, think it not strange concerning the fiery trial which is to try you, as though some strange thing happened to you: but rejoice, inasmuch as you are partakers of Christ's sufferings; that, when His glory shall be revealed, you may be glad also with exceeding joy." 1 Peter 4:12-13 KJV

1997

They celebrated their one-year anniversary with a dinner out and the cake top from their wedding cake. It tasted wonderful. Jack sent flowers to her work and she bought him a card and a new Bible.

His drinking continued. She went to church by herself a lot because he was either out of town or at the bar. She finally broke down one Sunday and told Pastor Mark's wife, Shary.

"Hey Jenna, how are you? I haven't seen Jack in a few weeks, is he out of town?" Shary was so sweet and always asked about Jack when she didn't see him. It was easy to see when he wasn't at church because they always sat in the front row together and Shary sat in the front across the isle from them.

Jenna tried to hold it together, but she couldn't; she started to cry. "Um, no he's at a bar right now. He has been out of town off and on a lot, but he's gone back to drinking and a lot of the time he isn't here because he's at the bar." She was sobbing now.

"Oh, Jenna, I'm so sorry. That must be so difficult. How long has he been drinking?" She sat down next to Jenna and put her arm around her.

"Since March of last year, about a month after we got married. I don't know what I did. I don't understand what is so awful that he drinks. Why doesn't he just love Jesus and be grateful that Jesus died for him? Why did God allow me to marry him knowing that he'd go back to drinking and turn his back on Him? I don't know what to do, I'm so scared, mad, hurt, frustrated, feeling like a failure and I don't know how much more I can take. He's mean and angry and says the most horrible awful things to me. I just don't understand." Jenna was beside herself. She'd held it in for a long time. She'd wanted to tell her pastor and his wife but felt like she was being a tattletale.

"Jenna, it's not your fault. It's sin. There's no rational explanation for it. Sin is just that, sin. It's destructive, illogical, incomprehensible and unreasonable. You'll never understand it. It's all about Jack and Jesus. That's it. It's that simple. He doesn't want to submit his life to Jesus so he's rebelling. He probably doesn't really know why he does it. It's a spiritual battle and it is going to be fought and won in prayer. We'll pray for both of you and you must pray for him. If he doesn't repent and turn from his drinking, the Bible says that drunkards will not inherit the kingdom of God. So, although I realize this is so painful for you, you have to look above that to the greater picture of his eternal position. Is it alright with you if I tell Pastor Mark?" Shary was one of the sweetest people she'd ever met. Everything she said to Jenna, Jenna knew was true and she'd said it in such an understanding gentle way, Jenna appreciated that.

"Of course, please tell him. I know what you're saying is right. I do think about that sometimes. I get scared for him. It's so hard to not take it personally especially when he blames me and accuses me of so many terrible things. I figure if I was a better wife some how he'd stop. I feel like if he thinks those things, then that must be how God feels about me." Jenna still had things left over from her childhood. She was working through them but feeling inadequate and that God was always judging her performance was a difficult one to shake. That was what her father had done. She didn't do it consciously, but it was there and would rear its ugly head.

"Jenna, Jack is not in his right mind. He is sin-sick because of his drinking. When we willfully choose to do things that are contrary to the will of God and the Word of God, we will get sickness in our soul. It affects every part of our life. We don't see things properly, think properly, assess situations correctly and we don't rightly represent God. Jack is lashing out at you because of his own guilt. He knows he's not right with the Lord and is angry and blaming you when, in fact, it's all him. Jesus isn't going to allow him to point the finger at you and say, she made me. Adam tried that in the Garden, it didn't work then either." Shary laughed and hugged Jenna.

"I'll try to remember that. I work hard at forgiving him, surrendering to the Lord and repenting so that I don't stay angry or bitter. I don't want my relationship with Jesus to be messed up. I need Him too much and I know what the right thing to do is, so I must do it. I just get so tired. Sometimes I fail. I get mad and give him the silent treatment, but I know that's wrong. I don't nag him or throw it in his face because I know that's sin, sometimes I just get so sick of the pain, I just want it to stop."

"I know. Do you believe that the Lord called you to marry him?"

"Yes, I do. I have gone over it in my head a thousand times. All the prayer, the confirmation even the fact that I almost didn't marry him, and it still comes up the same. I wasn't desperate to get married; in fact, I didn't want to get married, so I know it wasn't that. I just feel so stupid, like how did I miss the signs that he was going to drink?"

"I don't think you missed anything. I believe you are where God wants you to be. It doesn't look like it right now, but He has a purpose for it all. Some day you will look back and be grateful for all that the Lord did in you through this time. I believe you hear from the Lord Jenna and all this is for the glory of God. Just be patient and keep your eyes focused on Jesus." Shary was gentle but confident.

"I don't see that right now, but OK. Thanks for listening. It helps to know that you will be praying. I so am thankful for you." Jenna hugged her and Shary prayed for her.

"For as the heaven are higher than the earth, so are My ways higher than your ways, and My thoughts than your thoughts." Isaiah 55:9 KJV

QUICK FIX

J ack was becoming increasingly angry. One Saturday in the summer of 1997 it all blew up in Jenna's face.

Jenna was in the loft cleaning their room. Jack was downstairs and was in a dark, brooding mood. She was trying to stay out of his way and not push his buttons. She had her back to the stairs but heard his footsteps as he approached.

"Jenna, I'm sick of you holding out on me. We're going to see a counselor and talk about your issues." He was matter of fact, but the anger was just below the surface. He sounded almost condescending. She had to tread carefully, or it would be an explosion.

"I don't have any issues Jack." She tried to sound as calm and gentle as she could muster. She was shaking inside from fear and rage. She knew that she'd done her work with the Lord before they got married. She had relations with him on a regular basis and had, on numerous occasions, at the direction of the Lord initiated it when he was drunk. It wasn't her issue, it was his, she just couldn't figure out the root of it.

"You can say whatever you like but either we go see a counselor or I'm through. I can't take it anymore and I'm sick of you living in denial. You act all spiritual and like you're 'Miss goodie-two-shoes' to everyone else, but I know the truth. I've already gotten a number from my sister and made an appointment. If you don't go, I assume it's because you don't care about this marriage." He was glaring at her, daring her to protest.

She was raging inside. She'd been so careful what she told people and whom she told, and he was talking to his sister about their problems? *I bet you didn't tell her about your little drinking problem, did you? How convenient for you to call her and disclose something so personal about me so I look like the bad guy.* She was angry that he would even suggest they go to some counselor. He knew exactly how she felt about that. They were pointless. It was man trying to solve man's problem, which is impossible. She'd had her fill of counselors when she was not saved, they'd never helped her then and the Bible was clear that man is incapable of helping their fellow man with anything other than the Word of God.

"Alright Jack if that is what you want, I'll go." She put down the clothes she was folding and walked into the bathroom and shut the door. *Father, I am going to choose right now to forgive my husband for his accusations, his violation of my privacy, and for forcing me into a corner with a counselor and something I so strongly disagree with and do not believe in. I am going to give my hurt, frustration and anger over to You right now. Please free me from it. Help me, as the time approaches for the appointment, to not get an attitude and help me Jesus to not have conversations in my head. Please give me wisdom as to what You want me to do with the counselor. I have asked You so many times Lord; if I have a problem, please show me, otherwise please deal with my husband. Fill me with Your Spirit and give me the ability to walk out of this bathroom and not have an attitude and to love my husband. In Jesus Name, Amen.*

The appointment was on Thursday; Jenna had five days to wait. She continued to pray every time it came to her mind because if she didn't, she'd find herself five minutes down the road in some conversation in her head. She didn't want that. Jack was happy and smug with himself. He totally had the attitude that all the problems they had in their marriage were due to Jenna and her unresolved issues and this counselor would straighten her out. As Jenna prayed through out the week the only thing that the Lord kept telling her was "be silent". She didn't want to rehash some problem that she'd already worked out with Jesus and even if she hadn't worked it out with Him, some woman who went to school with all her fancy big words and psycho-babble wasn't going to fix Jenna, only Jesus could do that.

Thursday came and as they were driving to the appointment Jenna prayed silently, *Lord, I need Your help. I am angry that I have to go into this place and even angrier that Jack has already told her "my issues" and I don't want to talk to her. But I am willing to go, just please give me strength and please tell me what to do"* She waited, and she heard the still small Voice, "be silent."

They went into the office and signed in. They only had to wait a few seconds and they were ushered into a different office by the counselor. She was probably forty-something with a medium to heavy build and blonde hair. She seemed nice enough.

"Hello Jack, Jenna, my name is Barbara. Have a seat." She had a warm inviting office with two comfortable sofas' and a non-threatening posture. Typical counselor posture Jenna thought to herself.

They sat down. Jack started.

"Well, as I told you on the phone. My wife was molested as a young girl and I believe that it is interfering with our relationship now. I was hoping that she would talk to you about it and maybe you could help us." He sounded so sweet and concerned. He spoke with his wrinkled brow, crossed leg, concerned businessman voice.

"Well, I can certainly understand how that could interfere with your relationship. That is very damaging and can take a long time to heal. Jenna is that true about you being molested?"

Jenna simply shook her head yes. She was fighting back

tears. Not over the molestation but because she felt betrayed by Jack. She was angry and hurt that he would force her into this corner, that he was accusing her in the first place, and he wouldn't address his issues.

"Do you feel it is a problem?" She kept her voice calm.

Jenna shook her head no. Still fighting back tears.

"Jenna, you need to talk about it with someone; it's causing us problems. Please talk to her." Jack sounded so kind and gentle. Pleading in his tone. Not the same person who had been so angry only four days before.

Jenna sat there for the rest of the hour in silence. The Lord had told her to be silent, so she was. She was fully crying by the time they left. Her tears were from frustration. She couldn't defend herself and Jack never mentioned his drinking, his tirades or the mean, and cruel things he said to her. He never bothered to tell Barbara that he was gone at least seven days out of every month, sometimes fourteen. He didn't tell her that many times he'd be gone for seven days and the day before his return, Jenna would start her period and so in his mind that was twelve days he'd been deprived. She could not and would not try to convince either one of them of the work that Jesus had done in her. She knew the difference Jesus had made and it was night and day. She couldn't say or do a single thing except obey. That meant she sat there and took whatever they hurled at her.

Everything went back to normal. He tried a few times, unsuccessfully, to sober up. When he did, he was just a sober drunk. His mind and attitude were still in opposition to the Lord, which made for a very difficult marriage. After the first few times, Jenna didn't get her hopes up. She began to realize that when he was done, truly done, she'd know it. It would be so obvious and radical that no one would be able to deny it.

He began to put on weight with all the alcohol he was drinking. Since he already had a thick build, he easily put on a beer gut and his face was very bloated. He'd tried at one point to take a new prescription drug called Fen-Phen to help him lose weight. It was the latest miracle weight loss pill, available by prescription only. He'd gotten them and been taking them for a few months before he told her. During the brief month or two he was on it, he discovered that if he took it in the morning after he drank, and then downed some Gatorade, his hangover instantly went away. When Jenna found out she was furious inside. She'd heard so many terrible things about it and knew for someone to drink alcohol, which slows the body down, and then take a drug that speeds it up, it could be very dangerous. Equally infuriating to her was the fact that the dumb doctor didn't care one bit for the reason of Jack's weight gain; he just prescribed the pills and said thanks for the money. When he told her, she didn't say a word out loud, inside she was screaming at him. She had to seriously pray through the whole ordeal, she couldn't believe he'd done it. To her, if he stopped drinking, he'd lose weight, simple.

One Saturday morning he decided he would walk about two blocks from their apartment to a pizza place that served beer and had a big screen T.V.

Around eleven that night a car pulled into the driveway and stopped outside their apartment. She looked out the window and saw a taxi. The backdoor opened and Jack got out. He walked into the apartment and was not only drunk but also sweating and exhausted. She had to ask.

"Jack, you were just around the corner at the pizza place, why did you take a taxi home?" She wasn't trying to start a fight; just curious as to the reason he'd need a taxi for less than two blocks.

"Well, I left the pizza place around 2:30 this afternoon, got within a block of my parents house, realized it was late, I was too tired to walk all the way back, so I called a cab." He was so tired he could barely move.

"Why did you walk all that way? That must be at least 12 miles if not more. What were you doing?" She couldn't believe what she'd just heard. It had to be that stupid Fen-Phen.

"I wanted to tell people about Jesus. I felt great, I had

energy, and so I started walking." The look on his face said a thousand words. Even though he was drunk, he knew it was a ridiculous thing to do. Jenna didn't know if she should bust out laughing or break down crying at the idiotic, foolishness of this man that she loved.

"Wow, you are gonna be sore tomorrow. You could have called me to come and get you." Jenna was amazed that his heart hadn't exploded.

"I didn't want to bother you with my idiotic, stupidity." He was more sober than she thought.

"OK, well, I'll get you something to eat or whatever you'd like. Maybe you should go take a shower, your kind of sweaty." Jenna needed to get away from him. She didn't want him to see that she was barely controlling her laughter. It really wasn't funny; it was ridiculous and sad. What was she going to do? He had to ride out his rebellion and all she could do was buckle up. She just hoped he didn't have a heart attack in the meantime.

She didn't usually ask a lot of questions unless he started the conversation and she felt that she had the go ahead from Jesus to ask. True to His Word, Jenna found out, one way or another everything Jack was up to. In the times that he was sober and trying to stay sober, he'd talk freely with her about anything. Jenna had asked him during one of those times how much he drank when he went out to the bar and what a typical day looked like for him when he did. When you spend twelve to fourteen hours away from home, it can make a person curious.

"Well, when I leave here first thing in the morning I drive to the store and get a paper and a tin of chewing tobacco. Then I drive to Rookies, that's the Sports Bar I like. I order breakfast and then as soon as they start serving beer at 10 a.m., I start pounding the pitchers. I have to down the first pitcher quickly because I feel so convicted about being there, that I'm sinning against God and hurting you. I usually read the paper and find a corner where no one will bother me. I usually drink about five pitchers while I'm there. The equivalent of a case of beer for easy math and usually eat some greasy, fried food around lunchtime. Their garlic-chicken pizza is awesome, and it absorbs alcohol so I can drink more. Sometimes I drive to the Corn-Husker bar to watch a game and then go back to Rookies and when everything is over, I make my way home. That's about it."

She was astounded at the planning and the exact science of his behavior. She couldn't believe he drove that drunk. She was shocked that he didn't get pulled over and that he could even stand after all that beer. That he would admit to the conviction and guilt and still sit on the barstool was beyond her comprehension.

During their second year of marriage he came home from a work trip looking more tired, defeated and haggard than usual.

"Jenna, I have to talk to you." He sounded as though he'd just lost the third world war.

"What's up?" She was scared. What was he about to say? She couldn't take much more. They were two years into their marriage, and she was worn out.

"Remember when we went on our first date? Remember how I couldn't sleep the night before and I told you what the Lord had spoken to me? Remember how weird it seemed to you at the time?" He couldn't look at her and was beginning to cry.

"Yeah of course. It was totally weird. I get it now but then it was weird. What about it?" She was torn between wanting the answer and wanting to run away.

"Well, you asked me how long it had been since I drank. I told you two years, that I hadn't had a drink since I had given my life to Christ."

"Yes, I remember." The familiar knot had just made its appearance in the pit of her stomach.

"Well, I lied. I didn't just start drinking after we got married. I got saved, was sober a month and a half and then went to a party with some friends and thought I could have one beer. I have been battling ever since then. At times I could maintain and only have a few drinks, nothing that anyone would notice. Other times I would get drunk all weekend, but since I started traveling again, well you know the rest." He sounded so dejected.

She felt like she'd been punched in the gut. Everything about her marriage was a lie. Now it made since. He'd never stopped drinking. All this time she was under the impression he'd started again after they'd gotten married. She was devastated. Every vow, every conversation it all seemed like a great big deceptive lie. She sat in stunned silence. She vacillated between being so angry she wanted to punch something and so hurt and devastated she wanted to break into convulsive sobs. She wished she could file all of it.

"Jenna, I'm sorry. I feel like a great big loser. I don't know what else to say. I have known all along that I was supposed to tell you, but I couldn't bring myself to do it. That was the reason God gave me that warning. Because I was already drinking, He was warning me that if I didn't stop, I wouldn't be able to keep it from you and so now you know the whole story. I'm truly sorry. I hope you can forgive me." He had his head in his hands and was crying.

"I forgive you. I just don't understand it. I don't understand why you lied, why you keep drinking, why God is allowing this, and I don't know what to do. I want a godly husband who will pray with me, go to church with me, talk about Jesus with me and serve with me. I want a spiritual leader. I don't understand why you refuse to surrender to God and why you don't want to be a spiritual leader. I feel like the worst wife in the world sometimes. I feel like no matter how hard I try it's never good enough. You love your beer more than me. I can't compete with a can of Coors Light. How can I ever live up to that?" Now she was crying. She didn't want him to feel condemned or attacked but she couldn't keep it in. She'd just been sucker punched.

"I understand. I want to be a godly man. I just don't know how." He got up and went upstairs. She sat in the living room crying. She could hear him upstairs sobbing. What was going to happen to them?

"...behold you have sinned against the Lord; and be sure your sin will find you out." Numbers 32:23 KJV

THE SURE MERCY
OF GOD

As they moved toward their third year of marriage, Jenna was still battling and wondering if she had missed every red flag that had been thrown at her about Jack's drinking and married him anyway. She was constantly fighting against feeling like the stupidest human being on the planet. She had a hard time believing that God had a plan and a purpose for her in all of this.

One Saturday morning she got up to go to Bible study and Jack was gone; he'd left his usual note on the counter. He'd been sober for 33 days. Now, he'd gone to the bar. Given up the battle and raised the white flag. She was tired and broken. It was such a struggle for her to obey God and His Word and not follow her emotions, thoughts and desires. She was constantly before the Lord affirming that she had made a commitment to Him regarding their marriage. Yes, she had stood before man and taken marriage vows, she'd said them to Jack, but to Jenna, first and foremost they were to God. If she didn't continuously remind herself of that, she'd never be able to stand. Jack wasn't behaving in a manner that demonstrated a commitment to his vows and everything in her wanted to back out. As she was driving to church to meet with the ladies, she cried out to Him who hears from heaven and is willing to move heaven and earth to help her.

Lord, please help me. I know that my husband is going to be gone all day at the bar. I can't take it anymore. I want to quit, to run away and never look back. I made the commitment to You and I will stand on that commitment, but You have to help me. I need something from You. You have to speak to me from Your Word, to give me something to hold onto. It seems so hopeless and I feel so alone and afraid. I don't want to live my life like this. I don't want to watch him destroy himself, see him go to jail or end up in hell. I need You, please speak to me, please give me something Lord.

Jenna cried all the way to church.

Her eyes were red and swollen but she went in and sat down. Jo began the study in prayer and then opened her Bible.

"I know we have been studying in the book of Isaiah, but as I was praying about today's message, the Lord had me study some place else. Please turn to Hosea chapter 14."

Jenna opened her Bible like everyone else. Jo began the study and began sharing at verse 1. As she expounded on the verses she eventually got to verse four.

"I will heal their backsliding; I will love them freely; for My anger is turned away from him." Hosea 14:4.

Jenna's heart almost stopped. She felt as though an arrow had pierced right through her and she knew it was directly from the Throne of God. He had heard her prayer and answered it. She broke down. She was glad that the ladies that were there loved her and knew that she was having difficulty in her marriage.

"Jenna, what's wrong? Are you OK?" Jo looked concerned.

"Yes, it's just that I was praying on the way here and I asked the Lord to speak to me about my marriage and my husband and as soon as you read verse four, I knew it was from Him. He answered me and I'm so grateful." She was sobbing, but these were tears of joy and release.

"Praise God. Let's take a few minutes to thank Him and praise Him." Jo bowed her head and led the ladies in thanksgiving and a time of prayer.

Jenna now had something to hold onto. She knew that at some point her husband would turn from his drinking and God would heal him. She went home and looked up the verse again and pulled out her Strong's Concordance. She broke it down and found it to be very specific. After she looked up each word in the original Hebrew language she found it to say, "I (God) will thoroughly make whole and mend their apostasy and turning away." She was so grateful. She got down on her knees and began to thank God.

Lord, how can I say thank You enough. You heard me call out to You from the pit of despair and answered. I know You heard me and gave me something to hold on to so I can walk through this trial and continue to face what comes my way. I will pray this for my husband as You have spoken it, You will fulfill it. You promised that You would heal him and turn him back to You, I believe You and will pray for him that he allows You to heal him. Thank you Jesus for hearing me, I love You. Amen

"Stand therefore, having girded your waist with Truth..."
Ephesians 6:14 KJV

1998 MOVING ON

Everything continued as before. He traveled, he drank, he tried to be sober, and he drank. He continued to have radical mood swings, throw false accusations at her, taunt her and worship his beer. His anger grew and his health began to deteriorate. He had terrible stomach trouble and he was so dehydrated that his fingers began to crack and bleed. Jenna held onto what the Lord told her even though it was getting worse instead of better.

They still had Captain Jack and now they had a cat named Sox. The neighbors had been feeding a few feral cats since before Jenna had moved in. She loved animals so she shared the feeding cost with them. There was a mommy cat that had two kittens that were almost twins. They were long-haired with white bellies and paws and black and gray on their backs. Jenna fell in love, so she set out to tame one of them and make a pet out of him. It took a bit of time, a lot of scratches and extreme patience but eventually she won out. Sox and C.J. got along great and were instant friends. Life was moving on.

Then one day Jack came home from work with news.

"Jenna, I don't know what is going to happen, but my company is merging with our sister company and I won't have a job anymore. I don't know what to do."

"Why will you be out of a job? Don't they need a product sales manager to work with the guys under the new company?" Jenna didn't know what to think. The first thought was fear, as she knew that he wasn't exactly in his right mind or spiritually on track. According to the Bible he was still her spiritual leader and she had to follow.

"No, they are combining positions and mine will be eliminated. I guess I need to start looking for another job or I'm going to have to go back out into the field and that would mean traveling more than I do now. I don't want to do that". His face showed all the fatigue of drinking, bad food, sleepless nights, travel and defeat. He wasn't the same person she'd married in 1996.

"Well, I guess we just have to pray. If the Lord is moving you out of this job, He has something else planned. We need to pray and wait and see what happens. When is all this going to happen?" She was trying to stay calm and silently prayed that God would help her to help him.

"Six months at the most. They've been working on it for a while apparently. I have a few people I can call and see if anything pans out."

They talked and prayed together. That was difficult for Jenna, but she tried to stay focused on Jesus and not on Jack.

Over the next few months he had several offers, one from a company in California and one from a company in Minnesota. They prayed and talked, and Jack stayed sober for a few months. In May, they concluded that the company in California was not where God wanted him, so they made plans to fly to Minnesota. Two days before they were to leave for Minnesota, Jack got a call from the sister company that his current company was being merged with. They offered him a job in Washington State. They went to Minnesota with Washington as another option.

Minnesota was beautiful. Jenna had never been there. They saw a few sights, met with the company executives and took the plant tour. When they were on the plane home they talked.

"What do you think Jack, do you think it's where the Lord wants us?" Jenna wanted to talk about it and see what he was thinking. She felt that it was a shut door.

"I want it to be a yes. This is a great company. I've known the president for years and I would be assured a steady job. But I don't feel peace about it. I want to do it, but I don't think it's what I'm supposed to do. How do you feel about it?"

"I've been praying, and I don't feel like it's what we're supposed to do either. It just doesn't seem right. I can't explain it; it's just what's on my heart. I'm willing even though the thought of being up to my backside in snow for six months out of the year is not high on my list of things I want to do, I'm willing if it's what God wants for us." She would go anywhere God wanted even if it was difficult.

"So now what should I do? I have the offer from our sister company. The last person that wanted to go from one company to the other, the president of my company wanted to charge them $20,000 to allow the guy to go work for them. I know they aren't going to pay no twenty grand for me." He shrugged his shoulders.

"Well, why don't we just throw out a fleece? We'll pray and ask the Lord to shut the door if it's not His will. You go and talk to your president and let him know about the offer and if he says yes, well, we'll know. If he says no, we have our answer then as well."

"That sounds like a good plan but I'm telling you, there is no way that he is going to let me go. He isn't a very nice person and he's ruthless. We call him little Napoleon." They both laughed.

They had three days before he went back to work to talk to his president. They prayed and asked Jesus to open or shut the door.

Jenna was driving to the store and praying about it and she heard that still small Voice, "Proverbs 21:1."

She got home and went straight to her Bible and looked up Proverbs 21:1, *"The king's heart is in the hand of the Lord, as the rivers of water, He turns it which ever way He chooses."*

"Jack, I was praying on the way to the store and the Lord

told me to look up Proverbs 21:1 and I did, look at it." She took her Bible over to him and showed him the verse.

"Oh, my gosh. That is from the Lord. I guess we have our answer. I will go in there on Monday and see what happens and God is going to move this guy in whatever way He wants for us and I just have to trust that." For all of Jack's drinking and rebelling against God, he wanted to know God's will for him.

Monday came and Jenna sat on pins and needles all day waiting to hear what happened.

"Jenna, I'm home."

"I'm upstairs, be right there." She ran downstairs. The look on his face was one of disbelief and excitement.

"What happened? Did you see him? Did you tell him? I've been praying that verse all day." Jenna couldn't wait to hear.

"Well, I went into Mr. Yashiro's office and sat down. I told him that Mr. Yakamoto had offered me a job at his company, and I was considering taking him up on the offer. I asked him if he had any objections to that. He sat there for a few minutes with his hands folded, just looking at me. I was sweating bullets. Finally, he looks me in the eye and says, 'Yes, you can go, when you want leave?'" Jack did a perfect imitation of a Japanese man trying to speak broken English.

"Oh my goodness Jack that's amazing. I don't know whether to laugh or cry. I'm freaking out and yet excited at the same time. I know the Lord is the one who did it because He gave us the verse, we threw it out there and let Him make the decision which is totally cool but scary all at the same time. What do we do now?" Jenna was breathless and was trying to control her emotions. She had that nervous smile on her face.

"Well, I guess I should go talk to Mr. Yakamoto and see what he says. Then we can go from there. I'll call tomorrow and see what I can do." He sounded hopeful for the first time in a long time.

"I guess we need to keep praying and trusting and see what happens. How do you feel about going back to Washington? I mean the last time you lived there it was with your ex-wife. What would it be like for you to go back, old haunts and all?" She was concerned.

"I guess I hadn't thought about it. It would be kind of weird at first, but I lived way down south, and we wouldn't be living there. I'd be working the I-5 corridor so we could live a ton of different places. Besides that was another life. I have you and Jesus and it will be OK, I'm not worried about it." He was trying to keep it light and reassuring.

Jenna had to process everything. If they moved she'd be leaving everything that she'd known her whole life. She'd be leaving her job, family, familiar surroundings, her church family and her support system to move to a place where she knew not a single soul. And Jack was still drinking.

Jack went to work the next day and made an appointment with Mr. Yakamoto for Thursday.

Thursday finally came.

"Jenna, I'm home, you upstairs?"

"Yea up here." She ran down the stairs to see him and hear the news.

"Well, so I saw him. He wants me to start in August up in Washington. I'll be working for my old boss from before and I won't have to travel other than going to Eastern Washington and twice a year down to California. I'd be working the I-5 corridor and so I'd have to be up in Washington by July. That's pretty much it."

"I don't know what to say. I guess I'm in shock. Oh, man I guess that means we're moving to Washington." As much as she'd prayed for the Lord's will to be done she didn't really think she'd be moving to Washington. She didn't know what she thought but actually moving never occurred to her or maybe she never allowed it to. Now, she had to face it. They'd prayed, left it up to Jesus and He'd spoken. They had no other job offers, he was going to be out of a job before the end of the summer and this was the door that, against all odds, had been opened for them.

"You're shocked? I didn't expect the answer to be yes. I thought one of them would shut it down; if for no other reason than Mr. Yakamoto and Mr. Yashiro hate each other! I guess I'll go back in tomorrow and try to talk to Mr. Yashiro and see what happens. He could still shut the door so maybe we won't be moving." He sounded hopeful.

"OK." Jenna wasn't so hopeful. She had a feeling in her gut that this door was going to remain open.

Jack went the next day and saw Mr. Yashiro.

"So, he asked, 'How much time you need? You get two week you go look for house, I pay you $2,000 for help you move, you go there in two week and you find place. I pay for you go. You take wife. You need anything you tell me. I help you. OK?' So, I said OK!" He had the most dumbfounded look on his face. Jenna had never seen Jack look so bewildered.

"Oh, my gosh. I have to tell my boss and my family that we're going to Washington. I feel like I'm on that bullet train again, the speeding conveyor belt that God's got His finger on and I can't get off. I'm trying not to freak out." But on the inside every inch of her 5'7 ½" frame was completely freaking out.

The difference between Jack and Jenna was Jack saw the whole situation as some grand adventure, to go scout out a new homestead, claim the wild frontier and maybe get a new start on their marriage. Jenna saw reality. She'd be leaving everything she'd known her whole life. Good, bad or indifferent it was all she'd ever known; Southern California. She had a job that she loved; it gave her a sense of purpose, a paycheck and sense of security if Jack just suddenly went A.W.O.L on her. She loved her church and there were women there who knew about her situation, prayed for her and supported her. They were strong godly women. If Jenna was out of line, they'd tell her. They'd let her vent and then direct her back to Jesus and what she needed to do. They never allowed her to stay in a pity party, bash on her husband or stay angry or bitter. They weren't going to be in Washington with her, how would she survive without that support? She also had three things in life that she hated and tried to avoid at all cost: throwing up, going to the dentist and moving.

Lord, I see Your hand in this whole situation. I can't deny it and I don't want to fight You. I freely admit to You, I'm scared to death. I don't want to live in the middle of nowhere, with no friends, family or a job and deal with my husband the way he is. I don't want to leave my friends and my family and all that is familiar to me. I don't want to leave my church and have to find another one and You know I don't make friends easy and I'm an introvert and You know that I struggle with feeling worthless. But, we have prayed, and you gave us Proverbs 21:1 and we trusted You. So, if this is Your will for us to move to Washington, I will purpose in my heart and my will to follow You and go where You direct. My emotions are going to go through the whole range, and I am going to feel sad at times, but I am going to choose to trust You. Please help me to have Your peace and joy in the midst of this trial and please help me to keep giving all my fears over to You. I will trust You, just help me.

She told her boss, Michelle and her family, Jack told his family and they booked their plane reservations. They'd be flying down the first week in June and looking for a new home and a new church. Everyone was in shock including Jenna. Michelle was supportive and excited for what the Lord was going to do in Jenna's life. Her family was a little upset of course and she could tell Rachel was scared. Jack's family was supportive and excited. No one expected them to move to another state. But it was happening.

"Now the Lord had said to Abraham, get out of your country, from your family...to a land that I will show you." Genesis 12:1 NKJV

LOOKING AROUND

They had decided that they would pray for God to direct them to the town they were to live in. Jack could live anywhere along the I-5 corridor of Western Washington. All his customers were accessible by the I-5 freeway and he would be working out of their house. So, they looked up churches that were part of Calvary Chapel in Western Washington. Jack found a little church in a small town called Clark's Town. He told Jenna and they prayed that if that was the place God wanted them, when they went into that church, they would feel instantly at home. Jenna was excited but scared.

They arrived in Washington on a Monday and went to a hotel in Lincoln. They'd be staying there for most of the time except the last four days when they were going to a Bed & Breakfast in Clark's Town. Jenna's first impression of Washington was awe. Everything was so green. It was June and in California everything was brown except for the palm trees. Everything felt clean, the sky was blue and the whole place seemed to be fresh. The freeways were even cleaner than those in California. As they drove around they saw Bald Eagles, horses, cows, sheep and farmland. Jenna couldn't believe how beautiful it was. Although she was born and raised in California, she'd always dreamed of living on a farm in the country where there were wide-open spaces, clean air, and a slower way of life. Washington seemed to fit the bill.

They checked the papers for houses around the area

where they wanted to live, and the choices were slim. There were two options in Clark's Town and the first was a bust. They went in and Jenna immediately got the creeps. It was dilapidated, old, and when she opened the wood stove, she found a bird carcass and an old snakeskin. Jenna wasn't superstitious, but that gave her the jitters. The second place was more hopeful. It was a little two-bedroom bungalow down by the beach. Jenna couldn't believe it. She'd always wanted to live by the beach but in California, that was next to impossible. It was located on a small road that was lined on both sides with houses. Little bungalows, big three-story custom houses, boats parked in the yards, kayaks on the side of the driveways and the beach a stone's throw away; could it be possible?

When they pulled into the driveway the garage was directly in front of them with a small apartment right over the garage. To the left was a small well-kept yard with rose bushes and rhododendrons. The house was set on the left back corner of the property up against a hill. It had a deck that went across the front and along the side with a big sliding glass door and huge windows that faced out toward the beach. As you walked in the front door you were immediately in the small kitchen. The fridge was right next to the door, then the sink was next to the fridge and as you made your way around the counter to the stove, the stove was on the side of a half-wall that faced the living room. The living room was a decent size with a pellet stove in the corner and to the left of the kitchen was a dining room with large windows. The master bedroom and bath were behind the living room and down the tiny hallway was a very small second bedroom with a full bath across from it. A little further down the hall was the laundry room with a built-in desk that Jack could use for an office. It had a high vaulted wooden ceiling that made it seem much bigger than it was. But they lived in a 700 sq. foot loft apartment right now, so this seemed like a mansion. It was an older bungalow but was cozy. There were skylights in almost every room except the living room. Washington gets a lot of rain, the skylights let in light even in the winter. It came with a king size bed; which Jenna was thankful for because they'd been sleeping in a queen bed and she never had enough room. They loved it and Jenna felt immediately that the Lord had appointed for them to live there. There was one problem. Someone else had first claim to it. They filled out all the paperwork anyway. The owners told them, that if the other people suddenly backed out, they'd be next in line, but she was certain they were going to take it. Jenna wasn't worried. She knew if Jesus wanted her to live there, that was where she'd live.

They fell in love with Clark's Town. It was small, very rural and beautiful. There were trees everywhere, houses spread out to give people space and no big retail stores to bring the crowds. They sold liquor only in the "liquor store" and that was closed on Sundays. The town rolled up the carpet by eight every night and there was one high school, one junior high and only two elementary schools. The neighboring towns were all small as well. They were twenty minutes from the freeway and civilization. It was very small and cozy; Jenna loved it. There was only one traffic light in Clark's Town. There were a few restaurants, a furniture store, two hardware stores, two grocery stores, one tavern, a bowling alley, post office and antique stores. It was very different than the crowded, bustling, busy pace she was used to.

By Thursday, Jenna was sick. She was so upset about it. The timing was terrible.

Saturday night came and she was still sick. Jenna and Jack were discussing church the next day. She wanted him to go and check it out even though she couldn't go with him. She was going to have to stay behind in bed. She needed to get well. They still had another week to be there and needed to find a place to live. He argued, but eventually decided he would go.

Sunday came and he went to church.

"Jenna, you awake?" Jack tried to be quiet as he entered

the hotel room. She had the curtains closed and lights out, so the room was dark.

"Yes, just laying here. My eyes are burning so bad I couldn't do much else. Tell me all about church." She had been sitting on nails waiting to hear.

"Jenna, you'll love it. I walked into that building and felt at home. It's a small church around 65 people or so. A lot of them I met are from California including the Pastor, his wife and the Assistant Pastor. They have a small sanctuary. The worship was great. I like the way the pastor taught the Word and the people were really friendly." He was excited but had a funny smirk on his face.

"Sounds cool but did you talk to the pastor? What's he like and what's his name?"

"Yes, I talked to him. His name is Trent. You won't believe what happened. I walk in the door, people greet me; ask me my name, where I'm from and all that jazz. I tell them we're from Cali, up here looking for a place to live and a new church, all that stuff. They call the pastor over, introduce me, we shake hands and then he looks at me and says, 'So what terrible sin are you involved in that God would bring you to this church?' I'm so shocked all I can do is laugh. But he is looking at me with this look like he can see right through me. I couldn't speak. I'm thinking 'how does this guy know?' I was a little freaked out."

He looked like he'd been caught with his hand in the cookie jar.

Jenna immediately prayed in her heart. *Lord, that is the most amazing thing I have ever heard. You are going to work on my husband, and this sounds like the place that you are going to do that. You called him out, right there. You are incredible. I can't thank you enough for that. You will not let him get away with his sin and you are not going to let him hide here in Washington. Thank you.*

"Wow, he said that out loud?" Jenna couldn't believe it and couldn't keep that nervous smirk off her face.

"Yes, he said it out loud, right in front of about four other people and he stared me down. He wasn't joking; it was like he knew. I'm still freaked out about it." He shuttered like he was trying to shake it off.

"Man, that's kinda weird. Guess God's got your number doesn't He? How old is he-- could you tell?" Now she was smiling, she couldn't hold it back.

"He's our age. I guess he started the church with his wife about six years ago and his assistant's name is Jack too, he's from California and came up to help him start the church. They both are ex-alcoholic/drug addicts and surfers. I think you are going to love it. You gotta get better so you can go. I told them about you, and they all want to meet you."

"I'm so excited, I hope I get to go there before we leave. We still have to find a place to live even though I think we are going to live in the beach house."

"I just don't see how that is going to happen. It's already taken Jenna; they paid money and are approved and everything. We need to keep looking and praying. We have to be up here by August, so we need to move next month. We can't move if we don't have a place to move to." He was skeptical.

"I know that. I believe that beach house is where we are supposed to be. I know it's supposedly already taken but nothing is too hard for God." Jenna felt peace in her spirit, the beach house was hers, but she couldn't make Jack feel that way. So, they kept praying and they'd keep looking until they had to leave. There were only two other places in the area that met their price range, so they'd have to widen their search.

Jenna finally started to feel better the following week. They hadn't had any luck with housing and Sunday had arrived. They had left the hotel on Thursday and moved to a Bed & Breakfast that was right down the street from the church. It was beautiful, peaceful and just what she needed to feel more refreshed.

"I'm so excited about church today, I hope they like me. I can't wait to see it and meet the people." Jenna could hardly contain the excitement she felt.

"I am too. You are going to love it. You ready? We need to go so we aren't late."

"Ready." They got in the car and drove the six minutes to church. They walked in and everyone noticed them. Since they'd already met Jack the week before they were immediately interested in his wife, so they all stopped them to say hi. They asked how she was feeling and said they'd been praying for her. They were praying for her and they'd never met her. God was so awesome.

They made their way to the sanctuary and sat down. The worship team took the stage and had everyone stand. As soon as the first worship song began, Jenna closed her eyes and knew she was home. It was nothing she could verbally explain; she just knew she was home. This was the place that God wanted her to be planted, to grow, to live and to be a part of. She couldn't help but cry as she sang and thanked Him who had given her life...for His guidance...protection...love and that He cared enough to put her somewhere that she'd be safe and cared for, He was wonderful. This would be her new family. It was as if the Lord Himself said to her, "I got your back Jenna. I know you are scared; I know this is the biggest thing you've ever done. I see your concern that you will be all alone with a husband that deserts you for the bar and you're afraid. But, I see it all and I am watching over you. I will never leave you or forsake you and I've got you covered. You'll be safe here and my people will be with you and you'll be part of this family." He truly loved and cared for her.

"I love it Jack. I know this is where God wants us. Jesus made it so clear to me in there; this is my new home, my new church family. I knew it the moment that worship began. I can't explain it, I just know it." She was so overwhelmed that she was crying.

"I knew you'd like it. I believe it's where we are supposed to be, and I feel it too. Isn't it a great church? The people are so loving and full of Jesus."

"Yes, yes they are." They were both in awe of the new home that Jesus was giving them.

The following day they headed back to California, without a secured place to live.

Jenna put in her two-week notice so that by the first of July she'd be at home able to pack, plan and get them on the road. She gave notice to their landlord, so they had until the end of July to move out of their apartment.

They had no idea what they were going to do for a house, but Jenna still believed the beach house was going to be theirs.

Two weeks after they arrived home, they got the call; the beach house was theirs.

Everything was set in motion. They were moving.

"Behold how good and pleasant it is for brethren to dwell together in unity." Psalm 133:1 KJV

GOOD-BYE

J enna had a hard time leaving her job. She'd been there almost ten years, she loved her work and the people she worked with, especially Michelle. Her co-workers gave her a going away party. She cried at the thought of leaving but knew that God had called her to go and to trust Him. Michelle was so supportive of her and it gave her great comfort to know that she'd always be there for Jenna even if many miles separated them.

She was leaving security and comfort, friends and family all for the unknown. She was afraid that she'd be alone. She'd been alone so much in her life, she hated the thought of that, and Jack's drinking only added to the fear. Even with the new church she had to look forward to, she was still scared.

Jack had to stay at his job until they were ready to leave so Jenna had to take care of all the arrangements, packing and getting life set up in Washington.

Saying good-bye to family and church friends was difficult. Jack's parents and sister were sad to see him go but excited. Jenna's mom and sister were not so excited. Rachel and Jenna had just started to rebuild their relationship after Rachel's salvation. They had been able to spend more time together; go to church together and even went on a retreat. Rachel had been spending more time at their house, which was a blessing on one side and difficult on the other. Since Rachel was there more, she saw more. Jenna had to tell her about Jack's drinking. Rachel was angry. She didn't want to see anyone treat her sister badly and the fact that Jack was a Christian man made the offense inexcusable as far as Rachel was concerned. Rachel and Jenna still weren't very close with their mom, so they only had each other. Since her conversion, Rachel had been trying to make new Christian friends and wasn't having a lot of success, so Jenna was her closest friend. When Jenna told her they would be moving, she cried.

"I don't want you to go. What are you going to do there all by yourself? What if Jack keeps drinking, you won't have anyone there. What am I going to do? I don't have very many friends and you are my only family. Mom is in her own universe with her boyfriend and now I'll be left to fend for myself. You can't go Jenna."

"I know Bean. I wish it were different, but God is calling us to go and I can't disobey Him. I don't know what is going to happen, but I know this, He called me to go there, He has already shown me what church He wants me in, and I have to trust that He is going to work it out. I don't have all the answers. I'm going to miss you terribly and it is going to be very hard, but you can come visit me. Right?" Jenna was trying not to cry herself. She'd miss her family, what was left of it, but she had no choice.

Moving day came. They had turned Jack's car back in because it was a lease, so they had her little sports car and a U-Haul. They got the truck loaded, said their final good-byes, put Sox in his carrier and started off. They had made an agreement; Jack would not push Jenna to drive beyond her ability. She'd try to go as far as she could on any given day, and he wouldn't get mad if it took them longer than he wanted it to. She knew that she would only be able to take so many hours of driving a day and she would get too tired and her body would begin to hurt and shut down. She couldn't risk getting sick on the trip, so he'd agreed. He originally wanted to make it in 48 hours; she knew there was no way that would happen, so they'd had to negotiate.

The trip ended up taking them six days. It was an adventure for Jenna who'd never been outside of California. They had a few bumps along the way. Jenna's speedometer went out before they were out of California, which freaked her out and caused a fight. Jack had trouble with the air conditioner in the truck through the hottest part of the trip and Jenna's radio went out. All in all, it wasn't a bad trip, not one she'd want to jump at the chance of making again, but it all worked out and they arrived in Washington and at their beach house on July 25th, 1998. It was cloudy and 65 degrees, a big change from where she'd just come from. Jack had talked to a few of the young men at the church when they'd visited and took them up on the offer to help when they arrived. He tracked them down and they helped get the truck unloaded in record time and it only cost a trip to Dairy Queen for burgers and fries.

Now came the unwelcome task of unpacking and getting settled. Because of Jack's new position as a salesman for the company, she was going to be a stay-at-home wife. His company sold multi-million-dollar machines that were used in the sheet metal industry and he had a base salary plus commission. The cost of living was much cheaper in Clark's Town and he wanted her to stay home. She'd been working since she was fifteen, now at thirty-three she'd be at home taking care of her house and her husband; things were different.

They had to find him a car that he could use to travel around the Puget Sound area for his job but until they did he would have to use hers. They had to get the office set up for him, phone lines and a computer and all the supplies he'd need. Fortunately, she was good at organizing, planning and details so she had his office ready in no time.

"And whatever you do, do it heartily, as to the Lord and not to men..." Colossians 3:23 KJV

CHANGE OF SCENERY

Jenna got them settled. She loved her new home. She could walk out her door, down her driveway, across a small road that was only wide enough for one car, down her neighbors' driveway and she was on the beach. The weather wasn't beach weather, but she didn't care. She'd go walking everyday that it wasn't raining. It was so quiet and peaceful she couldn't believe she was still amongst civilization. She saw Bald Eagles almost everyday; she even had a raccoon that lived behind their house up the hill. Around the corner her neighbors had a horse and a donkey. She knew when the owners arrived home because she would hear the donkey, "hee haw, hee haw". She giggled every time she heard it. To her, it was the sweetest sound she'd ever had the privilege of hearing. Her neighbors had dogs that ran around the neighborhood. Their street only had about 25 houses on it and most of the people only lived there in the summer or visited for a few weeks every summer so it was very quiet, and the dogs could run freely. She enjoyed petting them and walking with them or throwing a stick for them on the beach. Captain Jack had gotten sick a few months before they moved and had died. She was devastated. Jack had to go into the room with him and the vet because she couldn't bear it. She'd had him since he was a baby. He'd been her one constant through so much. He was a huge comfort to her in the difficulty of her marriage. He made her laugh and she loved to walk him in their old neighborhood. It was a reprieve from the house and Jack. She missed him terribly and cried about him often. The neighborhood dogs were a gift from Jesus and filled that void in her life.

Jack started work almost immediately. He went out to visit his customers, introduce himself and started making contacts. He'd been sober since May when they went to Minnesota. He seemed to love living back in Washington and didn't mind driving around. He figured out the best and worst of the drive times and planned his days accordingly. He'd spend at least two days a week just doing paperwork and phone calls in the office. He had to learn a new program that managed his customers and familiarize himself with the different documents and procedures. Jenna helped him as much as possible. She spent hours on the phone with the computer software tech learning about the program so she could help him manage his customer base, filed paperwork for him and put all the customer information into the system once it was up and running. She answered his phone when he was gone and took messages for him. She asked him questions and learned about the different people he interacted with. She missed the work world but loved being at home and taking care of him.

Jenna saw each person that he worked with as someone that needed Jesus, including his new boss. They all knew that Jack and Jenna were Christians. None of them had any idea that Jack had returned to drinking. Some of his customers and co-workers were rough characters and his new boss was an old party buddy. They all took every opportunity to take shots and make fun of his new "religious" life.

Everything was moving along well. They had gone to an auction and picked up an old Crown Victoria that was once a police car for him to drive for work. They loved their new church and the people that were there. They went on Sunday morning, Sunday evening and Wednesday nights.

Then September came.

September is the start of football season and Jack still loved football. Unfortunately, Jack couldn't watch football without drinking. Sports were not the problem; the real problem was between Jack and Jesus. Sports were a convenient excuse for indulging his rebellion and so it began all over again.

She thought it was God's sense of humor that he would drive that old cop car on his excursions to the bar. Only it wasn't very funny. But at least he had his own car to drive to the bar and wouldn't take hers.

"As a dog returns to his vomit, so a fool returns to his folly."
Proverbs 26:11 KJV

LOST YEARS

When Jack began to drink again in September of 1998, Jenna knew it was going to be a long road. He had been sober since they arrived. For him to turn back to his sinful ways told her that he had a long way to go before he was done. The Lord had given her the promise of Hosea 14:4 and she clung to it, but it was a difficult, painful, long-suffering road. Shortly after he began to drink again, she had to tell their new pastor. It was a small town, a small church and a small community of believers so everyone knew everyone else and noticed everything. The first few times Jack wasn't at a Sunday service she could tell them he was out of town or not feeling well, but she couldn't keep that up for long, so the truth came out.

It was business as usual. Same pattern. Same anger. Same manipulation of the money. Same accusations.

Jenna was blessed to have people in her new church that loved her, loved Jack, were godly, supportive people that prayed constantly for the situation. Which was a good thing for many reasons, but she especially needed it for what was coming down the road.

In January of 1999, Jack decided that he was tired of driving to the bar to get drunk and wanted to be able to do it in the privacy of his own home.

One Sunday she was gone to church under the assumption that he was at the bar because he'd left a note. She went home expecting to find an empty house that would remain that way until sometime around 11 p.m.

Jenna pulled into the driveway and noticed immediately a small satellite dish attached to the house. She walked thru the door into the kitchen where she saw a cutting board that was covered with blood and meat scraps, a dirty butcher knife and dirty dishes all over the counter. She walked into the living room and saw the door to the spare room was closed; she knew it was open when she'd left for church. What in the world is going on? *Please God let me be wrong, tell me he didn't put up a satellite dish and that he is not sitting in our house getting drunk--please I can't take that.*

Jenna was so angry she didn't know what to do. It was bad enough that he was drinking but to bring it into their home was beyond what she could handle. Her house was her safe place, her place of peace and it belonged to Jesus and now he was defiling it with his drinking. She wanted to go break down the door of the room he was in and ask him what the heck he thought he was doing. But, her conviction got the better of her and so she went about her work of changing her clothes, cleaning up his mess and making lunch.

She was in the kitchen making lunch when she heard the bedroom door open. She held her breath and prayed a silent prayer for help.

"Jack is that you?" She tried to sound casual.

"Yeah, what do want?" He was obviously irritated and was headed to the bathroom

"Um, is that a satellite dish on the roof? We don't have a T.V. What is going on? You didn't tell me you were getting cable." She tried to control the anger in her voice and not sound like a nagging wife. She wasn't very successful.

"Yes it is and we have a T.V. now and I'm going to go to the bathroom and then go back in the room and finish watching the game. Any problem with that?" He was drunk and angry, and not even attempting to hide his anger.

"So, you're drinking beer in our house?"

"Yes, got a problem with that?" He was begging for a fight.

"Yes, but I'm not going to talk to you about it right now. Have fun watching the game." She went into their room and closed the door. She broke down. She knew that the Lord didn't want her to have an attitude or say what she'd said to him. She didn't want to live with him sitting in the room getting drunk. What was she going to do?

For the rest of the afternoon she tried to stay out of his way. She ate lunch, took a nap, listened to Christian radio and waited for time to pass. He only made an appearance if he had to go to the bathroom.

She went back to church that night and told Pastor Trent. They prayed for her. She felt better until she had to go home. He was still in his room when she arrived. She didn't sleep much that night. She cried mostly. Well, broke down and sobbed convulsively is more like it. She couldn't bare the thought of him sitting in there destroying his life. It broke her heart to think of him drinking himself to death right under her nose and she couldn't do a thing about it. She knew there was nothing she could say or do, no magic words, no magic wand, nothing. The Lord had told her to be silent and trust Him. Over and over she'd been given 1 Peter 3:1, "Wives, likewise, be submissive to your own husbands, that even if some do not obey the Word, they, without a word may be won by the conduct of their wives." She was crying so hard that he heard her, over the T.V. He kept stepping out of his room and listening, trying to figure out what the noise was. She would hold her breath and stifle her cries when she heard the door click open. It was a long night.

The satellite dish stayed along with the T.V. It was the most difficult time so far. She cried out to the Lord. She needed something from Him so that she could walk through this time. One day she was home alone crying and praying, *Lord, I don't know what to do. I can't handle him being in the room, drinking, destroying his life and our marriage. He is drinking more than ever; I don't even know how much he is drinking now but he is doing it more frequently and I can see that his health is deteriorating. The only thing we have is a marriage on paper. There is nothing left, it is desolate and barren. It is empty and I feel like I'm the only person that cares. He doesn't seem to care about anything except drinking. Please, please help me Jesus, please I need You to speak to me. I can't go on; I feel so alone and afraid. Please help me.*

Then she heard that still small Voice, "Jeremiah 33:10-11". She turned to the passage in her Bible.

"Thus says the Lord; Again there shall be heard in this place which you say is desolate without man and without beast, even in the cities of Judah, and in the streets of Jerusalem, that are desolate, without man and without inhabitant and without beast, the voice of joy and voice of gladness, the voice of the bridegroom and the voice of the bride, the voice of them that shall say, Praise the Lord of hosts: for the Lord is good; for His mercy endures forever; and of them that shall bring the sacrifice of praise into the house of the Lord. For I will cause to return the captivity of the land, as at the first says the Lord." (KJV)

She was so blown away. Once again she knew that He'd spoken to her. He was telling her, again, that He was going to heal her marriage. Nothing in her circumstances had changed but she had peace. She had something to hold onto again.

Now she had to continue to trust and wait. He'd given her the strength to carry on.

Jack had a few weeks here and there of sobriety. Some of the men in the church tried to reach out to him and help him but he wouldn't follow through for any length of time. He always went back to beer and self-destruction.

Thanksgiving 1999 came, and they were invited over to a family's house for worship, Bible study and dinner. She went ahead alone because Jack wanted to go talk to one of the men in the church. She was there for about two hours when the phone rang.

"Jenna, it's for you, it's Jack" Karen handed her the

phone.

"Hello Jack, what's up? When you gonna get here?"

"Well, that's why I'm calling. I'm not showing up. I wanted to know if you could come over here. I'm at Sid's house. I need to talk to you." His voice sounded nervous and somber.

"Um, sure. I'll be there in about 20 minutes. Is everything OK? What's going on?"

"Yes, everything is fine. I will tell you what's going on, but I want to do it person. Can you come over here please?" He sounded scared.

The butterfly in her stomach took flight. She hated that feeling. She was scared and didn't want to face whatever it was, but she had no choice. She said her good-byes and got in her car. She prayed the whole way, asking for help with whatever was about to come her way and for wisdom to handle it. She got there and went in. They sat on the couch together and Sid started the conversation.

"Jenna, Jack and I have been talking and he has a few things he needs to tell you. I know that it won't be easy, but he needs to tell you. Jack, go ahead." He gave Jack the nod.

"Jenna, I have to tell you a few things. I know this is going to be hard for you to hear but I know it's what God wants. Remember when we had the conversation in the car before we got married, you know about whatever I do you'll know? Well, besides drinking I have been looking at pornography. I used to look at it before I was saved with my ex-wife and after I got saved I stopped for a few months but then I started again. I'm sorry to tell you this Jenna. Please forgive me, I'm sorry." He was crying.

"What do you mean?" Jenna had never dealt with pornography before. She didn't understand what he meant.

"Well, when I'm traveling I watch porn on T.V., sometimes movies that are pay per view, sometimes just on HBO and sometimes I buy magazines." He had his head dropped down and was looking at the floor.

"Oh, I see. Have you ever cheated on me with another woman?" Jenna was calm, not crying but in shock.

"No, no Jenna, no way. I know that looking at porn is bad, but I've never touched another woman. Please believe me. I know that I haven't been honest with you about my drinking and the porn and you have no reason to believe me, but I haven't cheated on you."

"Alright, is there anything else? I don't know what else to ask or what else to say." She felt sick and wanted to run.

"No, I've told you everything now. I'm sorry that I didn't tell you before and that I've kept it from you this whole time, but I have no other secrets Jenna, as God as my witness I have no other secrets." He looked scared.

Sid was very calm. He could tell that Jenna needed to get home and process what she'd just been told.

"OK, we should pray. Jack you start and ask God to forgive you."

Jack prayed. He asked for God's forgiveness and for God to help Jenna forgive him. He prayed to be set free from the addiction and to live as a godly man. They got done and left. Jenna got in her car and Jack in his.

Jenna felt like a magnitude eight earthquake had just moved through her body.

She started her car and pulled out of the driveway. She had 20 minutes worth of drive time before she'd land in their driveway and face Jack, their house and sleeping in the same bed. She was so angry and hurt she knew that her only salvation was Jesus and that if she didn't cry out to Him immediately, she'd never be able to step foot in the house and look Jack in the face.

She finally began to pray out loud. *"Lord, I am going to chose by faith to forgive this man. I am asking You to help me to let go of everything that I am going through right now. I'm mad, hurt, frustrated and so angry with him I want to smack him, scream at him and run away. Please Jesus help me to forgive him, I am begging You to take the images out of my head that are there now. I don't want to think of all the naked women and sexual garbage that he has looked at and I don't want it in my head."* Jenna began to cry and couldn't restrain herself any longer. She slammed her hands down on the steering wheel and screamed at the top of her lungs through her tears. *"I CAN'T TAKE ONE MORE THING FROM THIS MAN! I can't take one more lie, one more surprise, one more deceitful, conniving, thing. How much am I supposed to take from him, when is it going to end Lord, I can't take it anymore."*

She was convulsively crying now and almost home. She didn't want to face him, talk to him or hear any more apologies. She desperately needed Jesus and wanted to be with Him. She pulled into the driveway and went into the house. Sox greeted her at the door as usual. She picked him up and rubbed his soft head. He purred and let out little meow asking for his food. Jack was already home and in their bedroom. She got food and put it in the cat's dish. On the ledge between their living room and kitchen sat their little portable stereo. It was always on the local Christian station and was playing softly. Jenna went over and turned it up to full volume, got on her hands and knees in the middle of the living room floor and sang at the top of her lungs and cried. Jack stayed in their bedroom. She must have been there for 30 minutes just singing and crying to one song after another. Finally, she felt as though she'd been lifted on wings and carried into the peace and safety of her Lord. She got up, got ready for bed and went to sleep, peacefully.

The next day, Jenna got up and immediately went into the living room, opened her Bible and began to read and pray. The moment she'd opened her eyes she was assaulted with images, thoughts, anger, hurt and fear. She felt that some how she was to blame for Jack's porn addiction. She'd never dealt with the issue of porn addiction. She had no idea how it affected men, why they did it, or what it looked like lived out in their lives. All she knew was that she felt like Jack had cheated on her and betrayed her. She felt dirty and vulnerable.

He was very quiet and somber when he got up. He acted

as though any minute she was going to verbally blast him. In fact, he acted like he wished she would.

Jenna continued to pray fervently for the Lord to heal her and free her. She began to realize through time and prayer that Jack's porn addiction was the reason for his anger and accusations regarding their sex life. She finally understood why she felt like there was an invisible wall between them; it was because there was. A wall built of lies, deceit, sin, guilt, drunkenness and porn. She also realized that her dad had a porn addiction. She'd never thought about it before but as she learned more about it through talking with Jack, seeing the effects of it firsthand and talking to their pastor, she realized that her dad was an addict. He always had Playboy magazines and other girly magazines around the house. It was a plague that invaded homes, minds, marriages and created sick and destructive behavior. Jenna had been exposed to it herself growing up with the magazines around the house and movies that she'd been allowed to watch, but she never understood what a destructive virus it was, until it was in her marriage.

Now, there were two issues to deal with when Jack traveled: drinking and porn. There was still nothing she could do about either one of them except pray and do her part to love, obey and serve the Lord. She was only responsible for her relationship with Jesus and how that affected the lives of others around her, she was not responsible for Jack. She was glad about that except she wished that she could pop open his head like a Pez dispenser and pull out all the junk and pour in the desire to repent and follow Jesus.

"For there is nothing hid, which shall not be manifested; neither was any thing kept secret..." Mark 4:22 KJV

Y2K - NOTHING
HAPPENED

J anuary 2000 came and went without much fanfare. Jack had to travel a couple times a year and was still drinking and looking at porn. He confessed to her now each time he looked at porn and that did make a difference in the frequency, however, he still looked at it and that still hurt!

Since Jack's drinking problem had been going on the entire time of their marriage, she had sought counsel on different occasions from a few pastors and several had told her that she should leave him. He was unrepentant, dangerous to himself and others and she needed to move away and let God deal with him. She didn't believe that was the will of God. He'd given her the promises that He was going to heal Jack and their marriage and every time she prayed, she knew she was to stay and trust in God.

In March, Rachel got married. Jenna and Jack were able to go, and Jenna was her matron of honor. The wedding was beautiful. Jenna cried as she watched her little bird take flight. Rachel looked breathtaking. She was all grown up. Now she would have her own house, her own marriage struggles, her own husband and lessons. It was hard on them both being separated by so many miles. Jenna wouldn't be able to be there if Rachel needed her to be because they were separated by two states. It was hard enough Rachel being single and far away but now she'd be married. She wanted Rachel to be loved, cared for, cherished and protected. She wanted her to have all the pain of the past washed away in the love and security of a home and a husband. But she had no control over any of it. Once again she had to surrender Rachel to Jesus. Pray for Rachel to continue to follow Jesus and for her marriage to be centered on Him. They had been able to build their relationship back up some as they stayed in touch over the phone. They missed each other so much.

May of 2000, Jenna had a breakdown. Jack had been on a binge for a few weeks, was drinking in his little "den of iniquity" as he called it and Jenna's health was beginning to breakdown dramatically. Her body was in constant pain, she was sick all the time. She could sleep for 12 hours and still be exhausted, and she was an emotional wreck. It was frustrating to her because she was doing all that she could to stay connected to the Lord, deal with her emotions and trust in God. But, she had to admit she was tired. Jack was constantly angry, nit-picking at her, spending money they didn't have and criticizing their church and their pastor. He would give her the silent treatment for days and on more than one occasion he'd pushed at her and picked at her until she finally blew her top and then he would mock her for loosing her temper. The pastor and some of the men in the church had tried to talk to him, been kind and gentle, honest and tough, called him out and tried to reason with him. They'd made themselves available to him any time he wanted to talk, was tempted or struggled. The pastor was always accessible, but Jack never took them up on the offers or heeded their advice, warnings or rebukes. Everyone in their new church loved him and prayed for him. They were very supportive of Jenna and were more like family than a church, but Jack continued his destructive behavior.

One Sunday she and Jack left the house in his car to drive to church, halfway there, Jack said he needed to go home because he felt sick. So, Jenna turned around and took him home.

She told him she'd just take her car in case he needed his and he told her no, he'd be staying home. Jenna had a very uneasy feeling about the whole situation but what could she do? She went to church in his car. After church was over she went home. When she pulled into the driveway her car was gone. She knew in an instant that he'd left and gone to the bar and had taken her car. Sure enough, she went into the house to find the note. She was so angry she completely lost control. She was ranting and raving and yelling at the top of her lungs at a husband who wasn't there. She couldn't believe he'd had the nerve to take her car and drive to the bar. After all this time, the four years of drinking and all the things he'd done, this one pushed her over the edge. She took great care of her car, it was like new, it was paid off and now he took it, was going to sit in a bar for 12 hours, drink the equivalent of a case of beer and drive for over an hour home, drunk. To her it was one of the most inconsiderate, in your face gestures he'd made. All the times he'd driven drunk and not even gotten pulled over, this would be the one time, he'd probably crash. It was a good thing it would be hours before he was home because it was going to take her a while to calm down. She knew what she had to do and eventually she'd get there, but she was angry!

She went back to church that night and talked to her pastor. He had previously told Jenna that it could get to a point where she'd have to separate so that she was out of the way. She could get the rest she needed and hopefully it would move Jack to repentance and brokenness. She'd balked at it, argued with it and felt that it was not even an option, until now. She acknowledged that she was just emotionally, spiritually and physically spent and this was the last straw. As minor as it was, it was the final push.

"To deliver such a one unto Satan for the destruction of the flesh, that the spirit may be saved in the day of the Lord Jesus." 1 Corinthians 5:5 KJV

FAITH

J ack came home in one piece along with the car. She said nothing to him until the next day. No use talking to someone who is inebriated anyway.

"Jack, we need to talk."

He was hung over and sullen. He never wanted to talk the day after he got drunk, maybe two days later he might apologize but not always.

"What about?" He sounded defensive and tired. His face was blank. He looked like the most miserable person on the planet. It was obvious to her that being in their house talking to her was the last place he wanted to be.

Jenna took a breath. She'd been praying practically all night and was scared out of her mind.

"Well, I think we need to separate. I talked with Pastor Trent and I've prayed about it a lot. I think you need some space and so do I. I don't want a divorce or anything like that, it would only be temporary and with reconciliation as the goal along with your sobriety." She was holding her breath.

"Alright, whatever you think, that's fine with me. I'll take care of the bills and you do what you need to do." He was so resigned and took it so well it was a little frightening.

Jenna hadn't realized that she was not only holding her breath but every muscle in her body was tensed up. She finally took a breath and let it all go, her body relaxed, and she was able to continue.

"Um, well, I'm gonna move in with Melody in town. She has an apartment and it has an extra bedroom and we talked about it last night at church. You can stay here because you have your job to do and all your work stuff is here. So, I'll just need money to help her with rent and to buy groceries and gas. I won't need much. Is that alright?" She felt bad. She just wanted him to break, repent and have it all fixed. She didn't want to move out, have a failed marriage, leave Jack alone, have people talk, most importantly she didn't want to be doing the wrong thing before the Lord.

"Thanks, I appreciate that. That's fine. Just let me know what you need. When do you think you are going to move?" He was sitting on the couch with his head back staring at the ceiling.

"Next weekend if that is alright with you. I won't need to take much. I'll take Sox, my clothes, a few books, my toiletries, the cat stuff and that's about it. I don't really need much else so it will be easy for me to move. I'll have to find a bed somewhere and I guess I'll take my dresser but that's about it. I'm sorry Jack. I don't know what else to say." She was starting to cry.

"It's not your fault Jenna. It's mine. I'm sorry to put you through all this. I am sorry I took your car; that was a messed-up thing for me to do. I didn't want our marriage to be this way. I'm sorry. I totally understand why you need to leave, and I don't blame you. I know I blame you sometimes when we fight and I accuse you, but I know deep down, it's my fault. I want to stop; I just don't know how. I wish God would just zap me and make me not drink." He was looking down at the ground now and tears were falling from his face. He was so dejected, defeated and miserable, but he still wouldn't reach out for help.

Jenna couldn't understand it. She knew in her heart of hearts that according to the Bible he had the power to overcome it; he was simply choosing to give in. For whatever reason, he wasn't done with his sin. As hard as it was to look at it that way and accept it, the Bible didn't lie and therefore the problem was with Jack and the choices he was making. As complicated as it seemed sometimes, she knew that sin was simply sin. It wasn't rational, reasonable, understandable or logical, it was just sin. The Lord had told her a year before to stop racking her brain and trying to understand it because she never would, she simply had to accept it and pray for his repentance.

People were always giving her suggestions to help him repent. Pin notes to his pillow with Bible verses on them, take his wallet, hide his keys, follow him to the bar and go in and sit down and make him have to drink right in front of her, put Bible verses up all over the house and the list went on. Jenna had to admit she'd battled through her own thoughts of "helping" him. She'd thought on more than one occasion that she could call the cops, give them his license plate number and description, tell them where he was and what time he'd be leaving and that if they waited they'd have an easy DUI arrest. She'd prayed that he'd throw up every time he took a sip of beer. She'd thought of getting all dressed up, walking into the bar where he was, sitting down, ordering a beer and watching him squirm. But, she knew these were all futile and sinful things of her flesh. So, she prayed, waited, forgave and loved him to the best of her ability in the power of Jesus. None of those things would change him anyway, but more importantly, she knew it wasn't God's will for her. She felt so helpless at times.

The weekend came and she moved. It was the hardest thing she'd ever done in her life. She felt like a failure. They'd said their good-byes and hugged, and Jack cried and said he was sorry about twenty times. She couldn't stop crying. She felt empty, defeated, alone and scared. What if he never sobered up, or if he got arrested or ended up in the hospital or dead? What if she never got her marriage back? What if he just dies alone in a drunken stupor? How could this be happening? They had Jesus! If you have Jesus this stuff isn't supposed to happen! She had prayed, waited and married at the Lord's direction. How could this be happening? Jenna hadn't felt this empty, alone, hurting and defeated since her pre-Jesus days.

She got settled into the apartment. It was June. She found a bed from someone in the church and got it moved in. She had to go shopping to stock up on food for herself and Sox and put stuff away but other than those things; she was at a loss as to what to do with herself.

Melody was young, twenty-one and sweet. She had a lot of spunk, was funny and shared a love of Jesus and the Bible with Jenna. They knew each other from church and Melody, although she was young, was wise in her approach to Jenna. She knew it was hard for Jenna. She knew the basic situation Jenna was in and didn't press her for information; talk bad about Jack or interfere in any way other than to say she was sorry and to pray for Jenna.

For the first two weeks all Jenna could do was cry. She couldn't process the whole ordeal. She believed that if Jesus was part of the equation, it could not fail. Especially when it came to marriage. Jesus never fails. So, if He is living in the hearts of those involved, He is the God of the Universe, then how could a marriage fall apart? She couldn't get past it. It was so confounding to her logical brain.

One night she was lying in bed staring at the ceiling, pondering and crying. She cried out to God for help, she was going insane trying to reconcile it and she heard the familiar Voice, "You must have faith" simple, direct, profound and exactly what she needed to hear. She finally was able to go sleep.

The next day she got up, spent time in the Bible and then began to clean the apartment. Melody kept it neat, but she wasn't exactly a clean-the-floors-and-scrub-the-sinks kind of girl, so Jenna did it. She was there, had nothing to do and nervous energy to expend, cleaning worked. She found a large piece of paper and some crayons and wrote in big colorful letters the word "FAITH" and taped it to the ceiling above her bed so that every time she lay in bed, she'd see it. Her daily devotions were all about faith and even those around her were constantly reminding her, she had to hold on and be obedient, trusting by faith that He had it all under control.

Now, being in a little church in a little community was a challenge for a couple that's separated. They had discussed with the pastor how they should handle church.

He looked at Jack and said, "Jack you need to get your eyes on Jesus and off your wife. If you want to be sober, you'll show up to every service and focus on Jesus and what He wants to say to you and not on your wife. Don't sit next to her, if she wants to talk to you, she will, otherwise you just hang out with the guys, get sober and God will take care of the rest. Jenna, you need to continue to serve the Lord like you have been. Don't worry about Jack; you'll see the change before you hear it and you won't have to wonder what is going on. If you want to talk to him, you can, otherwise you need to get refreshed and refocused." He was compassionate and understanding but firm in his direction to them. They needed that.

They followed the advice of their pastor and although it was weird, it wasn't uncomfortable. It was helpful to know where they stood, what needed to happen and the desired goal. They weren't on hostile terms or in the middle of a bitter disagreement. He was understanding and kind if Jenna needed something. They still loved each other very much and Jack understood Jenna's heart in all of it so there was no animosity.

They'd been separated almost two months when one day the pastor called Jenna.

"Hey Jenna, I'd like you to pray about something for me. I need a secretary to run things down here at the church, help me with my appointments, keep me organized and to help the church, I've spoken to Jack and he agrees with me. We both think you'd be an excellent secretary. Would you pray about it?" Jenna was caught off guard.

"Um, I guess, yeah sure. But, why did you pick me? I'm not church secretary material, I mean that is like a huge deal."

She was so shocked. She remembered one Sunday when they'd been at the church for about a month, she was standing there listening to the pastor, assistant pastor and another guy discuss who was responsible for some paperwork that didn't get filed on time. She stood there thinking, *wow, they need a secretary to help them be organized.* She'd never said it out loud, hadn't thought about it since nor had she thought she'd be the one for the job.

"Well, I believe that you are mature enough in your faith to handle it for one thing. You'll see all my weaknesses and mistakes, hear a lot of private things, see a lot of the inner workings of the church and I believe you are mature enough to handle them and to continue with your work and service without it changing your view of me or the church or shaking your faith. I also believe you have the integrity to handle it. Jack feels you can as well, but I know you will want to pray about it and talk to him about it so let me know." He was so confident and sure of what he felt God wanted him to do.

"OK, I'll pray about it. Thank you for thinking of me and for feeling that I could handle it, I don't know what else to say. I'll talk to Jack, pray and let you know by next week. Does that work?"

"Yes, that's great."

Jenna hung up the phone and sat in stunned silence. Why would anyone think those things about Jenna Clark Jenkins? She wasn't church secretary material--that was for holy people, people that had some special something from the Lord and that definitely wasn't her. She was just ordinary, struggling to survive, not godly, Jenna. She didn't know what to do with it all. She was flattered that her pastor thought that highly of her, but she couldn't figure out why. She was separated from her husband, what was he thinking? She collected her thoughts and decided to call Jack. She didn't know what it would accomplish but she wanted to ask him what had transpired in his conversation with their pastor.

"Hey Jack, how are you?"

"Good. I bet I know exactly why you're calling me." He sounded sober and a little mischievous.

"Yeah, well, I just got off the phone with Pastor Trent and I don't know what to think. I guess you talked to him and so I wanted to hear what happened."

"Well, he called and asked me what I thought about you being the church secretary. He wanted to know if it was OK with me, did I think you could handle it physically, did I think you'd be alright with all the drama and privacy stuff and seeing his shortcomings and I said yes to all of them. How's that for a summation?" He sounded proud that the pastor would ask his wife to do that. *Weird!*

"You said yes? What did you say that for? I'm not church secretary material. I've never done that before. It kind of freaks me out and what if I can't do it?" Jenna was trying not to sound panicky and trying not to cry. Her emotions were so raw that anything made her cry these days.

"Jenna, I totally think you can handle it. You're awesome at helping me, you worked for cops for goodness sake, how much more top secret and difficult can it get! You have kept me organized and done so much for me here in the office. You're smart, you're a fast learner, you're godly, and I believe you can do it and that God wants you to do it. I'm not saying you have to. You pray about it and make the decision yourself but I'm just saying I have peace about it and feel like it's the Lord." In that moment he sounded like the man she had married four years before. She missed that man.

Jenna sat in silence for a minute. She didn't know what to say. She was shocked, overwhelmed, and insecure and now she was being asked to take on this responsibility.

"Alright, thanks for all that. I'll pray about it. I just hope I can hear what the Lord wants me to do. I feel off kilter right now, super emotional and kind of scared. I hate being scared. I'm gonna go and just try to think and pray. Thanks for talking to him and for the encouragement, I appreciate it. And thanks for the confidence you have in me. I love you."

"I love you too Jenna. Don't be afraid, it's gonna be alright. You just have to trust the Lord. I'll talk to you later."

Jenna prayed about it for a few days and although she didn't feel very confident, she believed it to be God's will for her to take the position. It wasn't going to pay much, but it would help her out. She'd be working Tuesday through Friday, eight to five. Jenna knew absolutely nothing about the inner workings of a church, the inner workings of her pastor or all that the job would bring her way. She could balance a checkbook, answer the phone, use the computer, type at a pretty good pace and had good people skills, but it was a church! This was another testing, strengthening and stretching of her faith. That seemed to be the theme of her life right now.

For the first eight weeks she worked on balancing the checkbook, rearranging the filing system, learning about the different things she would need to be responsible for and trying to get the office organized. She went home brain tired everyday. She had a few phone calls, but she basically worked on organizing and rearranging. It was hard to get used to being at work again, but she had the advantage of it being casual. She could listen to Christian radio, and she had a Christian boss.

She talked to Jack on a weekly basis because they had to discuss bills, money and various things. He had gotten rid of the satellite dish, which was a relief to her. He was staying sober, working, going to church and had started to attend Alcoholics Anonymous. Jenna felt a little weird about that but if it was helping him to stay sober, then she figured God would work it out. She wanted him to be accountable and develop friendships with the men in the church and not a sponsor through AA that didn't even believe in God. But she knew that she had to allow him to work that out and that the Lord would be faithful to bring him around, some day. He had promised her.

They stayed separated until November. Jack had stayed sober and wanted Jenna to return home. She didn't feel confident that he was completely done. There were things that nagged at her gut, things that she had always figured when he really got sober would be talked about and changed. She couldn't articulate that to anyone, nor could she say that it had been clearly demonstrated in Jack, but she was being encouraged by her pastor to go home. So, in November she went home. Everything went fine. Jenna still had a lot of hurt that needed to be healed and still had a nagging sensation that it wasn't over, but she did what she was supposed to do and gave him space and God time.

In January of 2001, they moved into their first house. Jenna was happy at the beach house, but Jack felt like they were wasting money renting. Jenna didn't care about owning a home. First, she loved living by the beach, secondly she reasoned that should something happen, and they could no longer pay the rent, they'd move to a cheaper place; no muss, no fuss, no bad credit. If they owned a home and finances went bad they'd have a big "f" on their record, she'd feel like a loser and they'd have to move. Who in their right mind would want to rent to someone who couldn't pay their mortgage? Jack worked on commission and their income was never steady, so renting was easier. She also liked the fact that should something break in the house, the landlord had to pay to fix it. If they had their own house it would fall on them. But, in the end, Jack won out and they moved.

Jenna liked the house well enough. She'd have preferred to live on acreage, she wasn't thrilled with the carpet in the house, but it was a nice house. It was around 1,900 square feet, three bedrooms and two baths. It was built in 1994 by the previous owner and had been sitting empty for two years. The kitchen was huge. It had an island that contained the sink and dishwasher and a ton of counter and cabinet space. There was a breakfast bar, a formal dinning room, and an office with a half wall so Jack could work and still be part of the rest of the house. It had huge windows without any drapes and several skylights. All the ladies in the church loved the kitchen but all of them said the same thing, "you need drapes". Jenna loved the windows and wouldn't dream of putting drapes on them. It let a lot of light in, allowed her to see the beauty of the Northwest and gave the house a bigger more open feeling. The bedrooms and bathrooms had blinds of course. There was a woodstove in the corner of the living room so they could burn wood to keep the house warm, a laundry room, two-car garage and a huge walk-in closet in the master bedroom. The house was on a small block. There were only twelve houses on it and at the end of the road was a huge pasture with a horse. They were only six minutes away from the church and oddly enough their pastor lived two doors down from them!

They settled in. Jenna struggled a little to work full-time, help Jack and take care of the house. She still had health issues and they had begun to get worse. She had a great deal of body fatigue, body aches and felt very tired but she kept going.

Work was going well for her. She was learning a lot, getting to know the pastor better and figuring out ways to help him be more organized, efficient and relieve some of the pressure and burden off him. He was enjoying having a secretary and they developed a very good working relationship. He was the same age as Jenna and had grown up in Southern California. He never finished high school because he was too busy surfing. He was Italian, 5'11", olive skin, blue eyes and black hair. He still dressed like he was in California, weather permitting, and he constantly had a coffee in his hand. He was a good Bible teacher, had a great sense of humor, loved hanging out with the kids, and enjoyed sports. He was also very forgetful. He lost his keys more times than any human being she'd ever known. She finally started carrying a spare set of his house and car keys with her so he could get in his house or vehicle if he lost his. The amazing thing was every time it happened, Jenna would pray and then he'd inevitably find them. He was terrible with organizing himself and keeping his appointments straight. Like Trevor from long ago it was difficult at times to have a conversation with him because he wouldn't stay focused. His mind was always wandering. Sometimes he had a drum beat in his head, other times a drawing that needed to be put on paper or canvas. They had two small children at home and his wife was home schooling a niece, so she had enough on her plate. She was beautiful. She was small at about 5'5" and around 105 lbs. She had brown hair and blue eyes, was sweet, gentle, smart and very godly. She handled his crazy hours and even crazier ideas like a pro. He was very unconventional, and she rolled with the punches smiling and supporting him.

Jenna was on the inside of the pastoral life and the inner workings of the church and it was very different than what she'd thought it would be. She understood now, why he'd made it a point to say to her that she'd see a side of him that other people didn't.

The Lord began to bring women to the office and Jenna found herself talking with them and giving them Biblical counsel. She'd never asked for it, or even considered it, but God brought them and gave her words to share with them. She tried to learn as much as possible from the leaders in the church and from her pastor. She listened, asked questions and was willing to help them and serve them in any way possible. Her job as secretary began to evolve over time into a "jack of all trades" position. She helped wherever she could; shopping, organizing, and cleaning out closets, and anything else that she could help with or that no one else was available to do. She began to feel like she was finally where God wanted her to be and fulfilling His call on her life.

Things were changing in her life, some good, some not so good but one thing was always constant, Jesus. She was grateful for that.

"Therefore, whether you eat or drink or whatever you do, do all to the glory of God." 1 Corinthians 10:31 KJV

LIFE GOES ON, WHETHER WE LIKE IT OR NOT

Shortly before they bought the house, Sox died. When he was around two, the vet discovered a heart condition. Although she had him checked many times at different vets, no one seemed to be able to cure or manage it. One day he'd had an episode and she'd taken him to the vet. It was the worse episode he'd ever had. They tried to help him but in the end she had to watch helplessly as he slowly began to suffocate because he wasn't getting oxygen, so they had to put him down. She cried for weeks over him. He'd been an amazing cat. He acted more like a dog than a cat the way he followed her around, played fetch and snuggled with her. So, after they bought the house, the ladies at church decided that Jenna needed a pet. She was, after all, an animal lover and she had an empty space to fill since Sox had died. Enter, Samson. They'd picked him up at the animal shelter at eight weeks old, wrapped a big purple bow around him and gave him to Jenna. Her initial reaction on the inside was dread. She knew the challenges of raising a puppy and her schedule was full. He was very cute. She couldn't send him back to the shelter, so she took him home. He was a German Shepherd/Burmese

Mountain Dog mix. He was black with a thick undercoat down his back. His muzzle was black, and his face was tan with black eyebrows, tan legs and large white paws. She knew he was going to be a big dog! She loved large dogs but it meant diligent training so he wouldn't be an obnoxious oversized puppy. Good thing she'd traded her sports car for a Toyota Land Cruiser, he wouldn't have fit in her car.

She took him home. The first night she slept on the couch with him curled up on her chest and from that moment on, he belonged to her and she belonged to him. He was as cute as any puppy could be but naughty as any puppy she'd ever seen. He was strong willed, and it took her quite a few months to figure out the best way to train him. Until she figured that out, she lost a phone charger, a comforter, a pair of sandals, the nose off a handmade doll and some plaster off the laundry room wall. He was a handful! And as much fun as he was work.

He got carsick every time she put him in the car. She would barely get out of her driveway and he would start throwing up. She started to carry a bucket and trained him to barf in it, but it had to change. She began to wonder if at some point it had become psychological, so she asked the vet about it. Her vet told her to give him a dose of Dramamine, gave her the amount and she tried it. It worked! He never got sick again.

Once he was potty trained, done being car sick and old enough to behave without constant supervision, she began to take him to work with her. Pastor Trent was a dog lover and Samson was pretty irresistible, so he gave her permission. Samson would stay in the office with her, wander around the church and at lunch she'd take him out and work with him. She trained him to stay within the church property lines and that was that. He became her constant companion. She took him to work, the store, running errands and anywhere else she could. He followed her around the house and never let her out of his sight. He became a part of her. She taught him the stand-ard things--sit, stay, lay down, and added many other things to his skill set.

He was a lot of work but well worth it.

Jack wasn't much help. He liked Samson but wasn't very patient with him and left the work up to Jenna.

Jack was beginning to show signs of returning to drinking. Jenna wasn't sure if it was the inner voice of the Lord preparing her for the inevitable or her observation skills, maybe a combination of both, but either way she could tell he was heading back down that road again.

"That which has been is what will be, that which is done is what will be done, and there is nothing new under the sun." Ecclesiastes 1:9

IS IT GROUNDHOG DAY?

I t was October. Jack had begun to drink again around June, picked up speed over the summer, and then dove in heavily in September when football season started. This time was different. He had taken on a whole different attitude. He had lost hope in ever stopping and resigned himself to the fate of dying a drunk. His anger was worse than ever. He was more combative than before and when he was sober he was depressed and didn't speak to her. His health began to show the years of alcohol abuse. Jenna noticed that not only had his weight gone up to well over 300 lbs., but his face was pasty and ashen all the time. He constantly had dark circles and bags under his eyes, his stomach and intestinal track was a mess and he looked like he was on the verge of death. For Jenna it was frightening. She was watching her husband slowly kill himself.

Jenna had battled five years with her doubts and fears. Fear that she'd not be able to endure. Wondering if her husband was even saved. Having an internal tug-o-war over the road God had chosen for her and she was tired. She had the promises that He'd given to her about her marriage, but she was still unsettled in her spirit. She began to pray for the Lord to speak to her, to show her with clarity her situation and her husband. The answer came in two parts.

First, she was at a women's retreat and the Lord spoke to her through the teacher as they were working in the book of Philippians. Paul was in jail in Rome when he wrote to the Philippians. He had wanted to go to Rome, he got there by boat in chains. Not his plan. Just like Paul, the Lord had her right where He wanted her, it just didn't look like what she'd thought it would look like. But then our plans and God's plans are rarely ever the same. The second answer came in September. She'd been at a conference and was plagued over her husbands' salvation. Again, the Lord spoke clearly to her through the "parable of the sower". He showed her that Jack was saved but due to his sinful choices he was not bringing fruit to "its full fruition" and that he was in danger. Jenna was comforted over the understanding that she'd gained but fearful for her husband and his eternal destiny. The Lord showed her that according to Luke 21:34 he was being overtaken by drunkenness and the cares of this life and at the very least he'd miss the rapture of the church. He then took her to Galatians 5:21 and 1 Corinthians 6:10 to show her that drunkards will not inherit the Kingdom of God. She was concerned that he was going to die and that he would go into eternity apart from God. She knew she couldn't tell him because he wouldn't receive it but felt like she needed to warn him.

She didn't have to wait long.

He went out to the bar on a Sunday and was gone all day. He didn't know that she had stayed home from church because she was sick. She was sitting in the living room watching a movie on the old console T.V. they'd inherited with the house. She heard his car pull into the driveway around 7:00 p.m.

"Hi Jack." She was trying to stay calm. She knew that he probably had beer and a movie in the car. He wouldn't be expecting her to be home. His normal pattern would be to take the TV, his beer and his chewing tobacco into one of the spare rooms to finish off the beer, watch the movie and pass out without ever having to talk to her.

"What are you doing home? You didn't go to church?" He was angry.

"No, I wasn't feeling very well. Sorry." She was trying to be cautious with her words. He wouldn't look at her and his whole body was tense.

"Sorry. Are you done watching whatever you're watching?"

"No, I'm right in the middle of my movie."

"Well, I need the TV so you're going to have to finish it later." He was trying to control his aggression.

"But, I'm watching a movie. I'd like to finish it." She wasn't trying to be argumentative or difficult. She didn't feel that she should have to stop watching a movie and then have nothing to do the rest of the night when she wasn't feeling well. She didn't want to argue with him. Not only would it be a disaster, but Jesus didn't want her to provoke him.

"Well, too bad. I need the TV and I need it now so get over it and let me take it." Now he was barely in control.

"What am I supposed to do just stop watching my movie? I don't really want you to bring your beer in the house and sit in the spare room drinking, watching some violent movie. I don't feel good and I don't see why you should get the TV just so you can drink." Now she was mad. Something inside her snapped. She wasn't yelling, her voice was calm, and she wasn't being disrespectful, she just had enough.

She had paused the movie and was in the kitchen looking for something to drink. He walked into the kitchen and was standing on the opposite side of the island in their kitchen. His fists were clenched, he was gritting his teeth and giving her the "angry Jack" look. He had this way of wrinkling his forehead, clenching his jaw, glaring his eyes at her, staring her down and it was an evil, angry look that she hated.

"You don't pay for anything around here. I pay the bills. This is my house. I can do whatever I please in it. You contribute nothing to this place. It's my house and if you don't like it you can leave. I'm sick of you and your prideful, self-righteous, hyper-spiritual attitude. You can leave for all I care. I pay the bills and it's my house. I'm going to take the TV and sit in that room and do whatever I want. You can leave." He was yelling at her and his rage was boiling over. He looked like he wanted to punch her. It was the first time in their marriage that she was truly afraid of him. She didn't let her fear show. She remained calm and didn't say a word. He was drunk and out of control. She did the only thing she could, she got dressed, put Samson in the car and left. Church was just about over, and she needed to talk to her pastor and his wife.

She got to church as the message finished up and went into the office. She had started to cry and shake. She'd managed to hold it together until she walked into the church.

"Hey Jenna, what's going on? You look a little sad. Did you forget someone's birthday?" Pastor Trent was lighthearted and joking around with her. He didn't handle crying women very well. He wasn't trying to be rude or disrespectful, just his way of handling the situation.

Jenna laughed. She couldn't help it. He had a way of always making her laugh even if she didn't want to. "No, yours isn't until November."

"Is our little buddy acting naughty again?" He knew Jack was drinking again.

"Yes, worse than ever. He came home wanting the TV so he could sit in the spare room and drink and watch some violent movie. I was watching a movie because I was sick, and we got into a heated discussion and he started yelling at me. He was telling me that I didn't contribute to the house... I did nothing... I was self-righteous and could leave the house because it was his. When I was at the conference the Lord showed me that his life is in the balance. If he doesn't stop drinking and the rapture happens, he'll miss it. If he continues to drink he will not go to heaven. I'm scared for him and his eternal destiny. He looks horrible, like he's on death's door. I feel like he doesn't have much time left." Jenna was crying and very frustrated.

"Well, I can see that he is in danger from his drinking and I'm sorry that he's gone back. What do you think you should do?" He didn't want to tell her what to do. She had to come to her own decision.

"I feel like I have to move out of the way. I am tired of it all, but I feel like the Lord is telling me that I have to get out of the way because it's a matter of life and death for him. I don't know what to do about that. I'm scared. He was so angry and looked like he wanted to hit me."

"Well, I think you have your answer Jenna. If you feel like you need to move out of the way you should." He was concerned for her but did not want to influence her decision.

"I feel like I need to tell him to move out and that it's for his own good."

"Well I think you need to tell him what the Lord showed you and let him know that you would like him to move out. You need to give him a time limit and if there is any problem you can let me know and I can speak with him. But, don't talk to him until tomorrow. Let him sleep it off so he's sober."

"OK, I will. I honestly don't want it to be like this. I wanted him to stay sober and now here we are again. Haven't we already been down this road? I mean now it's the second separation in a year. I feel like if he doesn't sober up this time, something bad is going to happen. I feel like he is either going to die due to complications from the drinking or he's going to get into an accident. I don't want to see that happen. I have no intention of divorce; we don't use that word in our house. I don't want to lose my husband or my marriage, but I know he is going to destroy himself."

They prayed and then Susan, the pastor's wife, suggested that Jenna stay somewhere else for the night to avoid any further conflict. One of the ladies in the church, Cindy, was still hanging around and knew the situation; she offered to allow Jenna to stay at her house. So, Jenna went home, got some clothes and took Samson's crate to Cindy's. Jack never knew she came and went. He wouldn't have cared anyway.

The next morning Jenna went home. Jack didn't say much to her, so she had to start the conversation.

"Jack, we need to talk." She prayed silently and asked for wisdom and strength from the Lord.

"Yea, what about." He wasn't going to make it easy.

"Last night, our situation, the Lord. I wanted to tell you something. Please listen to me and know that what I am about to say, I say because I love you and because I believe that Jesus wants me to say it to you." She was trying to stay calm, be kind, and stand in the power of the Lord without sounding condemning or disrespectful.

"Fine I'll listen. What is it you want to tell me?" He didn't sound mad or anything, he sounded resigned, indifferent and tired.

"Well, I have been praying for you and about our situation. The Lord showed me that you are in danger. You are in a very delicate and difficult place. If you don't get right with the Lord you are going to end up separated from Him forever. You need to stop drinking or something is going to happen to you. You may think you are fine because you said a prayer and you have Bible verses memorized but Jesus showed me in His Word that you'd miss the rapture if it happened right now, and if you continue you will go to hell. I don't want to see that happen and more importantly, He doesn't want that to happen. He loves you and died for you, you keep turning your back on Him and He will continue to let you but not without consequences. I know that I need to get out of the way so that you can just be faced with Jesus and your choices. I would like you to move out by the end of this month. I know that we have been down this road before, but I believe it's what I'm supposed to do. I want our marriage to be healed and I believe that He will do that. But more importantly, I want you to be right with Jesus. He's given me two promises from His Word, but you must be willing to repent and follow after Him. I have no plans other than to follow Jesus." She sighed a sigh of relief that she finally got it all out.

"You're right. I'll move out. Sorry to put you through all this garbage. Sorry that my drinking hurts you so much and that you have to go through being separated." He had no emotion in his voice or expression on his face. He was done.

"Um, that's all you have to say?"

"Yea, what else is there? You're right and I don't feel like arguing with you and I don't want to say something that will cause an issue or hurt you or make you mad. So, it's better that I don't say anything at all. I'll look for a place to live and don't worry, I'll take care of the bills so you can stay in the house." He was resigned to what he perceived to be his fate.

"Well, um, I guess that's that. I do love you and I want you to be right with the Lord and for Him to use you. I know He has a great plan for you and wants to show Himself mighty in your life. He wants you to share His Word with other people. I want to see you succeed and serve the Lord." She was trying not to cry.

"Thanks, I love you to." He left and went into the spare room and shut the door. Jenna went into their room and sat down on the edge of the bed and cried.

Jenna couldn't believe they were at this place again. Her heart was crumbling in her chest and her faith was barely hanging on by a thread. If you could measure the tiny little half-moon at the base of your fingernail, you'd be able to see the size of her faith in the matter of her marriage being healed.

"Know you not, that to whom you yield yourselves servants to obey, his servants you are to whom you obey; whether of sin unto death, or of obedience unto righteousness?" Romans 6:16 KJV

ONLY THE LONELY

J ack couldn't believe that he was separated from Jenna for a second time. He had a beautiful house and an even more beautiful wife, and he was sleeping on a mattress, on the floor, in the basement of some lady's house that rented out rooms to people that needed a place to live. It was humiliating. He felt like he was alone in the world. He'd tried to visit his sister the last time he was in California, but she told him to stay away due to his drinking. He didn't have friends. He lived between two worlds, the world of unsaved-drunken-business acquaintances and those that were within the church. He didn't fit in anywhere. Those who were outside of Jesus knew he claimed to be a believer and believed him to be sober. Those inside the church who loved Jesus knew that he was living a lie and drinking his life away.

He had originally planned on moving about 45 miles south from Jenna and living in a singles only apartment complex. He'd gone down to look at it. It had everything. Lots of single women, a pool, tennis courts, activities and no one would care about his drinking; in fact, they'd probably join him. Standing on the balcony looking at the pool, he imagined all the women that would be lounging there come summertime. In a flash, fear welled up inside of him. He knew if he took that apartment, he was committing marital suicide. It was the closest he had ever come to feeling the end of his marriage in his heart. He knew he would not be able to fight off all the temptations that he would face living there. He shook the thoughts from his mind, wrote a deposit check and left.

For days he was tormented by it. He wanted to move there and just commit marital and spiritual suicide and get his miserable life over with. Sleepless nights, tossing and turning, fighting and kicking with the Lord, it was a Jacob moment. But peace would not come. Finally, he cancelled the hold. Finally, he got sleep.

So, he found the room for rent and moved in. He was able to work out of the house--well his room and had a place to sleep. His life was pathetic. Jesus was supposed to be the big fix, and this wasn't the way it was supposed to happen. He had so many internal arguments going on that it sounded like a session of congress inside his head. On one hand he just didn't care. He wanted to sit and drink until he died. He was angry that Jenna made such a big deal about it and that it even affected her because he didn't think it should. He hated the guilt he felt when he looked at her and blamed her for the unhappy side of his drunks. Then there was the section of congress that told him he didn't want to live without Jenna in his life. He loved her more than he'd ever loved anyone. He hated hurting her. He wanted to stop but didn't know how and couldn't understand why God didn't just take his drinking away. The third and loudest section could not be silenced, no matter how much he drank. The Jesus section. No matter how much he tried to convince himself that he'd go to heaven he knew it was a lie. He knew that if the rapture of the church happened he'd be left. He couldn't get the vision of Jesus on the cross out of his mind. Every time he drank he saw Him hanging there with those eyes that said, "I love you Jack", the eyes that saw right through him. He knew every time he went to the bar that he was risking going to hell. The reality that he was turning his back on the One that had given His life for him was more than he could bear at times.

Jack's plan was to work, drink, support Jenna and eventually die. At times *he* didn't even understand his willful rejection of the love of Jesus. All he could hope for was to keep his job so he could support Jenna and drink.

No one understood the battle that raged inside of him. It never ended and he could never win it. He had so much pain inside of him and no idea how to process it. It was constantly reaching up and grabbing him by the throat choking out his life. Growing up Catholic he understood that hate and unforgiveness were wrong, yet he felt them for his ex-wife and for his father. His father had been a drunk for the first 20 plus years of his life and during that time was an angry, spiteful, violent person and it all got unleashed on Jack. He belittled Jack, beat him mercilessly, made fun of him, called him names and did nothing to encourage him. Because his ex-wife had cheated on him and then bankrupted him he hated her. God's Word was clear that he was to forgive but it raged on inside of him.

At times it was hard to see Jenna at church and to know that everyone there knew he was a drunkard. There were times he wanted to go to a different church, but the Lord wouldn't let him. Jack drank and rebelled, but inside the Word of Life was always speaking, nudging, convicting, and drawing him. He was grateful for that on one hand and on the other he wanted to drown it out because he felt so powerless to obey. So many times, he'd cried out begging God to make him stop drinking, begging God to take it away. But, still he drank. He thought getting married would help him to stop. But, still he drank. Then he'd start to think about what his life would be like without alcohol and he came up boring, empty, frightened and bewildered. He'd been drinking since he was nineteen and been a full alcoholic since he was twenty-one. Who would he be if he didn't drink? How would he function? How would he cope with all the difficulties and the battles inside? He didn't have the answers to those questions. What he had was fear, so he drank.

Jack had despair, fear and hopelessness before him. He hoped that some how God had the power to change him, even against his own self-destructive will.

He was alone, lonely and had no one to blame but himself.

"But now I have written unto you not to keep company, if any man that is called a brother be a ...drunkard...with such a one do not even eat." 1 Corinthians 5:11 KJV

WAITING

I t was February. Jack had moved out in October. Winter was hard. The days short and cold, the sky dreary and Jenna and Jack were not living under the same roof for the second time in less than a year. She was coping. Working at the church plus attending, put her there six out of seven days a week. She had Samson and the Lord, friends at church, but it was painful. Every day she felt the absence of her husband. She had to build a fire in the wood stove just about every day, carry wood in and out, take care of the trash, cleaning, shopping and gassing up her truck; things that he did for her even when he was drinking and grumpy. She slept alone, ate alone, watched her old movies alone and went to church alone. At times she had to fight being angry that her life was falling apart. They had Jesus, wasn't that supposed to make everything all better? She went through times of self-pity, doubt, fear and then the opposite. It was so peaceful, easy and even joyful without the warfare, conflict and eggshells that she had been walking on. Jack wasn't in her face every day and although it wasn't what she wanted; she could be a single married woman for the rest of her life if she had to.

She held on to the promises that Jesus had given her, but her emotions and circumstances got the best of her sometimes.

She had given up wanting to be married, submitted to being married, now she was married and separated. Life was so weird and hard. She was very thankful to have Jesus, or she wouldn't have made it this far and Jack, well she probably would have kicked him to the curb long ago.

She prayed for Jack and their marriage all the time. She knew that was still the battleground and where it would be won or lost.

One rare sunny March day as she was driving into town to do the grocery shopping, she was praying. A thought struck her like lightning. *What if after all this time, Jesus does fix Jack and then I mess up our marriage? What if I can't be a good wife when all of this is behind us?* Her whole life had been crisis management. She knew how to function in that, but what about regular life? What about life that was truly being lived for Jesus? A marriage where both of them served Him together? In truth she had never experienced that. Their whole marriage from the beginning until now had been nothing but crisis management. Jenna started to cry. Fear began to overtake her. *Jesus, please fix me. Please make sure my heart is clean and right with you, that the forgiveness that you have taught me to practice is real and deep. I don't want to be the one to ruin my marriage. I want to be a godly wife and follow You and serve You and be able to love and follow my husband. But I know I am capable of being a total screw up and I need your help!*

She had never thought about it before. Not that she ever believed that she was an amazing wife or that she even knew what that looked like. She had been so focused on trying to deal with the problems at hand and how Jesus wanted her to live in those moments, she'd just never thought about the other stuff. She'd been thrown into a swirling tornado and was just trying to make it out alive. They'd never had the chance to figure stuff out like two regular sinners trying to do marriage.

There began to be a new focus now in Jenna's heart. She was always praying for Jack but now she began to pray for herself. To ask Him who knew all and had the power to change anything, to help her, to fix what needed to be fixed and to heal her broken wounded soul. The power of God's Word could change a life and heal hurts, she believed that, so she stood on that knowledge and waited.

"They that wait upon the LORD shall renew their strength; they shall mount up with wings as eagles; they shall run, and not be weary; and they shall walk and not faint". Isaiah 40:31 KJV

HOPE IS BORN

I t was August. Summer had arrived and hope came with it. Jack and Jenna had been separated almost a year. Jenna noticed sometime back in March that Jack had begun to show up at church, for everything. He didn't sit by her or try to force her in anyway. He just quietly showed up. Emptied trash. Mowed the lawn at home and at church. Cleaned the church. Served in the nursery. (Even got initiated by a small child pooping on him and another sliming him with a giant sneeze right to the face). He seemed different. He smiled more. His countenance was softer and kinder. He was slimmer than he had been since they were married and no longer looked like the walking dead. He was spending a lot of time with Pastor Trent. She was hopeful. Cautious. But hopeful.

Since their church was small it was inevitable that they would be face to face. There was literally no way to avoid him, not that she wanted to but it would have been impossible. They had begun to have brief conversations.

One evening, church had long since ended and everyone, but Jenna and Jack had gone home. She was always the last to leave. She made sure everything was shut off, cleaned up, locked up and ready for the next time the church would be used. He had taken to being the last to leave as well. He secretly didn't like her being the last to leave even though she had Samson.

He began with, "can we talk" which brought fear and

trepidation to Jenna. They had never been able to talk about the issues in their marriage, his drinking or anything of real substance. They could barely talk about groceries because he was usually very hostile, but not this time.

"I want to tell you first and foremost, I'm so sorry for all of the things I've put you through. I cannot begin to comprehend what you've been through. I'm sorry I lied and deceived you when we got married. I'm sorry for all the things I've said, and I know that my sorry isn't going to magically fix everything but I'm asking for your forgiveness. I know we need to talk about a lot of things, and I will probably be apologizing for a long time to come, but I had to start somewhere." With a hint of fear in his eyes, he held his breath and waited for Jenna to respond.

She took a deep breath and spoke as calmly as she could, "I forgive you. I have continuously had to choose to forgive you over the course of our marriage because it was what Jesus asked me to do. Thank you for apologizing to me and acknowledging that you don't understand all that I've been through. I know that you've been through a lot yourself and I hope that we can finally begin to talk about things." Jenna wanted to run. She had such fear in her heart about all the conversations that needed to happen and what his reactions would be like.

"Me too. I love you and I want our marriage to be healed by the Lord. I hope we can move forward. I have to go, but thanks for listening to me. I love you Jenna, more than anyone in the world." He was afraid but knew that he had obeyed the Lord in taking this first step. He knew he deserved for her to reject him at the least and unleash years of pain at the worst, but he also knew that he couldn't blame her. He had put her through hell and caused her so much hurt. He loved her more than he ever thought possible and it broke his heart to think how much he had wounded this woman who was a daughter of the King.

She gave him a hug, "I love you too."

Jenna was shaking inside but left feeling hopeful that

maybe, just maybe he had really changed. She thanked God that night for the work He was doing and for His faithfulness to her. She prayed for the Lord to help her with her fear and to give her wisdom on what to say and when to say it. She wanted to handle the whole thing His way. Not run ahead or lag behind, but His way.

"...Which hope we have as an anchor of the soul, both sure and steadfast..." Hebrews 6:19 KJV

SHUT THE DOOR

J ack had moved out in October; it was now January. It had been three months and he drank only once. Although he was technically sober, he was still a mess in his head and heart. It was a fight every day to not give up hope and go back to drinking.

He was eventually able to move from the mattress on the floor to his own apartment. He hated that he lived in the apartment and Jenna lived five minutes down the road in their house, but he had no one to blame but himself.

One day in January he'd gone over to the house to pick up some bills that he needed to take care of. Jenna was home. He hadn't intended to get into a conversation with her, but it happened anyway.

"Jenna, I just want you to know I'm trying to stay sober and hope I'm done with that life."

"Do you mind if I share something with you?" Jenna didn't like sharing anything with him; it always ended badly.

He knew that. Again, that was his fault.

"Sure." He really didn't want to hear anything.

He saw her take a deep breath, "The only way you are ever going to stay sober is to pull your toe out of the door. What I mean is, right now, going back to drinking is an option in your heart and mind. If life doesn't work out for you or gets too hard, you can always go get drunk. Jesus isn't going to force you. You have to be willing to pull your toe out of the door, ask Jesus to shut it and decide that it's no longer an option. Then you will be sober. Jesus has to shut the door, but you have to let Him. He has to be more important than you and your life or your choices or whatever it is inside you that rules over you instead of Him." Now she was holding her breath waiting for the backlash.

Jack stood there in silence. He knew she was right. He always had "that option". He always had his old life to run back to and hide in. He knew deep down that he was the one that had kept his toe in that door.

"Yea, OK I gotta go. I'll talk to you later." He had to leave. Part of him wanted to lash out and part of him wanted to melt into the driveway. He loved this woman and hated her words all at the same time.

So, he left.

But her words never left him. They rolled around in his heart and mind everyday. They hurt, they poked, they jabbed, they stung, because they were true, and he knew it. He'd begged God to snap His finger and take the drinking away, but He never did. In his heart he blamed God for his unquenchable thirst. He wanted to have the easy way out and Jesus refused to give it to him. He knew Jesus didn't want him to be a drunk and that it broke the heart of the Lord. He knew that Jesus loved him, but He wouldn't make him stop. He was angry and frustrated.

But her words were eroding away his arguments.

Over the next few weeks he realized that no matter how much he tried to shift the blame; the whole of the responsibility fell on him. He made the choice to go and drink, to look at porn, to refuse to turn from his sin, every time it happened; he knew it happened because he chose it. He finally admitted to himself that Jesus had taken it from him, once. When he first came to Christ, Jesus had delivered him. He had taken it away, but Jack had made the choice to pick it back up again. He finally admitted that if Jesus were to snap His finger and make it go away, it would be unfruitful, and Jack would just believe that he could go back and forth without dealing with his own sinful choices. It was a hard truth to face, but Jesus wouldn't let him turn from that truth.

He began to walk through these things with Jesus in his prayer time. As hard as it was to face, he did it. He didn't feel any different and was still very uncertain of the future, but he knew if he just kept talking it out and facing it, Jesus could and would do the rest. He finally believed that.

One morning in February, he woke up and knew in his heart he had been freed. The repentance, prayer, facing the truth, trusting Jesus to do His part finally came to be a reality in his heart. He knew he'd never drink again. He was done. In his heart, he wanted to love Jesus more than anyone or anything. He knew that loving Him, serving Him, obeying Him, following Him was going to be his life. No turning back. He was done with his old life and old ways.

He fell on his face before the Lord.

Jesus, I know that I am a wretched sinner and I've wasted so many opportunities and so much time. I know that I have messed up my marriage, my witness, my walk with You and that it was my choices that brought me to this apartment, separated from my wife and living alone. I realize that I have kept my toe in the door, and I am asking You to shut that door that no man can open it. I don't ever want to go back there again. I don't care what comes my way. If my wife and I never reconcile, if she gets cancer and dies, if I lose everything, I don't care, I just want to follow You, love You and serve You. I will do whatever You ask me to do, go wherever You ask me to go. I'd love to be reconciled with my wife and to have the chance to love her and have all that You desire for us to have. But, nothing matters more than You. Just tell me what to do and I'll do it. Thank You for saving me and for freeing me and forgiving me. I love you Jesus."

As Jack was there weeping and rejoicing he heard that familiar still small Voice, "Go to Pastor Trent, tell him I sent you and that you are to do whatever he asks of you."

So, Jack called his pastor.

"Hey Pastor Trent, I was wondering if you had a minute maybe we could grab some coffee and talk?" Jack was nervous. Trent knew everything that had gone on in their marriage. Either Jenna told him, or Jack had told him in one of his brief times of trying to stay sober.

"Sure, how about in an hour at Denny's?" Trent and his wife had prayed for Jack and Jenna and he hoped this call was the answer.

"See you then." Jack knew it was what he was supposed to do and that he deserved anything his pastor might feel needed to be unleashed on him. He didn't deserve grace or forgiveness or even to have time with Trent, but he was willing to obey even if it meant rejection and humiliation. For the first time in his life it didn't matter what anyone said to him, he wasn't turning back. He got dressed and went.

When Jack arrived, Pastor Trent was already seated sipping on a cup of coffee. Jack walked up to the table and Trent stood up and gave him a hug. Jack sat down.

"First, I just want to say that I know I've blown it big time with Jenna. I know that you and many others have prayed for me and been willing to help me, but I have just refused. That is all on me. I have been praying and seeking the Lord and repenting. Not feeling sorry for myself, truly repenting of my sin. This morning I was praying, and I told Jesus I would do anything He asked me to do. I realized that I have been unwilling to say that to Him before and obviously unwilling to do it as well. Anyway, He told me to get a hold of you and do whatever you tell me to do, so here I am. I am truly sorry for everything I have done and all the lies and deception and drinking, I'm done, and I want to go forward. So, boss, what should I do?" Jack got it all out in one big breath. He felt relieved. He was finally able to say it out loud to his pastor and mean it.

Pastor Trent sat in silence for what seemed like an eternity just looking at Jack. It felt like he was looking right through him. Trying to determine if Jack was for real or if this was just another sales pitch. He'd said many times that Jack could sell ice cubes to Eskimo's. Trent had been around the block enough to know that drug addicts and alcoholics are the best salesmen in the world.

"Well you need to show up to church every time the doors are open. Get there early, be the last to leave. Bring your Bible and notebook and no matter how you feel, what is going on in your head, how tired you are you show up. If you see trash that needs to be emptied, empty it. If you see someone who needs help, help them. If you have some down time, are done with work early, have time off, get a hold of me and we'll have coffee, you can go on calls with me, be ready and willing to do whatever is needed. If your head is getting squirrelly, pick up the phone and call; don't let the squirrels have free rent. Know that the enemy is going to attack, and you will have to learn to battle through it. Being honest about the stuff that swirls around in your head is key to winning those battles. You have a lot of garbage in there and it needs to be thrown out; that gets done through prayer, transparency, the truth of the Word and more prayer. And last, trust Jesus for Jenna and your marriage."

This began a friendship and accountability that Jack had always needed. They talked, went out on calls together, hung out and had coffee or ate a meal and all the while, the Lord was building in Jack the foundation that had been lacking due to his sinful choices. Jack appreciated his pastor and was grateful for the grace, wisdom, encouragement and forgiveness that he received from him.

Jack had hope for the first time in his life. Life wasn't easy, but there was hope.

"Stand fast therefore in the liberty by which Christ has made us free and do not be entangled again with a yoke of bondage." Galatians 5:1 NKJV

TALKING IT OVER

Over the next few months Jenna and Jack talked more than they had since before their marriage. They discussed his sobriety, his commitment to following Jesus, and the problems they had in their marriage and where they were headed. It was a strange time, but it was refreshing.

Some conversations were easier than others. He brought a lot of things up himself without Jenna prompting him. Some were painful for both of them. He cried a lot and asked a lot of questions because there were things he didn't even remember. She never tried to make him feel bad or pour salt in his wounds. She truly felt bad for even bringing stuff up, but they both knew it was the only way for true healing and reconciliation to begin.

Jack was giddy. Like a young child whose favorite uncle just gave him the greatest toy a boy could ask for. Life was fresh and exciting for him. He saw everything through new eyes. He had a new attitude; was excited about Jesus beyond what she had ever known him to be. He'd never been so open and honest. He had never apologized, genuinely, as much as he had in recent months. Jenna, however, was scared. Scared that it was not over. That she would trust and then get slammed again. She was afraid she'd end up on the roller coaster and never be able to get off. She knew she couldn't take going through the last six years all over again. Emotionally, physically and spiritually she had been pushed to her limit. Jesus could take her through it, but she wasn't sure that she was willing. Despite all that, she couldn't hold off the inevitable forever. She was going to have to reconcile with her husband and eventually live under the same roof with him. She'd have to take the chance, like it or not.

Lord, I know that You are in control. I believe that You have been working on my husband and he has been sober longer than ever before. Our conversations are going in the right direction, he seems very different, but I'm scared. Scared to trust and scared to get taken advantage of. Terrified of what will happen if I allow myself to let my guard down and trust him. How can I trust him when I have been betrayed so many times? When we have been through this so many times. What do I do? How do I have a marriage without trust? Jenna was lying in bed crying out to the Lord. Trying to sleep but knew she needed to pour out her heart, so she did. When she was finally spent, she lay there quietly and heard the familiar gentle Voice.

"You don't have to trust your husband, you need to trust Me. If you trust Me I will do the work that needs to be done in your marriage. I will heal you and Jack, and I will be the center. It's about trusting Me."

Jenna sighed a sigh of relief. She only needed to trust Jesus. That she could do. He had proven Himself to be faithful, trustworthy, loving, gentle and able to do above and beyond what she could imagine. She had no idea what that would look like or how it would play itself out, but she knew what she had to do and the One she needed to trust was worth trusting.

It wasn't magic fairy dust, but it was a start. She was still tired from the long ordeal of her marriage and knew she had a long way to go. But she had a clear direction and the One who was leading her loved her completely.

"Trust in the Lord with all your heart and lean not on your own understanding, but in all your ways acknowledge Him and He will direct your path." Proverbs 3:5-6 KJV

THIS CAN'T BE HAPPENING

October 2002

I t was 6pm when Jenna pulled her Toyota land cruiser into her driveway. Samson, her faithful sidekick sat in the passenger seat, tail wagging and ears perked. It had been a long day and she was tired. She loved her job as the administrative assistant to her pastor. She had learned so much and grown to enjoy all the ways she was able to serve.

Samson had just turned two and was finally coming out of his puppy stage. She was grateful for that. He had calmed down a bit and was now fully trained but still had enough puppy playfulness in him that he made her laugh. He was full grown and weighed 110 lbs. And was quite intimidating looking to those who didn't know him. He'd finally grown into his huge feet. If he stood on his hind legs he could put his front paws on her shoulders. He shed a lot but she didn't mind. He was always there offering comfort and loved her no matter what kind of day she had. He was such a blessing in her otherwise crazy life. She was glad that she was able to take him to work. She was in the office most of the time by herself and he was great company and a good watchdog.

"Ok buddy, release. Let's go in and get some dinner." He was trained to enter or exit her vehicle at her command. He would sit eagerly waiting for the word, his ears perked forward and a little wrinkle on his forehead, waiting for the signal. Sometimes he could hardly contain himself wondering if he was going to be allowed to go with her or be left behind. He was very smart. When she put him in the truck if she said, "we are going to work" then he was excited and eager to get out when they pulled into the church parking lot. If she said, "we are going to church" he would relax and sit patiently as she went inside for service. All the kids would run up to her after service was over asking if they could get him out of the truck. He loved them and was always excited when one of them set him free. He'd lick their faces, wag his tail wildly and run around the churchyard then run straight for the door to find Jenna.

As they walked into the house, B.C. her cat met them as usual. Samson would give him a good sniff all over. Thoroughly but cautiously. It was their ritual whenever Samson came home with Jenna. B.C. and Samson had a love/hate relationship. One minute they were best buds, curled up on the couch sleeping, the next Samson was bobbing and weaving trying to avoid the cat claws. It was a ridiculous sight because Samson could have put one paw on the cat and held him down or picked him up and flung him. But he never took advantage of the size or weight difference. Jenna had no intention of getting a cat but B.C. (Brat Cat, named because he was a complete brat) showed up on her deck in the middle of winter. It was thirty-two degrees outside, she'd gone out to get some wood for the stove and there he was. Shivering in the cold, meowing his head off. She brought him in intending to find his owner the next day. She tried, but no one claimed him, so he stayed. Samson didn't mind at all. But B.C. wasn't sure he wanted to share his new home with a dog. After a few tussles and some scolding by Jenna, he decided that he would let the dog stay.

Jenna was looking forward to putting on her pajamas,

feeding the animals, eating her dinner and crashing. She still had health struggles and all she had been through had taken its toll on her body. Although things had changed in recent months, she was still worn out and recuperating.

The phone rang. She checked the caller ID and let out a long sigh. She had to answer it. It was Jack. If she didn't answer it she would feel guilty the rest of the night. She'd feel like she was lying. Pretending not to be home when in fact she was. Besides, if she didn't answer it now, she'd have to call him back sooner or later. It wasn't that she didn't want to talk to him she was just tired. Although things had drastically improved, it still took a lot of energy for her to handle some of their conversations in a Godly manner. Right now, she was very low on energy.

She decided she'd try to keep the conversation light, not get into any long discussions or heavy topics.

It started out fine. The usual small talk, "how was your day?" and "how are you?"

But then the conversation turned.

"What? Are you serious? You've got to be kidding." She tried to keep the fear, no, it was stark raving terror, out of her voice. She didn't do a very good job, so it made her sound snarky. She needed to get off the phone before she said something she'd regret.

"I have to go; I don't want to talk about this right now." She quickly hung up the phone.

Jenna didn't want to be rude or seem harsh, although that was how it came out. She was in shock. He'd finally answered a question that she'd asked him a few days earlier. It had been a simple question. She didn't think it was a big deal. She didn't expect an answer of any great revelation or weight. What she got was both!

"Remember you asked me the other day what I thought Jesus was going to do with my life or if I knew how He wanted me to serve Him? Well, I do know the answer to that." He hesitated, took a breath and said, "He is calling me to be a pastor."

Given the circumstances they were in, the answer seemed completely out of left field. They were in the middle of a separation, their second one in fact. It was October and they had been separated since the previous October. Did no one else in the universe remember that? Who says that in the middle of being separated from your spouse? How was that even going to happen given their track record and the long road that seemed to be ahead of them? The first six years of their marriage had not been a model marriage. Certainly not one you would want to write a how-to book about. A how-not-to guide seemed more appropriate. Jack's answer was like a lightning bolt through her soul and her mind was reeling.

If she was honest with herself, the disbelief and shock was more about Jenna than Jack. Considering her life, her struggles and all they had gone through and where they were, it seemed, at the least, impossible, if not completely ridiculous.

Jenna sat on the couch and started to cry. It was so overwhelming for her to think about. Samson laid his head on her leg, looking up at her with his big brown eyes, the little wrinkle in his forehead, eyebrows twitching from side to side and he let out a whine. "It's OK boy, I'm just having a meltdown, but I'll get it over it." She stroked his head. He was always such a comfort and so in tune with her.

You have got to be kidding me! Lord why in the world would You do that to me? I simply asked Jack what he thought you were going to do with his life. He has been sober a year, we're separated and I'm in no way shape or form, by any stretch of the imagination, pastor wife material! He must have heard You wrong. You wouldn't really tell him that you want him to be a pastor. It's ridiculous! Absurdly, completely insane! The most ridiculous part is not about him, it's about me. I know You take the broken, most unlikely people and often put them in those places. They are Your favorite people in fact because it shows Your power and glory. But, really! I could never be a pastor's wife. I am a secretary, behind the scenes, organize, file and help other people to do their job, not the in the front, smiling, sweet pastor's wife. Pastor Trent's wife, she is PW material, me not so much. I can't even talk about this right now. I'm just gonna have to process so You go ahead, do whatever You are gonna do but believe me, I'm the wrong chick for that job.

"The things which are impossible with men are possible with God." Luke 18:27 KJV

MOVING IN

I t took Jenna a few weeks to process what he had told her. She wasn't happy about it, hadn't changed her mind about being a pastor's wife but she had come to the place where she was willing to follow Jesus wherever He would lead her husband even if it meant her being a pw! It was more than she could assimilate. She had other more immediate stuff to sort through so that could take a backseat. Anyway, if it was what He wanted, she wasn't big enough to stop it.

In November of 2002, Jack moved back in. Jenna didn't feel ready, but she knew it was what the Lord was calling them to do. She was scared, still trying to recover from the wounds and scars that had come from her marriage. Neither Jack nor Jenna knew what to expect. They had never lived under the same roof while he was sober, truly sober. He had been doing well living on his own, growing in his relationship with Jesus and serving at the church. She had been working through her hurts and fears while they talked and worked on their communication. But living in the house together was an entirely different story. It came with all kinds of challenges that they had never experienced before. It was like they were just married only they had a huge history haunting them.

The first year of living together under the same roof was as difficult as the previous six. Jack was learning how to fight spiritual battles, to live life on Jesus' terms and not his own, how to be a godly man, a husband and how to communicate with his wife, which he had never done, all while living under the same roof. Jenna was still trying to heal. She was tired, overwhelmed, struggling with her health and didn't even know the man she was living with because he was not the same man that she'd married. It was hard to navigate all her emotions and his. Even though she'd had lots of practice, it was still new, different and difficult.

It was all new territory and yet they had been married for six years. Life was hard and full of twist and turns.

There were times when he would exhibit old behavior and she'd start to get fearful that he was going back. She had to work hard at giving that over and trusting Jesus just as He had told her to do that night months back. They had some big fights and some more hurts. But they kept going. Each of them, individually had to keep their relationship with Jesus as the priority, run to Him with everything, trust Him for everything, and depend on Him for everything. They were in uncharted territory and determined to make it safely to shore.

Time, they say, heals all wounds.

But Jenna and Jack had more than that. They had Jesus Himself and the promises that He had given to her. They had already begun to see them come to pass. The Hosea promise had stated, "I will heal his backsliding and return him to Me..." Jesus had done that in Jack's life already and He was in the process of fulfilling the promise in Jeremiah.

The road was hard and bumpy, twisting and turning, but Jesus...

"For we walk by faith not by sight." 2 Corinthians 5:7 KJV

TIMES, THEY ARE
A CHANGIN'

As 2003 ended, Jack and Jenna were still struggling but things were getting easier. They began to find their footing in their home life. Jenna was still serving as the administrative assistant; girls still came to her and Jack was working and serving in any way he could at the church.

In September, Pastor Trent had asked Jack to start a drug and alcohol recovery study. He wanted Jack to take all that he had gone through and learned and use it to help others who were making their way into the church trying to get freedom from their addictions.

It started out as a small group of men and quickly grew into a large group of men and women. Once the ladies started to show up Jack and Trent both felt that Jenna should step in. So, she began to go and help. It was an amazing thing to listen to Jack share with the group, challenge them, direct them and even correct them. She was listening to a man that loved Jesus and was radically changed. He was humble, broken, honest and it was so refreshing. He would say things that were so obviously from Jesus sometimes it would make her eyes well up with tears. She was so proud of who he was becoming, how he loved Jesus and how committed he was to following at all cost.

As the group continued to grow, they began to separate the ladies from the guys. Jenna and the girls, worked through a Bible based workbook, talked about their struggles, prayed for each other, encouraged each other and held each other accountable. It was such an amazing thing to watch the transformation of lives right before her eyes. It was also a huge blessing to take all she had been through and learned living with Jack and use it to help others.

They began to have people come and ask them questions, ask for prayer and wisdom concerning their own marital struggles. So many in the church were aware of all they had gone through and could see in front of them the results of prayer, counsel, walking with Jesus and what getting help could do for a marriage. They began to do couples ministry with couples that were struggling in their marriage.

Jack and Jenna were serving Jesus together.

When Jenna looked at him and where they were, her heart would well up with joy and gratitude for all Jesus had done for them. She realized He had done so much and so far above and beyond what she could have ever imagined.

"Now unto Him that is able to do exceedingly abundantly above all that we ask or think...Unto Him be glory in the church by Christ Jesus throughout all ages, world without end." Ephesians 3:20-21 KJV

EPILOGUE

October 2004

J enna had played the scenario in her head a thousand times. Standing at the front of the church, alone, her future uncertain. Where would she go, what would she do. What was life going to be like? It was her worst fear. Standing there without Jack because he had been killed in a drunk driving accident. Standing there, waiting. Waiting for the people to show up, the pastor to come up to the front, the music to start.

But this was not the scenario that was getting ready to be played out. How did she get here? This wasn't her plan for her life. This was a different life. Very different. It still frustrated her at times that life was so beyond her control and this, well this was way beyond. She had ideas in her mind of what their life would be like when Jack sobered up. She'd imagined many things, godly things. But nothing even came close to where they were now and what was about to take place.

When life felt out of control or was just so far beyond her, she went to the only safe place she knew to go.

Father, I know You are here with me. I know my life is in

Your hands and there is never a moment that You have said oops. Nothing is ever a surprise to You. Nothing is beyond Your reach or control. I gave my life to You 12 years ago and said I would follow You. I have reaffirmed that commitment to You more times than I can count. I know You are good. I know You love me. I know if You have allowed this to happen in my life, it is for a good reason, Your purpose and that it will be for Your glory. I just simply don't see that right now. But, again, I know You love me and I am choosing right now to trust You and surrender my will and life. Please calm my nerves. Please, please help me to hold it together in front of all these people. I don't want to cry like a blubbering baby. Please in Jesus name, help me. Thank you for all You have done for me Jesus.

Jenna looked up and smiled at Jack. She was not alone at the front of their little church; he was there with her. Alive, sober and loving Jesus. She was so humbled and in awe of what the Lord had done. She stood there, not alone, not living her worst nightmare but with Jack by her side.

Pastor Trent began to speak.

"Tonight, before we begin our service I have asked Jack and Jenna to come up here. This couple has been through many trials and tribulations. Most of you know their story. Most of you have prayed them through this story." Laughter and agreement rang out in the little church. "It is my privilege and honor tonight to pray for this couple and to announce that Jack has been ordained and will be serving as an assistant to me. He has been doing that in reality for the last two years, without a title or an ordination. We are just making it official. There was a time when I didn't see hope for Jack. He had given up hope that he would be sober, that his marriage would be restored, and that God would ever use him, but he was wrong and so was I. I have been blessed to walk with Jenna through this time. Although she has struggled and at times barely held onto the promises God gave her, she never let go. It has been an encouragement to me to see her faith. I can't wait to see what the future holds for them. So, will you please bow your hearts and heads before the One who holds our lives in His hands and the One who has brought these two people from ashes to beauty."

Everyone in the little church bowed their heads. With tears streaming down her face, so did Jenna. She was humbled beyond words and grateful to the One who loved her and died for her. Jesus was very present in that room as Pastor Trent, Jack, Jenna and the little congregation brought their hearts and thanksgiving before the One who rules the Universe but stoops down to hear the cry of the lowly.

"Thus says the LORD; again there shall be heard in this place, which you say it is desolate without man and without beast, in the cities of Judah, and in the streets of Jerusalem, that are desolate, without man and without inhabitant, and without beast. The voice of joy, and the voice of gladness, the voice of the bridegroom, and the voice of the bride, the voice of them that shall say, praise the LORD of hosts; for the LORD is good; for His mercy endures forever; and of those who will bring the sacrifice of praise into the house of the LORD. For I will cause the captives of the land to return as at the first, says the LORD." Jeremiah 33:10-11 KJV

"To console those who mourn in Zion, to give them beauty for ashes, the oil of joy for mourning, the garment of praise for the spirit of heaviness; that they might be called trees of righteousness, the planting of the LORD, that He may be glorified." Isaiah 61:3 KJV

AUTHOR'S NOTE

This book has been an amazing journey for me personally. The events you read about in this book are all true. I know because I am Jenna, it's my life. I changed names, places and times and of course omitted things to protect those involved, but it's all-true. I have been through many things in my life and Jesus has used it all to grow me, teach me, bring me to Himself and to encourage others in their struggles.

I never wanted to write a book. I'm not a writer. I'm just a woman who loves Jesus and like so many others, has been through many difficulties in life. This life is hard. But, Jesus can bring healing and redemption. Over the years I have used my personal story to encourage and comfort many women. I had many tell me "you should write a book". I always thought, "there is no way—I'm not a writer. I can't tell my story because people are still alive. And, oh, did I mention I'm not a writer?" But one day, when I was trying to nap, Jesus just gave me the prologue, the names, the intro and laid it all out for me. I tried to ignore it. He wouldn't let me. So, I put it on paper— well, computer actually. I didn't do an outline or plot or plan. I sat down and He wrote it using my fingers on an old laptop with Microsoft Word 2000. It took me a short time to write the whole thing, and then it sat for two years. I figured it was a lesson in obedience or maybe another step in my healing. But then one day, He sent me to Amazon Self-Publishing and said,

"Do it." Scary! But, here it is. I'm not looking for a best seller. I am just being obedient. My hope, my prayer, my wish is that just one person will read this book and give their life to Jesus. Maybe one person will read this and be encouraged to keep following Jesus even though the road is hard and unexpected. That somehow, some way, Jesus will use this broken imperfect vessel to shine His glorious grace, love and beauty into another soul.

If you are either of those people, my prayer is that you will follow Him. Know that when I stepped out in faith, I did so with you—whoever you are—in mind. I hope one day we meet in heaven and we can rejoice together as we worship at the feet of the One who deserves all the credit, all the glory and all the praise.

I hope this book blessed you. If it did, you can email me your thoughts or questions or if you just would like prayer. My email is 2019differentlife@gmail.com.

If you are interested in reading my blog you can find it at www.brokenandmadewhole.wordpress.com. You can find the ladies bible study teachings at www.islandchristianfellowship.com.

SPECIAL THANKS

I'd like to take a moment and say thank you to some people that are very special to me and without them, you wouldn't even be reading this page!

Thank you first to Jesus Christ, to my Savior, my Lord, my Redeemer. Words are not enough to say thank you and I love you. My life was broken, and I was dead in my sin until you rescued me, saved me and called me Your own. I love you, Jesus, and I cannot wait until I see your beautiful face—when I get to live with You for all eternity in the light of your glory and beauty.

To my husband Michael; thank you for all your prayers, your love, your encouragement and the kick in the pants I needed to see this project through to the end. Thank you for all the hours you let me sit at the computer, for making dinners, for sacrificing time with me so I could work on this book. Thank you for listening as I talked things out and read whole sections to you, multiple times over! I love you second only to Jesus and I can't imagine my life without you. You are an amazing husband, a godly man and a great pastor. Thank you for loving me and staying in the battle with me.

To Shannon Forsythe, Michelle Unger, Sarah Ayling and Frances Henning—you ladies are so amazing, and I am so very grateful for you. Thank you for your prayers, your love and support through this whole ordeal and in my everyday ordinary life. Thank you for your countless hours of encouragement and for believing in me and helping me to press on even in my fear and insecurity. You are treasures, each of you, and I adore you and love you beyond words.

To Robbie Quigley for reading, rereading and rereading again. For correcting my grammar and laughing with me at my inability to get "to" and "too" in their proper places! This book would not have happened if you had not been willing to spend hours poring over it. Thank you for all your encouragement and prayer. I'll buy you some more post-it notes and your next pair of glasses!

Thank you to Belva Meanor who spent countless hours proofreading and correcting! For your encouragement to persevere and not quit and for your willingness to reread this book in its entirety more than once!

Thank you again to Sarah Ayling for your help with the cover, helping me figure out difficult sentences and helping with the computer work that I have no skill or brain power to figure out! The hours of formatting and editing, you are amazing! You made this book possible.

Thank you, Bri Walther for your infinite patience with shooting the cover photo as your toddler was in the middle of his clingy stage! And Hallie Pennington for your willingness to pose as our cover model. You are awesome!

Special thanks to Sasha, my faithful furry friend that is no longer with us. You were the inspiration for Samson and truly the best companion through so many hard times. I will always miss you.

Run 2 Rescue

All proceeds from this book will be sent to Run2Rescue, a non-profit Christian organization dedicated to reaching, rescuing and restoring girls from the sex-trafficking industry. They have been in operation since 2012 and have helped hundreds of girls. Their goal is to rescue, restore, and lead each girl to Jesus. I have had the great privilege of walking beside them, praying for them, supporting them and watching the amazing things Jesus has done with and through them. To find out more, you can visit their website at:

www.run2rescue.com.

Made in the USA
Middletown, DE
09 December 2019